**"May, are you up**

"Why should there be

huffed.

"Why does your tone say differently?" Thad tried to search her eyes.

"Listen, Thad." May's voice lowered to a controlled tone. "You made a fool of me once before. You're not going to do it again. I'm moving to Indiana. I suggest you have someone else care for Leah."

He took a couple steps backward. "May, I'm not seeing anyone."

She shook her head. "Your personal life is none of my business. I'll watch Leah until you can find someone else. I'll see you tomorrow." She closed the kitchen door and that was that.

Stunned, Thad stared at the door. He carried Leah down the porch steps to the buggy and set her bassinet on the seat. It was his fault trying to rekindle their relationship. There would always be that doubt in May's heart. He'd never be able to convince her that he did care for her. That he had always cared for her...

**Marie E. Bast** grew up on a farm in northern Illinois. In the solitude of country life, she often read or made up stories. She earned a BA, an MBA and an MA in general theology and enjoyed a career with the federal government, but characters kept whispering her name. She retired and now pursues her passion of full-time writing. Marie loves walking, golfing with her husband of twenty-seven years and baking. Visit Marie at mariebastauthor.com and mariebast.blogspot.com.

**Rebecca Kertz** was first introduced to the Amish when her husband took a job with an Amish construction crew. She enjoyed watching the Amish foreman's children at play and swapping recipes with his wife. Rebecca resides in Delaware with her husband and dog. She has a strong faith in God and feels blessed to have family nearby. Besides writing, she enjoys reading, doing crafts and visiting Lancaster County.

# MARIE E. BAST

*The Amish Marriage Bargain*

&

# REBECCA KERTZ

*Finding Her Amish Love*

Recycling programs for this product may not exist in your area.

ISBN-13: 978-1-335-40244-8

The Amish Marriage Bargain and Finding Her Amish Love



This edition published by arrangement with Harlequin Books S.A.

For questions and comments about the quality of this book, please contact us at CustomerService@Harlequin.com.

Harlequin Enterprises ULC
22 Adelaide St. West, 40th Floor
Toronto, Ontario M5H 4E3, Canada
www.Harlequin.com

**Printed in U.S.A.**

## CONTENTS

# THE AMISH MARRIAGE BARGAIN

Marie E. Bast

To past and present dairy farmers in my life:
my husband, Darrell; brothers Robert and Richard;
and my extended family, Jesus Návar.

In loving memory of Michael, my brother, and
Richard Walline, my father, who wisely raised me
on a milking farm—one of the best times of my life.
I love you both dearly and miss you.

To the Iowa Amish organic dairy farmers,
and all farmers who work hard
from sunrise to sunset and beyond.

Also, to Melissa, my superhero editor, who has a
keen eye, a fierce red pen and spot-on guidance;
the Harlequin publishing team (my white knights);
and Scribes202: Laura H., Linda M., Linda H., Heidi,
Christy, Kathy and Julie. I love you all.

And to Cyle Young, my agent, who gives subtle,
awe-inspiring nuggets of advice.

Last, but certainly not least, Kayla Caudle,
who mentioned she lived by a dairy farm…

But if ye forgive not men their trespasses,
neither will your Father forgive your trespasses.
—*Matthew* 6:15

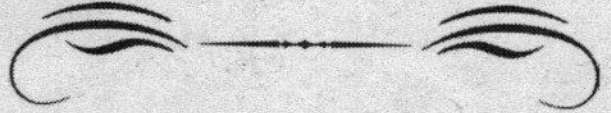

# *Chapter One*

*Washington County, Iowa*

May Bender had made her decision, but how could she possibly tell him?

Conjuring up the strength of a Goliath, she readied herself for battle. But first, she set dinner on the table, lifted her year-old niece, Leah, into her high chair and handed her a piece of bread smeared with jelly. Leah tilted her head and gifted *aentie* with a very toothy smile.

She was going to miss this little pumpkin. May wrestled a tear from her cheek with the tip of her finger.

Tucking that sad thought away, she eased onto the chair across the table from Thad and bowed her head for silent prayer. After the blessing, she took potatoes for her and Leah's plate, then handed the bowl to Thad. His hand glided over hers as he grabbed the bowl. She jerked her hand back as a tingle shot up her arm.

Thad, toting a farmer's appetite, loaded his plate and took a bite of pork chop. "Mmm, *gut*."

The compliment stunned her. He didn't often hand them out. In fact, they didn't often talk much at all. "*Danki*, it was just a little seasoning. That reminds me, the door on the spice cupboard sticks and a couple of the others are swollen from humidity."

Without raising his head, Thad nodded. "I'll take care of them on the next rainy day."

May took a slice of bread, buttered it and pushed a few crumbs off the table, watching them drop to the floor like pieces of her life. Her faith taught her to forgive, but how could she forget April and Thad's betrayal when he sat across the table from her every day?

Leah picked up a few peas with her index finger and thumb. Dropping a couple, she managed to shove a few in her mouth, giggling at her achievement. She smacked her lips and handed her soggy bread to *Aent* May. *"Mamm, Mamm, Mamm..."*

"Oh, *danki* for sharing, but you can keep it, sweetie."

Pushing her hand in her pocket, May touched the letter, to draw encouragement. "Thad, my *aent* in Indiana has offered me a job. She wants me to help run her café and bake shop in Shipshewana and take it over when she retires. Edna has given me three months to make up my mind."

He took another bite of food but didn't respond.

May didn't need twelve weeks to think it over; she just needed to box up all her belongings and make the arrangements. It was time she moved. Time she got away from Thad Hochstetler, her brother-in-law. A man who had once courted May, then dumped her for her beautiful sister, April.

She raised her chin to face him. "You know you'll need to hire a nanny?"

He took another bite of pork chop, then nodded.

May glared at him. Nineteen months ago, Thad had brought May home from singings, and April rode with his *bruder* Alvin. Her sister must have loved Alvin. They had both been baptized, joined the church and their banns were set to be read on the next Church Sunday. Six weeks after Alvin's death from his buggy accident, April and Thad wed.

Thad cleared his throat. Deep lines creased his forehead just under a dark brown swatch of hair that had fallen forward. He raised his head and locked eyes with hers. His mouth twisted into a weak smile, the edges nervously twitching. "Would you…consider postponing your plan to move to Indiana? I hate to ask this, but I'd appreciate it if you would stay on a little while longer and watch Leah."

"What?" A tear pressed at the corner of her eye. "You're joking, right?"

"The farm's income has declined by almost 35 percent this past year with the problem The Amish Dairy Association has been having with the USDA and its inspection agencies. Small farmers are losing money by the day trying to compete with the big dairy producers out west when they violate the organic rules and overproduce." His voice quaked. "The inspection agencies have been lax in suspending violators and writing citations for fines. I can't afford a full-time nanny right now with a mortgage, and *Mamm*'s arthritic hips won't allow her to chase a one-year-old all day."

May drew a deep breath, holding it deep in her chest

before blowing it out. "The longer I postpone the move, the harder it will be on Leah." *And me.*

"Look, May, I'm in dire straits here… I could lose the farm."

Contempt for him boiled her blood. "You mean my *mamm* and *daed*'s farm that you inherited from my sister. It's been in our family for 170 years." She spit out the words as if they were wrapped with barbed wire.

"Small dairy farmers are being driven out of business all over the Midwest." He let his gaze drop, then raised his eyes to meet her glare. "I'd really appreciate it if you could stay a while longer."

May fisted her hands. Her world was tumbling, as if a spool of thread dropped to the floor, unraveling before her eyes.

She heaved a sigh but caught the look of pleading cross his face, then vanish in a heartbeat. "I'll think about it."

Thad nodded, scooted his chair away from the table, snatched his straw hat from the peg on the wall, plopped it on and headed outside.

May clutched her chest while pain arrowed through her. Why had she told him she'd think about it? She had thought about it, and the time was right to move.

She dropped her fork and covered her face with her hands. *Nein. Nein. Nein.*

April's words whirled through her head. *"I'm dying, sister. Promise me you'll take care of Leah and Thad."*

"Nein, *April, I can't do that. Not after what Thad did..."*

*"I feel the life draining from me. You must do it, May, please! Forgive me. Thad and I never meant to hurt you. Things just happen."* April exhaled a long breath and closed her eyes. Her hand fell limp.

May steered her mind back to the present.

Why had she made that promise?

A blast of evening air squeezed through the screen in the door and circulated around the room, giving it a fresh scent. While Leah played on the floor with her blocks, May stowed her decision for now, washed the dishes and straightened the kitchen.

When Leah started to fuss and rub her eyes, May snatched her up and snuggled her close. "I won't be able to do this much longer if I decide to go, little one." She kissed Leah's sweet little head when she laid it against her shoulder, almost falling asleep. "*Nein*, let's get you bathed and settled in bed."

After putting the child to sleep, May closed Leah's door with Thad's request still whirling in her head. How could she stay here? He was certainly insensitive to her need. Her fingers twitched with the impulse to start packing now. She'd never be able to sleep. Tiptoeing quietly down the hall, she headed to her sewing room.

Sewing always calmed her nerves.

She grabbed her basket of long strips of cloth she'd torn from old clothes and started sewing them together to make rag rugs. She finished connecting the last strips together, then glanced at the battery clock. *Ach*. Midnight. After tidying the sewing room, she trudged down the hall to her room and collapsed on her bed.

She rubbed her hand over her quilt. The softness of the cottton reminded her of Leah when she was born. Her sweet *boppli* softness, and even then, she was as lovely as April with dark blue eyes like Thad's. She'd hated her sister for stealing Thad from her, but how could she stay angry when April was dead? She would have been so proud of her *tochter.*

*Oh, April, you were so careless in caring for yourself and letting the diabetes get out of control, like it had with* Mamm.

May pressed her hand over her eyes to blot out all the ugliness she'd silently heaped upon April.

*Lord, please forgive me for my sins. It was sisterly rivalry, or maybe jealousy that I coveted what she had. April always got what she wanted, and I got her hand-me-downs. Thad had a right to choose, and he chose April. I can't even tell her I'm sorry. Your scripture says I must forgive, but it's hard to forget the trespass. Help me to learn.*

A deep yawn coaxed her out of her shoes. She removed her prayer *kapp*, letting her long auburn hair cascade over her shoulders. After putting on her nightgown, she burrowed under the covers, drowsiness tugging at her eyes.

She loved Leah so much, but she couldn't pass up the opportunity that *Aent* Edna offered. Could she? A once-in-a-lifetime offer?

Could she pass it up to help Thad? For the sake of the farm?

But Edna's offer was a vote to move.

The next morning, sunshine poured in between the curtains and roused May from sleep. She glanced at the clock. *Ach*, 7:00 a.m. The thought of Thad waiting in the kitchen hungry pushed the cloudiness from her head. A *gut* Amish woman always saw to it that the men had a nourishing meal before they started their workday.

Although *Daed* assured May she could stay in the

*haus* until she married, it was uncomfortable living with Thad. That was another vote in favor of moving.

She dressed and hurried downstairs. When she entered the kitchen, the aroma of strong coffee assaulted her nose. Thad stood over the stove, bacon in one pan and French toast in another. Her eyes roamed from the stove to Leah in her high chair, smiling as she ate scrambled eggs. She held her little hand out and offered May a gob of egg.

"*Danki*, *lieb*, but you eat it." She turned to Thad. "I'm so sorry I overslept. I don't know what got into me." Something she never wanted to have to do…apologize to Thad Hochstetler.

He turned and swept his arm in the direction of the table. "Sit. Your breakfast awaits you, Miss Bender."

He was being nice, too nice. Now what did he want?

Thad smiled. "I noticed you worked late in your sewing room. We're a family and that means we help each other out. Occasionally, we forget to set our alarms. No harm done. Sit. Breakfast is ready." He placed the platter on the table and sat.

After silent prayer, May dribbled syrup on her French toast and took a bite.

He scooted a slice onto his plate and ladled strawberries over top. "Mmm, your garden strawberries are *gut*. I picked them fresh this morning."

May tossed him a she-could-hardly-believe-it stare.

A knock on the door pierced the silence, then the screen door popped open. Lois Plank, the midwife, and her son Elmer stepped in.

"*Hullo.* Come in and sit." Thad motioned with his free hand.

"It smells *gut* in here." Elmer stuck his nose in the air and took a couple of deep whiffs. "Only it's a little late for breakfast."

Lois raised a brow at Elmer's nosy remark. "I'm sorry to interrupt, but I've come to give Leah her twelve-month checkup."

"Of course!" May stood and pulled Leah out of her high chair. Lois followed May into the other room.

"How's the cheese business, Elmer?" Thad leaned back in his chair and glanced at his guest. "Looks like you dashed over here right from your factory."

Elmer brushed a hand down the front of his shirt. "*Jah*, *Mamm* doesn't like to drive all over the township by herself when she makes her rounds."

Thad listened to Elmer drone on, naming all the other homes they would visit today. When the women returned to the kitchen, May sat Leah in the middle of the floor with her toys.

"Lois, Elmer, would you like a cup of coffee?" May grabbed the pot off the stove and placed it on the hot-plate as she sat. "Please sit."

"*Nein.* I have other appointments. We need to get going." Lois motioned for Elmer to head for the door, which he ignored.

Thad cut into another piece of French toast, put it in his mouth and watched Elmer scurry to May's side, slipping into the chair next to hers.

Thad sniffed and breathed in a tangy whiff of cheese stuck to Elmer's shirt. The smear of ripened cheddar from Elmer's aging room seemed to mingle with his blue cheese spot. Thad stifled a smile. Elmer called himself a cheese artisan.

"How are you, May?" Elmer's voice dripped with concern. He leaned toward May, put his arm around the back of her chair and pressed in closer. "I'll stop by tomorrow." He tossed Thad a better-not-try-to-stop-me look, quickly adding, "Thad, are you attending the meeting tonight over at the Millers' dairy on the USDA's organic standard?"

"Wouldn't miss it." Thad glared at the cheesemaker. He wanted to tell Elmer to stay away from May, but she'd resent his interference.

Elmer leaned even closer to May. "I noticed your garden has a lot of beans ready to harvest, and you'll probably want them for your vegetable stand. Why don't I stop back later and help you pick them? It'll be cooler this evening."

"*Danki*, Elmer, but aren't you going to the meeting?"

"I'll go late. They chew over everything before they get down to business." Elmer threw Thad a sly smile.

"Are you sure you don't want a cup of coffee?" May started to stand.

Lois shook her head. "*Danki*, we need to go if we're going to stick to our schedule. Elmer, it's time."

The screen door squeaked open and the distinctive shuffle that followed pulled Thad to his feet. "*Gut* mornin', *Mamm*." His cheeks burned as he caught a hint of judgment in her eyes.

"What's going on in here?" Gretchen took a deep breath and looked around. "Are you still lollygagging over breakfast? You should be out in the field, *jah*?" She tossed a sour glance at Thad, then turned toward the table with a stern look. “May, you need to get up earlier and get the food on the table by five thirty. April never ran her *haus* like this. There are beans in the garden to be picked and canning that needs to be done.”

Elmer stood and gave a nod. “*Gut* mornin’, Gretchen. Nice to see you. I forgot you and Aaron were staying in Thad’s *dawdi haus* while the one on Jonah’s farm was being refurbished.”

“It’s nice to see you, too, Elmer. Lois, you checking on our Leah?”

“Indeed. She’s a sweet little thing and in *gut* health. No worry with her, Gretchen. May, don’t forget about the quilting frolic in three weeks.”

“*Jah*, it’s on my calendar.”

Elmer held the screen door for his *mamm*. “See you later, May.”

Thad pulled his hat from the peg on the wall and headed out the door with a sideways glance at May. She sent him a glare.

He’d hurt May when he’d tossed her aside for her sister. There was no way to apologize for that but his sharp-tongued *mamm* only made things worse. “Come on, *Mamm*, I’ll walk you out.”

In the evening, May and Leah sat on the porch and watched Thad disappear into the barn after he’d hitched Tidbit to the buggy. Twenty minutes passed. Her gaze swung from the barn door to Tidbit as he pawed the ground nervously, waiting to stretch his legs. Why was Thad taking so long getting ready to go to the dairy association meeting?

A buggy turned into the driveway, the wheels

crunching over the rocks as she watched Elmer park it in front of the *haus*. He stepped down and waved as he walked toward her.

Elmer was handsome and his bronzed skin set off his sky blue eyes. He'd definitely be a *gut* catch for some woman, but not her. She only thought of him as a friend, and he deserved a *frau* that would *liebe* him.

Thad closed the barn door and stalked toward the *haus*, a grimace plastered on his face as he nodded to Elmer. Ah, now she understood why Thad had stalled after hitching Tidbit. *Elmer.*

When they were all *kinner* in school, Thad and Elmer had some kind of rivalry. It seemed like everything was a competition to them, horseback riding, swimming, but it was more than that. But she couldn't quite tag it. If she didn't know better, she'd think Thad was jealous. *Nein*, that couldn't be. It was just their old silliness, like two small *buwe*.

A smile tugged at her lips as Elmer got closer. He had donned a clean blue chambray shirt and trousers. *Gut.* He had smelled like cheese curds earlier in the day.

Before Elmer reached the steps, Thad smacked the reins across Tidbit's back, and the buggy shot off down the driveway toward the gate. May gripped her apron as she watched the speeding buggy. She relaxed as Tidbit slowed before he crossed the road.

"*Gut* evening, May. How are you this evening?"

"A bit tired."

"*Jah?* I'll stay only a little while."

She faced Elmer, then glanced at the road after Thad. A twinge of sadness washed over her. She couldn't believe that Thad might lose the farm. Her family's farm.

*Daed* and *Mamm* fought hard for years to keep the farm, to make the payments and to put food on the table every day. This land ran through her veins almost as much as her blood did. It was who she was. Even if she had to go door-to-door in town with a bucket of vegetables to make a sale, she'd do it.

Her heart pounded. That was a bad sign. Why was it that the mere sight of Thad made it hard for her to breathe? To walk in a straight line? And when his hand touched hers when she handed him the potato bowl, she nearly melted on the spot.

*Jah*, she either had to hide her heart or convince the angel Gabriel to protect it, or Thad would steal it away. *Nein*, not again! She didn't know what was worse…losing the farm or losing her heart.

But could she risk sticking around to find out?

## *Chapter Two*

The next morning, Thad ran his hands through his hair as he entered the kitchen. "Mmm, sausage and eggs smell *gut*."

"Thought it was my turn to treat you to breakfast this morning," she turned and faced him. "How'd the dairy association meeting go last night?"

He pulled a chair away from the kitchen table and plopped down. "It doesn't look like the USDA is in any big hurry to make changes. That means that many farmers are going to have to sell organic for the regular milk price. We'll lose money, about 33 percent, by doing that, but it can't be helped."

"I'm sorry to hear that. I know how hard you work."

"*Jah*, well, times are changing."

"Maybe you could sell the cows and put in all produce?"

"The reason why we diversify is because a storm could wipe out the whole crop. This way we still have milk money to fall back on. The president of the association called the newspaper and a reporter showed up. He was going to put a story in the paper. Maybe the *Englisch* politicians will take notice. I'm praying for that."

May flashed him a hopeful smile.

"How's Leah? When I'm outside, I don't see her much.She's not up yet?"

"She was up earlier playing and had her breakfast. Now she's napping. We were outside all yesterday afternoon. She missed her nap, and went to bed early. It threw her off schedule."

"How is your vegetable stand doing?"

"It's doing very well. Lots of *Englisch* stop by the roadside stand wanting to buy fresh produce."

"Ah, *gut*. At least there is something we grow that the consumers like to buy."

They hadn't talked this much since they'd courted. Yet, if he was going to persuade her to stay, they'd need to be getting along a whole lot better. She set the breakfast on the table and sat opposite Thad. After the blessing, she poured his coffee and dished up her plate.

She only tolerated him, but in all fairness, he had dumped her and married her sister. He truly regretted that.

They both wanted the farm to succeed. And he sure hoped her *liebe* for it and Leah made her come to the right conclusion. But he needed to know where he stood with May.

A flash of fear tugged at his gut as he aimed his gaze across the table. "Have you made a decision yet about leaving Iowa?"

She raised her head and he could read the surprise on her face.

The words popped out before he could bite them

back. He knew he shouldn't rush her. She needed time. He'd only push her into making a hasty decision. That probably wouldn't be in his favor.

"*Nein*. I'm taking my time—a move to Indiana is final. It's a big decision, and I want to get it right."

A sigh whooshed out before he could stop it. That meant he still had time to sway her decision.

But how could he convince her to stay?

May lugged the baskets of tomatoes and bins of green beans and peapods to her roadside stand she had put at the end of the driveway by the white fence. She arranged the quart-size cartons of strawberries in rows, then sat the plastic bags and cash box on the opposite end of the table.

She blotted her forehead with her hand as she glanced at the blanket on the ground where Leah sat playing. Her pumpkin was the only sweetness in her life. For sure and for certain, she was going to miss that little bit of sugar if she headed to Indiana. She'd told Thad she hadn't made a decision, but in truth, it was for the best that she moved. But she needed to consider it from all angles.

Someday Thad would want to remarry, and that would make it uncomfortable for her. Edna's offer was only for a short while, and she needed to take advantage of her generosity.

A warm breeze danced across her face, drying the perspiration on her forehead. She turned in that direction, stood for a minute and fully enjoyed the blessing.

It reminded her of the times she and April had sat under a tree one summer and talked about *buwe*. Who was the cutest, which one had the best personality, and who owned the broadest shoulders? Thad and Alvin tied for the win in all categories. A few pangs of homesickness stirred in her, knowing these would be her last few weeks on the land if she decided to move.

May glanced toward the barn where Thad stood looking her way. It was hard even imagining losing the family's farm.

She finished arranging her vegetable stand, then took a step back and glanced at the display in front of the white fence. Perfect.

She'd miss her garden and the stand, but surely *Aent* Edna had a patch behind her café and bake shop.

She picked up Leah and the blanket she was sitting and crawling on. Leah smiled so sweetly that it stole May's heart as she swung the tyke around. Leah giggled while little wisps of taffy-colored hair bounced around her cherub face. "*Mamm*, more!"

"*Nein*, it's time for your nap, little one."

*"Mamm,"* Leah laughed.

May reached the porch and laid the blanket on a chair. She turned when she heard wheels rumbling into the drive.

Bishop Yoder climbed out of his buggy and walked a few steps in her direction. "*Gut* afternoon, May. Another hot July day, *jah*? Is Thad around?"

"I believe he's in the shed boxing vegetables, Bishop. Would you like a glass of lemonade?"

He looked toward the shed, then back at May. "That does sound *gut*. Just a small one."

He followed her into the kitchen and plunked down on a chair waving his hat across his face.

"Would you rather sit on the porch?"

"*Nein*. This is fine."

She sat Leah on the floor by her toys, cut a piece of banana bread, poured a glass of lemonade and set them in front of him.

He took a bite of bread, then washed it down with the cold drink. "Mmm, they are both *gut*."

"I'm just going to put Leah down for a nap, but I'll be right back."

She laid Leah in her downstairs crib and returned to the kitchen.

She poured herself a glass of lemonade and joined the bishop at the table. "It's a hot day for visiting."

"Indeed. Tell me, May, does Thad work the farm every day, and do you cook his meals?"

A chill ran up her back. *"Jah."*

"How's this situation working out for you?" He took another sip and waited for her reply.

"I'm not sure I understand the question, Bishop." She rubbed her finger down the glass through the condensation.

"*Jah*, he jilted you years ago, is that right? So is it uncomfortable for you to live here? Together?"

"This is my family farm that Thad inherited from April, but *Daed* said I could stay here until I married."

"But he's here all day." The bishop gestured with his hand to the outside.

"He lets me stay, so I watch Leah and cook the meals. That's all. Otherwise, I see very little of him during the day."

The bishop finished his refreshment, pushed his chair back and gave May a nod. "See you on Sunday."

She froze in her chair, and waited until his footfalls left the porch. She looked out the window. What was that all about? Why was he asking such questions?

May sipped her lemonade, sat the glass down and dried her hand on her apron. No doubt, she wouldn't like the answers to those questions.

Thad took off his straw hat, slapped it against his leg to shake the dust and soil off, and plunked it back on his head. He watched the *youngies* he'd hired to pick vegetables leave for the day, then he sealed the cartons of tomatoes, beans and peas going to market.

It was a hot day, but at least it hadn't rained. He'd prayed for a sunny day, and *Gott* had answered. He sighed as his mind drifted to May.

They had started getting along, putting the past behind them. At least he hoped so. Their conversations seemed more relaxed, and she was at least still considering staying. Maybe her hesitation to make a decision about moving was due to the thought of leaving Leah.

The shed door squeaked open and pulled his attention to footfalls approaching. He tried to hold back a smile. *Jah*, May was coming out to talk. He peered over his shoulder, then jerked around in surprise as he saw the bishop approaching. "Bishop Yoder, *hullo*."

"*Hullo*, Thad. I was visiting with May. She made some delicious banana bread and lemonade. Did you have some?"

"Ah, no, not yet, probably for supper. What brings you out here today?"

"An elder brought it to my attention that you and May were still living together."

Thad's back stiffened. "*Nein*, we aren't living together. I inherited her family's farm, and my parents are staying in the *dawdi haus*. Why bring this up now? April has been dead a year."

"Exactly, your year of mourning is over and now it is not acceptable. So you live in the *dawdi haus* with them?"

"I still sleep in the same bedroom that April and I shared."

The bishop kicked at a few peas that had landed on the floor before aiming his gaze at Thad. "To others in our district, they think this is not a *gut* arrangement. You are here all day and all night unchaperoned in the same *haus*. I heard that she was moving to Shipshewana to live with an *aent*?"

"*Jah*, that's what she said, but I think she is having a hard time leaving Leah."

"Is it just Leah that she is having the hard time leaving?"

Thad took a step back and clenched his teeth, then released. "I'm not sure I understand what you are talking about, Bishop."

"You courted May before you married her sister, *jah*?" The bishop's tone was the one he used for preaching.

"What are you saying, Bishop?" A rigidness seized Thad's shoulders.

"It's time May was married."

Thad felt the blood drain from his face.

The bishop walked to the door, then glanced back over his shoulder. "You need to think seriously about how this living arrangement looks to others. It cannot be allowed to go on much longer." The bishop walked out, letting the barn door bang closed.

Thad stared after him and scrubbed his hands over his face. *Why,* Gott, *why have You done this? I was hoping May would decide to stay but this...this will drive her away. And if the bishop finds out Elmer is always hanging around, he'll try to matchmake them. I had hoped to win her back.*

The next morning, Thad's gut clenched when he saw Elmer's buggy pulling into the drive. What did he want? But he already knew. *May.*

Perhaps the bishop had sent Elmer out here to see May. Thad settled his feet like a bulldog with his paws planted squarely in the center of the walkway.

"*Gut morgen*, Thad." Elmer smiled as he approached.

Thad nodded. "Elmer. What brings you out this way?"

"Come to help May in her garden and visit with her a while."

Thad shot Elmer a cold stare, stepped off the walkway and stalked across the barnyard, the dust flying off the heels of his boots. He grabbed his toolbox off the shed's workbench and headed back to the *haus*.

He shook his head and tried to clear May out of his brain. She had a right to a life of her own but all he could see were her smoky-gray eyes staring at Elmer. Those same eyes made his heart swell until he could hardly breathe. Her hair and skin smelled like strawberry blossoms on a sunny June day.

He took the porch steps two at a time, stopped and caught his breath before entering the kitchen. Bumping the screen door open with his hip, he maneuvered his toolbox through the doorway and set it on the floor, letting the door bang closed.

May and Elmer turned and scowled at his abrupt entrance. He looked up and locked on to her eyes, then let his gaze drop to her peaches-and-cream cheeks.

"What are you doing, Thad?" She squared her shoulders and lifted a brow. "Forget something?"

"*Nein.* I just remembered you wanted the doors fixed. Since Elmer was here, I thought it would be the perfect time to take off the swollen cupboard doors and fix them. Leah's door also sticks from the humidity. It squeaked when I opened it. We can take it off the hinges and plane a couple of spots to make it level. Since Elmer has two *gut* hands, I figured he'd want to help." Thad felt his face trying to smile but he controlled the urge.

Elmer pursed his lips and tossed Thad a displeased stare. "*Jah*, okay. Let's get to it so I'll have a few minutes to visit with May."

"We'll start with the kitchen doors." Thad's instincts kicked in and told him he was in trouble, but he wasn't going to let Elmer have the upper hand before he tried to work things out with May.

He felt Elmer's glare as they finished up in the kitchen. Of course, he forgot a couple of tools and had to go to the shed twice. Thad nodded toward the stairway that led to the second floor and to Leah's room, but as he did, the glare in May's eyes and her furrowed brow signaled he'd upset her plans for a nice afternoon with Elmer.

*Gut.* A pang of uneasiness settled in his stomach. May deserved a nice man to court her, and Elmer was a *gut*-hearted man with many skills that kept him in demand, like his cheese business. But Elmer was also a stern man who worked his employees hard and no doubt would demand his *frau* do the same.

As Thad picked up his toolbox, he shot another glance in May's direction. A rosy blush tinged her cheeks like a January wind had just whirled through the room. She held her back straight as a yardstick and stared him down. He'd made his choice, married April, and now he should step aside and let May find happiness.

But he just couldn't. After speaking to the bishop, he wanted one more chance. With May.

*Jah*, he had no right disrupting her time with Elmer. Regret crept up his back but a smile curved his lips as he turned to head upstairs.

He had tossed May aside to marry April, now he was trying to prevent her from courting Elmer. What was wrong with him? Why did he keep hurting her? She was a *wunderbaar* woman any man would be proud to have as his *frau*.

Guilt pushed out a frustrated sigh, and his insides warred. He needed to back away and let May have her chance at happiness. Elmer needed his chance at winning May's heart. Thad owed her that, but why did it feel like a pitchfork was stabbing his heart?

May fumed under her breath as the men tromped up the stairs. She heard banging and pounding, feet shuffling around the wood flooring and a loud clink when the door hinge pin slid back into place.

When they came back downstairs, Elmer let out

a loud sigh as he sat in the chair next to hers. Thad stomped toward the door, his toolbox clanging with tools shifting around as he gave her a nod. Her cheeks burned hot enough they could fry an egg.

"Job is done," Thad announced as he clomped out the door and down the porch steps.

May turned to Elmer. "I'm sorry you got roped into helping him."

"*Nein*, I wanted to help. Your cupboards are all fixed. I wouldn't want a loose door to swing open and bump your head when you weren't looking." He smiled like a *bu* who had just received a dollar to buy some candy.

"My cheese factory is doing very well." He glanced at May. "The artisanal cheese is a big seller. It's fancy cheese for the *Englisch*, they *liebe* it with crackers. The cheddar with bacon bits is my most popular seller. My shop is even in the Iowa Cheese Club and on the Iowa Cheese Roundup." He cleared his throat. "I'm building a *haus* and will be well established enough to marry soon."

The twinkle in his eye warned May he wasn't here just as her friend. She dropped her gaze as his hand started inching closer to hers. She jumped up, twisting her foot but stifled the yelp. "I'll make some coffee and we'll have a cookie. I made them the other day. Snickerdoodles."

"That's okay, May. Don't go to any trouble. Please, sit and talk."

"*Nein.* You deserve a little refreshment after driving all the way here and then helping Thad." She hurried to make a small pot of coffee, and in the meantime, set a plate of cookies on the table. When the coffee was ready, she poured two cups, set them on the table and collapsed on the chair.

"You seem tired, May."

"*Jah*, I am." When they finished their coffee, she stood and walked him to the porch. As she waved goodbye, a movement caught her eye and she turned toward the *dawdi haus*.

Gretchen was watching them from her flower garden.

It was for the best that he went home. She needed time to think of a way to tell Elmer she didn't *liebe* him and didn't want to marry him.

And she needed time to think of an answer for Thad...and what was best for the rest of her life.

# *Chapter Three*

Thad helped his *youngies* stack the vegetable boxes of tomatoes, carrots and bush beans onto the truck bound for Des Moines. This load would complete the contract he had with a local market chain. He heaved the last box up into the waiting hands of the Vickerson Transport Company man inside the truck, stacking and securing the boxes. Done.

The truck driver handed Thad the clipboard with the receipt. He reviewed it, signed it, took his copy and handed it back. It was 6:30 a.m. when the truck pulled away.

Thad pulled a hanky from his pocket and wiped his brow as he watched the truck pull out of the drive. "Ethan Lapp, you and Carl Ropp head to the barn and start milking, it's getting late. The rest of you are on cleanup, follow me."

While Thad supervised, the *buwe* cleaned the packaging room of vegetable scraps, foam pieces and boxing debris, then he had them scrub the area and store the unused cartons back on the shelves. When they completed the task, he had them disinfect the milking room when Ethan and Carl had finished with the last cow. After lunch, they spent the rest of the day weeding the north forty acres. At four o'clock, he gathered the three summer hires for a short meeting. "*Danki* for all your help, you work hard and did a *gut* job today. You can come back on Friday morning for your pay. If you don't make it, I'll drop your check in the mail."

Daniel, the newest of his summer hires, stepped forward while the other two walked away. "*Danki*, Mr. Hochstetler. If you need help with anything else, give a shout."

Thad patted him on the back. "*Danki.* I'll do that."

As the *buwe* stood by their buggies talking, Thad overheard a few discussions of what they were going to do with their money. He chuckled. Most planned to save it. However, a few sounded like they were going to fix up their buggies to attract a pretty *mädel.*

Rumbling wheels on the drive pulled his attention from the *buwe* to his *daed*'s buggy heading straight toward him. *Daed* parked under the shade of the oak tree and stepped down. He walked toward Thad with an uneasy look on his face.

"Something wrong, *Daed*?"

The older man took a couple of purposeful strides closer. "The bishop stopped to chat with me in town." He kicked a stone with his foot as he stopped abruptly. "He said the elders didn't like you and May living in sin together. Your year of mourning is over. What was allowed before, won't be tolerated now."

Thad's jaw dropped. "That's not true."

*Daed* held up his hand. "Stop right there. Whether

you are or not, it goes by appearance and what's decent. You're out here on the farm with May inside the *haus.* You wander in and out all day and spend the evenings together."

"Who said that?" Thad's back bolted up straight.

"Is it true or not?"

"*Jah*, but it's my *haus* and May lives here, too. It was her *daed*'s farm, but you know all that."

"You must marry May, or she must move out. I know what her papa said about her staying in the *haus*, but no doubt, he would thank me for looking out for her reputation. I worry that no nice *bu* will want to marry her."

Thad stepped back so fast he almost fell. His hands and face turned cold as his blood drained to his feet. His throat tightened so he could barely speak. "Who… is spreading rumors?"

"The bishop said that several elders have mentioned it to him. Not just that, but he doesn't want the *Englisch* neighbors to think that we condone living in sin. Not my words, his." *Daed*'s voice turned sullen. "Did you tell May that the bishop paid you a visit?"

"She knows he was here, but we never talked about what he said." Thad's gaze dropped to the grass. His mind whirled. He didn't want to lose May when they were just starting to get along. This would humiliate her, and for sure and for certain she'd move the three hundred miles to *Aent* Edna's.

Thad rubbed a hand over his heart. It felt as though a hundred stampeding Holsteins had trampled on his chest. Gott, *how do I make May understand? We need to get married—and fast. When I tell her, please ease her pain and confusion.*

He paced the ground, then faced his *daed*. "How much time did the bishop say we could have to think about this situation?"

*Daed* hooked his thumbs under his suspenders and locked eyes with Thad. "She has to be told today. Either she moves out in the next couple of days, or you marry." He gave Thad an easy pat on the shoulder. "She's a fine woman and would make Leah a *gut mamm*. Do what's right, Thad." He nodded and headed back to his buggy.

Thad wandered to the bench he'd made a year ago and sat in the front yard. He stared at his *daed*'s buggy kicking up dirt and sticks as it sped across the barnyard to the *dawdi haus*. The dust swirled in the wind, then disappeared like May would probably do when he told her about the gossip.

He kicked at the grass underfoot. He could give May back the farm, and she could pay someone to run it. The outcome would no doubt be the same. Someone would gossip about her and that man. Then the bishop would make her marry him.

They were getting along better. Maybe she'd consider a proposal. *Nein*, what was he thinking? She had told him once she hated her sister's secondhand clothes. She'd never want her secondhand husband.

He stood and walked around the *haus* toward the porch while a million reasons why their marriage was a bad idea bombarded his senses. Was it possible one of the *buwe* who worked for him was gossiping about him and May and his *daed* just didn't tell him?

He reached the porch steps and halted, one foot still in mid-air, then he slowly lowered it to the step. He tried to budge the other foot from the ground, but it felt as if glue clung to the sole of his shoe making the task difficult. Finally, one step after the other, he reached the top, knocked on the kitchen door and entered.

May glanced his way, then finished taking Mason jars from the processing kettle. She checked the Kerr lids and set the jars to cool. She pushed the previous cooled jars to the back of the counter out of the way. She wiped her hands on a towel and turned from the sink. "Why did you knock, Thad? Did you want me to come out and help with something?"

"*Nein*, we need to talk."

"Let me dish up the food and we can talk during dinner. Leah's napping so it gives us a few minutes." May set the bowl of boiled potatoes next to the meatballs, sauerkraut, green beans and cinnamon bread already on the table. She pulled her chair from the table, letting the legs scrape against the wood flooring, then sat. They bowed their heads for silent prayer.

Thad rubbed his hands across his trousers. "It was a warm one today." His voice shook on the last word. *Lord, please help me say what I must.* After taking a bite, he took his napkin and blotted his mouth. "Mmm. This is delicious, but then your cooking is always *gut*."

The hot food and warm kitchen teamed to coat his brow in perspiration. He swallowed hard, laid his fork down, took a deep breath, and told May about the bishop's visit the other day and the bishop's conversation with his *daed* today.

Her face went blank and her smoky-gray eyes turned stormy black.

"May, I adore you. I cared for you, *nein*, I loved you in a way when we courted, and I think you cared for me, too. We can get that back if we work at it. I'd like you to marry me. But if the answer is *nein*...then you'll have to move out of the *haus*."

His words speared May in the heart. "Who is gossiping about us?"

"If the bishop told *Daed*, he never told me." Thad lowered his gaze. "I must say, you're not as surprised as I thought you'd be." He raised his chin to face her again.

"Your *daed* never indicated who complained, or maybe named a neighbor?" Her eyes locked with his.

"*Nein*. It might be one of the *buwe* that work on the farm. Maybe they told the bishop, or their folks, that I walk in and out of the *haus* whenever I please without knocking or something like that. Did they ever stop to think, it is my *haus*, and you are only the...nanny?"

May's heart nearly stopped. *Only the nanny?*

"Look, May, I care about you, and I owe it to April to take care of you. We can get married and all will be well. What do you say?"

May stared at him in utter disbelief.

Leah let out a cry from her crib in the other room. She hurried and picked her up, changed her and snuggled her close as a tear threatened but May batted it away. How was she going to survive without seeing this sweet little girl?

She carried Leah to the kitchen, and set her down in the high chair. "I'll get her food ready so we can talk." She got her food and set her plate and cup on her tray.

"Okay, where were we?"

"May, you didn't answer my question."

She swallowed hard and looked Thad in the eye.

"Before April died, she asked me to take care of her *boppli*. I stayed here to do just that, instead of going to Indiana, where *Mamm*'s family lives. Now I'm repaid by my friends and neighbors gossiping about me?"

"I—I'm sure it's not like that..." Thad stuttered.

"*Nein*, apparently it is." A knot tightened in the pit of her stomach. "I appreciate your offer of marriage, Thad, but that would keep you from marrying someone you loved."

"*Nein.* I did not say it right before. I *liebe* you and want to marry you. We could make it work, May. If I hadn't married April, we might have..." He stopped.

Her cheek twitched and heat rushed up her neck and burned all the way to her ears. She was sure her eyes shot lightning bolts.

In the silence, the ticking of the kitchen clock pulsed like the heartbeat of the *haus*.

Her life had just changed in a few seconds. The *haus*, the farm, Leah... Thad had everything. She had nothing once again. At least he'd given her a place to stay, for a little while anyway. Now, *Gott* had taken that away, too, but He stretched out two roads before her and she must choose.

"Thaddaeus Thomas Hochstetler. What's going on? You should be in the field."

May jerked around at the same time Thad did to see Gretchen with her hands perched on her hips.

"*Mamm*, people are gossiping about us living together, and we are discussing whether to marry or not."

"You want to marry May? *Nein.* She's nothing like her sister." Gretchen huffed and glanced at the dozen jars of canned string beans on the counter, then her gaze dropped to the bucket sitting on the floor still full of beans to be canned. "April worked twice as fast as her."

A flash of heat stormed through May's body as she listened to Gretchen berate her. Ha, three votes against staying: Edna's offer was one, her discomfort around Thad was two, and now Gretchen's unkind words.

Thad grabbed his *mamm*'s arm and escorted her out of the *haus*. When he stomped back into the kitchen, his face was as pale as a whitewashed fence.

"I have a lot to think about, Thad. Can you look after Leah for a little while?"

He nodded. "I'm sorry about all this, May."

Before she reached the stairs, Leah started to cry. She stopped and glanced at Thad. "You sure you're okay with her?"

"*Jah*, we're *gut*."

Before May reached the stairs, Leah was crying. This was a *gut* test for Thad to see how he handled his *tochter* on his own.

May closed her bedroom door and collapsed on the bed. She didn't want to marry Thad. She didn't love him. She could barely talk to him.

But she loved Leah and that little *mädel* loved her like a mama. She could sell her rag rugs to help Thad and she could bake bread, rolls, pies and cookies and sell them at her roadside stand.

But the whole idea was just crazy. She and Thad didn't *liebe* each other, not anymore, if they ever did.

She could hear Leah crying downstairs, then the sniffling grew closer, and closer and stopped. A tap sounded on her door.

She hesitated, then opened it. "Janie, what are you doing here?"

"That's a nice greeting for a friend. I hadn't seen you for a while so thought I'd stop by on my way to town. *Mamm* keeps me busy canning, but I wanted to see you. Thad said you were up here doing some thinking. He couldn't quiet this one's crying." Janie gave Leah a squeeze.

Leah sniffled and held her arms out to May, sobs rocking her little shoulders while her nose ran. When Janie handed her over, Leah almost jumped into May's arms.

May enveloped her in a hug, then wiped the tears and her nose. Leah laid her head on May's shoulder with her arm stretched around her neck. "Shh. Everything will be okay."

May pointed toward the bed and her friend sat. She confided her dilemma and watched Janie gasp with each new piece of information.

"What are you going to do? If you ask me, I think you should give Thad a second chance," Janie whispered. "I think he's cute, and I've always liked him. Plus, he's tall with a muscular back and strong arms. Now, what *mädel* could resist that?"

"You're guy crazy." May lifted a brow. "I believe I have two choices—marry Thad or move to Shipshewana, where I would probably never see Leah again. And right now, she is the only joy in my life."

"The decision to marry is for life. Amish don't get divorced. I know you realize that, but I just wanted to remind you. Oh, here's another idea. If they have a lot of *gut*-looking guys in Indiana, send me a letter, and I'll move out there with you." Janie chuckled.

May rolled her eyes at her sweet and funny friend. "Again, you're guy crazy. The scary thing is, I've never been to Shipshewana, and I have no idea if I will like Indiana."

"You know you could always come back later, if you weren't happy there. I'll pray for you, May, but here is something else to consider. Your sister, Sadie, is pregnant with twins. I heard she was looking for a mother's helper, so you could go live with her. She'll soon have five *kinner* all under the age of five. Oh, but you'll have to share a room with Sadie's oldest, your niece Isabelle. What do you say? Think about it. I'm sure Sadie would *liebe* to see you come and stay."

May laughed. "I'm glad you stopped by. You certainly cheered me up." She gave Janie a one-armed hug.

"If you move, can I have Thad?" Janie's eyes widened almost as much as her smile.

May ignored the question. "If I go to *Aent* Edna's, I'll be working in a bakery for the rest of my life. That is, unless I find someone in Indiana to marry. Or I could stay here with this little bundle of joy that I *liebe* like a heartbeat." She gave Leah a jiggle up and down and listened to her musical giggle. "No more tears when you're with *aentie*, huh? I've prayed, but *Gott* has been silent so far."

"*Jah*, He might want you to search your heart, May, or He might want to see if you'll reason it out and make a practical decision. Here's another offer—come and live with us. *Mamm* would *liebe* another pair of hands to help out around the *haus*."

Footsteps echoed in the hall followed by a knock on the door. "May? I need to talk to you for a second." Thad's voice cracked.

Janie put a hand on May's shoulder. "I need to go, but if you want to talk later, stop by the *haus*. I'll see you on Church Sunday."

May opened the door and her friend slipped out, waving as she flew down the hallway. "Sorry, Thad, you're probably starved since our lunch got spoiled with talking. I can warm lunch back up."

"*Nein*, that's not why I'm here. The bishop is downstairs waiting to see you."

May's heart dropped to her stomach. "What?"

"*Jah*, I'll just take Leah and walk over to the *dawdi haus*. Give you some privacy."

May made her way downstairs and into the kitchen. The bishop sat at the kitchen table but nodded when she entered.

"*Hullo*, May. I'd like a minute of your time, if you're not too busy." The bishop casually sipped a mug of coffee that smelled as if Thad had warmed the leftover brew from lunch.

"Bishop, what can I do for you?" She sat, rested her elbows on the table and clasped her hands.

He shot her a stern look. "I drove out to see which day next week I should clear in my schedule for your wedding."

# *Chapter Four*

Thad's heart felt stretched, as if he wore it on the soles of his shoes and he was walking on it. If May decided to move to Indiana, what would he do without her? He and Leah would both miss her.

May loved Leah and he hoped enough to stay and marry him. If they married, he'd shower her with so much happiness, she'd have no choice but to fall in *liebe* with him again.

But if May ever found out the real reason why he married April, she would hate him.

A lump rose in his throat. What if May decided to move away, and he never saw her again? She was the only woman he wanted.

He glanced at the clock. One hour past the last time he looked. What was the bishop saying that it was taking so long?

Ethan entered the barn, letting the door bang as he walked toward Thad. "I'll start the evening milking, Mr. Hochstetler."

Thad nodded. "*Gut*. I'll help, and you can follow me."

*Jah*, he needed to concentrate on something to keep his mind off May. He applied the iodine mixture to the cows' udders while Ethan followed along behind with the alcohol wipe. Ethan was a *gut bu* and a hard worker. Thad appreciated the loyalty the young man gave him.

He finished his barn chores, stepped out of the barn and noticed the bishop's buggy still parked in his drive. He heaved a long sigh. It was not a *gut* sign that the bishop was still talking to May. That could only mean one thing—May said no and the bishop was trying to talk her into marrying him.

When the screen door banged closed, Thad gave a grunt and walked toward the bishop's buggy. His heart pounded like a blacksmith's hammer with every step.

The bishop met him at his buggy wearing a long face. Then he smiled at Thad. "*Jah*, she will marry you in two weeks. Since you have been married before, and her *mamm* and *daed* have passed away, she wants just a small gathering instead of inviting the whole community. Until then, you will sleep in the *dawdi haus*. I'll read the banns on Sunday."

After the bishop left, he felt numb. This seemed too *gut* to be true. He inched his way to the *haus*, pulled the screen door open, entered the kitchen and stopped cold. May was standing at the sink, her back toward him. He gawked at her, unsure what to say. Should he wait for her to speak first? His gut clenched as he pulled a chair away from the table and sat.

Though it was summer outside, a coolness filled the distance between them. Was she going to back out?

Had she truly forgiven him?

The minute she turned from the sink, his heart raced,

and his tongue felt like a piece of toast. He stood up, his knees shaking, when she approached the table.

*"Hullo."*

He nodded and smiled.

May motioned for him to sit. She sat across from him, laid her hands in her lap and straightened her back. "Were you surprised to hear the news from the bishop?"

"*Jah*, but *gut* surprised." He dropped his gaze to his hands folded on the table and studied them. Each callus, each skinned knuckle and each chipped nail had a story. He raised his eyes to hers. "I have just one question. Your answer won't stop the wedding, but I want to know…are you marrying me because you have forgiven me, or because you *liebe* Leah too much to leave her?" He held his breath for a second before blowing it out.

May glanced at the window, then returned her gaze to him. Her demeanor seemed more businesslike than happy that she'd just accepted a marriage proposal.

His pulse quickened. Something wasn't right. Had the bishop threatened a shunning or something if she didn't marry him?

He bit his lip and braced for the worst.

Silence stretched across the room. All he could hear was the pounding of his heart. It just occurred to him… he might not like what she was going to say.

Dampness beaded his brow.

May's heart nearly stuttered to a stop. "Thad…" She kept her gaze on her hands, then lifted her eyes to meet his. "I'm not going to lie to you or pretend this is something that it's not. I'll tell you the truth, and if you want to call off the wedding afterward, that's fine. I'll understand and move to Indiana."

He shifted in his chair, and she noticed the moisture dotting his forehead. Maybe she should have made this easy and bought a train ticket to Shipshewana.

"Listen, Thad. April asked me to take care of you and Leah, but she didn't tell me to marry you. Two things are keeping me in Iowa. I want to be the one to raise Leah, and I want to help you save the farm."

She peered into his face, then glanced away. He looked shocked. "Not quite what you wanted to hear?"

"I'm listening."

"Scripture tells us we must forgive or *Gott* will not forgive us. It's hard, but if He said I must, then I will… I have. Yet at times, like when I look at Leah and see your features, it floods back into my memory that you tossed me aside for April." Her voice quaked.

"May." Thad started to speak, but she held up a hand.

"You said you loved me. I'm not sure about that, but maybe so. We were always the best of friends. Back then, did we even know what *liebe* was? But if you had truly loved me, you wouldn't have married my sister. You'd have married me."

Discomfort lined his face.

"I'll try to make you a *gut frau*. It might take some time, but maybe after a while, I'll be able to put the past behind us and move on. But I can't promise that on some days it won't surface. If this doesn't work for you, I'll leave tomorrow."

"*Nein*, I want you for my *frau*, and I will do everything in my power to make you forget the past." He unclasped his hands on the table and reached his right hand across to her. She slowly put her hand in his. He clasped his fingers around hers and squeezed, then she squeezed. "The bargain is sealed."

Her cheeks burned and her heart nearly stuttered to a stop.

"We'll be married in two weeks and have the service here on the farm." His eyes held hers captive for several seconds before letting go.

He pulled his hand slowly away from hers as he stood, and a lonely feeling gripped her as he walked away.

She brought her hand to her face, curled her fingers and braced the knuckles against her chin as her elbow rested on the table. May took a deep breath and could smell the lingering scent of soiled straw.

The next day, May called her sister, *aents* and close friends to tell them her big news. Sadie insisted everyone come to her farm for the planning.

The following day dawned with a brilliant sun to chase away her cloudy mood. Fear started to shimmy up her spine. Had she made the right decision? She could still buy a train ticket. *Nein*, she shook his hand. She'd made a bargain.

She forced those thoughts from her head and hitched Gumdrop, her favorite horse, to her buggy and headed to her sister Sadie's farm to plan the wedding. The clip-clop of Gumdrop's hooves had a calming effect. She watched the yards of daffodils and roses go by, the birds sitting on the fence chirping take flight, and the occasional motor vehicle zip past.

She guided Gumdrop up the drive and passed the

toolshed. John, Sadie's *ehemann*, greeted her with a wave. "Mornin'."

"*Hullo*, May. Congratulations. Sadie is excited and started planning without you so you better hurry on in."

"*Danki*, John. That's what big sisters are for." She laughed as she ran to the *haus*.

Sadie flung open the door. "*Ach*, May, I can't believe you and Thad are getting married. I had no idea you two were back together. That's so *wunderbaar*."

Her *aents* and cousins from her *daed*'s side were there and took over the planning while May worked on her wedding dress. It would have been nice if *Aent* Edna could have made it, and her other relatives from Indiana, but it was too short notice to make travel plans. And some of her cousins didn't have the extra money for such things.

She held up her dress. It was the same material as her Sunday dress, only this one was in her favorite shade of blue. A sense of hope seemed to cling to the cloth as she laid it down and ran her hand down the bodice. A string of emotions wheezed through her one right after the other. Regret, turned to excitement, then slid into nervousness. Moisture gathered and clogged her throat. *Mamm, I wish you could have been here to see me married.* At the sound of shuffling feet, she cleared her throat and fluttered her eyelids to bat away the extra moisture.

"May, congratulations." *Aent* Matilda whirled into the room with her *tochter* Josephine close behind. "We are so happy for you."

"*Danki* for coming, and Josie, *danki* for being one of my attendants."

"Cousin, I'm thrilled you asked me. I'm so excited for you." Josie knelt on the floor beside May's chair and squeezed her hand. "This is so *wunderbaar*, and now Leah will have a real *mamm*."

Matilda flounced into a chair next to May. "*Jah*, and Josie and I will organize your kitchen help and see that all the food is prepared on time. Your wedding will be a very special day, indeed."

Matilda gave May a one-armed hug and shared what May's *mamm* and *daed*'s wedding day was like. The day flowed with joy and excitement, and Matilda remembered the stars in both her parents' eyes. "*Jah*, now we must go and help plan and prepare and you must finish your dress." She patted May's hand as she stood.

The air stilled after Matilda and Josie swished through the room like a broom, and May stared at her wedding dress and the stitch she just made. Her hands shook as she stuck the needle in the hem of the dress. It was really happening. She was going to marry Thad. Her heart beat fast and hard, but she wasn't quite sure why. It was only a marriage of convenience. *Nein.* A marriage bargain. Nothing more.

Before she'd left the farm, Thad had given the *youngies* instructions to clean the yard and barnyard, and when they finished with that, they were to start plucking the chickens for the wedding dinner. The women were planning to serve baked chicken, mashed potatoes, gravy, creamy celery casserole, coleslaw, pies, donuts, pudding and several cakes, which included two special ones that her friend Sarah and her sixteen-year-old *tochter* Mary would make.

When she got home from Sadie's, it was non-stop

work of washing walls, floors, fixtures, dusting from top to bottom, borrowing dishes and silverware, and planning the seating to feed one hundred guests. Although Matilda had organized and delegated a job to each of her cousins, May still insisted on helping. Most Amish weddings would have as many as three to four hundred guests. When an average Amish family was nine people, it didn't take long to fill the guest book. *Aent* Matilda and Josie were in charge of organizing the kitchen and cooks and May knew not to interfere.

Since Thad's farm had belonged to her parents, it made sense for her wedding to take place there.

On the eve of her wedding, May twirled around in her room like it was the last time she'd ever see it. Of course it wasn't, but why was that feeling stirring in her stomach? She stopped moving and blotted a tear that had collected in the corner of her eye. She glanced out the window and toward heaven. How she wished *Mamm* and *Daed* could be here with her right now. But if they were, what would they truly think about her marrying Thad? Would *Daed* have given his blessing?

May woke early and bolted upright in bed. Ach, *it's my wedding day!* A shiver of fear swept over her. Had she made the right decision? It wasn't too late; she could change her mind.

*Nein*, she'd given her word.

She jumped out of bed and slipped into her wedding dress. The noise from downstairs with Matilda and her helpers preparing food for the noon wedding meal seeped through the floor.

May took special care with her hair, pinning it back

and into a bun as her *mamm* had taught her when she was young. She carefully placed her new prayer *kapp* in just the exact place. This would be the only time she'd wear these clothes, then she'd pack them away for her funeral.

May smoothed her skirt and slipped her apron over it. The *Englisch* liked to wear fancy dresses to their weddings, but she was content with the Plain ways. If everyone in her community wore Plain clothes, then no one would appear wealthier than another, and she liked that thought.

A tap sounded on her bedroom door. "May? Open up, it's Janie and Josie."

She ran to the door and threw it open. "I'm so glad you're both here." She wrapped them each in a group hug, then stepped back. "How do I look?"

"That blue is the perfect color for you," Josie said, and Janie nodded in agreement.

"Are you getting cold feet?" Janie raised a brow. "Your face is saying take me out behind the barn and hide me."

"*Ach*, just a little bit. I hope this is the right choice. The bishop pressured me to make a decision, and now I'm not sure."

"Don't worry, you'll be fine. You've liked Thad ever since you were fourteen."

"*Jah*, but don't forget, he married April first."

Josie grabbed May's hand and held it tight. "Forgive like Jesus did."

"I'm trying." She glanced at the clock on her night-stand, then turned to her side-sitters. "It's almost nine o'clock… We'd better go downstairs."

They hurried to their bench in the family room as Thad and his attendants, his brothers Jonah and Simon, took their places.

At 9:00 a.m., the congregation started to sing the first song from the *Ausbund* while the ministers motioned to Thad and May to follow them to the back room, or rightfully called the council room for her wedding, for their twenty-minute premarital talk. Her stomach clenched as she stood. She'd seen other couples get marched off, but no one ever divulged what a twenty-minute talk was, not even Sadie. But it was considered part of the ceremony so it had a great significance. She blotted her hand on her skirt as the ministers entered the room first. Thad pressed a warm hand to her back as they entered. His strong support and nearness calmed her, knowing she wasn't in this alone. He turned and closed the door.

When they stepped from the room, Thad grabbed her hand and walked beside her. May almost jerked her hand away, but didn't. They were a couple now. They returned to their benches. Thad and his two attendants sat and faced May and her side-sitters.

After the ministers gave their sermons, Bishop Yoder delivered the main sermon that focused on the Old Testament marriages, their relationships and the obstacles their marriages faced. Just before noon, the bishop called May and Thad up front for the wedding ceremony.

Thad said his vows first.

The bishop glanced toward May. "Do you promise…?"

May froze. The words wouldn't come. Her heart

raced and her throat tightened. She drew in a deep breath of air, but her throat was too tight to speak.

Thad stared at May with a pale mask covering his face. "May?"

"*Jah*, take your time, May," Bishop Yoder whispered.

May squeezed her eyes closed. What was it Janie said? This was final. Forever. What was she thinking? She should have thought about this longer.

A faint shuffling of feet from someone on the benches caught her attention. *Jah*, she had to answer.

The bishop touched her elbow. "Do you need to sit?"

"*Nein*. I feel better."

The bishop repeated the question.

She cleared her throat. "Yes."

Bishop Yoder quickly pronounced them *ehemann* and *frau*. May froze as his words settled over her like a thin dusting of flour. It was real. She was Thad's *frau*.

After the closing words, Thad took her hand and pulled her gently to face him. "Don't look so scared. We are now one, forever and always, May." He pulled the back of her hand to his lips and bushed it with a kiss. A smile slowly spread across his face until it reached his eyes and tugged at May's heart.

She turned her head trying to hide her face, until she finally gave in and smiled back.

When Mildred's helpers had everything ready, she called to the wedding party to take their places at the bridal table.

They sat at the *Eck*, the bridal table, and ate their meal. There was little talking since everyone was hungry after the long morning. May took a sip of lemonade and let her gaze wander to Thad. He was talking to his *bruder* Jonah. She hadn't really paid much attention lately, but when he was cleaned up, he was a handsome man, her *ehemann*.

May turned toward Josie and Janie and joined in on their discussion, chattering as if they were at a frolic.

Thad reached over and gave May's arm a quick pat.

She pulled her attention from her side-sitters and focused on Thad. Her face twisted into a playful smile.

"It will be nice having a *frau*. Now I won't have to take out the garbage." His voice teetering toward the loud side.

Knowing he was trying to break the tension between them, she tossed him a not-on-your-life look with a raised brow. "You're not getting off that easy." They both chuckled.

Their laughter lightened the mood, and it helped May forget that he was April's *ehemann* first and she was once again getting April's hand-me-down clothing. Only this time it was her husband.

Thad glanced at her. "Are you sure you're okay, May?"

"*Jah*, it's just…my head is spinning. Two weeks ago, I had planned to buy a train ticket to Indiana. Now I'm married."

"But you're okay with it, right?" He caught her hand in his and squeezed.

"I'm fine."

"We need to walk around and greet our guests." He swung his legs over the bench and pulled her to her feet, wrapping his arm around her.

She shook aside the image of April eighteen months earlier, in this very spot, and clung to Thad's side as they walked around all afternoon and evening visiting with their guests.

When the last few buggies finally pulled away, Thad helped the *youngies* pick up the benches, and May stole her way back into the *haus* and up to Leah's room. She cracked the door and peeked in.

Josie, dressed in her nightgown, sat next to Leah's crib. She waved her in.

"I missed this little one," Josie whispered.

"Me, too." May quietly pulled the rocker over next to Josie's chair by the crib and sat.

"You should be with your new *ehemann*." Josie nodded toward the door. "I'm watching Leah. Go."

"I just wanted to check on her. He is helping the *buwe* stack the benches on the wagon so they'll be ready for Church Sunday."

"How does it feel to be a *frau*?"

The question bounced around in her head. She wasn't quite sure of the answer. She wanted to be Leah's *mamm*, and Thad came along as baggage. "It's a new feeling."

That was a lie. She felt numb.

Josie gave her a hug. "I'll help clean the mess tomorrow. You go get ready for bed. You're a married woman now. I'll sleep on the twin bed next to Leah's crib. And don't worry about a thing."

May slid out of the rocker, walked to the door, and glanced back at Josie and Leah. Leah looked like a little angel, and after the long day, Josie looked like she was asleep already.

She hoped her married life was as simple as that.

## *Chapter Five*

At noon a week later, Thad looked toward the *haus* and noticed May standing in the kitchen doorway waving her hand vigorously to get his attention. He stopped the buggy and stepped down to hear her words.

"Dinner is ready," she said with a pleasant voice but a weak smile tugged at the corners of her mouth.

The past week had been tense. May had married him, but ever since that day, she'd acted as if it were a mistake. He certainly didn't profess to know the mind of a woman, but if he had to guess, it seemed like she regretted her bargain.

Thad crossed the lawn and headed up the porch steps, dread dragging his heels. Another dreary lunch with May, watching her stare at her food until it was gone, then she'd jump out of her chair and start clearing the table. Anything else was better than a conversation with him.

Where was all the happiness he was going to shower on his *frau*? Forcing this marriage had been a bad idea. But he knew if May ever left the farm, she'd never come back. He had to be patient and give her time to warm up to him. They had only been married a week.

He'd always heard that the first year of marriage was the hardest. Maybe everyone who said that was right.

He hung his hat on the rack, washed his hands and quickly scooted to his chair, trying to stay out of May's way in the kitchen. The scent of fried chicken, mashed potatoes and gravy wafted through the air, not her usual lunch menu. May was a terrific cook, and even if her company was lacking, her meal more than made up for her coolness.

After silent prayer, May cleared her throat. "Thad, I want to apologize for the way I've acted toward you this past week and your marriage to April." He could see the tears run down her cheeks. "There is no excuse for my actions. You are my *ehemann* now…" the word stumbled out "…Leah is now my daughter, and I'd like to try to get along. Start fresh again. The marriage happened so fast. I made a decision." Her voice cracked.

His face burned as shame inched its way up his back. He set his fork down and swallowed hard. "I'm sorry, too. I should have told you that April and I were getting married instead of letting you hear about it when they read the banns at church. That was wrong. Instead, all the unspoken words have been hanging between us, creating a big ugly storm cloud. I'm sorry it had to come to this."

She wiped a quick hand down her cheek and glanced his way. "*Jah*, I agree."

For the rest of the meal, May talked to him and even smiled. She chatted about the garden, the strawberries she had picked and her expectations that she'd have an ample amount for canning. "If you bring in some cream, I'll make strawberry ice cream. Leah would like that."

"*Jah*, okay."

After milking, Thad headed across the barnyard toward the north forty to see how the pickers were progressing in the field. The tomatoes were a bumper crop this year. That would help offset what he lost on the milk, but even a bumper crop wouldn't save it if he lost much more income.

He watched May carry a basket of laundry out to the clothesline. She shook out her dresses and hung them in a row next to his shirts.

His heart raced. The sudden urge struck him to run over to May, pull her into his arms and press a kiss to her lips. When she was nearby, he couldn't take his eyes off her. Her slim form and that auburn hair peeking out from beneath her prayer *kapp* made him want to stand here all day and watch her.

He swallowed hard. Sweat beaded on his forehead. He searched his shirt pocket for his hanky. Empty. He checked his pants pocket. Nope. He removed his hat and rubbed his shirtsleeve across his forehead.

Somehow, he had to get May to fall in *liebe*, but he could see that wouldn't be easy. *Jah*, she said she was sorry for the way she acted toward his marriage to April, but had she really forgiven him? Actions spoke louder than words. And some days she barely tolerated him. He'd bide his time and think of a way, but his arms were sure itching to hold her.

He swiped his stained and sweaty hat against his trousers, then thumped it back on his head. He glanced at May one more time before continuing to the field.

* * *

May finished hanging the laundry, grabbed the basket and headed for the *haus*. When she noticed Thad watching her, her heart gave a weird jump.

*Lord, please grant me a double portion of patience and tolerance for Thad. Please help me stash my personal feelings and help save the farm. And sometimes, Lord, I feel I married Thad for the wrong reason. Forgive me.*

As the week went on, she saw less and less of Thad as he stayed busy with the harvest. He ran in the *haus* for dinner and supper, then worked until dark, barely seeing May or Leah. *Jah*, she knew farmers were busy, but he had an obligation to his *tochter*, didn't he?

When Leah awoke from her nap, May peeked around the corner of the crib. "Peekaboo!"

Leah laughed and held out her arms.

"There's my big *mädel*. Would you like your diaper changed so you'll be all sweet-smelling for your *daed*? Some day, we will start potty training. Won't that be fun?"

*"Nein."* Leah giggled.

"*Jah*, it will be fun."

*"Nein."* She laughed at the game they were playing.

Leah's eyes brightened and she jabbered away. She didn't really know what the words meant, but it sounded like a great idea.

May reached out her arms. "Let's go see *Daed*."

She carried Leah to the barn. Walking through the barn, she heard noise coming from Tidbit's stall. She stuck her head around the corner and Leah followed suit.

Thad looked up and smiled. "Ah, so my two girls

have come out to see me." He set his pitchfork against the wall, walked over and gave Leah a kiss on her head.

"Ew." May wrinkled her nose.

"Ew." Leah winkled her nose, than patted it with her hand.

"What brings you two out here? Wanting to help, maybe?"

She smiled. "Not hardly. Leah misses you. When you walk out the door, she watches it a long time for you to return. At least spend a little time with her when you come in to eat."

He nodded. "*Jah*, you're right. I'll spend some time with her at meals."

She held Leah out toward Thad. "Would you like to hold her now?"

"My hands are dirty and I'm smelly. Wait until I come in and clean up."

"Okay. Barbecued spare ribs will be ready in an hour." She wrinkled her nose and made the trip out of the barn faster than on the way in.

Thad smiled and shook his head as he watched May leave. For sure and certain, she didn't want him around but was willing to sacrifice her happiness for Leah. His heart ached each time he saw her sad eyes. How he longed to take her in his arms and hold her until her pain went away.

Whirling around to retrieve his pitchfork, his foot smashed a bug that darted across his path. *Jah*, it was evident that May's love for him was as dead as that bug. But what did he expect? This was a marriage of convenience and nothing more. Unless he could strike a spark in her, but how would he go about doing that? Maybe there was another way to win her heart…

He finished cleaning Tidbit's stall and would tackle the others after dinner. Parking his boots by the barn door, he slipped his feet into his shoes and headed to the *haus*. May's barbecued ribs were his favorite.

After dinner, Thad picked up Leah and set her on his lap. Her little eyes stared up at him intently, studying his features. She'd brought along her baby doll and he had to hold that on his other leg. Leah reached for his whiskers, but Thad turned his head fast and they slipped through her fingers. She giggled and giggled. He turned back, she grabbed for them again and he jerked them away.

She laughed and squealed. *"Daed."*

"What did you say?"

She laughed and showed her little teeth.

"May, did you hear what she said?"

"*Jah*, it was plain as day, she said *Daed*."

Leah's tiny fingers gripped his blue chambray shirt as if she were the one keeping him safe and secure. His heart melted. He stroked his finger over her velvety soft cheek. There was nothing he wouldn't do for these two girls. But this wee one needed all the protection he could give her.

She giggled and squirmed around on his lap, playing with her doll. She finally set her doll down and leaned back against him, her eyelids slowly starting to droop. She popped them open, but slowly they closed in sleep.

The sound of a dish breaking in the sink jerked his attention in time to see May lose her balance standing on a stool and fall. Her arms flying in every direction, she smacked hard against the sink, then crumpled to the floor. He hurried and laid Leah in her crib and ran back to help May.

She stuck her hand up. "*Nein*, don't touch me." She grunted as she tried to move. Then froze. And moaned as she slumped against the sink, her bottom firmly planted on the floor.

"Did you hurt your back?"

"*Nein.* I hit the sink with my arm and shoulder and probably bruised them *gut*. I twisted my ankle when I fell, so I can't stand on my left foot."

"Let me help you up, and I'll take a look."

"You're not touching me, Thad," she ground out through clenched teeth.

"Well, it's either that or I'm going to the barn to call an *Englisch* ambulance to take you to the hospital."

"Are you crazy? I'm perfectly fine." She tried to stand but the movement and exertion caused a flush to rise on her cheeks. She inhaled three deep breaths. "I might need a little help."

"I'll put my arm around your waist and lift you straight up. If you want me to stop, just say so."

She threw him a glance with fear-filled eyes as the colored drained from her face.

"I'll try not to hurt you." *Jah*, like that was really going to happen. He could already see a huge lump on her foot, and the way she held her shoulder, it might be broken, too. "I'll try to inch you up slowly. Take a deep breath."

She inhaled deeply, and before she could exhale, he had her on her right foot holding the left up off the floor.

"What happened to the inching idea?" She groaned and her cheeks paled.

He touched her hand, then her cheeks. They were cold and clammy. Fear crept into his heart.

"I'm so weak. Let me sit and rest a minute."

He helped her to a chair and slowly lowered her down. "Okay. I'm calling a driver and taking you to the hospital. I think your foot is broken and maybe your shoulder, too." He held his voice steady, but inside, he was shaking like a fall leaf in the wind.

"I'm feeling a little better, but my foot really hurts." Her voice cracked. She tried to move it but he could see tears in her eyes.

"If it's broken, it will hurt until the doctor sets it. I'm going to the barn to use the emergency phone to call for a car. Leah is sleeping—will you be all right?"

"Yes."

Now he knew something was broken or she'd never have so readily agreed. He watched her for just a second to make sure she looked settled enough that he could leave her for a few minutes.

When he returned to the *haus*, he crouched down next to May. "Are you okay?"

Her voice shook. "Sure. What will we do with Leah, take her with us?"

"*Nein.* I called the neighbors, Caleb and Sarah Brenneman. They'll come and pick her up. Since Sarah is pregnant, the bishop let them have a phone and Caleb just happened to be in the barn when I called."

"She'll be scared to go with someone she doesn't recognize." May heaved a nervous breath.

"I know, but it's probably time she got used to it.

Something like this could happen again." The minute the words left his mouth, he wanted to bite them back.

"I certainly hope not." She cringed when she leaned back against the chair.

He propped a hip against the counter. "So do I, but we need to plan for what could happen."

"I know. I just think about how she will miss us." Her voice wavered with worry and pain.

"I need to go to the toolshed and write out instructions for the *youngies* I hired to help weed the crops this week. With the past few days of rain, the weeds are out of control." He left a note on the workbench, then hurried back to the barn to give Tidbit a quart of oats and fresh water. The strong smell of soiled straw assailed his nostrils. He'd neglected his maintenance duties while trying to get the fields worked, but mucking out the stalls would need to wait a couple more days.

When he entered the kitchen, May had her arm propped on the table, and the other lay next to it, the hand curled closed and white-knuckled. The gravel in the driveway crunched under buggy wheels and hooves. Thad glanced out the window. "Sarah and Caleb are here."

He opened the door as Sarah flew to May's side. No doubt, Sarah's years of experience in the bakery business had prepared her for many unforeseen emergencies. "May! How do you feel?"

"A little better. *Danki* for taking Leah."

"*Jah*, of course. I'll pack enough bottles and clothes for a few nights, and Caleb will take her mattress so she'll have a familiar place to sleep." Sarah and Caleb dashed upstairs and returned to the kitchen with the mattress and a box and bag stuffed with Leah's things. Caleb carried it all out to the buggy.

Sarah bustled over to the downstairs crib, picked up Leah, her eyes big and round with puzzlement, and snuggled the tyke close.

Leah puckered up to cry. "Shh, little one," Sarah cooed softly until Leah settled back in the crook of her arm and closed her eyes. "She'll be fine." Sarah was still crooning to her when she disappeared out the door and Caleb latched it closed.

Silence filled the room as May stared at the door.

Thad noticed May shift on her chair and a pained expression crossed her face, but not like the one when she fell. This look, he imagined, was more about separation anxiety from Leah. He turned toward the window as a lump lodged in his throat and watched the buggy pull out of the drive, nearly colliding with the SUV that pulled in.

"Our ride is here." He helped May get to her feet and wobble out to the SUV. He hadn't wrapped his arms around May since they'd married. It felt strange as the swish of her skirt touched his leg when he tugged her close to give her support. Her warmth and the smell of strawberry shampoo evoked a memory tucked safely away. Until now.

Gott, *don't let me stumble.* He had a plan to win May's forgiveness, not just in words but also in her heart, and he didn't want to ruin his chance.

# *Chapter Six*

May held her breath. She squeezed Thad's hand tightly as she slipped into the SUV and settled on the seat. She blew out a long sigh. "My arm is so sore I can barely move it, and I can't step on my foot without excruciating pain. It's so swollen. What am I going to do if I'm in a cast? How will I take care of Leah or myself?"

"Take it easy and don't worry about all that. We'll be there in a few minutes." He tried to give her an encouraging look, but she could see he was worried, too.

The eighteen miles to Iowa City felt like it took hours. Each turn and sway of the vehicle caused pain to rip upward and over the top of her arm. She gasped and tried to watch the scenery passing by the window to take her mind off the trip. That didn't work. Her mind kept replaying Leah leaving the *haus* with Sarah and Caleb. Loneliness crept into May's heart knowing that little tyke wouldn't be there to greet her when she got home.

Her left hand moved to her temple and massaged the throbbing pain that had started there when Leah left the *haus*. Sarah would take *gut* care of Leah. Of that May had no doubt. But she still was worried about her.

The SUV jerked to a stop at the emergency entrance of the hospital and May bumped into Thad. She groaned.

"Are you okay?" He wrinkled his brow, then tossed the driver a warning look.

The man looked back over his shoulder. "Sorry about that."

Thad paid him, then helped May. She moaned and scooted to the edge of the seat, swung her legs around and pushed herself gently out of the SUV with her good arm, and gently eased into the waiting wheelchair that an attendant had pushed over to the vehicle.

With the advent of warmer weather, summer brought farm accident victims and several children with broken bones to the Emergency Room, all of whom were in line ahead of May to see the doctor.

"They'll call your name when it's time for your X-ray," the woman in Admitting said as she directed May to the waiting area.

Thad pushed May's wheelchair to a private corner away from the others. "Would you like some coffee?"

She nodded, and watched him saunter over to the coffee maker and pour her a cup. Guilt worked its way through her. What would she have done without Thad's help? She was hard on him, but this was the Thad she remembered, always so kind and willing to help a friend in need.

*Jah*, his tenderness was probably nothing more than a friend helping a friend. Except she wasn't only his friend. She was his *frau*. Like the bishop said, he was her forever helpmate.

* * *

May sat on a gurney in a cordoned-off area of the emergency room, waiting for the results of her X-ray. The cold room made her shiver all the way from her head to her feet. She grabbed the edges of the gurney with her left hand to support her aching body. The pain and soreness were making her tired. She wanted to lie down and sleep. If she could just rest a bit, she'd probably be fine.

She moved to the right, trying to get more comfortable. "Oh, it hurts to even move."

Thad walked over and stood next to her. "Lean on me."

She bumped against him and felt his warmth. His closeness stuttered her heart for a second. He slid his arm around her shoulder. "Feel better?"

She drew a ragged breath, but this time it wasn't from the pain. *"Jah, danki."*

The door opened and a handsome young man in a white coat hurried in and stuck out his hand. "I'm Dr. Kincaid. Nice to meet you, May. We're going to have you fixed up and on your way very soon. I'm just going to examine the injured areas."

He felt her shoulder, moved her arm around and looked at her hand. Then he took off her shoe, tenderly touched her ankle and examined her foot. He glanced up and looked at her face as he felt around. "What's your pain level from one to ten when I move your foot?"

"Maybe eight. If I try to stand on it a ten."

The doctor nodded. "Your shoulder and arm have bruising, but they're not broken. There is a lot of tissue damage so there will be discoloring and swelling for a few days."

He pushed a plastic-looking sheet onto a lighted box on the wall, then pointed. "This is the X-ray of your foot. Right here, in the fourth metatarsal in the left foot, is a crack and a tiny chip out of the bone. We'll need to immobilize the ankle so it won't move and put pressure on the cracked bone. That will allow it to heal and prevent further injury."

"But, Dr. Kincaid, I have a one-year-old daughter. I can't be laid up a few weeks."

"I'm sorry, but you really don't have a choice. You could injure it further if you don't let it heal properly. I'm going to put your foot in a boot support and after the swelling goes down, you'll be able to move around comfortably. You'll have limitations, but you should still be able to care for a small child. Your shoulder and arm are fine, just bruised. They'll heal in a few days but they might get a little stiff. But until then, you won't want to pick up or hold a child. I can write an order for physical therapy on that arm, if you like?"

Thad stepped forward. "*Nein*, we don't have money for that. Isn't there something she can do at home that I could help her with?"

"Of course. Just have her start with stretches, then in a day or two add light exercises like lifting a can or fruit jar. When the shoulder heals some, she can lift the can over her head to stretch out the muscles until she gets her strength back."

Her heart gave a cold shiver. "How many weeks will I need to do the exercises?"

The doctor glanced up from writing on the chart.

"Keep them up until the shoulder and arm are totally healed, three, maybe four weeks until it's totally healed. Start the stretches right away. In a day or two start the exercises. Also," he pointed to an egg-shaped lump on the top of her foot, "that bone chip torpedoed up and into your muscle when it broke, causing tissue damage. That's why you have this swelling. Apply ice packs when you get home. Twenty minutes on and twenty minutes off for two hours and that should take the swelling down. Later today or tomorrow, dark bruising will spread over the top of the foot, but it'll go away. It will take about four to six weeks for that bone to heal."

She tamped down the nausea that threatened. Fear twisted her stomach into a knot. "Four to six weeks? I live on a farm. I can't be laid up that long."

"I'm sorry, but you don't want to do permanent damage to that foot."

"Still, with the restrictions, I'll need to hire a mother's helper."

"That shouldn't really be necessary, but suit yourself. Just no running, and stairs will be awkward to maneuver with the boot. For the next few days, you're going to be very sore and walking may be difficult until the swelling goes down."

May slumped back against Thad.

"May, don't worry. I'll help you. We'll work it all out together."

"I've heard that the Amish always helped each other out in times of need."

"*Jah*, we do." May nodded. "I just hate to impose on others. It's canning season and everyone's gardens are ready at once. But it can't be helped."

Dr. Kincaid placed May's foot in the walking boot and fastened the straps snugly around her foot and leg. "I want to see you in six weeks. In the meantime, remember, no work, stay off the foot and apply ice three times a day until the swelling is gone."

May thanked the doctor for his help while Thad left her for a moment to go call a driver to bring them home.

She slumped back in the chair next to Thad while they waited for their ride. A dark cloud pressed down on her as she thought about Leah. She'd be worried and confused when she awoke in the morning at the Brennemans and not in her own bed, in her own home with May snuggling her close.

"May, are you okay?" Thad reached over and lightly laid his hand on top of hers.

"*Jah*, just thinking about Leah. I hope she's not scared."

How was Leah ever going to handle this? *Nein*. How was she ever going to handle this?

Sixty minutes later, the SUV arrived at their farm. May clutched the sheet of instructions for her medicines, the care of her injured foot and her next appointment written at the top. As Thad ran around to her side of the car to help her out, she stared out the window at the porch steps. "I never noticed before, but there are so many steps."

"Don't worry, I'm here to help you." He held the car door as she slid out and gingerly stepped on the ground. "Are you okay?"

"*Jah*, but can I hold on to your arm until we get inside the *haus*? I'm still getting used to walking in this boot."

He closed the door and held his elbow out for her to grab. Her boot clunked on each step until they slowly reached the top.

She stopped, released his arm and heaved a sigh.

Thad slid his arm around her waist. "You okay?"

"Just needed to rest a second." She drew in a deep breath. "I can make it the rest of the way on my own now."

Thad took his arm away from her waist and opened the door. May stepped in, stopping just inside.

Gretchen's voice shattered the silence. "What's been going on in here? It looks like you two were fighting, broken dishes and the stool turned over. Shame on you both! Thad, you're too old to act like a hooligan. You never fought with April like this."

May's back stiffened. "We didn't have a disagreement." She hobbled to a chair and sat down feeling Gretchen's scalding glare on her back.

"I've cleaned up the mess you two made."

"*Mamm*, May fell off the stool putting away dishes and broke a bone in her foot. *Danki* for cleaning up the mess. I had planned on doing that when we returned."

"Where is Leah?"

"I called Sarah and Caleb Brenneman and they came and got Leah. They will keep her a few nights until May is feeling better."

"You had me worried sick. I didn't know what was going on. You should have run over to the *dawdi haus* and told me."

"May was in a lot of pain, and I didn't want to leave her. I figured we'd be back before you even noticed."

"Of course I noticed. I worry about what goes on over here."

"*Danki*, Gretchen, I appreciate your concern. And *danki* for cleaning up the mess."

Thad stepped toward his *mamm*. "May isn't feeling well and I'm going to help her into bed. You can visit with her tomorrow."

He pressed a hand to his *mamm*'s back and escorted her swiftly to the door. "I'll let you know tomorrow how she is feeling."

Gretchen huffed and strutted out the door, as she headed back to the *dawdi haus*.

When Thad closed the door and turned, he shrugged. They both knew Thad's mother was a handful. "Are you going to pick up Leah at Sarah and Caleb's?"

"*Nein*, not for a few days. You're tired and need rest. Tomorrow, we'll talk about new arrangements for Leah and about hiring someone to take over your work."

"I'm worried about her."

"I know, but the Brennemans will take very *gut* care of her. Quit worrying. Right now, you think about yourself."

"I… I can take care of Leah just fine." A nervous laugh belied her words. Her arm and shoulder throbbed and her foot was so swollen she could hardly move it. But she was sure Thad saw through her ruse.

"*Nein*. You cannot. I don't want you hurting your foot any further or risk you dropping Leah. Maybe when the swelling is down and you're stable on your feet, but not now. You wobble like a pregnant cow ready to calve. Let's get you upstairs so you can rest and I'll bring you some ice for that foot." He helped her to stand up, placed his arm around her and gently supported her.

At the touch of his strong arm pulling her close, an unexpected spark of excitement coursed through her. Her traitorous heart raced as she tried to control it, to dismiss it like it hadn't happened. Only it had. She focused her attention to the staircase just ahead and tried to bring her breathing back to normal.

She took a step but swayed as the boot and swollen foot interrupted her balance for a second.

She hadn't realized just how much strength the ordeal had sapped from her. Her head began to pound. She gulped a breath and tried to flash Thad a smile, but no doubt he could see through her efforts.

She was sure pain, worry and weakness etched lines around her eyes.

Thad shook his head. "*Nein*, I've made the decision, you are too weak right now to take care of Leah. I'll see if I can hire a mother's helper. Do you know of a girl who might take the job for a couple of months, or for at least the next two or three weeks? We'll need her to live here."

May thought for a moment. "My cousin Josie. She is the only one I can think of." Fear edged into her throat as her voice shook the last sentence into existence. She loved her cousin but she was as bossy as *Aent* Matilda.

Thad noticed the strained expression on May's face as she sat on her bed, and he couldn't decide if it was from physical pain or the pain of missing Leah. He patted her back. "Is there anything you need right now?"

She pushed his hand away. “I’m fine. I can take care of myself.”

From what he’d seen, that didn’t seem to be the case, but he let it go for now.

May rubbed her free hand over her injured right arm. “I could rest for a while, and then we could go over and see how Leah is doing.”

“*Nein*. Let’s not confuse her any more than she probably already is with staying with them. To visit her and leave would just upset her. When they picked up Leah, Sarah said since she is expecting her first *boppli*, she’s anxious to have Leah around for the experience and to get her household in a routine of helping with a wee one.”

He walked to the door, glanced back and caught the lonely expression that crossed May’s face. She spent every waking hour with Leah. He could see it was upsetting for her to let her pumpkin stay somewhere else just a few nights, not to mention a week or more. “I’ll offer Josie a little more if she’ll come right away.”

“*Danki*, Thad.”

He couldn’t tell by the sound of her voice if she was feeling relief or dread. “I’ll call her right away.”

“*Aent* Matilda’s number is on the pad in the barn.”

He nodded. “I won’t be a minute.”

Thad hurried to the barn and the phone that the bishop had allowed him to have ever since April was pregnant and went long overdue. He’d used it to call the emergency unit when April died after she delivered the baby.

He swallowed back that memory and dialed the number of the phone shanty by May’s *Aent* Matilda. He explained their dilemma and asked if Josie would be available to come and stay a few weeks. He left his number and hung up.

Since May was napping, he strolled to the north forty to check on the *youngies* and see if they had completed weeding the field. Carl was supervising the others. As he approached, it looked like Carl had everything under control. The field looked clean. He waved and Carl ran between two rows to where he was standing.

"How's it going, Carl?"

"Real *gut*. We're almost done."

"We'll pick on Friday. Will you tell the other *buwe*?"

"Sure, no problem. Ethan has gone to the barn to start the milking process. When we get done here, would you like us to go help him?"

"*Jah*, that would be *gut*."

"How's May?"

He shook his head. "Her foot really hurts and doc said it would be a few weeks to heal but she is in a boot and getting around for the most part."

"That's *wunderbaar*."

Thad headed back to the barn and as he got close, he heard the phone ringing, which set his feet to hard run. He yanked open the door, and got the phone just in time.

"I almost hung up." Josie chuckled. "I was just planning on leaving a message. I can't come right away. I have other commitments and can't come until a week from today, is that okay?"

"*Jah*, that'll work. *Danki*."

Thad panted, trying to get his breath back as he entered the kitchen. May would probably be awake, stewing about where he was and if he heard back from Josie.

He tapped lightly on her door in case she was asleep, then edged the door open and stuck his head around the corner.

"I'm awake."

"How do you feel? But that's probably a stupid question."

"I feel a little better. Why are you panting?"

He took a deep breath and blew it out. "Sorry, I ran to the *haus* from the barn. Josie can't come for a week, so we'll need to let Sarah and Caleb take care of Leah until Josie can make it."

It was the first smile he'd seen on her face since he'd broken May's heart. "Why the smile?"

"I was afraid that Josie might have gotten another job and wouldn't be able to make it. That's a big load off my mind knowing that Leah can come home in a few days."

Leah was her ray of sunshine. He hoped someday he could put a smile like that back on her face. "I'll make you a cup of tea."

May gave him a thankful nod, her eyes brimming with softness like clear, turquoise ocean water covering a warm sandy beach. It was funny how that image just flashed through his mind. One day when they were courting, May confided how she wanted to see the ocean wash up on a beach. She wanted to walk through the surf with her bare feet and let the wet sand squish between her toes.

When the teakettle whistled, he put a tea bag in each cup and poured in hot water. He put a few cookies on the tray and carried it upstairs. He pulled a chair up by the bed and set the tray on her lap. He swirled the bag around in his cup, eventually pulling it out and setting it on the tea bag holder sitting on the tray.

He glanced over at May, still swirling her bag. "You must like strong tea."

"What?" She looked up, then back down at her tea. "Not really." She tugged the bag from the cup and set it next to his. She gingerly put the cup to her lips and took a sip as her eyes stared at the quilt.

"Something bothering you, May?"

"I just keep thinking about Leah. She'll miss me."

"Sarah and Caleb's son Jacob will entertain her, and their daughter Mary will fuss over her, no doubt. She'll *liebe* it there."

"That's what I'm worried about. I'll seem like dull company when she comes home."

"What? Don't be ridiculous! You're her *mamm*. She will always *liebe* you. Maybe we should get her a kitten or dog to play with. No doubt Jacob will introduce her to his cat, Tiger."

May wrinkled her nose. "We'll see. She's only a year old. Maybe later."

"I know you miss her. Whenever you want to see Leah, and you're feeling strong enough, I'll take you to the Brenneman's *haus*."

Her face brightened. *"Danki."*

"Now, you look tired and need to rest. I'm going to check the refrigerator. Was there any ribs left over?"

May jerked her head in his direction. "*Nein*, but I don't think I can make supper."

He nodded. "I'll fry some ham and make us French toast, how does that sound?"

"Great. I'm going to take a nap." She picked the tray up off her lap and handed it to him.

"Do you want to eat downstairs? I can come up and get you."

"The swelling in my foot is down. I think I can manage."

"I'm going to make sure. I'll come up and help you. You are too important of a commodity to have anything happen to you."

She smiled for the second time today. "You're too late, I'm already damaged goods." She pointed to her foot.

He gave her a wink as he stood. "*Jah*, but now you are captive company."

After chores, Thad washed up, sliced the ham and then made the batter for French toast. The sizzling maple-glazed ham permeated the air with an aroma that teased his stomach.

*Thump. Thump.*

He stepped back from the stove and listened. *Thump.* He sat his spatula down on the spoon rest and ran to the stairs. "I thought you were going to wait until I came and helped you?"

"I wanted to see if I could maneuver this boot around." Under his cautious eye, May shuffled through the door and slumped into a chair at the table. "Mmm, that smells *gut*. I didn't know I was so hungry."

"I'm glad you're not too picky. My skills as a cook are limited, I'm afraid."

"*Nein.* I'm very grateful to you for all your help.

You know your *mamm* wouldn't approve if she saw you waving that spatula like you know what you're doing."

Thad grinned. "What she doesn't know won't hurt her. When I was young and hungry and *Mamm* wasn't home, I cooked all the time." He raised his spatula up and down in the air as if he was lifting a hundred-pound bale of hay.

"*Ach*, my hero," she laughed, and their eyes met for a second before she pulled away.

A soft knock sounded on the door. Thad put down his spatula. "I hope it's not *Mamm* again," he whispered as he passed May.

He opened the door to three wonderful women holding baskets of what smelled like food. "Come in, come in. And if that is what I think it is, I can retire my spatula for a few days."

Hannah Smith, Minnie Miller and Mary Brenneman, her neighbors and dear friends, crowded through the door, laughing at Thad and rushing to May's side. They each swirled an arm around May and hugged her gently.

"We were so sorry to hear about your fall." Hannah set her basket of food on the table. "There's a couple casseroles here, plus breads, meat loaf and desserts. You—or Thad—won't have to cook for several days."

"*Danki*, that's *wunderbaar*."

"So how is married life treating you?" Minnie asked, with a teasing tone. "Maybe we shouldn't ask since you broke your foot and you'll be chained to this *haus* for several days."

The ladies chatted, sharing the latest news of Jesse and Kim Kauffman, who were moving to Indiana, and Turner and Naomi Lapp were expecting another *boppli*.

They teased May and Thad a little before saying good-night and then headed home, promising they would be back soon to visit.

Thad closed the door after them. "Supper is almost cold."

"That's okay. I'm starved. You made it, and I'm going to eat it."

Something in the way May said that warmed his heart. It had a pleasant tone and even a fondness. Could it be that she was finally setting the past on the shelf and going to give their marriage a chance?

# *Chapter Seven*

A golden stream of sunbeams poured through May's window and warmed her face. Reluctantly her eyes opened. She glanced at the clock. 10:00 a.m. She'd slept all through the night and almost all morning. She had slept for twelve hours. Thad would think her lazy.

She jerked upright, then stopped. A wave of pain seized her foot, and a pronounced ache traveled from her shoulder down her back to her hips. It was as if a horse and buggy had driven over her. She threw her legs over the side of the bed, stepped into her ankle brace and stood. Another wave of pain washed over her. She moved slowly toward the hook where her dress hung on the wall.

Each step was a challenge. She stopped, pulled in a deep breath and blew it out.

Her muscles felt tight and needed stretching. The fall yesterday must have pulled and bruised every muscle in her body. She rested for a moment, then sucked in three deep breaths and walked to the wall where a peg held her dress. She pulled her dress off the peg, draped it over her head and slipped her injured arm through the sleeve, then the other. *Ach*, it hurt more than she thought it would. She bit her lip and braced her back against the wall for a moment. She felt a little dizzy from the pain. In a minute, it cleared.

A soft tap sounded on the bedroom door.

"Yes. Is that you, Thad?"

The door cracked open. "Can I come in a minute?"

"Stay right there. I don't have my prayer *kapp* on." Her hair was a mess. She couldn't let him see her like this, and she probably needed to pinch her cheeks and bring a little color to them.

"Caleb called while I was in the barn. They will bring Leah back to us next Friday, if we decide that you're feeling better and ready to handle her."

"That would be *wunderbaar*."

"Do you need help getting dressed?" His voice seemed hesitant.

"*Nein.* I'm just sore and moving slow as a caterpillar. I'll be down in a minute to fix breakfast."

"Not necessary. I've already fixed scrambled eggs and sliced ham. So when you come down, it'll be waiting for you."

Had she heard him right? She pushed away from the wall and took a step in his direction. "You made breakfast?"

He chuckled. "Don't be so surprised. I told you last night, just because I'm a man doesn't mean I don't know how to cook a little or take care of myself. I'm heading back out. I left a note on the table, but I wanted to check on you. I'll stop back later." He pulled the door closed.

She smiled.

A small spark of relief surged through her as she fought with her prayer *kapp* to get it in place over her bun. The next time Sarah or someone stopped by, she'd ask them to help her with her hair. She sighed at the effort it took to get dressed. It would have been noon before she had breakfast ready, moving at this pace.

The aroma of strong coffee hit May's nostrils when she entered the kitchen, followed by the tantalizing whiff of honey-glazed ham that set her stomach growling. She reached for the orange juice in the gas-powered refrigerator and gasped at what she saw. Thad had made meat loaf sandwiches, all wrapped up and stacked on a shelf ready for lunch.

A tinge of guilt nudged her. He was trying to be nice, and she appreciated that.

A smile pulled at the corner of her mouth although she tried to resist. For sure and certain, he had a sweet way about him sometimes.

A knock sounded on the screen door, then it opened. "*Ach*, Janie, what are you doing? Come in, come in."

Janie rushed to May and gave her a big hug. "It's all over town that you fell and some big handsome man caught you and saved your life. That big strong man wouldn't happen to be your *wunderbaar ehemann*, would it?" She gave her a knowing wink.

"He didn't exactly catch me. I wish he would have, then I might not have broken my foot. *Danki* for stopping by."

"Of course. I baked you some cookies. Chocolate chip." Janie held up a plate covered with plastic wrap. "What else would you like help with while I'm here?"

"Could you help me wash my hair? My arm and

shoulder are sore and it's hard to lift my arms above my head."

"I can do that while I tell you my big news. Let's go to the sink. Where's your shampoo?"

"Under the sink. *Ach*, what big news?"

Janie giggled. "Jonah Hochstetler asked me out."

*"Nein,"* May gasped.

"Yes, yes, yes. He is every bit as handsome as his big brother Thad."

"When did all this happen?"

"At the wedding while you were busy being a new *frau*. We spent most of the afternoon together."

"I can't believe you waited so long to tell me."

"Now, May, as you well know, courting is a private matter to the Amish. Besides, I wanted to make sure there was some kind of spark. Some real feelings there. *Ach*, then he asked me out again." She gave a little scream, then quieted. "I hope Gretchen the Grouch didn't hear me."

May smiled behind her hand. Her mother-in-law was rather grouchy. But it wasn't right to agree with Janie openly. "So how many times have you gone out with him?"

"Several times. It's been so *wunderbaar*. I really like him, May. I was hoping that Simon would ask Josie out, but it didn't happen. I think she sort of liked him."

"For real? I hadn't noticed any of this going on at my wedding."

"*Jah*, well, you were a little busy with that handsome *ehemann* of yours. Don't think I didn't notice you two holding hands and snuggling at times."

"Oh, stop. He just had his arm around me, and he is my *ehemann* after all."

"I know. I just wanted to see if you did, too. How are you two getting along in your bargain marriage?"

"I shouldn't have told you about that. You must never tell anyone. Promise me, Janie."

"May, anyone could figure it out. You hated him something awful after he married April. I'm actually shocked you gave in to the bishop."

May shot Janie a stern stare. "I had my reasons."

"How does your hair feel? It's all clean and back up in a bun."

"I forgot to tell you, Josie is coming to stay a few weeks and help me take care of Leah while my foot is healing. If she likes him so much, maybe we could have Simon over for dinner."

"Now, May, don't go playing matchmaker. You didn't like it when the bishop first came to you."

"That was different. I'm only going to ask him if he is interested."

Janie chatted away, listing all the pros and cons to a match between Simon and Josie. "If it did happen, and she married Simon and I married Jonah, we would all three be sisters. *Ach*, that would be *wunderbaar*. *Jah*, and now before I go, I'm going to tidy up Thad's messy kitchen." Janie cleaned the stove and washed dishes, the whole time talking and sharing her dream for her and Jonah.

May smiled and got a word in sideways occasionally.

Thad had cooked breakfast. He was good to make eggs and sandwiches, even though he hadn't cleaned up.

She was grateful to Thad, and to Janie, for all the help around the house. But a veil of shame covered May's heart. She was careless to have gotten up on the stool and fallen. Now Thad had to spend his valuable time helping her, or paying others to do her work. Josie would work for free, but she knew Thad would want to pay her. Money he didn't have right now. She felt useless. Instead of helping Thad, she was a burden to him.

The week passed slowly. May rested as much as possible to keep the swelling down. She scratched around the boot. Her foot was already mending. She could feel it getting stronger every day. The bruising was gone.

She puttered around the kitchen. When she opened a cupboard door, she noticed Thad had rearranged the contents so the dishes they used every day were more accessible on the lower shelves. It was nice how he surprised her with these little helpful gestures without asking her, just taking it upon himself to make things more convenient.

She smiled to herself when she thought of him working in the kitchen, and an image of him with his beard tickled her memory. When they courted, he was single and clean-shaven, but Old Order Amish followed the law Moses gave that a man at adulthood wasn't to cut his hair or beard. But May didn't mind. The beard matured his face and even gave him a dignified appearance. With some men, the beard changed their appearance, and it wasn't for the better. She couldn't say that about Thad. His dark hair and beard framed his dark blue eyes.

When he was in the *haus* with her, his gaze often followed her when he thought she wasn't looking. He wanted to help her, but she had to show him she was strong enough to take care of Leah.

May scooped up a dust cloth. She worked alone for two hours, dusting and cleaning until her good arm started to tire. But it was important she show Thad she was getting stronger and ready to have Leah come back home. She straightened her back and stretched to ease the tightness. Today, her arm was only a little sore but felt stronger. Her foot felt comfortable in the boot. Tonight, a nice dose of liniment smoothed over the foot and arm would help them heal even faster.

She glanced at the clock. Almost noon. May opened the refrigerator and pulled out the sandwiches she had noticed earlier that Thad must have made again, poured the lemonade and set the plates on the table.

At noon, she heard Thad's boots thumping up the porch steps and the screen door squeak open. He hesitated when he saw her and jerked his head toward the table. "How are you feeling today?" he drawled in Pennsylvania Dutch.

"A little better. *Danki* for rearranging the cupboards." It amazed her how simply that gratitude rolled off her tongue, with no bitter undertone.

Thad must have noticed, because his bunched shoulders relaxed as he washed up at the sink, then he took an easy gait to his chair at the table.

A playful smile pulled at the corners of his mouth for the briefest second before he wiped it away. She could see he wanted to make another comment but thought he'd better not tempt the light mood.

After silent prayer, May took a bite of her meat loaf sandwich. It actually felt *gut* to eat a sandwich that Thad had made especially for her.

A knock sounded and the screen door opened. "Yoo-hoo! Is anyone home?"

May's back stiffened.

Thad called out, "Come in, *Mamm*."

"*Hullo*, dear. I came to see how May was doing and if there was anything I could do to help."

"That was very nice of you to stop by, *Mamm*, but we have everything under control."

May threw Thad a sidelong look. She liked his vote of confidence. "*Danki* for stopping by, Gretchen. I'm doing much better and up on my feet. It is a little slow going in the boot, but I'm managing." Hopefully, this was Gretchen's way of trying to make amends.

"Well, if you don't need any help right now, I'll stop by again tomorrow."

May and Thad finished their lunch, and Thad set his napkin down on the kitchen table.

"I have a dairy association meeting at four o'clock this afternoon. Will you be okay staying here by yourself for a little while?"

"Of course, but could you lift that bucket of string beans to the table so I can snap them?"

May grabbed a towel and laid it on the table, and he set the bucket down. "I'll stick my head back in before I go. Anything else?"

"*Nein*, I'm *gut*."

After an hour of snapping beans, she stretched and exercised her arm, then finished snapping the beans. She rinsed the beans in cold water, drained and stored the bowls in the refrigerator.

Thad poked his head in the door and called out. "May, I'm leaving for the meeting."

"Fine. See you later."

She had just enough time to rest, then she'd have to start thinking about supper, although that would be easy. So many members of their community had dropped off food. May laid her head against the back of the chair in the living room for just a minute to rest.

Sometime later, she heard someone call her name. "May. May?"

She opened her eyes and noticed her *ehemann* standing over her, the sweet smell of the goat's milk soap wafting in the air. "Oh, you're home. How was the meeting?"

"Not *gut*." He sat down next to her. "Because there is an overproduction of organic milk, the association is only selling 85 percent and the rest is being sold at regular price. This is on top of the price of the organic milk dropping, too."

May gasped. She reached over and covered his hand with hers. "How long can we last with just the crops for income?"

He leaned his head on the back of the chair, then lifted it and faced her. "Not long. The only way we are surviving this year is because of our vegetable crop. Let's pray we don't have weather that will ruin it. But if the dairy association can't get a response from the USDA, we might have to take drastic action."

"What kind of action?" Panic swept through her.

"Sell out!"

Fear prickled the hair on her arm as her gaze met his. Besides Leah, saving the farm was the reason she made the marriage bargain. Selling wasn't going to happen.

*Nein*, not if she had to sell every stick of furniture they had, she wouldn't let them lose the farm.

# *Chapter Eight*

May stood at the kitchen sink while the Friday morning sun streamed in through the window onto the African violet sitting on the windowsill. She checked the plant's soil. *Jah*, still moist.

Her thoughts wandered to the farm. What could she do to bring in a significant amount of money? Get a job? Who would take care of Leah? *Nein*, she'd miss her pumpkin too much to get a job.

Hearing buggy wheels and horse's hooves clomping up the drive, she glanced out the window, hurried across the porch and clunked her boot down each step. Thad raced from the barn and they reached Sarah and Caleb's carriage at the same time.

Caleb helped Sarah and Leah down, and as soon as Leah saw May, she nearly jumped into her arms.

"*Mamm*. Home, *Mamm*."

"I'm so glad you're here, sweetheart. *Danki* for taking care of her."

Sarah gave a flip of her hand to wave the thought away. "We were glad to do it. We loved having her. She missed you, but Jacob and Mary kept her busy and entertained."

She hugged Leah as her arms encircled May's neck. She kissed her pumpkin's cheek. "It's so *gut* to have you home. I have missed you."

Seven-year-old Jacob lifted a box from the carriage and set it on the ground. "*Jah*, I can carry her easy."

"*Jah?* You must be very strong." May winked.

"She even has a loud burp, louder than my *boppli bu* cousin."

"Jacob. A gentleman doesn't tattle on a lady." Caleb smiled. "She was the perfect *haus* guest. We will watch her any time you want us to."

Thad put his arms around both Leah and May and gave a hug. Leah turned to her *daed* and planted a big kiss on his cheek. "*Danki*, Leah, I missed you, too. Come in the *haus*, all of you. I'm sure May has some coffee she could brew."

While Caleb pulled Leah's crib mattress from his buggy, Thad and Jacob carried in the rest of her things and toted them straight up to her room.

May headed to the stove. "The coffee is hot. Would you like a cup, Sarah?"

"*Nein*, we have other errands to run and thought we'd drop her off first. I knew you'd be anxious to see her."

The men tromped down the stairs and returned to the kitchen.

"Come on, Jacob, time to go." Caleb headed for the door, held it open and motioned for Sarah to go before him.

Sarah turned back toward May. "Let me know if you need any more help. We'll be glad to watch Leah again."

"*Danki* for everything."

Thad came back in the kitchen from seeing them off. He walked over to May, and kissed his *tochter* on the cheek. Leah reached her arms out to her *daed*. "Oh, so you are going to come and see me. I was feeling bad that May was the only special one." He glanced at May.

"*Jah*, she loves her *daed*."

"I have a surprise for you, Leah. Mama cow has a new baby. Shall we go see it?"

Leah nodded.

"Want to come, May?"

"*Nein*, not right now. You spend time with your *tochter* alone."

May unpacked Leah's boxes of bottles. Filled them and placed them in the refrigerator.

The slamming of a car door pulled her gaze to the window. She hurried to the door and pushed it open. Her cousin stepped out of the car, as the driver lifted her luggage out of the trunk. She paid him and dragged her suitcase to the porch.

"*Ach*, Josie, how nice to see you. *Danki* for coming."

"It's no problem, I wanted to help. How are you feeling?" She gave May a hug.

"Would you like a cup of coffee?"

"*Nein*, sit. I'm here to help you."

"*Danki*, but I'm getting along much better." May started toward the cupboard. "I'll probably just need your help a couple of weeks or so."

The screen door banged as Thad stepped inside with Leah in his arms. He set Leah on the floor with her toys, then bent down to pick up Josie's suitcase. "As long as she is here and ready to stay a few days, we will accept her offer of assistance. Leah and I just went out to the pasture to see a new baby calf."

Josie smiled and looked at Leah. "*Hullo*, sweet girl. Did you go out and see the baby calf?"

Leah squealed and pointed her finger.

"Did you see mama cow, too?"

Leah jabbered on and on, laughing and giggling, then jabbered more about her adventure.

Josie glanced at Thad. "You are a very popular *daed* right now."

He motioned to the door. "*Danki* for coming, Josie. I'll take your suitcase upstairs so you can get settled in your room."

Thad tossed May a what-are-you-doing look with a raised brow. She raised her brow right back at him. She knew his concerns. She'd told Josie she didn't need to stay too long, and he wanted to make sure May had all the help she needed.

She shrugged, picked up Leah and laid her in her downstairs crib for a nap. She followed Thad and Josie to make sure Josie was comfortable with the room.

Thad had plunked the suitcase down on the bed and gave May a cautionary look. "I'm glad you're here, Josie. May really needs the help. She needs to stay off that foot or it will never heal." His tone carried a note of concern.

"We're fine. Go do the chores. Supper will be ready when you're done." May rewarded his thoughtfulness with a gentle smile. "I can be on the foot. I just need to rest, too."

"*Danki* for coming, Josie." Thad got the last word in. When they'd courted long ago, she had thought *Gott* had handpicked Thad for her. Who knew? Maybe this had been God's purpose and plan for her all along.

Thad heaved a sigh as he unhitched Honeydew, and laid the collar and breeching off to the side. An image of May looking fetching today fought its way back into his mind. Her cheeks had a glow that he hadn't seen in a long time. Had Josie's visit put it there?

He brushed the horse down, hooked a fresh bucket of oats on the fence and closed the gate. He had hoped that eventually May would forgive him for the past, and it seemed like she had started to do just that. He just hoped and prayed that she never found out the true reason he'd married April or she'd never forgive him. Never.

Thad finished his chores and made his way back across the barnyard to the *haus*. It bothered him that he'd lied to May, or rather, that he hadn't told her the whole truth, but he knew it was for her own *gut*. He shuddered to think what she would say or do if she knew he had lied to her. To everyone. If she ever found out, this little bit of heaven with her that he'd found would be over.

He approached the driveway, looked up and saw a buggy there. *Nein*... It was Elmer's horse and buggy nearly blocking his way. What was he doing here?

His stomach twisted into a knot as he opened the door to the aroma of baked ham, gravy and biscuits swirling through the air around him.

May gestured him to the sink to wash up. "*Gut*, you're here. We are ready to sit down."

Thad nodded. "Evening, Elmer."

Elmer nodded back. "It is indeed, Thad. I thought there for a minute you were going to leave me with these two ladies to enjoy their company by myself."

He raised a brow. "Not a chance."

Back when May had turned sixteen, Elmer had told Thad he wanted to ask May if he could court her. Thad had known that his brother Alvin and April would drop May off at the singing, so Thad ran over and asked May out first. He had done it to spite Elmer, not because he had any real interest in May. Since they were *buwe*, he and Elmer had always had a rivalry. They competed over everything. Who had the best horse, the nicest buggy, took the prettiest girl home from the singing.

Elmer was plenty miffed at him when he asked first to court May. But he unintentionally led May to believe he cared about her. He did like her, but not true love. At least, he didn't think he was in *liebe* with her. After Thad married April, Elmer had made it known what he thought of Thad for hurting May. He knew then how much Elmer cared for May.

Sitting down at the opposite end of the table from May, Thad bowed his head for silent prayer.

Moments later, he tapped the fork against his plate, then speared a piece of chicken from the platter sitting in front of him. "So, Elmer, how is the cheese business?"

"*Gut.* Since they invited our cheese factory to join the Iowa Cheese Club and the Iowa Cheese Roundup, business has been booming. The artisanal cheese flavors that we developed at Sunnyhill Cheese Factory are popular. The bacon and dried tomato flavors are our two favorites. Now, we ship cheese to people all over the world."

"That's impressive. I'm glad to hear it." Thad nodded as he took a bite of food.

Elmer glanced across the table at Josie. "So you're May's cousin? I don't believe we've ever met before, or I would have remembered you. You and May look so much alike, you could be sisters." His mouth opened as if he had something more to say, but he closed it again.

"May, have you ever been to Elmer's cheese factory?" Josie asked pointedly.

May sat her fork down and glanced at Elmer, then at Josie. "Not for a long time. I'm probably way past due for a visit. Would you like to go sometime?"

"*Jah.* Maybe Elmer will show us around." Josie smiled at him.

"I'd be delighted. How about Monday?" His gaze bounced from Josie to May. "I'll be expecting you both then."

Thad liked the idea of Josie's sudden interest in Elmer. Maybe then Elmer would go over to her *haus* to visit instead of parking his buggy in his driveway.

"And, May, dear," Josie interjected, "if you get tired, you can sit and rest while Elmer shows me around the factory."

Thad glanced at May's face. She was smiling, which told him that she might have the same idea as he did about Elmer and Josie. In fact, perhaps she was even matchmaking at this very moment.

Only time would tell.

On Monday, May asked Thad to hitch up Gumdrop to the buggy for their trip to the cheese factory.

"Sure you don't want me to hitch Honeydew instead? He's big, but gentle."

"No, *danki.* I appreciate the offer." She gave him a wry look. "Gumdrop needs the exercise. And besides, I might be in a hurry on the way home and want a younger, faster horse."

"I'll have the buggy at the door in a few minutes." A chuckle followed his words.

Josie talked nonstop the whole way over to Sunnyhill Cheese Factory about Elmer—he was nice, handsome, caring, etc., etc., etc. May nodded in response but hoped Josie didn't talk nonstop on the tour.

Elmer was waiting when they pulled in the drive and helped them down from the buggy. "I cleared my schedule so I could show you around this morning."

He escorted them to his office, where May left the *boppli* bag and tied Leah to Josie's back. That way, she could sleep and wouldn't be so hard to carry. Elmer started the tour by taking them to a large white building.

After pointing out the different areas first, he started explaining the process from the beginning, with the arrival of the milk. He showed the fresh, foamy milk, supplied by the surrounding small-herd Amish farmers, pouring into a large vat. He waved his arm at the large sign that read:

> Sunnyhill uses only organic milk from Amish farmers' pasture-fed cows.

May tried to linger behind them as much as possible to give Josie and Elmer time alone to get acquainted. *Jah*, she was going to make sure Josie was the first thing he saw every time he turned around. She hoped it worked out between them. They were both special to May and they deserved happiness.

Elmer showed them the process for making cheese, then explained the ripening process. He took them into the aging room so they could see the large wheels of cheese stacked on shelves all the way to the ceiling. May surveyed the huge amount of cheese that Elmer had stacked and aged that would bring him in money months from now.

Josie stood next to Elmer. Very close, in fact. "I have never seen so much cheese before. It's definitely macaroni and cheese for supper tonight."

"I'll happily supply the cheese," Elmer volunteered, "so you can see how *gut* the cheese is that we make."

"*Nein*, Elmer." May shook her head. "I've been here before and bought your cheese. You don't need to give us any." She tried to keep the tease out of her voice and make it sound serious.

"But I'm anxious for Josie to try it. Then she can come back and tell me how she liked it."

Josie beamed. "*Jah*, I'll do that."

"While you two finish the tour, I need to change a diaper. I'll wait for you in Elmer's office." She untied Leah from Josie's back, turned to leave and caught Josie batting her eyes at Elmer. "Don't be long, Josie."

She guessed Elmer wouldn't be stopping by the house to help her out any more. Not that he ever really did, except for the time Thad requested he help him fix the swollen doors.

At the time, she'd been angry with Thad for disturbing them. Farm life could be lonely, and it was nice when Elmer paid a visit. Yet she'd known that at some point she'd have to tell Elmer she wouldn't marry him. Now it appeared Josie had set her sights on him. So that was one task stricken from her to-do list.

May sat Leah upright and she smiled and pointed here, then over there, then somewhere else. "So many new sights in Elmer's office for little eyes, huh?"

Leah smiled as if it was some fun game to play. May picked her up and snuggled her close.

"What are you telling me, sweetheart, some really big story about the cheese factory?" May tickled Leah's tummy.

She giggled. "Stop, *Mamm*." She pulled herself up on the back of the couch and gave May a toothy smile.

Josie hurried into the office. "Elmer is bringing our buggy to the door. I've asked him to come to dinner tonight." She held out a big brick of cheese. "I promised I would make macaroni and cheese for him with this. What do you think?"

"I think if you are cooking, then that is a terrific idea. So are there sparks flying between you two?" May stuffed Leah's things back into her bag and handed it to Josie. "Do you mind carrying this? My leg is tired from lugging this boot around, and I don't want to fall. That's all I need, another injury."

Josie led the way to the buggy. "We're just friends, Elmer and I," she said, shooting May a coy look. "For now anyway."

After Elmer brought the buggy around and helped them up into it, May shook the reins and Gumdrop took off with a jerk, but soon settled into an even trot. Before they were out of the drive and past the big buildings, Leah was fast asleep.

May glanced at Josie, who was staring out the window. Her cousin looked deep in thought worrying her bottom lip. "Something wrong, Josie?"

"*Nein.* Do you think Elmer is courting anyone?"

There it was. May had wondered when Josie would get around to asking that question and how she should answer. In the Amish community, courting was a private affair and not talked about, and folks never knew who was courting who until the reading of the banns at church.

Elmer had never officially asked May if he could court her, but at times when she was single, she thought he might. Yet that seemed like it was ages ago, and today, on the cheese tour, she was sure she'd seen Elmer stare at Josie.

May felt Josie's stare, waiting for an answer. "You know courting is a private matter. He has not mentioned anything to me, so I don't have the answer for you. I'm sorry, Josie."

"*Gut.* I'm going to take that as *nein*." Josie settled back in the seat and crossed her arms.

Josie talked a lot and Elmer had his quiet moments; they would be a *gut* match.

If that was true, was it also true that the bishop saw some qualities that were compatible between her and Thad? That he at times seemed resigned to give up the farm but she had a spark of energy that could get them through these hard times.

And just like that, she knew how to save the farm…

# *Chapter Nine*

At the end of his long workday, Thad crossed the barnyard toward the *haus*, sweat running down his face and trickling down his back. He'd sleep *gut* tonight. His pace slowed as he approached the *haus*. A spanking-clean buggy sat in the drive. *Elmer.* Was he here courting Josie?

He climbed the porch steps and paused for a second before opening the door. Elmer's deep voice had said something he didn't catch. May and Josie both laughed. Did the man ever work? Thad blew out a breath, plopped his hat on the wall peg, then washed his hands at the metal basin in the sink in the kitchen.

May hurried into the kitchen from the sitting room and began uncovering serving bowls and setting them on the table. "Thad, you look tired and hungry. Dinner will be on the table in a minute. Sit down."

"How is your foot after walking on it for the factory tour?"

"*Gut*, but I'm a little tired."

Thad looked Elmer up and down as he made his way

to the table. There were no cheese curds on his clothes. He'd cleaned up for his visit. "Not busy at work today, Elmer?"

"On the contrary, business is booming. Tour buses come in every weekend. I had to hire more help. Mondays are slower, and it's the day I usually catch up on paperwork, but I reserved this morning for May and Josie's tour."

Thad nodded. *Tour buses.*

Josie helped set the food on the table, then sat across from Elmer. "He gave us a *wunderbaar* tour and a brick of cheese, so we're having mac and cheese for supper along with the pork chops."

"My favorite." Thad's voice went a little flat with fatigue stretching across his shoulders and down his back. He bowed his head for prayer, then silence swept over the room.

Thad listened to Josie go on and on about their visit to Sunnyhill Cheese Factory. Her face glowed as she spoke about his operation. The way Elmer looked back at Josie, Thad was sure he was only waiting until he knew her well enough to ask to court her.

Thad's heart thumped against his chest as he watched Elmer talk to May and smile at her. The three of them laughed and enjoyed reminiscing about the morning they'd shared together at the factory.

"Thad?"

He jerked his head to the other side. "I'm sorry, Josie, did you say something? I'm so tired even my ears are sleeping." Everyone chuckled at his joke.

"What do you think of the macaroni and cheese? I

made it with cheese from Sunnyhill." Josie looked earnestly at Thad, waiting for an answer.

The three sets of eyes and ears at the table were not going to let him off without hearing his opinion. "It was very tasty. Maybe the best I've ever had."

After Josie and May heaped mountains of praise on Elmer's cheese, they finally expanded their conversation to other wonderful dishes that could benefit by Elmer's prize-winning cheese.

"Elmer, what do you say to one day we take these ladies on the Cheese Roundup? It could be a fun outing. We could hire a car." Thad picked up the bowl and piled more mac and cheese on his plate.

"What is the Cheese Roundup?" Josie glanced toward Thad, then back to Elmer. "I've heard of it but not quite sure what it is."

"That would be a *wunderbaar* time." Elmer nodded. "It's a mapped trail around Iowa that hits all the cheese factories. Along the trail are other places to visit like state parks and the Amana Colonies. It goes through Des Moines, Iowa City, Cedar Rapids, with all kinds of things to do. And there are lots of fun places to stay—lodges, inns and campgrounds. Of course, we wouldn't be gone that long, but cheese-tastings have been paired with all kinds of other events and festivals, so the customers can take a vacation, along with visiting the factories and shops."

"But if you want me to tag along," Thad pointed his fork at himself, "we'd need to go on a late fall day when harvesting was over."

May's head snapped his way. "We could take Leah. She'd love it."

"*Nein.* That would be too much for her, and it would give us time away together."

"I could carry her on my back, and she'll sleep while we walk."

"May, that would be too much for you and her. We'll think about it. We're not going tomorrow." The more he thought about time away and alone with May, the more he liked the idea.

"Well, I want to go," Josie cut in, already starting to plan the trip. She glanced in Thad's direction occasionally, and he nodded when appropriate. While they hashed it all over, he listened.

He glanced out the window. Still daylight. "If you'll excuse me, I have a few more chores to finish up. Always *gut* to see you, Elmer."

Thad retrieved his hat from the peg, tromped down the steps and headed to the shed. *Jah*, if he never heard any more about cheese or cheese factories, he'd be a happy man.

Queasiness roiled his stomach. Thad pulled the scythe and sickle from their hooks, carried them to the sharpening stone and sharpened their blades until they sliced through a piece of straw without resistance. Tomorrow, he'd work out his frustration on barnyard weeds.

He heard cows pushing against the barn door, bellowing in impatience, wanting to be milked. He'd lost track of time. Hurrying to hang the scythe and sickle back on their hooks, he washed and gloved his hands.

The barn door creaked open and Ethan's head appeared in the crack. "Need help with the milking, Mr. Hochstetler?"

"Perfect timing, Ethan. *Jah*, I got busy with other tasks and fell behind. Help me lead the Holsteins into the stanchions. I'll apply the iodine mixture to the udders, and you can follow behind with the alcohol wipe."

"Sounds *gut*. Do you want me to get a couple of the other guys to help so it goes faster?"

"*Danki*, *gut* idea." Thad blew out a long breath. His *onkel* Edward once told him idle thoughts were the devil's work and busy hands were *Gott*'s antidote.

He needed to wipe his jealousy from his head and from his heart. This was the perfect remedy.

May stood. "You two sit and visit. I'm going to clear the dessert plates off the table." She returned to refill Josie and Elmer's coffee cups.

Gathering the leftover bread from their meal, she threw it out on the lawn for the birds to nibble on. She glanced over at Thad's horse and buggy sitting in the same spot they were an hour ago. He usually unhitched the buggy right away. Maybe he started doing something in the barn and forgot about Tidbit. Concern poked her, then worry. Many a farmer had gotten hurt doing hard work and by the time they were found, it was too late.

The barn door squeaked as she opened it. May held her skirt close to her legs in case any daddy-long-legs spiders were lurking about, her dress swishing as she entered. She made her way back to the milking room. "Thad?"

"I'm back here, cleaning the stanchions. Did you want something?" His voice held a note of surprise.

She found him busy, but unharmed. "You looked

tired at dinner, and I wanted to make sure you were okay."

His face brightened. "*Danki* for thinking about me, but I'm fine."

"Okay, but did you know that Tidbit was still hitched?"

"Oh… I forgot about him." His voice wavered as his back straightened.

"You do have a lot on your mind these days. Ethan was on his way home and I asked him to unhitch Tidbit. I figured you forgot when I saw him still hitched after you checked the pasture."

"*Jah*. Is Elmer still up at the *haus*?"

"*Nein*, he had a tour bus coming in early in the morning so he wanted to get home."

"I'm done here, so I'll walk you back to the *haus*."

When they entered the kitchen, Josie was finishing up the dishes while Leah sat in her high chair having a treat.

May checked Leah's hands after she shoved the last bite greedily in her mouth with most of the crumbs appearing to have stuck all over her face. "What a mess."

"I'll get a washcloth," Josie said, pulling open the drawer.

May heard scuffling on the porch, then came a knock on the door.

Caleb Brenneman stuck his head through the kitchen door. "Anyone home?"

May laughed. "What are you doing, Caleb? Come in, come in."

Caleb's son Jacob strolled in first, with Sarah and Caleb following close behind him. Jacob lifted his hands until May finally noticed a midnight-black kitten wiggling in his hand.

"Oh, she is adorable. Have a seat. Would you like a cup of coffee?" She gestured to the pot on the stove.

Sarah looked at Caleb, and he shook his head. "*Nein*, *danki*, we just finished supper."

Caleb slapped Thad on the back. "You look as tired as I feel, my friend."

Thad nodded. "*Jah*, summer makes for long days of work. What brings you by?"

Caleb tilted his head toward his *sohn*. Jacob held the kitten out in front of him. "This is Blackie. She's a gift for Leah."

Silence filled the room as May glanced from Blackie to Thad, then back at Jacob.

"Tiger has taught her well," Jacob said. "She's a *gut* mouser."

May shot Thad a serious look. "Was this your idea? You didn't talk to me about a pet. Don't I have a say in the matter?" She tried to calm her voice. Glancing back at Thad, she noticed his flushed cheeks. She hadn't meant to voice her opinion so strongly. But this should have been a private conversation between her and Thad. "Sorry, I suppose she is old enough to treat one gently."

Caleb took a step forward. "Every farm could use a *gut* barn cat. Keep her in the *haus* in the winter, and you won't have field mice sneaking in. I'll guarantee you."

May picked up Leah from her high chair. "Come and see your new kitty." She carried her over to Jacob.

Leah's eyes widened. She smiled and reached her hand out toward the kitten, then jerked it back. She reached out again, her hand getting closer, then finally touched the kitten with her fingertips. She giggled and jerked back.

"Is she soft and wiggly? Touch her again," May coaxed.

Jacob held out the kitten to May. She sat and held Leah and Blackie.

May looked at Thad. "*Jah*, a *kind* needs a little animal to *liebe* and play with." She raised a brow at Caleb.

Caleb put an arm around Sarah and guided her to the door. "Now that we've upset your whole night, we'll be going."

Thad walked Caleb, Sarah and Jacob out to their buggy. May pet the kitty and showed Leah how to stroke his back. The little girl smiled and watched it until her eyes grew heavy and she fell asleep.

Thad walked back in. "Sorry, I had no idea they were going to do that. I might have mentioned to Caleb that we wanted to get Leah a kitten someday, but I never thought that they had one to give away right now."

"It's okay. Leah will like playing with her, but she'll have to do it tomorrow. It's bedtime."

"For me, too. I'm tired. *Danki* for letting her keep the kitty, May." Thad kissed her cheek, then walked upstairs.

His kiss knocked the wind out of her. She dragged in a ragged breath and tried to calm her racing pulse. She hadn't expected the kiss, nor had she expected her reaction to it. After all, he was her husband. Her eyes followed him until he was out of sight.

She sighed as she got Blackie a bowl of milk and watched her lap it up. She found a box in the storage room and set the kitten in it alongside one of Leah's fuzzy stuffed kitties. The next time she checked on Blackie, she had fallen fast asleep snuggled next to her friend.

A tear welled up in May's eye until it spilled over and ran down her cheek. She brushed it away as she sat in a chair and stared at Blackie. That was the kind of unconditional love, like *Gott's* love, she wanted. She didn't want secondhand love or someone who pitied her, or someone who wanted her out of loneliness. She wanted to feel loved by someone who was content being next to her.

May wanted an adoring *ehemann* by her side, working hard as they planned their future together. She deserved that. Could she find that kind of *liebe* with Thad? Did he *liebe* her at all?

Sometimes she thought he did. Sometimes she wasn't so sure. Only *Gott* knew for certain.

# *Chapter Ten*

Thad entered the kitchen to the unfamiliar sound of May's laughter filling the room. A cheesy aroma made his stomach growl. "Something sure smells *gut* in here so where are you three off to?" He stepped around Elmer and Josie, who was holding Leah.

Elmer lifted the picnic basket he held in one hand and nodded to the pie in his other. "Wherever these two take me, but today it's going to be to the park. Josie even made mac and cheese again."

"Do you need any help getting out to your buggy? I could hold that pie for you, Elmer?" he teased.

Elmer laughed. "There's no chance I'm handing you this cherry pie after I've been standing here for the last ten minutes smelling it. It has my name written all over it."

May followed them out on the porch. "Are you sure you want Leah along? You don't have to take her."

"Me go, *Mamm*."

"I invited her along. We are going to have a great time with this sweet one." Josie gave Leah a little shake and Leah squealed with delight.

Thad walked over and stood next to May on the

porch. They watched Elmer place the picnic basket in the back of his buggy, then help Josie and Leah into the front seat. He climbed in and settled on the seat next to them, tapped the reins on the horse's back and spurred him into a trot. They drove down the lane and onto the road, heading to the park.

Thad slipped his arm around May. "Why are they taking Leah with them on their date?"

She looked up at him and smiled. "It was Josie's idea. I think she is testing Elmer to see if he likes *kinner*, and if he is helpful with a *kind*."

"Hmm. I didn't know women set traps like that to test us poor unsuspecting men."

"I'm not saying any more on the subject. Today, I finish canning beans, so tomorrow Josie, Leah and I can attend a frolic." She tossed Thad a wry smile. "So what are you up to this afternoon?"

"I heard you say earlier that you had canning to do, and I thought I'd come and help. With twice the hands, you'll have to spend less time standing. How is your foot feeling?"

"It's been three weeks since I broke the bone and it feels *gut*. So, you ran out of work to do?"

"*Nein*. Always plenty of work on the farm. I just wanted to be helpful."

"*Datt* is *gut*. You are a man after my own heart." The look on her face told him that the words slipped out, surprising even her. She paused, then whipped out a smile that stole his heart and made this whole canning idea he'd come up with worth it.

"So what do you want me to do?"

"I already have the beans cut and the jars sterilized. So we need to start packing."

She set what they needed on the counter, set a pan of beans and clean jars in front of him, and nodded. "Go to work."

He held up his spoon. "Ready." He started scooping spoonfuls of beans and packing them into a jar. "Do you think it's getting serious between Josie and Elmer?"

"Neither one really talks about it, but they are both very happy and bubbly when they are around each other." She filled her jar and reached for a lid. He reached at the same time and his hand touched hers and lingered. The feel of her soft skin sent a streak all the way up his arm and pierced his heart. He took a deep breath, waiting for something to happen. Anything.

She didn't pull away.

"We could hurry to get the beans done and take a buggy ride into town for an ice cream cone, or just go for a ride since we don't have Leah for a little while." The words spilled out a little breathy.

She hesitated, then pulled her hand away. "I'll probably be too tired when we're done to go for a ride."

"A ride could be relaxing."

She raised a brow. "I better wait and see how I feel. I don't want to commit to that just yet."

The stop sign she held up released that streak that had hit his heart. *Jah*, he got the hint, she wasn't ready. But as the *gut* Book said, patience is a virtue. He'd wait. Little by little he was getting a little closer to her. It was only a matter of time before she'd come around.

"Hurry, Josie." May looked back as she hurried to the door. "We don't want to be late to the frolic to finish Sarah's *boppli* quilt. I'll hitch Gumdrop while you get your basket of scraps of material."

May drove the buggy to the *haus* and parked. Josie stepped into the buggy hugging Leah to her side and settled on the seat next to May.

"Giddyap, Gumdrop. No loafing, we don't want to get there when it's over."

When they turned onto the road, the horse lengthened his gait and stepped out smartly. The buggy jiggled and Leah let out a laugh as if someone were tickling her tummy.

In twenty minutes, May turned Gumdrop onto the Yoders' farm and trotted him up to the front door.

"Good mornin'," David Yoder greeted them as he took the reins. "I'll take your buggy and park it in the shade."

"*Danki*, David. We seem to be running a bit late." May grabbed Leah, Josie snatched the scrap basket and they hurried into the *haus*.

David's daughter Jane met them at the door. "Come in. We were all wondering where you were." She waved toward the stretcher where the others sat stitching their patches on the quilt.

"*Ach*, you made it." Sarah hurried over to May and stole Leah from her arms. "Here's my sweet girl. She is getting bigger every time I see her."

Mary, Sarah's daughter, stuck her head out of the kitchen. "Is Leah here?"

"*Jah*, come see how big she is," Sarah called.

Mary scooped Leah out of Sarah's arms. "I'll take this hungry little critter back to the kitchen with me, and we'll find a cookie and lemonade."

Leah laughed at Mary as she made funny faces.

"How old is she now?" Mary asked.

"My little pumpkin has been spreading her joy for a year, but you might want to watch her. She pulls herself up now and tries to get into everything."

May sat in the empty chair next to Hannah Smith. "Hannah, it is so *gut* to see you. How are Ezra and the family?"

"Everyone is healthy, and we are looking forward to our new addition." She patted her stomach and beamed with joy.

"I see that. I'm so happy for you." May wrapped her arm around Hannah and hugged.

Christine Glick scooted over and patted Hannah's shoulder. "We will start your *boppli*'s quilt as soon as Sarah's *boppli* blanket is finished."

Janie breezed through the door as if a butterfly caught on a breeze. "*Ach*, sorry I'm late."

"Would that handsome Jonah Hochstetler be the reason why?" Christine teased. "My *ehemann* Carter said he saw you in his courting buggy."

"*Ach*, he just gave me a lift to the store." Janie batted her eyes and tilted her head with a coy smile.

"Oh!" Sarah moaned, placing her hands around her protruding belly. "I think you better hurry with the quilt."

Christine shot to her feet. "I'll run and call the midwife! She can meet you at your *haus*, Sarah. I thought she was supposed to come to the frolic…"

"*Danki*, Christine," Sarah gasped. "Caleb is waiting outside. He brought me since it's so close to my time."

Caleb hurried in and helped Sarah out to the buggy.

May couldn't help but notice his face was flushed with excitement. His and Sarah's first *boppli* was something special to both of them.

After the rush of Sarah's departure, the frolic continued until the quilt was finished. May wrestled Leah away from Mary, and Josie gathered up her scraps and basket, then they said their goodbyes and headed to their buggy to go home.

"Even though it ended a little early, I had a great time," Josie said. "But thankfully we got Sarah's *boppli* quilt finished. I have never sewed so fast in all my life." She slid onto the seat and settled next to May, situating her sewing basket on the floor of the buggy.

May handed Leah over to Josie. "She's almost asleep. The rocking of the buggy should do it."

The trip home was relaxing with the methodical clip-clop of Gumdrop's hooves tapping out a rhythm. May settled back in the seat and glanced over at Leah sleeping and Josie softly singing a hymn from the *Ausbund.*

Josie stopped singing and glanced toward May. "Do you think Janie and Jonah are courting? She said he was only taking her to the store. Do you believe that?"

May dipped her head to the side to dodge the glare of the sun. "That's two questions, but the answer is the same for both. I don't know." Amish women loved to gossip, but May wasn't going to talk about her best friend's love life.

Gumdrop turned into his home driveway without being coaxed, ready for his treat when he got back to the barn. May stopped in front of the *haus* to let Josie and Leah out. "I'll unhitch Gumdrop and be right in."

"Don't hurry, I'll put Leah down for a nap." It was

nice having Josie here to help. For sure and certain, May would miss her when she went home.

May hooked the pail of oats to the stall door and headed to the *haus*, excitement bubbling in her to hear the news of Sarah's new *boppli*. She was happy for her friend. Sarah had been married to Samuel for ten years but they had never had *kinner.* After his death, she'd never planned on having the joy of a family until she married Caleb a few years ago. Now Sarah would finally be a *mamm*.

May entered the kitchen in a daze of happiness for her friend. She turned to see Thad and his mother hovering over the canned string beans on the counter. They both turned at her entrance. Thad's face was covered in regret, Gretchen's was a glare. "What's wrong?"

"What's wrong? I'll tell you what's wrong," Gretchen began. "Most of these beans you canned the other day are spoiled. The lids never sealed, and you apparently never checked them. Every woman knows to check to make sure they sealed."

May ran to the counter and gasped. Gretchen was right. The lids weren't sealed and the beans were bubbling with fermentation. She glanced up and locked eyes with Thad. "I guess I forgot."

"You forgot! Such carelessness!" Gretchen hissed.

"*Mamm*, May feels bad enough. What's done is done."

"Well, I'll leave you two to take care of the mess." Gretchen huffed to the screen door, letting it bang on her way out.

"May, I'm sorry, I must have distracted you. We started talking about other things when we were done and just forgot. I'll start taking off lids while you can get a bucket."

She hurried back and helped Thad empty the jar contents into the bucket. "I checked the first few jars when they came out of the canner. They sealed, and I guess I got busy and didn't check the others. I feel like such an idiot."

"*Nein.* I'm sure *Mamm* knows by experience, she just doesn't want to say it. Besides, it's always a lot easier to criticize someone else's work." He gave her a reassuring pat on the shoulder.

She turned toward him and he hugged her. It felt *gut* to have him stand up for her against his *mamm*, but she still felt stupid. But that wouldn't happen again.

She ached from embarrassment as she dumped a lot of hard work into the slop bucket.

Thad took a jar, opened it and dumped. "You don't have to help me," May said.

"Of course I do. We're partners. You're helping me out keeping the farm, why shouldn't I help you? We're in this together. Don't feel bad. It's the kind of error that we all make. The ones you checked should have been a *gut* indication of the whole group. It just so happened in this case they weren't."

"*Danki* for your understanding."

"How was the frolic?"

"Very exciting. In all the fuss over the beans, I forgot to tell you about it. We were all talking and having a *gut* time and all of a sudden Sarah Brenneman goes into labor. Christine called the midwife to meet Sarah at her *haus*. Fortunately, Caleb had driven Sarah over to the Yoders' and was waiting outside for her, so they could get right home."

"Wow, you don't get that kind of excitement at a frolic very often. So has she had her *boppli* yet?"

"We haven't heard yet."

It was nice just talking to Thad about her day, Sarah thought to herself. They didn't often do that. He was always so tired after working on the farm all day, and now, with her foot healing, sometimes the effort of getting around wore her out and she went to sleep early.

She glanced over at Thad. "*Danki* again for helping clean up the mess. That was so thoughtful."

When they finished the cleanup, Thad went out to do chores and May leaned a hip against the sink and stared at the counter where the beans had sat. She'd make sure that never happened again, but what hurt most was that Thad's *mamm* had scolded her like a child. Her sharp tongue cut faster than a double-edged blade.

At 7:00 p.m., a buggy came up the driveway and stopped at the *haus*. May ran to the front door. "Caleb, how is Sarah?"

"She is doing well." His smile stretched from ear to ear. "It's a boy!"

"Congratulations! Jacob will be a *gut* big *bruder* to him. Have you named him?"

"He is named after his two *grossdaedi*, Michael Paul Brenneman."

"*Datt's* a fine name. Is Mary at the bakery?"

"*Nein.* We closed the bakery for a couple of days. Mary wants to stay home with Sarah and the *boppli*. The whole family is excited."

"Of course. Tell Mary I can help when she needs it.

Josie is here to watch Leah, but if Josie goes home soon, I'll just bring Leah with me."

"*Nein*, that won't be necessary. Mary has hired a friend to work in the bakery. I need to get going, I have a couple more stops to make."

"*Danki* for letting us know, Caleb." She closed the screen door and watched Caleb rush to his buggy. He waited when he saw Thad walk over from the barn. May heard the excitement in his voice as he told Thad the news.

Sadness drifted over her heart. Right now, it was doubtful she'd ever have *kinner*. After all, her and Thad's marriage was only one of convenience.

Wasn't it?

The next morning, May sat with Leah and Blackie on the grass in front of the *haus* and watched them play. Blackie hopped around jumping at bugs and birds and chasing her tail. Leah played tug-of-war with her with her chew toy. She'd hold it out, Blackie would try to get it, she'd pull it away and laugh. Leah tried to push herself to stand, but was wobbly.

"Oh, are you going to try to walk? You are so big."

Leah plopped back down, then picked up the chew toy and poked it at Blackie.

Wheels crunching over rocks and horse's hooves tromping the ground stole May's attention as Janie parked her buggy under the oak tree by the *haus*. She stepped down and ran toward May, her eyes and cheeks glazed with tears.

May jumped up and wrapped Janie in a hug. "What's wrong?"

Janie gasped for breath. "Jonah says he can't court me any longer."

"Why, did he give a reason?"

"His *mamm* told him I wasn't the right girl for him."

May could hardly believe her ears. She had no idea the extent of Gretchen Hochstetler's sway over her *buwe. Nein*, they weren't *buwe*, they were men. "What? He listens to his *mamm* when he wants to find a *frau*?"

"Apparently so, and you know Gretchen, she is pushy." Janie looked around. "I hope she isn't close by to hear me. That's all I need."

"*Nein*, I saw her and her *ehemann* Aaron leave the *dawdi haus* earlier and they're not back yet." May motioned at the blanket Leah was sitting on. "I'm afraid I know Gretchen only too well. Now, sit and tell me the whole story."

Her friend wiped away the tears from her cheeks and sat down. "Not much to tell really. He stopped by yesterday and said that we could no longer court, that his *mamm* said she had someone he needed to meet, and she just knew he'd *liebe* her. She wouldn't quit pestering Jonah about it until he broke it off with me." Janie sniffled, took a hanky and dried her eyes.

"He told you that?" The heat burned its way up May's neck. "So without even seeing or talking to this *mädel*, he breaks up with you?"

"Apparently so." Her shoulders shook with each sob. "I'm sorry, May."

"For what?"

"For not realizing how much it hurt you when Thad dumped you for April." Janie blew her nose. "I was really insensitive. I remember I joked around about how Thad was so cute, you should marry him. I never stopped to think how that must actually have felt."

Stunned, May straightened her back and rubbed a hand across the grass. "For Leah's sake, I pushed that behind me and haven't thought about it since Thad and I married."

"I just wanted you to know that now I understand what you went through." She patted May's arms. "I didn't mean to open old wounds and hurt you again."

"It's *oll recht*. But now that I think about it, Gretchen always did like April better than me. I wonder if she told Thad the same thing?" She swallowed hard as the thought settled upon her like the dust stirred up from galloping hooves.

If Gretchen *had* poked her nose into her and Thad's courtship, that would explain so much.

# *Chapter Eleven*

May finished sewing her strips of rags together, then started rolling them in a ball. *Jah*, this group of blues and yellows would make a beautiful rug when she had it woven.

Thad stepped in the doorway. “So here you are.” He crossed the sewing room and sat in the chair next to hers. He smelled *gut*. She tried to keep the smile off her face, but it was hard. The scent of his goat’s milk soap was a little intoxicating, and he’d combed his hair. He looked so handsome.

“How’s the new rug coming along?” he asked, his voice almost startling her.

“Your old shirts are going to look great alongside the yellow of this old tablecloth. What’s your dairy association meeting about tonight?”

“They want to start dumping milk in protest for having to sell it at regular price. Other small farmers across the country are starting to dump.”

May laid her ball of strips down and faced Thad. “What do you think?”

"I hate to dump perfectly *gut* milk, but I feel it's important to follow what the majority wants. The association members need to stick together. They'll probably take a vote tonight. But I shouldn't be home too late. They might just have a discussion, then take the vote, if not tonight, then at the next meeting. They are letting everyone think about it."

"Does discussion mean argue? Dumping sounds like a touchy subject when it comes to money. There could be strong opinions on both sides of the issue."

Thad chuckled. "*Jah*, I'm afraid you're probably right." He glanced at the clock. "I better get going. See you later."

At 7:00 p.m., May glanced out the window. Black clouds rolled and rumbled across the evening sky. The air had turned a greenish-gray. She laid her ball of strips down and hurried downstairs to close all the windows.

When she entered the kitchen, Thad burst through the door, turned and slammed it closed.

"What's going on, Thad?"

His face was ashen. "There's a tornado coming across the field. Grab Leah and head to the basement. Where's Josie?"

May gasped. "She and Leah are both upstairs."

"New plan. I'll run up and get them. You get a lantern and go to the basement and get into the southwest corner. We'll be right down."

May scurried downstairs, hurriedly cleared the southwest corner and dragged an old mattress close so they could cover themselves with it. Within seconds, Thad was marching down the stairs holding Leah, followed by Josie close on his heels. By the time they reached her, the day had turned as black as night and the wind's howling was deafening, sounding like a freight train passing directly overhead. Thad passed Leah to May, then grabbed the mattress and held it over them.

Before the mattress covered her eyes, May glanced at the window. She could see the trees bending so far over, she feared they'd snap clean off. She heard a loud cracking, like a tree falling. Crashing sounds next to the *haus* and farther away in the distance made her squeeze Thad's arm. Glass breaking upstairs along with thumps, bumps and bangs made her huddle closer to Thad and Leah, with Josie clinging close on the other side of Thad.

Leah began to cry. May attempted to soothe her. "Shh, it'll be all right."

"*Nein*. Stop it! Stop it!" Leah screamed. The louder the storm raged, the louder her cries grew.

"I know you're scared, but we are here to protect you," May cooed next to Leah's ear. "Shh."

Thad wrapped May and Leah in his arms. "Josie, stay close."

"*Jah*, don't worry, I will."

The wind died down and the crashing noises stopped. But the rain continued, and the hail pummeled the roof and the side of the *haus* so hard, May feared it might break the walls down. After what felt like hours, the storm finally quieted, and Thad pushed the mattress off them.

The brightening sky pulled May's attention to the basement window plastered with mud. Apparently, the pounding rain had splashed mud up from the ground. A shiver of fear ran through May's heart.

Thad started to stand but Leah clutched at his shirt. *"Nein, Daed. Nein."* He kissed Leah's head and held her close.

"Shh, the storm is over. It'll be okay. The worst is over. It's just rain now." When she quieted, he handed her back to May and started to stand.

*"Nein, Daed!"* Leah screamed.

"Okay. We'll all stay here a while longer to make sure the storm has passed. Is everyone all right?"

"*Jah*, just scared." Josie's voice quaked.

"I'm fine." May clutched Leah close to her chest to soothe the little *mädel.* After a while, she checked Leah. "She's finally asleep," she whispered to Thad. "We need to see if we should board up windows or doors so the rain doesn't make things worse."

"I agree." Thad kissed Leah on the cheek. "Hand her to Josie and let's do a walk-through upstairs before we let them come up." He looked at Josie. "Do you mind waiting down here?"

"*Nein*, but could you bring us some blankets?"

"Sure, give us a minute." He grabbed May's hand as if it was the natural thing to do and helped her up the basement stairs. He paused and drew in a deep breath before he unlatched the basement door and peered out. He pushed the door open and pulled May up to the top of the stairs. She held the lantern up and moved it around in an arc as they assessed the damage.

May stared. The two west windows in the kitchen were broken and glass was scattered all over the room. The table and chairs were overturned. The cupboard doors were open and it looked like the storm had sucked everything off the shelves of one of the cabinets and thrown them around the room. They walked through the mess, Thad still clutching her hand.

The sitting room was untouched. Thad led the way upstairs. May stayed close behind, her heart pounding against her ribs at what they might find.

The empty west bedroom had a broken window and water had drenched the flooring. The rest of the second floor was untouched by the storm.

Thad looked all around. "I'll need to get the windows boarded up tonight. Let's check the outside."

"Okay, but let me run some blankets down to Josie first."

Thad was waiting in the kitchen for her when she came up from the basement.

"Ready?" He flashed an encouraging smile. She nodded and he threw open the door.

He stepped onto the porch first, and she followed. It was 7:40 p.m. The sun breaking through the clouds was just setting, giving her enough light to see around the farm as they stepped off the porch.

May swept her gaze from one side of the barnyard to the other. The barn and shed roofs lay scattered over the barnyard and field. Several trees were down and debris strewn all around. She pressed a hand to her chest. "It's going to cost a lot of money to repair these buildings."

Thad nodded. "Money we don't have for something as massive as this damage. I'm going to walk out into the pasture. Do you want to come along?"

"*Jah.* We do this together." She glanced his way, trying to focus through tear-filled eyes. He wrapped his arm around her shoulders and held her close to him as they walked out to the pasture. She scanned the land and saw that several cows were dead.

Thad murmured, “I count twelve down.”

May’s throat tightened as she burst into tears. “What are we going to do? There is so much damage.”

“I’m not sure. I don’t have the money to repair all this. We can borrow from an Amish lender but the farm is barely making ends meet right now. I’m not sure where the extra money for the loan repayment will come from. Look at that field.” He pointed to the fall crop of squash and pumpkins. “It looks like a total loss but I’m hoping in the morning I can salvage some. I’ve been counting on the fall market. In order to survive, we’ll need a bumper crop next year and for milk prices to go up.”

May surveyed the *haus* as they walked back. It didn’t look bad, but a lot of shingles were missing, which meant the *haus* roof would have to be reshingled. Thad let go of her hand and turned all around examining the land again. His shoulders slumped.

Raindrops hit May’s hand, then quickly turned to a light shower. She ran up the porch steps while Thad kept looking around.

“So much destruction, but it could have been worse. If every Amish farmer around here has this much damage, there won’t be enough money in our community to pay for all the damages. Everyone chips in, but that won’t work for this much damage.” When it started to rain harder, he jumped up the porch steps two at a time and plopped down in a chair next to May.

He glanced her way. “I don’t know how we will ever recover from this.”

She reached over and patted his arm. "The bishop will put the word out to the other Amish communities asking for help. We don't know, maybe it's just our farm that got this much damage."

"You're right, and it could have been a lot worse." He gave her an encouraging smile. "I'm going to check the milk room and get a hammer and some plywood to cover the broken windows until we can get them fixed. You better let Josie know she can come up but Leah needs to stay off the floor until we sweep."

"If she's still asleep, I'll just put her to bed and start cleaning up."

Thad gave her a hug. "We'll get through this." The feeling of his arms was comforting on so many different levels. He kissed her forehead and took his arms away. The cool air that passed between them when he stepped away let her know what she was missing.

She smiled up at him. "*Jah*, we will. Together."

Thad's gut wrenched as he gazed out over his farm. *Nein.* His and May's farm, and it was barely breaking even now. This would be devastating, but he couldn't let May know just how bad it really was for them. If he lost her family's farm, she'd never forgive him. It had been one of the stipulations in their marriage bargain. *Jah*, they were getting along better, but was their relationship *gut* enough to withstand a catastrophe like this? The farm meant everything to May. He swallowed against the glumness.

He opened the barn door and made his way to the milking room. Doing a careful walk-through, he surveyed the whole area. Aside from the roof being gone, he didn't observe any other damage inside of the barn. First thing tomorrow, he'd see if he could get a tarp put over the rafters until he could make arrangements to replace the roof. The barn had numerous floor drains, but nonetheless, he had to stop the rain and other elements from entering and doing any further damage.

When the rain finally let up, he dashed over to the shed and cut several pieces of plywood for the *haus* windows. He carried them to the *haus* and May helped him nail the pieces in place.

When that was finished, he and May helped Josie sweep all the glass off the floor and clean up the mess in the kitchen.

Thad glanced at the clock. Midnight. "Let's go to bed. We'll need our rest for tomorrow."

The next morning, Thad quickly ate his breakfast. He kept glancing outside as dawn began to light the barnyard.

"More pancakes, Thad?" May asked.

"*Nein*, I need to get out and assess the damage in the daylight to determine how much to request on a loan. Looking down the road, there is a lot of damage to neighboring farms. I need to get our application in before the Amish lender runs out of money."

"Josie, will you watch Leah while I go out and help Thad?"

"Of course, May. I'm here…to help."

Thad grabbed a tablet and pencil. They stepped into their boots by the door and walked out into the field.

He opened the tablet and handed it to May. "Your handwriting is better. I'll let you write it down." He walked down a field row and May followed. "Last night,

I'd hoped that we could save a few pumpkins and squash but this is a total loss for sure. The storm uprooted the vines and smashed the pumpkins and squash back on the ground. Some even looked like they had exploded."

Next he checked each field, all the livestock, and did a thorough assessment of the buildings.

Thad gazed out over the barnyard. "I'll have the *youngies* clean all this up. Let's go check the barn." He glanced over at May. Her face told him how hurt she was to see all the damage. "We'll get it fixed, May, don't worry." He wrapped an arm around her, and she leaned into him for support.

"Last night you sounded like the loan repayment would probably stretch us beyond what we could afford," she said.

"We'll talk to the lender and see what we can work out. Don't worry just yet." But her face told him she didn't believe that.

He opened the barn door, and she went in first. The stanchions and stalls all looked intact. The flooring and walls of the barn were unharmed. Thad told her what needed marked down that he thought needed repair. He wanted to make sure to request a loan that would cover all the repair costs.

After their evaluation of the farm, he went to his desk and tallied up the damages. His estimate ran in the thousands of dollars. Money he didn't have and wouldn't for a long time. He had to decide if he wanted to go with the traditional shingle roof on the barn or change to a steel roof. If he wanted to go cheaper, he could go to aluminum. But the *haus* definitely needed shingling, too. The roofs alone would probably run over $100,000.

He stood up and paced the floor behind his desk, running his hands through his hair. He finally looked up and saw May standing in his office doorway.

"Thad, how does it look?"

He swiped his hand down his beard. "I'm worried about borrowing all this money and getting it repaid, but there's no choice."

May took a step forward. "I know, but I have an idea on how to get the money and pay off the debt."

"My first priority is to get the loan papers filled out and sent in. You can tell me about your rug business or whatever after that. The loan is the best way to get this much money." He patted her arm and smiled.

## *Chapter Twelve*

May's gaze swept over Thad's face. The second day after the storm, and he looked tired after a stressful day of filling out forms to borrow money.

"Now that the loan papers have been sent, would it be possible to get a cup of coffee while I listen to your plan to get money or make money? I have a feeling this might be a long talk."

"Of course. Let's go sit at the kitchen table." She poured two cups, set them on the table and sat in the chair next to his. "Before you left for the last dairy association meeting, you said they wanted to start dumping milk and they were going to take a vote. In all the commotion since the storm, I forgot to ask, did the vote pass?"

"Yes. They want to start dumping milk."

May pressed her back against the chair. "We can't afford to waste milk like that. So I've been thinking..."

"What about?" His voice sounded tired.

She laid her hand on his arm, then quickly pulled it away. Her cheeks burned at her familiar gesture. She gulped a breath. "Elmer showed Josie and me all around his cheese factory. He said they ship all over the world and that his business was doing *gut*."

"So why are you telling me this?"

"I think we should make cheese instead of pouring the milk on the ground. We could even make ice cream."

Thad leaned back in his chair. "I don't have the time or the money to make cheese in addition to farming. And it would cost a fortune to set it up. Not to mention, I don't know a thing about cheese. Elmer sells a lot, but he makes all kinds of fancy artisan cheese and sells it to the tourists, the *Englisch*."

"But listen…"

He held up a hand. "*Honig*, I don't have the money to start up a cheese factory, and especially now after the storm."

"But I do."

He straightened his back. "Where did you get that kind of money?"

"I've worked all my life selling rugs, quilts, doilies and baked goods. I've operated a vegetable stand and saved all my money. I have always lived here, and *Daed* or you have always supported me. I have over $100,000 saved."

Thad gasped. "I can't believe it. But even if you have the money, we don't know a thing about making cheese or starting a factory."

May laid a hand over his hand. "We can learn. Let's at least check into it."

She noticed his gaze drop to her hand on his. His voice shook. "I don't have time to learn how to start a cheese factory and then run it, while keeping the farm going."

"Why don't we hire more *youngies*? And I'll help, too. Maybe I'll run the cheese factory."

"You know what the bishop thinks about women working outside the home." He gave her a serious look.

"*Jah*, but we have to make money soon or we'll lose the farm. Our fall crop is gone, we have lost almost half our herd of cows and we have to borrow money with interest. We have to have some way to get back on our feet. It doesn't have to be a big factory like Elmer's. I can make cheese and sell it at my vegetable stand. I will have to start small anyway while I'm learning."

He leaned over and gave her a sweet kiss on the lips. "May, you are one gutsy lady."

Heat rose from her neck onto her cheeks and burned her ears. Her voice nearly stuck in her throat. "I'll take that compliment as a yes."

"What is a yes?" Gretchen asked as she opened the screen door and entered, followed by Aaron, Thad's *daed*.

May tried to stare Thad into silence.

"*Mamm*, we are thinking of starting a cheese factory." Thad's words seemed to suggest he was aiming to shock more than inform. "Elmer is very successful at his cheese business."

"Indeed he is. He is a cheese artisan. You are not. You are a farmer."

"He farms, too."

"He doesn't farm the land. He only has his milk cows," Gretchen huffed. "You'd have to build the factory from scratch."

"We know that."

"I wouldn't be surprised if this was May's idea."

"It is *our* idea to try to save the farm. We can't keep selling cheap milk or dumping it on the ground because we have no buyers. Cheese can be packaged and sold all over the world."

"You'll lose the shirt off your back if you waste your money on starting a factory. And who will do all that work?" Gretchen jabbed her fists on her hips. "It's a crazy idea. You are foolish to sink your money into such a business."

Aaron pulled his *frau* toward the door. "Gretchen, it is their business, not ours."

"Thad is not sinking a dime into this business. I am." May let the truth slip out, then was angry with herself for letting Gretchen provoke her into saying it. "The money is mine, and don't forget this farm has been in my family for 170 years. Thad inherited it from my sister. The farm isn't making enough right now to pay all the bills and support us."

"Apparently it does if you have enough money saved to sink into a cheese business," Gretchen hissed.

Thad placed a firm hand on May's shoulder. "*Nein. Mamm*, *danki* for the advice, and we will take it under consideration."

Aaron pushed Gretchen out the door, then turned back. "I'm sorry about that, *sohn*."

Thad patted May's arm. "*Mamm* is not an adventurer when it comes to money. She still has a coffee can on her kitchen counter filled with money saved up for a winter coat for me when I was a *bu*."

May raised a brow. "So you didn't get a new coat?"

"She decided to save the money and sewed those little knit cuffs on the end of the sleeves of my old coat. I was growing up, not out, so it still fit just a little short. The cuffs did the trick, and she's been patting herself on the back for her thriftiness ever since."

"When winter comes, I'm going to check the sleeves on your coat and see if you need a new one."

He laughed. "*Jah*, I believe you will. Don't let *Mamm* get you down. She grew up in a family where they didn't have much money, and every penny was saved and not spent frivolously."

May stood. "So you think I'm frivolous?" His words were like a punch on the arm. "If I have $100,000 saved, that doesn't sound frivolous to me."

"*Nein*, I didn't say that."

"It sure sounded like that to me. Are you taking her side? Do you think the cheese factory is a bad idea?" She punched her fists on her waist.

Thad stood. "Look, I know nothing about making cheese, or how to run a business like that. Yes, I see people doing it. Cheese is big business in Iowa. It might work. I just don't know." He let his gaze drop to the floor, then looked back at May. "I just don't want you to lose all your hard-earned money." Worry lined his eyes.

"So you think this is a boondoggle idea?" Her voice softened.

"Don't put words in my mouth and start a fight I don't want to have. We have been getting along so *gut*, *jah*?"

May walked to the sink, took a rag and wiped up around the edge. "So you just want me to put my money back in the coffee can?"

"I'm saying it's a lot of money, so we need to be certain what we want to do with it. Yes, let's inquire about starting a cheese business. Maybe we can begin small. We can always start with a couple of different cheeses and you can try selling it on your vegetable stand."

"We can start out small to learn but a small business that makes a few dollars doesn't pay very many big bills. We have to invest in our future and in our children's future." What did she just say—their children? "We will have to ensure we have enough money to make the loan payments."

Thad walked to the sink and stood next to her. "We haven't even discussed what kind of cheeses we want to make. Do you know what kinds sell the best? Didn't Elmer start out small, then add his fancy cheese the *Englisch* like?"

"*Jah*, you're right," May said. "Let's think about it and decide if it is truly right for us. In the meantime, I'll just keep making quilts and rugs and selling my vegetables."

He put an arm around her shoulders and hugged. Then his arms encircled her and pulled her close. He dropped his mouth to hers for a tender kiss.

She stepped back and exhaled. "I know what you're doing, Thad. And I don't like it. You're trying to change the subject, and you're hoping this all goes away."

"May, I have to run the farm and oversee the repairs. I don't have time to run a cheese factory, too. I'm sorry."

"I know, but the money is mine. I'll take care of running the cheese factory."

Thad's face turned somber. "The bishop won't like you running a factory, but he probably won't be against you selling a few homemade cheeses." He headed toward the other room, but looked back at May. "I'll help as much as I can. See if you can find some classes we can take, but not from Elmer." He raised a brow. "Maybe there is a book we can buy or some recipes."

She ran over and gave him a hug and a kiss on the cheek. "*Danki*, Thad. I know we can do this."

He raised a brow. "Hope so."

A burst of excitement flooded her heart. *Jah*, she could do this and the cheese factory would be a success. And she knew the perfect place to start.

The next morning, while Josie watched Leah, May hired a driver and had him drop her off at the library in Iowa City. Thad stayed at the farm to oversee the first day of repairs, but May needed to start the factory research before her boot came off and Josie went back home. She asked the librarian to show her how to find the online cheese-making class. The computer was an awkward device, but with the help of the librarian, she managed. It was a long day of studying and note taking.

On her second visit to the library, Thad went along with May. They took the advanced online cheese-making class to learn how to make the artisan cheese, then ordered a suggested recipe book and information on how to start a cheese-making business.

The following day, Thad accompanied her to visit a factory. The tour guide was helpful and answered their questions. On the way home, she asked the driver to stop at a shop so they could pick up a vat, press and other supplies. After selecting a few items, May looked up to see Thad frowning. "Is there something wrong?"

"The vat and warmer are pricey. But I guess we have to have a little outlay first. I just worry about the bills."

"*Jah*, and I forgot to tell you, we need to buy a goat or two so I can make some goat-milk cheese."

He frowned.

She knew the factory was a big risk for their family but they had to take it. They'd start out small and only increase production if it looked like the customers liked their product. With the over-production of organic milk by the big producers, it made sense to have another outlet for their milk instead of dumping it. *Jah*, she was sure she could make the cheese and sell it.

Maybe she'd offer a cheese-tasting when she officially opened her business. In the fall, she would add apples and pears to the stand from their trees. It would be easy to add cheese to the wares offered.

This had to work. Gott, *please bless the cheese idea so it will work and save the farm.*

May made her first batch of cheese and tasted it. Terrible. She threw away her second attempt. Cheese-making was a little more complicated than she'd thought. She hadn't realized that it was the aging process that actually gave cheese its distinctive taste and texture, which produced thousands of varieties. That aging caused sour, sharp or tangy tastes over time, so some of the cheeses would take several months to age properly for the taste to develop. She hadn't planned on that.

May selected a few cheeses to start with: Colby, cheddar, provolone, Monterey Jack and Parmesan. Fortunately, all cheese started with the same basic ingredients: milk, from either a cow, goat, sheep or buffalo; bacterial culture; rennet and salt.

While some of the cheese aged, she still needed something to sell. Leafing through her recipe book, she found cream cheese, sour cream, ricotta and feta cheese recipes.

For two weeks, May worked hard making cheese, throwing away batch after batch. Her stomach ached from worry that they'd lose the farm. *Nein.* She had to keep trying.

Finally, the batches started to develop good flavors. This might actually work!

A horn honked from the driveway, and May ran to look out the window. "Josie, the driver is here to take me to the doctor's office. Hopefully it won't take long."

"I'm going to pack so I'll be ready to go home when you get back."

May slid into the car and handed the driver the address. "It's a medical building."

"Yep, I've been there before, ma'am. Have you there in no time. I'm James, by the way. I'll drop you off and wait for you in the lobby."

"Thank you. That will be *gut.*" Her hands fidgeted on her lap. After six weeks, she was so ready to get this boot off.

She blew out a sigh as she exited the car and hurried to the doctor's office, leaving James to follow behind her. She signed in, took a seat and waited.

"May Hochstetler," a lady in blue scrubs called.

The nurse took her information, then led her to a room to wait for the doctor. In only a minute or two, she heard paper rustling outside the door, then the doctor entered.

Dr. Kincaid held out his hand and shook hers. "Good morning, May. Good to see you. How's the foot feeling?"

"*Gut*, Doctor. I'm anxious to get this boot off."

He loosened the bootstraps and helped her slip her foot out. He felt around her ankle and foot. He moved the foot this way and that and rubbed his hand across the top. "The foot feels like it's healed. You don't need to wear the boot in the house, but if you walk on the ground where it's uneven, wear the boot outside for another month. That'll ensure the foot doesn't twist and get reinjured."

"Do I need to come back?" She held her breath.

"Not unless you have trouble with it."

"Then I can stand on it and run my cheese business?"

He nodded. "You sure can but let your foot tell you if it gets tired. If it does, let it rest. Don't push it. It might still be weak for another few weeks."

She hopped off the examining table. *"Danki."* May shivered as excitement streaked through her. Now she could officially start her business. Her plans for her factory were already down on paper. She was ready to go.

Her happy energy propelled her out of the car when it stopped in front of the *haus*.

She paid the driver and hurried inside.

Josie met her at the door, her suitcase packed and sitting in the kitchen. She flagged May's driver and he agreed to give her a ride home.

"I'm going to miss you so much, Josie. And so will Leah."

Josie gave her a big hug. "I know, but I have to get

home and help *Mamm*. Leah is in her high chair having lunch. Oh, and she is toddling around today."

"Tell *Aent* Matilda I said *hullo*, and that I appreciate her lending you to us for a few weeks. I hope your stay here wasn't too boring, but meeting a handsome cheesemaker may have eased the boredom just a bit, I think." Her cousin raised a brow, then hurried down the porch steps toward the waiting driver.

May stuck her head in the *haus* to check on Leah, then stepped back out on the porch to watch Josie drive away.

A feeling of loneliness settled in her chest. Waving at Josie only made it worse. She was going to miss her terribly.

Now May and Thad were truly alone as a married couple. Was she ready for a real relationship with him?

# *Chapter Thirteen*

May gazed out the kitchen window and smiled. Without fail, every morning Thad always brought her fresh, foamy milk to use in her cheese business.

As he passed by the *dawdi haus*, Gretchen dashed out the door and appeared to be talking to him. Gretchen was always interfering. What did his *mamm* want this time? Her cucumbers picked or her carrots and potatoes dug?

May regretted her unkind thoughts. But why did that woman have to be so narrow-minded? Gretchen was always belittling her to Thad and keeping him busy so he couldn't help her with the cheese business.

Thad smiled as he finished talking to Gretchen and continued on to the *haus*. His *mamm* disappeared back into the *dawdi haus*. Letting the screen door bang behind her. That was odd, since Gretchen never banged a screen door. Ever.

"Here's your morning milk, May," Thad said upon entering the kitchen.

"*Danki* for bringing it up to the *haus*. How are repairs going on the barn?"

"They will soon be done. These men from Shipshewana really know their business." He headed for the door. "How is your foot feeling today?"

"*Jah*, it feels *gut* without the brace and I'm glad. My foot is so much cooler without all that plastic wrapped around it."

"I think it's called thermoplastic. Where is Leah?"

"Making cheese." Leah pushed herself up from sitting on the floor on the other side of the table. She held up the ball of cheese she was trying to push into a mold.

"Oh, you are a big helper, aren't you?" he praised her, then winked at May. "I can see you have a big helper."

"The best helper. I told her she could make you some cheese." She gave him a wry smile.

"I'm sure I'll like it very much." He tossed May a grin before disappearing out the door.

A knock sounded on the door before she could even count to ten. Thad must have forgotten to tell her something. At the continued silence, she looked up. "*Ach*, Janie, come in. I'm so glad to see you."

Janie gave her a hug, then sat at the kitchen table. "How's the cheese business going? *Mamm* is finished with her canning, so I thought I'd come over to see if I can help you. It's all over town about your cheese business. I think Elmer is even a little worried about his Sunnyhill business falling off with you making cheese so close to him."

"Did he say something?"

"*Nein*, I don't think so. He is just used to getting all the business around here. You will be his competition, don't forget."

"The dairy farmers around here are all dumping

milk. Once I get the business going, I'm hoping to be able to buy more milk."

Janie shook her head. "Why doesn't Thad just buy more cows and supply the milk for you?"

"Maybe, we'll see. But I might need a bigger *haus*. I converted the pantry to storage for the cheese business. Thad made floor-to-ceiling shelves in there to accommodate the cheese that needed to age. And I've realized that I need an assistant. Would you be interested in the job?"

"*Jah*, I'll help. I have plenty of free time."

"Are you and Jonah still not back together?"

"*Nein*, that's over. Whatever Gretchen said to him, she killed our relationship."

May walked over and gave Janie a hug. "I'm so sorry to hear that. When do you want to start helping?"

"Now is *gut* for me. I heard Josie went home, so I thought I'd help you if you needed it." Janie's face was somber, then brightened. "Who knows, maybe I will meet some tall, handsome man by working for you."

May shot her friend a sympathetic look. "If Jonah has to have his *mamm* pick a *frau* for him, you don't want him."

"*Jah*, I know. Just tell my heart that, it's breaking in two."

"We are going to be so busy making cheese, you won't even have time to think about him."

"I hope that is true, and that your business makes lots of money," Janie laughed.

"Saturday, I'm going to have my vegetable and fruit stand. I'm going to make a few apple pies and strudels, and have a cheese-tasting here on the wraparound porch. So you can help with that."

"Do you have cheese ready to sell?"

"I have some, but I was hoping to take some advance orders. Most of our clients will probably be *Englisch*. Mr. Kolb from the gift shop in town where I consign some doilies and rugs has a computer and made me a few signs and flyers to hand out. He also said I could leave some samples with him on Friday and Saturday, and maybe some coupons to encourage the *Englisch* to drive out here." She finished the goat-cheese cheesecakes and set them aside. "We will sell these on Saturday."

"You're definitely going to give Elmer some competition. He's not going to like that."

"Elmer is on the Iowa Cheese Roundup and in the Iowa Cheese Club. He has plenty of customers."

"I don't know. He's very protective of his business."

"He has tour buses that stop at his factory. I'm sure he's not worried about a little competition. Besides, it's more than likely that *he* will drive *me* out of business, not the other way around."

"Who is Elmer driving out of business?" Thad entered the kitchen silently, almost as if he were in stocking feet.

"How long have you been out there listening to us?" May asked.

"I just came in. You two were so busy worrying about Elmer that you didn't hear me. It might serve Elmer right to have a little competition. He acts so smug, with all the tour buses stopping by his factory."

Thad took off his hat and tossed it on the peg by the door. "What's for supper?"

"Baked chicken smothered in cheese. Janie has come to work for me and help out with the cheese business."

"*Gut.* Now I won't have to dump milk." Leah toddled over to her *daed*, and he picked her up and set her on his knee. "Are you going to be a cheesemaker, too?" She shook her head and smiled.

"Repairs are done," he told May. "The *youngies* are going to milk the cows the rest of the week, and I am going to help you make cheese so you will have plenty ready to sell on Friday and Saturday." He flashed her a smile.

"Really? Or are you just teasing me?"

"*Nein*, no teasing. I'm going to help, for sure and certain. Whatever you need me to do. At your tasting, I have two *youngies* that are going to stand by the road at your vegetable stand and their sister will be on the porch selling the cheese and taking orders."

Her eyes locked with his, and sent her heart racing.

Leah jumped off Thad's knee and toddled to May, holding out her arms. *"Mamm, Mamm."*

"You want a taste of cheese?"

Leah smiled and nodded.

May gave her a small taste of the feta cheese. Leah smacked her lips and chewed, then made a funny expression. She took a piece out of her mouth and handed it back to May.

"*Danki*, sweetheart, but you are a bad advertisement for my cheese," May laughed.

The rest of the week, they all worked making feta and ricotta cheese, cream cheese and mascarpone. Some of the Gouda had aged and she had mozzarella sticks. She added flavoring, tomato bits and avocados and then made cheese spreads for crackers. She made cheese dips out of the sour cream to serve with chips, and she made mascarpone and used it for a cannoli filling.

Janie prepared many of the foods to complement the cheeses and when Saturday arrived, Thad assisted her in setting up the porch with display areas. As customers started dropping by, he helped take orders. The prepackaged feta, ricotta, cream cheese and mascarpone were big sellers.

May watched Thad's brother Jonah approach the house and take a plate of food. He glanced toward Janie but didn't approach her.

May could see the blush on Janie's cheeks rising to a cherry red, and tears begin to form in her eyes. She brushed them away when she thought no one looked.

"I'll get more samples," Janie said, and disappeared inside the *haus*.

May's sister Sadie parked her buggy under the oak tree and brought her three children up the porch steps.

May gave her sister a hug. "*Danki* for stopping by." She gave the *kinner* a piece of pizza and a glass of lemonade and had them sit in chairs by a table. They were very happy with that. They didn't get pizza that often, she imagined.

"May, I can't believe you made all these cheeses by yourself. Who would have guessed you had a talent for this?" Sadie filled her plate with several samples and sat by the *kinner*. "These are all so *gut*."

"Hope you spread the word to your friends and neighbors, *jah*?"

"*Mamm* would have been so proud of you. I haven't seen Gretchen yet. What does she think about all this?"

May sighed. "Don't really think she approves."

"She will when she sees what a big success it is. Making all these dishes and letting everyone sample the flavors of the cheese was a great idea. Has Elmer been here yet?"

"*Nein*, not yet."

Sadie smiled at her sister. "I always thought Elmer was sweet on you. I wonder what he's going to think now that you are going to be in competition with him."

"There is plenty of business for all of us, and besides, Elmer is well established in his cheese factory. I'm sure he doesn't have to worry about our little business."

"I need to get going, or my *kinner* will eat you out of all your sample pizza. See you on Sunday."

Just as Sadie drove her buggy out onto the road, Elmer steered his into the driveway. May watched him park. She wondered if he would stop by and sample her cheese. She watched as he walked up to the porch.

"So you are starting a cheese business?" He took a piece of pizza and nibbled on it. "*Gut* cheese and pizza. What gave you the idea?"

She wasn't going to confess that they needed the money. It was none of his business. "We didn't like the idea of dumping milk, and this was a good way to use it."

He nodded. "You are right, this is a better idea. I wish you success in your new endeavor."

"*Danki*, Elmer. That means a lot coming from you. And I hope you don't feel that we are stepping on your toes."

"*Nein*, there is enough business for all of us. But you

will give me some stiff competition if you keep serving food with your cheese products on them." He took a piece of the Gouda and popped it into his mouth. "*Gut* tangy flavor. All the best, May." He gave a nod to Thad as he headed back toward his buggy.

Thad worked his way through the crowd of customers on the porch over to May. "What did Elmer say?"

"He said the cheese had *gut* flavor."

"That is high praise coming from him." He watched as Elmer's buggy headed down the road. "Think he is worried just a little bit?"

May chuckled. "*Nein.* He's not worried about me making a few dollars. But he did grow quiet when he tasted a couple of my cheeses. I'm so pleased at the turnout today, and I think we have made a few regular customers."

Thad patted her shoulder. "Your cheese is *gut*, and I'm sure you will have a lot of repeat customers." He sounded impressed and that sent warmth straight to May's heart.

Could they really do this? Would this cheese-making business really help them save the farm?

May knew only *Gott* had the answers to such questions. But it didn't hurt to ask Him for guidance.

## *Chapter Fourteen*

On Monday morning, May had set to work early starting new batches of cheese when she heard the wheels of a buggy crunch over the rock in the driveway. She glanced at the clock. Janie was early. Which was *gut*, since there was lots to do that day.

A knock sounded on the door "Come in, Janie. Don't be shy." She stayed at the sink washing some bowls.

"*Gut* mornin', May." Bishop Yoder's voice startled her.

"Bishop, I'm sorry, I thought you were Janie. Come in. Would you like a cup of coffee?"

"That would be nice." He pulled out a chair at the kitchen table, and by the time he sat down, the cup was in front of him.

"Are you looking for Thad? I think he is in the barn."

"*Nein*. I've come to see you." He blew on his hot coffee, then took a generous sip. "I heard you made quite a stir over the weekend, giving away samples of your cheese from your new business."

May glanced at the bishop, not liking where this conversation was headed. "Many enjoyed the samples. Would you like to try any cheese?"

*"Nein."* He shook his head as if to reinforce his reply. "May, it is Satan whispering in your ear that makes you think that a job outside the home is more rewarding than homemaking. You must not be fooled by his lies."

May stopped what she was doing, rinsed her hands and faced the bishop. "Bishop, we are losing money every day on the farm. The dairy association wants us to dump milk on the ground. We cannot afford that. We lost our fall crop in the tornado, and if that wasn't enough, we had so much damage that Thad had to take out a loan. A loan that we cannot repay without a bumper crop next year, which we cannot plan on."

"A *gut frau* has many talents to utilize in order to make money. In fact, I hear you have several thousands of dollars stashed away from your numerous projects."

"That money is still not enough to pay for the tornado damage, not to mention the loss of money in crops, and the continued dumping of milk. We won't even have money to buy seed next year at this rate."

"That is not an excuse for you to work outside of the home."

"I am not working outside the home. I am here in this *haus* every day, cooking my *ehemann*'s dinner."

"You are starting a cheese business as witnessed by everyone in the community."

"It is up to my *ehemann* and me what kind of business we own, Bishop. We do not need the community's approval to keep body and soul alive. I am not doing it for pride but to save my family's 170-year-old farm. We Amish all dress alike so no one will look wealthier than another, but we all know some have more money than others."

"May?"

Thad was standing in the kitchen doorway, his face red. His eyes shot a warning to her. "We do not talk to the bishop like that." His voice trembled.

May dropped her gaze. "You are right." She leveled her gaze at the bishop. "I'm sorry, Bishop Yoder."

The bishop stood up and slowly walked to the door, shaking his head. He turned back. "Thad, make sure it is for the right reason you start this business." He walked out the front door.

Silence fell over the kitchen.

When May heard the buggy wheels heading down the driveway, she turned toward Thad. "Your *mamm* told him."

"There was no need. Everyone in the community knows about the cheese business," he retorted.

"He knew I had saved money, so your folks—or better yet, your *mamm*—must have told him."

"We don't know that."

"No one else knew except your parents."

Thad's gaze dropped to the floor.

"Unless…did you tell others, Thad?"

"I…may have."

"I cannot believe you did that!" May turned her back on him and got busy at the sink. "You had no right to do that. And you didn't stick up for me. You never do. When your *mamm* is browbeating me, you never say a word."

"She is my *mamm*, I can't sass her."

"And I am your *frau*. I am doing all this work to save the farm. Our farm. It is what we discussed. It's what we decided to do. I'm not losing this farm. I thought we agreed on that?"

"May, you know what the *Ordnung* says as well as I do. Women take care of the home, and they should find satisfaction in that."

She stared at him. "And men are to make the living. I shouldn't have to help with that. Whether the bishop likes it or not, I'm not stopping the cheese-making until we can save the farm."

"Then you plan to stop?"

"It's a lot of work, and I don't enjoy standing on my feet making all that cheese, in addition to the cooking and taking care of the *haus*. But I will do it as long as we need to earn extra money to save the farm. Who knows, maybe I'll have enough customers that I can sell my recipes and the business."

Thad smiled. "I said it before, and I'll say it again. You're one gutsy lady." He walked over and gave May a hug. "I'll talk to Bishop Yoder and smooth things over with him. Tell him you working like this is only temporary."

"*Danki*, Thad. We have to do what we have to do."

Footsteps climbing the porch echoed into the room. Only they were lighter of foot than a man's and May knew whom they belonged to, but a second heavier set followed. She was glad of that.

The screen door squeaked open. "*Hullo*, Gretchen, *hullo*, Aaron."

"Well, I see the bishop paid you a visit. No secret what he was probably doing here. Did he tell you that you needed to stop this nonsense of running a cheese business?" Gretchen spit out the last few words.

May bit her tongue. She'd had enough of discussing her business with people that shouldn't be sticking their noses where they didn't belong. Just then she heard Leah wake from her nap.

She headed for the stairs. "Excuse me."

After May left the kitchen, Thad turned to his mother. "*Mamm*, May is a hard worker and she is only doing what she thinks is right to hold on to this land. Why do you keep needling her?"

"She is nothing like April."

Thad rubbed the back of his hand across his mouth. "April was *gut* and kind, considerate and a hard worker. May is all those things, too. We are married now. I wish you would try to get along with her. Were you the one that sent the bishop over here?"

"Everyone in the community knows she is starting a business. That is not a secret."

"Here is one thing that you and the rest of the community might not know. May has my blessing to run the cheese business, and I plan to spend as much time as I possibly can with her to make it a success. The cheese she makes is actually delicious. Did you try any of it?"

His *daed* shook his head. "*Nein*, I was too busy in my woodworking shop to try samples of cheese."

"Like I said, they were *gut*. Even Elmer said they were *gut*. And by the look on his face, he actually seemed a little concerned that she might just steal business from the Sunnyhill Cheese Factory."

Gretchen harrumphed. "That'll be the day."

"You should try the cheese, *Mamm*, before you make a statement like that. I'm telling you, it is really *gut*."

Thad watched Janie pull her buggy up to the *haus*. "I'll walk you two out. The girls have a lot of work to do, and I know May does not want to stand around arguing with you about whether she should have the cheese business or not."

Thad paused on his way down the porch steps. "May is upstairs with Leah. Give a call and let her know you have arrived."

May was already downstairs waiting in the kitchen when Janie stepped through the door. She peeked out the window to make sure Gretchen was headed back to the *dawdi haus*.

"Something wrong?" Janie asked. "You are all acting strange."

"The bishop paid me a visit this morning. He lectured me on what the *Ordnung* expects of a woman. That she is to find satisfaction working in the home only, not running a business. I think Gretchen put him up to it."

"That doesn't sound like Bishop Yoder. I've never known him to listen to anything a woman said." Janie tried to hold a straight face, then burst into laughter.

May laughed. "I'm fine, But how are you? Did Jonah talk to you at all on Saturday?"

Janie walked over to the high chair. Leah held out the piece of bread she was eating to her. "Hmm, is that *gut*?"

Leah nodded, took another bite, then offered it again to Janie.

"Oh, *danki*, but you can eat it." She walked back toward May. "It hurt to see him. I thought I could keep my feelings under control, but it was difficult to do. Have you heard if he is courting someone?"

"I haven't heard. I can ask Thad if you want me to and see if he knows."

"*Nein*, please don't do that. I don't want him to know that I was asking about him. Not that it really matters. I just don't want to give him the satisfaction that I still care about him. I would be mortified if he found out."

"Don't worry, I won't say a thing, but I'll keep my eyes and ears open."

"I was just curious as to whom Gretchen set him up with." Janie's voice dipped.

"I can't believe how her sons think the sun rises and sets on her opinion. Thad is the same way. We had words this morning because he didn't stick up for me. I'm certain Gretchen was the one that sent the bishop to my door."

"Maybe if we ever have sons, they will think that about us." Janie took a deep breath and stood up straight. "Are you ready to start making the cheese? I need to keep my hands and mind busy."

"We are going to make the same cheese recipes again for this weekend, and I have a few special orders that we need to get started on."

"Before we do anything, I have a little gossip to tell you." Janie had a twinkle in her eye and seemed, at least temporarily, back to her old self.

"And what is that?"

"Guess who I saw in Elmer's courting buggy the other day?"

May's heart nearly stopped. If it was anyone but

Josie, she'd never be able to tell her. She'd seen the hurt in Janie's eyes and didn't want to see it in Josie's eyes, too. Why was it that all three of them seemed to be unhappy in *liebe*?

"Who was it?" She nearly choked the words out.

"Josie."

May felt overwhelming relief. "Really? I'm so happy for her." At least there was one Amish man in their community who was loyal.

# *Chapter Fifteen*

On Church Sunday, May relaxed on the buggy seat next to Thad as he steered Tidbit past the white picket fence and onto the road heading toward the Brenneman farm. The bishop's preaching always had a *gut* message that seemed to settle in her heart and brought her a little closer to *Gott* and His ways.

Her gaze roamed over the farms during the three-mile ride. It was a breath of fresh air to sit and enjoy the countryside around her. She held Leah on her lap and pointed at the chickens and the cows and the pigs, making their sounds each time.

Leah laughed. "Again, *Mamm*, again."

May stiffened. It was the first time Leah had called her *mamm* so clearly that the meaning finally sunk in. *Mamm.* Yes, she supposed she was the only *mamm* this little *mädel* would ever know. She hadn't thought about what hearing that word would be like. It was *wunderbaar.* She kissed Leah on the head as she practiced her animal sounds until she grew tired and leaned back against her.

May settled in to enjoy the rest of the short drive. She gawked at a neighbor's yard peppered with yellow chrysanthemums and white dahlias. Even their bird-house had a new coat of paint. *Jah*, she would need to ask Thad to paint theirs, too. It was starting to look shabby. Two squirrels scampered around on the road bank, chasing each other, and she chuckled.

A wheel dropped in a pothole, and the buggy jerked, bouncing the seat and jiggling her closer to Thad. She could feel the heat from his body next to her. May caught her breath at his nearness. She held her gaze out the window and hoped the horse's hooves drowned out the pounding of her heart. Even though a cool breeze swirled through the buggy, she raised her hand and blotted the moisture from her forehead.

"You recieved a lot of orders and are bringing in a lot of money with the cheese business. I'm so proud of you, May. We won't have to worry next year where the seed money will come from or the money to repay the loan." Thad glanced her way and smiled.

"*Danki.* I do it for us, for Leah and to keep our farm."

"I know." He reached over, grabbed her hand and squeezed.

While Thad parked the buggy at the Brennemans' and talked to the men milling around the house, May carried Leah to a bench on the women's side and settled next to Janie. She rocked Leah back and forth until she fell asleep again.

After the singing of the *Loblied*, Preacher David stepped to the front and gave the opening words, in Pennsylvania Dutch, to remind the congregation why it had gathered and called each member to humble their heart before *Gott*. When he concluded, May knelt with the others for silent prayer, then stood for the Scripture reading.

Preacher Paul delivered the main sermon, and May felt her heart open as the Holy Spirit worked His way in. When he finished, Bishop Yoder gave his testimony on denying thyself. *Jah*, he amazed her at his deep love for *Gott*.

The bishop cleared his throat before the reading of the banns. May smiled and often thought he did that as a little stalling tactic because he knew everyone loved to hear them.

"Now, I have a *wunderbaar* announcement. Elmer Plank and Josephine Bender will be married in four weeks."

May grabbed Janie's hand and whispered, "He asked Josie. I am so happy for them."

"Your cousin will be very happy. Elmer has a *gut* business and is a hard worker. And she will have a nice mother-in-law," Janie chuckled.

May nodded. "And Lois is a midwife so that will be handy."

Later on, they headed to the kitchen to help serve the common meal. Janie helped carry food out to the serving tables while May kept filling glasses with lemonade at the tables. She reached over Howard Lantz's shoulder to refill his drink as he remarked, "I might have to sell the farm."

A hush fell over the table.

"*Jah*, me, too," Tim Lambright said. "Milk prices are too low and the storm did a lot of damage."

May walked toward the end of the table where Jonah

Hochstetler, Thad's youngest *bruder* who had already taken over the farm since he'd inherit it from Aaron and Gretchen someday, sat. "*Jah*, I'm in the same boat as all of you," Jonah confessed. "What with milk prices so low, the storm and losing some of this year's crop, I might lose *Daed*'s farm."

May watched the expression on Thad's face as he spoke to Jonah. "Why didn't you ask for a loan?"

"By the time I got to the Amish lenders, their money had run out. They said they would check with Indiana, but storms ripped through the whole Midwest. I could maybe get a regular loan but the interest would be so high I couldn't afford the payments." Jonah sipped his lemonade.

"What?" Thad stared at Jonah. "Why didn't you say something?"

"You have your own problems, Thad, but at least you have a *gut* woman to help you out."

May caught Gretchen's reaction as she set food on the table and glanced from *sohn* to *sohn*. It was a table full of men, so Gretchen would not interrupt them. But by the look on her face, it was the first time she'd heard that her youngest *sohn* might lose their family farm.

May could see the shock settle on her face as she turned pale and walked to the porch steps and sat.

"Thad, how is the new cheese business doing that you and May started?" Jonah asked, quickly changing the subject.

"It was the answer to our prayers, but May does most of the work. She took classes, studied hard and practiced the recipes. She learned all about making cheeses." Thad looked at May. "She has even gotten orders from some bigwig local real estate agent who likes to serve cheese and crackers at her fancy open houses. And she has other customers who give her weekly orders. Mr. Kolb has a gift shop. He made her a webpage and brings out her orders. May is very successful, aren't you?"

The table of men glanced her way.

"*Jah*, we are doing very well. But I only have two hands, well, four with Janie Conrad helping me. But the two of us can only handle so much business. We have too much business now so we are turning orders down. If your *frau* or *tochter* would like to help, we can take you into our business and share the profits."

The men at the table all started talking at once.

Thad held up his hand. "Wait a minute, May. Are you talking about taking on business partners?"

"I'm saying if the bishop doesn't want me to have a business, then all those who need extra money, if they want to contribute and help make cheese, they can share in the profits. It will be a community business."

"That's a *gut* idea, but if many want to help, our kitchen isn't big enough," Thad emphasized with a pointed look.

"They could make it in their own kitchen. Or maybe we could rent a building in town. It would keep us all busy," May offered.

She watched Jonah walk over to Janie and talk to her. She tried to inch closer, but she was still too far away to hear a word they said.

While May continued to pour lemonade, Thad canvassed the table to see how many were interested in taking part in their cheese business. When May poured

Thad a glass of lemonade, he showed her the list he had put together.

"*Gut*, that means we can make more cheese," she said. "All those who want to learn the recipes and the tricks to making cheese will need to come or send their *frau* to our *haus* for training. What about Jonah, since he doesn't have a *frau*?"

Thad glanced at his *bruder*. "Jonah will supply more milk and cream, and he is *gut* at making ice cream. We could expand the business into yogurt and ice cream and maybe hire some *youngies* to help."

Jonah smiled and nodded in response to Thad. May noticed Bishop Yoder heading to the table. While the men gave it further discussion, she wandered over to the bishop. "What do you think of my idea, Bishop?"

"That's a fine idea. It's very generous of you to share your knowledge, May, and make this a community project. That's what we are all about, community and thinking of others before ourselves."

"It's no different than a barn raising or helping someone with their crops when they have been sick. It's all about community service, *jah*?"

He smiled. "*Jah*, but it was nice that you offered to help teach the others."

May cleared the table when the men were through eating. Janie joined her, holding a big tub for the plates and cutlery that weren't disposable.

May set some serving bowls in the tub. "I saw Jonah talking to you. How did that go?"

"All right. It was hard talking to him. My heart was fluttering so badly. He just wanted to know how I was, and if I liked making cheese. Small talk."

May smiled. "*Jah*, I know. Just don't let him break your heart again."

Janie nodded. "I'll take this tub inside and come back."

When May finished wiping down the table, she turned toward the next table, but Gretchen was standing in her way.

"That was very nice of you to let others join in your cheese business, May." Her voice held a tone of humility; it was almost timid.

"It was the right thing to do. We are a community, *jah*? We help each other out."

"It must have taken hard work to learn the craft. It was thoughtful that you are willing to teach others. Maybe I will come over and help one day a week."

"That would be nice, Gretchen." May smiled and gave her a gentle pat on the arm. It was going to be easier being friends with her mother-in-law rather than not.

After the meal, May headed her buggy to her *onkel*'s farm only a mile away and parked by the other cousins already there.

*Onkel* Thomas ran across the barnyard and helped her down. "You gave him a *gut* workout getting here after church," he laughed. "I'll brush him down a bit."

*"Danki, Onkel."*

*Aent* Matilda met her at the door with a big hug. "You heard Josie is getting married in four weeks?"

"*Jah*, I'm so happy for her."

"Go upstairs and tell her. She expected you to drop by."

May ran up the stairs and knocked on Josie's bedroom door. "I'm really mad at you," she called from the hallway.

"Come in," Josie sang out.

May ran in and wrapped her arms around Josie, hugging her tight. "I'm so happy for you." She sat on the chair next to Josie and watched her work on her wedding dress.

"I was actually surprised when Elmer asked for that first buggy ride," Josie said.

"I think once he met you, Josie, he only had eyes for you."

Josie smiled. "*Danki* for stopping by."

"I'm going to let you sew in peace, and head downstairs and see if your *mamm* has something for me to do."

Josie beamed with happiness.

May found *Aent* Matilda in the kitchen. "What would you like me to do?"

"I'm still making the list. Would you want to help me empty the hutch and set the *gut* china out for washing?"

May helped them until it was almost dark. Weary and alone, she and Tidbit made their way back home.

May was so happy for her cousin, but she couldn't help but wonder if she and Thad would ever be as happy. *Jah*, they'd become closer the past few weeks. But she still wasn't sure if Thad truly loved her.

Or if he ever would.

# *Chapter Sixteen*

Thad heaved a sigh. He'd volunteered to take care of Leah today while May attended Monday's quilting frolic. He packed Leah's diaper bag, put her coat on and trudged across the yard to the *dawdi haus*. She coughed, fussed a bit rubbing her nose, then fell back to sleep on his shoulder. His *mamm* wanted to see Leah, and that would give him time to work in his *daed*'s wood shop.

The sharp October wind blew in his face as he carried her across the barnyard to the *dawdi haus*. The aroma of fresh brewed coffee was a pleasant welcome when he stepped into his parents' kitchen.

"Mornin'." His *daed* rushed to his side and grabbed Leah's bag. "A raw day to be out and about."

"*Gut* mornin'. I was wondering if *Mamm* could watch Leah for a bit while I work on some shelves in your workshop. May is at a frolic, and I volunteered to take care of Leah."

"Sorry, but your *mamm* is sick in bed with the flu. Probably not a *gut* idea to have Leah here."

"Sorry to hear that. Tell her I said to take care of

herself." Thad hurried out the door. The short walk back seemed longer with Leah fussing and squirming.

She reared up, coughing and crying, as he hurried into the *haus*. He set her down, and slipped her out of her coat. Her little body was sweaty and all her clothes clung to her. He wiped her off, changed her and gave her some juice. She spit up the juice and pushed the cup away. When she fell asleep, he laid her in her downstairs crib. She woke up and cried. He picked her up and rocked her until she fell back to sleep. Later when he checked, she was very warm to the touch. He paced the floor as a shiver of fear crawled over his heart.

At 3:00 p.m., Thad heard a buggy pull into the drive. He peered out the window, then raced out the door to help May. "Leah is sick. You go in, and I'll unhitch Gumdrop."

May gasped and sprinted to Leah's crib. She laid a hand on her forehead and cheeks. They were burning.

Leah raised her head, her nose was running, but she smiled and held her arms out.

"*Hullo*, sweetie." May lifted the *boppli*, wrapped her in a hug and kissed her cheek.

Leah's breathing was wheezy and her chest rattled, but she snuggled close and laid her head on May's shoulder.

She waited for Thad to get back to the *haus*. "She's really sick. Call a driver. We need to take Leah to the hospital right away."

By the time he returned, Leah was quiet, too quiet. Her cheeks were red and her eyes glassy. Everyone was bundled and ready when the car arrived.

May was grateful for the warmth when she slid across the seat of the car. Thad set Leah in the middle and strapped her in the car seat. His quick actions helped May relax. The eighteen miles to the hospital in Iowa City seemed endless as she prayed.

When the car stopped at the emergency room entrance, Thad jumped out of the car and ran around to help May. *Gott* answered one prayer, there was no one ahead of them at the hospital admittance. As quickly as possible, a nurse took them to an examining room.

A few moments later, the door opened and a tall man in a white coat entered. He shook hands with Thad, then May. "I'm Dr. Evans. I'm the pediatrician on call. You're Mr. and Mrs. Hochstetler?"

Thad stepped forward. *"Jah."*

Dr. Evans's gaze jumped from Thad to May. "Tell me what's going on with Leah?"

May filled him in while the doctor examined her.

He ordered X-rays and several other tests. Then he left the room. After a while, he came rushing back in the exam room. "She's a very sick little girl. She has bacterial pneumonia. You're Amish?"

May nodded. *"Jah."*

"When Leah goes home, she needs to stay in the house as much as possible."

"Okay, for how long?"

"Preferably the rest of the winter. We don't want her catching pneumonia again."

"She's going to be all right then?" Relief washed over May.

"I'm admitting her for now. Her temperature is 103 degrees. She has an advanced infection. We need to monitor how she responds to the antibiotics. Has she ever been on antibiotics before?"

"*Nein*. No."

After they settled Leah in a crib, May sat next to it and rubbed her back until she fell asleep. Tears filled May's eyes. Thad pulled up a chair and wrapped an arm around her. She settled into his embrace and laid her head on his shoulder.

The rest of the day they stayed with Leah only taking turns when they stretched their legs and got something to eat.

Monday evening, Thad left the room and came back with two blankets. He wrapped one around May, and he curled up in the chair next to the window.

She pulled the blanket tighter around her shoulders as the tears slid down her cheeks. If anything happened to Leah, it was her fault. While Leah had been sick, she'd traipsed off to the quilting frolic. May had wanted some time away with her friends. Now this little girl was in the hospital fighting for her life. Thad never said a word, he wouldn't. But her place was at home taking care of a sick *kind*.

Leah hadn't moved a muscle in a long time, and her breathing was still labored. May stood and lightly laid her hand on the tiny back. Leah snuffled, moved her head back and forth but didn't wake. She drew in a deep ragged breath.

May woke during the night and stood at Leah's bed. She sounded a little better. Her sleep seemed more comfortable. Her cough sounded looser, and hopefully, the tightness in her chest was relaxing and the infection was starting to clear.

She needed to keep her promise to April and take care of Leah…and Thad.

Her sweet pumpkin still looked pale as a snowflake on a winter's day. Beautiful and unique like *Gott* made all his creations, yet fragile as a flower to remind May that she needed Him. Needed His grace and forgiveness for all her sins and for forgetting about Him except at times like this. May's heart swelled with the knowledge that *Gott* was beside her, helping her carry this burden.

When Thad took a walk, she pulled her Bible out of her quilted bag, turned to Psalms and read. She had faith that Leah would fight off this infection and would return home soon with her and Thad. They were a family now and May realized she needed to work with Thad more to make that feeling strong. It wasn't her versus Thad. They had made the decision to marry and that was a lifetime commitment. She needed to honor that obligation. And if she would admit it to herself, the more time she spent with Thad, she felt safe and secure. By his side was the place she always wanted to be, beside him and Leah. Her family, a family that she never really had. Her *mamm* died young, her *daed* stayed busy, and she and April had differences. This was the first time she felt like she was really in a family.

Tuesday Morning, Thad woke and glanced at the clock on the hospital room wall. 5:00 a.m. He stretched and the aroma of coffee out in the hall awoke his mind and pried his eyes all the way open. Leah was quietly whimpering. She was probably hungry. He'd get a couple cups of coffee and tell the nurse.

May had finally drifted off to sleep. He'd woken during the night and heard her crying. She felt bad because she went to the frolic and blamed herself. He should have stayed home with Leah instead of dragging her over to his parents' *haus*. *Nein*, it was just as much his fault. If that wasn't bad enough, *Mamm* was sick and he'd exposed Leah to the flu.

Thad wiped away the moisture from his eyes. He opened the hospital room door a crack, squeezed through, got two cups of coffee and told the nurse—Dottie was her name—that Leah was waking up.

She nodded. "I'll be there in a minute."

When he went back to Leah's room, May was awake and sitting up and watching her. He handed May the coffee. Dark circles were like half-moons beneath her eyes. Her mouth pressed tightly into a straight line, and a tear was rolling down her cheek.

"We need the nurse," she whispered. "I've touched her cheek, and she's very hot."

"She's coming." He set his coffee down. "But I'll make sure." Before he reached the door, it opened and Dottie walked in.

She checked Leah and her fluids, took her temperature, and looked into her eyes and ears. Leah started to fuss. "I'm calling Dr. Evans," Dottie said at last. "Her temperature is up to 104 degrees." She rushed to the nurse's desk, leaving the door open. A minute later, she returned. "They're going to page the doctor. He's in the hospital making rounds."

The few minutes they waited seemed like an eternity. Finally the doctor ran into the room. He looked Leah over and listened to her heart. He ordered the nurse to start a new IV with a different antibiotic. She got the new bag, hung it and fiddled with the lines.

Dr. Evans glanced at Thad and May. "She is not responding to this antibiotic. So we're going to try something else."

May threw her hand over her mouth as her body began to shake.

Thad wrapped both arms around her and held her tight. "Shh. Let the doctor work. Do you want to step out into the hall?"

*"Nein,"* she said through gritted teeth.

Thad pulled May back toward the window and whispered in her ear, "We need to pray to *Gott.* That's how we must help the doctor and Leah."

May nodded, and he knew she was doing everything she could to prevent herself from crying. He placed his hands on her shoulders and pulled her to him. "Are you with me on this?"

*"Jah."*

"Heavenly Father, You took April and Alvin from us, please do not take Leah, too. She is so innocent. Please fill the doctor with the right knowledge, give him swift hands and a sharp mind. Please heal Leah, Father. Amen."

May stayed in Thad's embrace. He rested his cheek on the top of her head and held her tight.

Wednesday morning, May pulled the Bible from her bag and turned to 1 John 4:8-20 and read the scripture. Gott *is love... * Gott *is love. Hate has no part of Him.*

She bowed her head. Gott, *please forgive me for all the hateful thoughts I had toward April and Thad. I was jealous of April. I wanted what she had, but please don't take my foolishness out on Leah. Please save her, Father. Please heal her, Father* Gott. *Please don't take this little bit of sunshine from my life.*

May prayed and cried until a calm settled in her heart.

Thad sat next to her and wrapped an arm around her shoulders. He whispered in her ear, "*Jah*, she will get well. *Gott* will bless this little girl who has lost so much."

When Dr. Evans entered Leah's room he asked the nurse to check Leah's temperature first.

The nurse flashed the results at the doctor. He nodded.

"The fever has started to come down. Her breathing should start to improve. The nurses' station has my number, and I'll stop back later to see how she's doing."

Thad nodded. "Thank you, Dr. Evans."

May tiptoed to the side of Leah's bed, and Thad stood by her side. Watching. Praying. And thanking *Gott*.

The rest of the day was a long one. May sat by Leah's bed for hours, staring at her. Drinking in her tiny face. Watching the movement of her fingers opening and closing as she slept, like she was grasping for something.

May rested her head in her hands and cried. If anything happened to Leah, it was her fault.

Thad sat next to her, wrapped an arm around her and whispered, "May, stop. Leah will get better. You're going to wake her. Let's go for a little walk down the hall, *jah*?"

She shook her head. "*Nein*, I don't want to leave her."

His voice was firm. "For one minute. You need to get up and walk."

"One minute," she repeated.

Dr. Evans returned Wednesday evening and examined Leah. "The fever is definitely coming down. Her breathing has improved, and she's started to respond to the new medication. She'll sleep a lot, so don't be alarmed at that. She needs the rest. It will help her body heal. I'll check her in the morning." He nodded to them and closed the door on the way out.

As soon as the doctor left, May felt Thad's arm relax on her shoulders, and she heard him sigh. She'd been selfish. Thad kept giving her comfort while his heart was breaking for his little *mädel*. She grabbed his hand and squeezed it. It seemed a vague attempt, but she was unsure how to comfort him.

Leah woke and smiled the minute she saw them. That frail little face warmed May. She picked her up and cuddled her warm body. After a few moments, she laid her back down in the crib.

"May, let's go for a walk and let Leah sleep," Thad suggested. "Or we could take turns and go on breaks to get food. Whichever you prefer."

"*Nein.* I can't leave Leah. She might need me."

Thad nodded that he understood and told her he'd get some food for them, returning as soon as he could.

Thad stepped back in the room from one of his walks and gave Leah a kiss. "I talked to the nurse. She said there were showers downstairs. If you wanted to freshen up."

May didn't take her eyes off Leah. "*Jah*, *datt* is *gut*. But I don't want to leave Leah just yet."

"I know." Thad leaned over and gave May a kiss on the forehead.

She didn't pull back. She might have almost liked it.

Early Thursday morning, Thad touched her on the shoulder. May opened her eyes to see him hovering over her. She glanced at the clock. She'd only slept a couple of hours. "Is something wrong with Leah?"

"*Nein.* The nurse said Leah's fever is down a little more and her breathing is much better. I have called a driver. He will take me home. I'll freshen up and bring you back clean clothes. Okay?"

"*Jah*, but don't be long."

Thad walked toward the door, turned and glanced over his shoulder. He winked as he closed the door. She tried to suppress a smile. Her heart raced at the little exchange and warmth flushed her cheeks. Did he just flirt with her?

When she glanced back at Leah, reality pinched her. Leah was April and Thad's *boppli*, not hers.

Why was it she could never get beyond that fact?

An hour after he left the hospital, Thad returned to Leah's hospital room. He walked to her crib, leaned down and kissed her head.

May tiptoed up behind him.

Thad wrapped his arm around her. "She's going to be fine. Leah is getting better hour by hour, and she's resting comfortably. Now you need to get some rest."

May stepped closer to him and laid her head on his shoulder. The touch of her hand rubbing his back was soothing. He felt like he could handle anything with her by his side.

He drew in a deep breath to slow his racing heart.

Leah was resting. The color had started to return to her cheeks.

Still, if anything had happened to Leah, he never would have forgiven himself.

Gott, *please forgive me. I am sorry for the burden this has placed on May. She feels responsible for Leah and me.* Nein. *May has been hurt enough. None of this is her fault.* He raised his arm and wiped his shirtsleeve over his face.

"Thad? Thad? Are you all right?" May's voice grew louder.

"I'm fine." He reached over and folded May's hand in his, squeezing tight. His heart thumped so loud he was afraid she could hear. The more time he spent with May, the more he never wanted to leave her side.

She was his now, and he never wanted to let her go.

# *Chapter Seventeen*

Five days later, Leah was finally home from the hospital and in her own crib. May smiled as she closed her pumpkin's bedroom door. She was still sleeping a lot, but the doctor said that was normal and essential for gaining her health back completely. May tiptoed down the stairs and started making breakfast.

Ten minutes later, Thad entered the kitchen. "Mmm, the bacon and eggs smell *gut*." He went straight for the table and sat down.

"*Gut* morning," May chirped. "You're a sleepyhead."

"With Leah safely home, I slept hard, awoke a new person, and thanked *Gott* for her recovery and that we're all together."

"*Jah*, feels *gut* to be home, but I was at the hospital so long and in a state of panic over Leah that I still feel anxious." And not just over Leah, but Thad. They had grown close in the hospital. How should she respond to him now?

"Are you still worried about Leah?" Thad asked.

"I'm heartbroken I didn't recognize the symptoms until they got so bad."

"Don't blame yourself. You're a first-time *mamm* and this was her first sickness. Anyone could have missed those signs. It came on all of a sudden."

"So you are not going to take any responsibility?" she huffed.

He jerked his head. "I… I didn't mean it like that. All I meant is, now we know more of what to look for when she has a sniffle. Check for a fever and listen to her breathing. We are *both* new parents, *jah*?"

May waved her hand in the air. "Never mind what I just said. You're right. I didn't mean any of that. It's as much my fault as any. I just felt like a failure that I went to that frolic, and I struck out at you."

"I know." His voice was sympathetic. "We'll both calm down and get our child-rearing confidence back in a few days."

While she cleared the table, he put on his coat and hat. "Later today, I've got a dairy association meeting. But I'll be in before I go. This meeting could take a while."

He strolled across the kitchen to the sink and stood next to May. He put a warm hand on her back. "We both need to forgive ourselves about not noticing earlier how sick she was." He slid his arm around her, leaned in and gave her a kiss on the cheek.

She could feel his closeness and hoped he couldn't hear her heart beating like an old windup clock. How could that be happening? How could her head know that he was completely wrong for her, yet her heart fluttered whenever he walked within six feet of her and looked forward to when he would come in at noon?

May couldn't wait for Thad to come in for lunch. She'd made his favorite, yumazuti, a goulash-type dish, with cherry pie for dessert. He deserved it for staying by her side when Leah was sick.

Her heart fluttered when he walked through the door and flashed her a big smile. Where he was concerned, she had trouble thinking in terms of *liebe*. *Jah*, she cared for Thad. More and more. But she found herself tamping down her feelings until they were hidden.

He had tossed her aside the minute April smiled his way. Now she had to remember this was a marriage of convenience and that was all. He'd never really said he loved her.

"*Danki* for making the yumazuti, it is *gut*, but not as *gut* as this pie. You spoil me. How is Leah?"

"She was up for a little while. She lingered over breakfast, not much of an appetite. She played with Blackie and her doll for a while, now she is back in bed napping. Her cheeks are rosy again, just not a lot of pep."

Thad patted her on the shoulder after lunch. "Spend your day with Leah and let everything else go."

She nodded. He walked to the door, opened and closed it in a hurry so only a small draft of cool air found its way into the kitchen.

After cleaning the kitchen, she slipped upstairs and checked on Leah. The little girl lifted her head off the crib mattress and gave May a big smile, holding herself up with her arms. *Jah*, she was indeed getting stronger.

May picked her up and sat in the rocker. Leah leaned against her. Blackie sneaked in through the open door and jumped up on May's lap. Leah giggled and petted the kitten.

"Here, kitty." She patted her leg and wanted him on her lap.

"Leah, you are my little bit of sunshine." May kissed the top of her head and smelled her apple-blossom taffy-colored hair.

Leah pulled at her *kapp* strings, patted her face, then leaned forward and placed a big kiss on May's mouth.

May chuckled. "You are feeling better. *Datt* is the first kiss I've gotten in days."

Leah clapped her hands together and giggled. Her dark blue eyes and perfectly arched brows were the exact image of Thad. He was handsome, and Leah was a delicate little doll, like April.

May hugged Leah and whispered, "Every time I look at you, I'll never forget who your parents are." She kissed Leah's cheek. "But I do *liebe* you, precious little one. You have stolen my heart for always." She squeezed and hugged her little morsel again. "It is time you ate, little one, then you can play with your blocks while I do a few things."

May hadn't been fair to Leah, Thad or herself. She had married him for the wrong reason. Leah deserved a *mamm* and *daed* who could show love and affection for each other as well as for Leah. Thad said that he loved May, but she knew that it wasn't true. He only needed a *mamm* for Leah.

May kissed the *boppli* on the cheek. "Sorry, little one, that I got caught in the past. We better get to work."

While Leah sat on the kitchen floor, banging her building blocks, May gathered her canning kettle, left-over jars and utensils, carted them to the pantry and set them on the top shelf for winter. The rest of the day was spent catching up on laundry and other work that she'd pushed aside while staying at the hospital. For supper, she fried potatoes and pork chops, then set them on a warming plate.

Thad stomped through the kitchen door and rushed in panting. "Sorry, I'm in a hurry. Dairy association meeting. I forgot."

"Supper is ready. Do you have time to eat?"

"*Jah.* Just a few minutes. I'll wash up quickly."

They sat at the table, bowed their heads for silent prayer, then dug in.

"You're quiet." She finished filling Leah's bowl, set a spoonful of potatoes on her plate and took a bite.

"*Jah*, I'm anxious to see if there is a new development. There is some kind of rumor about a letter. I'm anxious to get there and see what's going on." Anxiousness laced his words.

He glanced up from his meal and locked eyes with her. Worry pulled his mouth into a taunt line. "I'm not sure what's going on. The big ranchers keep producing more and more milk and will soon infringe on our smaller markets. They produce faster and cheaper. Our milk is organic from grazed cows, which makes the amount produced less, but it's better quality. I think tonight they want to talk about reducing the price… again." His voice was strained.

"We could expand the business, but after Leah's illness, I had hoped to spend more time with her."

"*Nein.* You take care of Leah and make cheese as you have been. The cheese-making was only to help out, not to be a full-time job for you."

"I haven't been making cheese at all since Leah's been sick. I could always take in sewing this winter."

The color in Thad's cheeks heightened. "*Nein*, not unless you really want to do that. But I don't want Leah to be out in the cold if a *youngie* can't come to the *haus* and watch her." He shot her a warning look. Then he stood up and walked out the door.

May hadn't meant to upset him, and she knew he had a lot on his mind. A twinge twisted in her gut. She wasn't helping him enough. She'd make more rag rugs and maybe work on a quilt while Leah slept. She could get quite a bit of money for a large quilt, slightly less for a *boppli* or youth quilt.

She glanced at the door Thad had gone out. They were a team. And they had to figure out how to save their farm together. But she could certainly think up more ideas to discuss with him…

Thad tapped the reins on Tidbit's back. "Come on, *bu*, it's not bedtime yet, you still got work to do."

Tidbit stepped out smartly and the trip to the dairy association meeting went quickly. When he got there, he pulled up the reins and parked his buggy next to all the others.

The meeting and discussion had already started. *Jah*, he was late and shouldn't have eaten supper. He quietly weaved between rows of chairs and stepped over feet to find an empty chair.

The president tapped a mallet on the table. "We need

a show of hands on the suggestion to write a letter to the USDA about tightening the regulations."

An Amish man from the other side of the room shouted, "We *have* to write the letter. The big producers from out west have flooded the market with what they call 'organic milk' but there is much doubt that it all meets the organic grazing standard. The USDA needs to ensure stricter inspection criteria so all the organic milk meets the standard. The overproduction means we have to sell some of our organic at regular price or we'll go broke."

A second man behind Thad shouted, "Another dairy farmer in Wisconsin had to sell his farm."

Thad stood. "*Jah*, I agree. We have to send the letter. Our prices keep falling. The word *organic* must be stated clearly as grass-fed, during the grazing season." He sat down and leaned back in his chair while others said their piece.

The talking and debating went on for another hour before the mallet hit the desk and they finally took the vote.

It was late and Thad was bone-weary by the time he made it home. May had left the flashlight by the door so he could find his way to the bedroom in the dark. But he already knew sleep wouldn't come easy tonight. It wasn't just the milk he was worried about.

He was worried about May, too.

# *Chapter Eighteen*

Thad stepped into the house and dropped down into a chair in the family room. Exhaustion and worry pulled at every bone in his body. The farm was losing money by the day. He scrubbed a hand over his face and ran it down his beard.

His mind kept wandering to thoughts of May standing at the sink in her blue dress. An image of her, with little auburn tendrils at her temples touching her cheek and teasing her smoky gray eyes, sent his heart beating faster.

Sleep tugged at his eyelids and pushed him out of the chair. He trudged up the steps to the second floor. Stopping to peek in on Leah, he saw May asleep in the rocking chair, her feet pulled up and scrunched under her afghan.

He removed his shoes and padded down the hall in his stocking feet. After a wide yawn, he hurried and got ready for bed, snuggled deep into the mattress, and covered with the quilt May had made him when she saw how tattered his was, then let his head sink into the softness of the pillow.

The ringing of the clock startled him. He bounded out of bed. The cold floor coaxed his feet into a dash across the room to retrieve his clothes and return to the warmth of the rag rug May had made.

A stream of daylight pulled his attention to the window. The sky was clear and the sun rose big and yellow, glowing like a bonfire chasing away the darkness.

He hurriedly dressed, and tiptoed past Leah's room, carrying his shoes in his hands. During the night, he'd heard May up twice trying to comfort Leah, cranky and still recovering from her illness.

The smell of hot maple syrup greeted him the second he entered the kitchen. Pancakes. His favorite. Plus May had opened a mason jar of canned peaches. He made a beeline to the table like a dog with his nose in the air. "Mornin'."

"*Gut* morning. How'd your meeting go last night?"

"We voted to send a letter to the USDA."

"Do you think it will help?"

He poured syrup on his hot stack of pancakes. "Can't hurt. Sorry, a lot on my mind."

"I know."

He let his eyes wander over May as she stood at the stove. Trying to ignore his feelings for her, he dropped his gaze back to his plate, and took another bite. After draining the last sip of coffee from the cup, he blotted the drip that dribbled down his chin. He eyed the remaining stack of pancakes on the platter. *Nein*, time to get busy. He pushed his chair from the table and stood.

"Would you like another stack?"

"*Nein.* Chores are waiting." He finger-combed his hair back, plopped his hat on, then shrugged into his coat.

The sound of wheels crunching over the frozen ground came closer and stopped by the house. Thad peered out the window, then darted out the door to the porch. "Caleb, what brings you out so early?"

"I wanted to get your thoughts on last night's meeting," Caleb said. "You look tired this morning. Didn't sleep well after listening to all that debating last night?"

"*Nein,* I got some sleep, but not much." Thad was silent for a moment, then blurted out, "I asked Bishop Yoder to play matchmaker for me and May, like you suggested, and press her into marrying me, but instead of a *frau*, I have a nanny and...*nein*, I didn't mean that. I'm just tired. I wanted to talk to May last night and bounce some ideas off her after the dairy association meeting, but she is always fussing over Leah."

May heard Thad and Caleb talking on the porch and noticed the door ajar. She set the dish she was washing on the counter, reached for the door and heard her name. She listened and clutched at her chest.

*Thad sent the bishop to pressure me to marry him?* She stumbled to a chair. Of all the cruel things Thad had done to her, this was the worst. He thought her life was that trivial that he could dictate whom she married? She'd trusted her heart to him once again, and once again he'd betrayed that trust.

The burning on her cheeks lasted all the way upstairs. She poked her head into Leah's room to check if she was asleep. May quietly ducked into her room, pulled her suitcase out from under the bed and heaved it on top.

Thad had not only ruined her life once before, she let

him into her heart, and he'd ruined her life again. She couldn't get a divorce, but she didn't have to live with him. Her body shook with sobs until her knees buckled, crumbling her to the bed. She let the grief drain from her soul.

After several minutes, she gathered her strength, pushed off the bed and packed her suitcase. *Nein.* He would not betray her trust again. She loved Leah and always would, but she could not stay with a man that had that little regard for her.

This was the last time that he would make a fool out of her. She wandered to the window and let her eyes feast on the red buildings surrounded by the white picket fence, the large garden area and the cows grazing in the pasture. A sight she'd probably never see again once she moved to Shipshewana.

She'd never come back. And never see her *daed*'s farm, the one she'd grown up on, ever again.

Squeezing her eyes closed, she turned from the *wunderbaar* view. Since she wouldn't be coming back to this *haus* again, she'd need to find everything she wanted and have it sent to *Aent* Edna's. There were a few of her mother's things in the attic that she'd like to take with her. The walnut whatnot shelves that *Grossdaddi* made *Mamm.* After April and Thad married, April put away several of *mamm*'s mementos so she could give the *haus* her own personal touch. If there was anything remaining after May left, she would tell Thad it should go to Leah.

She took her dresses off the hangers, folded them as neatly as she could with her hands shaking like a kite in the wind, and placed them in the suitcase. She'd never imagined that Thad would treat her with such a cold heart.

Hurrying around the *haus*, she gathered boxes and the belongings she had to have, then packed them for the three-hundred-mile trip to Shipshewana. She closed the box lid and hesitated. The finality of her actions spun around in her head as she glanced around the kitchen. If she moved out, she'd never return.

The screen door opening startled May. She jumped out of the pantry so fast it reminded her of the time *Mamm* had caught her dipping into the cookie jar between meals.

Thad stuck his head through the crack in the door. "I'm going over to Caleb's to help him with some work. I'll be back for supper."

"Okay." May blew out the breath she held as the door banged closed.

Leah let out a cry. May left the box in the pantry, poured a cup of milk from the refrigerator and took it upstairs.

Leah stopped crying as soon as May entered the room, her little mouth turning into a sweet smile.

"Oh, *datt* is such a charming face, it chased away all those big tears."

Leah laughed and smiled again, batting her lashes.

"Yes, you will be a heartbreaker like your *mamm* so your *daed* better keep a close eye on you, for sure and for certain."

May sat in the rocker while Leah sipped her cup of milk and fiddled with May's dangling prayer *kapp* strings, her deep-blue eyes big with mischief. She grasped the strings and let go, grasped and let go, then batted them back and forth with a fist.

"So you found a new toy, huh?"

Leah smiled like she understood every word May said. When she finished her milk, they played with the blocks on the floor.

A lump grew in May's throat. How was she ever going to leave this child? She carried her downstairs, put her in her high chair and gave her the blocks. "And don't be tossing them off the tray."

May's heart was splitting in two. Stay or go? But how could she stay? She pulled a hanky from her pocket and blotted the tears streaming down her cheeks. Her grief tucked away, she stood at the stove and browned the stew meat, then cut up potatoes, onions and carrots. She let it all simmer in a big pot.

While Leah played, May packed a few more things. With the *kind* watching, it made boxing up her things very difficult.

After a few hours, Leah's eyes couldn't stay open. Ever since her pneumonia, she wore out earlier than usual. May fed her, tucked her into her crib for the night and returned to the kitchen.

When she heard Thad's buggy in the drive and go to the barn, she dished up the stew and waited. When Thad entered, he hung his coat, washed up and joined her at the table.

They sat and bowed their heads for silent prayer.

"It's cold out there," Thad said at last. "Wouldn't be surprised if we have snow soon."

"I imagine so, it's late fall." She took her fork and stirred it around in her stew.

"Is something wrong? You seem quiet."

May took a deep breath. "I heard you talking to

Caleb today on the porch. Is it true? You went to see Bishop Yoder and had him press me for an answer? And tell me people were talking about me when that wasn't really true? You tricked me, forced me into marrying you so I could take care of your nanny problem. You told him I was the best person for the job."

His jaw dropped.

"You trapped me in a loveless marriage?"

At first, Thad couldn't believe it. How could he convince her of the truth?

"May, please believe me. I *liebe* you."

"I can't believe you went to Bishop Yoder. You lied to me about everything. Everything, Thad. My whole life with you was a lie. I'm leaving and moving to Indiana. You'll need to find a real nanny for Leah."

"You can't leave! We're married," he said.

She raised her chin. "Yes, I can, and you can't stop me. I've had it with you and your lies. Tell the bishop that."

"What about Leah? She'll miss you so much."

Her voice caught. "I'll miss Leah, but she's little and will soon forget me. I can't stay with you, Thad. I can't forgive you this time. You've gone too far. I'm all packed. I'll find a place to stay here in town until I can catch the train to Shipshewana."

His voice turned raspy. "I'll take Leah over to *Mamm*'s tomorrow. We can stay in the *dawdi haus* for a few days until you can move. But I'd like to try to work this out, May. I do truly *liebe* you. I don't want you to go."

"I'm boxing up what I want, and the rest can go to Leah. I'll let you know when I'm leaving."

May walked out of the room—and out of his life.

# *Chapter Nineteen*

The next morning, Thad hurried to pack a bag while May gathered Leah's belongings. The mood in the *haus* was tense, and he needed to get away so he could think clearly, figure out what his next steps should be.

He carried their things out to the buggy, then came back inside for Leah. He'd take Leah over to his parents' *dawdi haus* on Jonah's farm for the night. "I'll come back and do the chores, but I won't come in the *haus*. I won't bother you any longer than need be." The words stuck in his throat and nearly choked him.

He'd never meant to hurt her. How could he make her understand that? How careless of him to even bring the subject up to Caleb. He felt like kicking himself. They had started their union with a marriage bargain. He should have been more sensitive, more careful.

She nodded. "It's your *haus* and your food. You can come in and eat."

*Nein*. He knew she couldn't stand the sight of him. "We'll call it quits right here. No more contact, no more uncomfortable moments or forced talking to be nice."

She shrugged.

His brain was too tired to figure out what that meant. The only thing he wanted was to get out of here. His heart felt like it was ripped out and dragged around like a piece of dirt. Sadness, bitterness, loneliness all washed through his body at once.

Gott, *I only did what You asked. I asked You to guide my steps and look where it has gotten me.*

He needed to get away. To put some distance between him and May. When he tried to step in the buggy, Tidbit paced the ground and jiggled the buggy. "Whoa. Whoa." He walked over, laid a hand on Tidbit's neck and stroked it. "*Jah*, big guy, I know you sense my tension, and you don't like it."

The horse calmed at his soothing voice. Finally, Thad stepped into the buggy and set Leah on his lap. He tapped Tidbit's reins and the buggy lurched ahead as the horse started to move.

In a few minutes, the motion of the buggy had Leah fast asleep. Thad glanced down at her face and sighed. He swiped away the tears rolling down his cheeks, then gazed out the window at the frozen ground, the harvested fields, the dead grass. Jah, Gott, *I get it. It's winter and time to let the ground rest and let my soul rest. Maybe I should have been honest with May instead of stacking lie upon lie.*

He'd had two marriages in eighteen months. He felt burned-out. Tired. He'd tried to *liebe* April as best he could, and he did *liebe* May with his whole heart and soul. Maybe his calling in life was just to raise Leah.

May was hurting. He got that, but he'd hoped she cared about him enough to forgive him. But *nein*, that was not going to happen. Tomorrow he'd go see Bishop Yoder and ask if it was possible, if he'd make a special exception and let him and May get a divorce. Their marriage was never going to work.

After a twenty-minute ride to Jonah's farm, he parked the buggy, carried Leah in, still sleeping, and laid her in the crib his parents had set up especially for their *Enkelin.*

He drew a deep breath, then found his *mamm* sitting in the kitchen and told her everything.

"Thaddaeus Thomas Hochstetler, you go back to that *haus* and make up with May right now! She is a *gut* woman and a hard worker. You hurt her feelings."

"I didn't mean it. I was tired."

"That is no excuse."

Thad sighed and looked down at his shoes. "*Jah*, you're right, *Mamm. Danki.*"

The next morning, he begrudgingly got himself out of bed, dressed Leah and asked his *mamm* to watch her while he drove to town.

Thad stepped out of the buggy in front of the bishop's *haus*. The door burst open and the bishop appeared, signaling him to enter.

"Morning, Bishop Yoder."

"You're out early and on such a bitty morn." The bishop steered Thad into the kitchen. "Rebecca, if there is coffee left, would you fetch us a couple of cups?"

"*Gut* morning, Thad, so nice to see you." She ran to the kitchen, then came back out with two cups of coffee. She set them down, and discreetly disappeared into another room. No doubt a prearranged courtesy when the bishop had visitors.

"So, what can I do for you this morning, Thad? You're already happily married."

"*Jah*, about that... May found out that I tricked her into marrying me and she is angry. Very angry. So angry she's leaving me."

"Thad, slow down, you're making no sense. What has happened?"

"May found out that I sent you to talk to her, to insist that we marry. She loves Leah like her own *kind*, and I thought it would work out. But she doesn't trust me or believe anything I say now, and I fear she never will. I broke her heart not just once, but twice. She wants to live apart, but that's not fair to her. I want to set her free. I want a divorce."

The bishop's eyes widened. "Thad, you know that is forbidden among us."

"I know, but since we just got married a few months ago, I thought you could make an exception somehow." He tried to send the bishop a pleading look.

"*Nein*. Absolutely not. Your request can't be approved. You'll need to work it out, you and May," the bishop said firmly.

"She doesn't want to live with me. May can't get past how much I hurt her." Thad's voice turned earnest.

The bishop folded his hands together on top of the table. After a silent moment, he spoke softly. "Yours is the first match I have made where the couple wants a divorce. I may have to throw away my matchmaking hat after this." He tried to lighten the air. "I hope this foolishness doesn't get around."

Thad was in no mood to listen to a joke.

The bishop patted the table twice with his hand,

scooted his chair back and stood. "Let me take your situation under consideration. No one has ever complained before. Give me a few days."

"Bishop, May wants to buy a train ticket and move to Shipshewana as soon as she can."

"Why, that's nonsense! Why would she want to do that? What about Leah? She needs a *mamm*." Bishop Yoder headed for the door.

Thad stopped in the doorway. "Because she hates me and wants to get as far away from me as possible."

The bishop lightly put his hand on Thad's shoulder, turned him around and pushed him out the door. The door closed firmly behind him.

Thad rubbed his chest. He already missed May, and she wasn't even gone yet. What would happen when she left Iowa for *gut*?

May trudged up the stairs, trying not to spill the bucket of water or the cleaning caddy she carried. She turned the knob, opened the attic door and gasped as a huge cobweb hit her in the face. She set the bucket down and wiped the cobweb off her mouth. The air smelled dusty and stale, as she batted a hand to circulate some fresh air. Dabbing a rag in the water, she wrung it out and wiped around the doorframe to remove other webs and dirt.

She turned the flashlight on and shone the beam around, grateful the bishop let them use the device when necessary. She held the light in front of her as she stepped through years of accumulated dust.

From one end of the attic to another sat old furniture, objects of many treasured memories. Things she had long forgotten about: lamps, shelves and boxes marked *Mamm*, April or *grosseldre*. A pang of longing touched her heart.

She sighed deeply. It'd take her a month to sort through this mess. Her footfalls echoed on the wood flooring as she walked through the maze of cartons and old dressers. She moved a stack of boxes and stared… April's oak *boppli* cradle. *Daed* had carved a fancy design on the head and footboard. May took the wet rag, wiped it down and cleaned the top edge where the name was carved. APRIL.

Her eyes filled with tears. It was as beautiful as her sister. She straightened and flashed the light all around. Where was her cradle? If her memory was correct, hers was plain with no carving on it. Finally she saw it, sitting farther back. She pushed a box of toys out of the way, picked up the dusty cradle and carried it to a cleared spot.

She dipped the rag in the bucket of water, wiped off a layer of years and flashed the light over the cradle. Astonished, she stepped back. It was made of a dark brown walnut. Plain, yes, but lovely inside and out. Carving would have destroyed the natural beauty of the wood.

*Nein.* Was that really her old cradle? She dipped the rag in the water and wiped a spot on the top edge. MAY.

She finished cleaning it and set the cradle with the other things she wanted to keep. May flashed the light around again and uncovered a big object that had been sitting next to April's cradle. *Mamm*'s oak buffet. Beside that, she saw *mamm* and *daed*'s bedroom set. What was it doing here?

May huffed. Thad, of course. Something as *wunder-*

*baar* as this bedroom set and that buffet, he hid away in the attic for the rodents to run across and gnaw on with their teeth.

Thad and April must have moved them up here on a day when May wasn't home. Since *Mamm* died, they didn't have large family dinners anymore. She had forgotten all these treasures were even here.

Tears welled up in her eyes as she drew in a ragged breath. She wouldn't be able to take any of these things to *Aent* Edna's *haus*. She couldn't afford to ship all this. And even if she could, there would be no space for these things there.

May stumbled back against the buffet, her body shaking in uncontrollable sobs. She wasn't just leaving Thad, she was leaving her family and all that she loved. Leah would never know what any of this was, who it belonged to, or what it represented. She'd never know her *mamm* or her *grosseldre*.

May calmed herself and dried her tears.

After dusting the top of the dresser, May set her rag down and opened a drawer. It wasn't empty...it was stuffed full of dresses. *Mamm*'s things? But she'd given all *Mamm*'s clothing to a woman who had lost everything in a *haus* fire. They must have missed these. Well, she could tear them up into strips and weave them into rag rugs.

May picked up one of the dresses and shook it out. A spiral-bound notebook dropped to the floor. She bent, retrieved the book held closed by a blue ribbon and laid it on top of the dresser. She held up the dress. This would never have fit *Mamm*'s stout frame. *Mamm* had loved her strawberry-filled jelly donuts every morning and pie for supper. Whose dresses were they?

She glanced at the spiral-bound book. She folded the dress, slipped it back in the drawer, closed it and lightly caressed the book with her fingertips before picking it up. She had never seen *Mamm* write in such a book. Maybe it was her recipe book. After she'd died, May hadn't been able to find it.

*Wait a minute!* She opened the drawer again, grabbed a dress and held it up. These weren't *Mamm*'s. They were April's before she got pregnant. She must have stored her old clothes in *Mamm*'s dresser.

A chill swept over May like the wind skimming over the pond on a cool evening. She picked up the notebook, untied the blue ribbon and slowly started to open the cover, then snapped it closed and threw it back on the dresser.

She stared at the book. What if it contained love letters to Thad? She choked back a tear and swallowed hard. *Nein.* She didn't want to read April's passionate words to Thad. And maybe his letters to her were inside.

She flopped in the chair, her heart racing. The pain from April and Thad's betrayal still stabbed at her chest.

Why had May ever married Thad? She could never get a divorce, and the reminder of his *liebe* for her own sister stared her in the face every day when she looked at Leah. The *kind* had April's face and Thad's dark blue eyes.

Maybe it was best for everyone if she did move to Shipshewana. *Why,* Gott*, after everything I've been through all my life living in April's shadow, did You allow this to happen to me?*

She noticed the blue ribbon dangling over the edge of the dresser. May grabbed the book. She didn't want to see April's words professing her love for Thad, but she needed closure.

She flipped the cover open and scanned the words…

Dear Diary—

Her heart raced. It was definitely April's writing. Did she really want to know what April had hidden away from prying eyes? Something that was personal to her and no one had a right to see…

May needed to know the truth. *Had* to know the truth. She gingerly flipped the page.

Alvin and I *liebe* each other so much we can hardly stand to be apart. We sneak out at night to meet down at the creek and lie in each other's arms until almost dawn. We talk for hours and plan our future.

May's hand shook as she turned the page. With each page, she devoured word after word, paragraph after paragraph, that spoke of April's love, but not for Thad, for Alvin, Thad's older *bruder.*

I'm pregnant! Alvin and I are so happy. We can't wait to marry and share our lives with our *boppli.* This is the happiest time of my life. The bishop will read our banns on Sunday.

She scanned down the page and stopped…

My life is a total shambles and my heart is breaking. Alvin died in a buggy accident. It's just the *boppli* and me. *Danki*, Alvin, for giving me a small part of you; I will treasure this gift always. The bad part is…when they know I'm pregnant, and as members of the church, they will shun the *boppli* and me.

Her hand flew to her chest as May read on.

Thad has volunteered to marry me so the *boppli* can have a name and the community won't shun us. I feel awful but I hope that someday May can forgive me. I'm desperate and have no place else to go.

May read for hours. About Thad, how his and Alvin's *daed* made Thad marry April to keep her and the *boppli* from a shunning. At last, May burst into tears. Thad gave up his own life for his brother, April and Leah. Thad had chosen to sacrifice his happiness for the rest of the family.

Her heart sunk to the floor as her tears drenched her cheeks. She crumpled back in the chair, wiping her eyes and face with her hanky. Thad was an honorable man. He had kept April and Alvin's secret all this time.

Now that she and Thad had separated, his *liebe* for her, like an old relic set in the attic and forgotten, would soon turn to dust.

# *Chapter Twenty*

The sun peeking through the window shone a warm beam on May's face and roused her from a restless sleep. Her mind sputtered to life after only a few hours of sleep, then began to focus. She regretted lying awake half the night rehearsing what she'd say to Thad. The thought of seeing him pushed her out of bed and hurried her to dress.

While the oatmeal cooked, she kept rehearsing what she'd say to him. She'd start by apologizing. Surely he'd understand. He had only moved out a few things so it wouldn't take long to move back.

She selected her dark blue dress to wear. It deepened the color of her eyes, he once said.

Her hands shook when she slipped the harness on Gumdrop and tightened the girth. Words and phrases danced around in her head. How was she going to apologize to Thad? Would he ever forgive her?

She tapped the reins against Gumdrop. "Giddyap." The horse trotted down the drive, past the garden, onto the road, and increased his gait as he passed the white picket fence. It was only a twenty-minute ride to Jonah's farm and his parents' *dawdi haus*.

May relaxed back in the seat, but the closer she rode to the Hochstetler farm, the faster her heart beat. Her palms were damp. It was like the first time Thad had asked her to go on a buggy ride. He'd been nervous and his tongue had stumbled over the words. All she'd been able to reply was *jah*.

Her chest squeezed her ribs so hard she could barely breathe.

She urged Gumdrop into a faster trot. May's heart raced, thinking about throwing herself into Thad's arms. She could feel his arms around her right now, pulling her closer for a kiss.

Her stomach turned somersaults.

"Hurry, Gumdrop, hurry." She took a deep breath and exhaled slowly. *Lord* Gott, *danki for setting me straight. I should have believed Thad all along.*

She'd surprise him with…what? Her newfound forgiveness because now she knew the truth? Would he be insulted because she hadn't trusted and believed him?

Another thing spun around in her head. Why hadn't he just told her about what was going on? Why did he feel the need to keep it a secret? Maybe he really had loved April.

She would never know for sure, but she had to trust Thad.

A tug to the right on the reins turned Gumdrop into the drive. She guided his steps to the *dawdi haus* around to the back of the main *haus*. Drawing a deep breath, she blew it out and stepped down.

May knocked on the door. No answer.

She knocked again and stepped back. This time she heard footfalls in the hall on the other side of the door.

The door opened and Thad motioned for her to enter. "Did you come to see Leah?"

"*Nein.* I was hoping she'd be asleep. I need to talk to you."

He led the way to the sitting room. "Have a seat."

He sat on a chair next to the heating stove opposite the couch, his glance darting everywhere, avoiding eye contact with her. His actions made her uncomfortable, but she didn't blame him after the way she'd treated him.

"Thad, I found April's diary, and I know what you did and why."

He was silent for a moment. "So what are you saying? Now you forgive me and everything is okay?" His manner was strangely calm. "You've forgotten about the past and that April and I were married?"

Her heart skipped a beat. What was he saying? She wanted it to work, she really did. She loved him… But she hadn't thought about if she had fully forgiven him. Had she really turned her back on what he'd done to her? All she'd really found out was that April hadn't loved Thad, and Thad hadn't loved April.

At least she didn't think so. Confusion stirred inside her.

Thad's eyes locked with hers. "Sometimes people just aren't meant to be together. People don't usually flip from hate to love overnight. I ruined your life—twice. I'm sure now, after reading April's diary, you want to forgive me. The thing is, you can't just want to. You have to do it. And in this case, it also means that you have to forgive me for marrying April and all that went along with that choice."

"I've loved you all my life, Thad."

He crossed the room, sat by May and placed his hands on her shoulders, and turned her toward him. "*Jah*, even when I was married to April? You realize if your sister hadn't died, we'd still be married."

May's heart felt like it had just been punched. "Why are you saying this to me?"

"I can read it in your eyes. Your heart loves me and has forgiven me…but your head is saying stay away from him."

His words stabbed her. She hadn't really thought it all through.

He patted her hand with his large, calloused palm. "I've asked the bishop to let us divorce."

"He'll never grant that. Amish can't divorce."

"Let's wait and see."

"You and Leah could come back and live at the *haus*." She wrung her hands in her lap.

"*Nein*. I think it's better that we are apart right now, and that we don't confuse Leah too much. *Mamm* is going to watch her for a few days. Let's each take some time away from each other. You could even go to Shipshewana like you've always talked about. Maybe then you could decide where you want to live. Edna wanted to leave the café to you if you'd move out there. That is a *gut* opportunity for you. She has no other close heirs and wants you to work with her."

He didn't want her.

He removed his arm from her shoulders.

Her heart had already told her where she wanted to be. She got up and walked to the door.

Thad followed. "May, it's for the best. I can see the distrust in your eyes. Your heart might want me, but that's not enough. No matter how much you think you want this. I want you to *liebe* me and to accept all that I am, including my flaws and the choices I made in the past, whether they were good or bad."

The heat from the stove and her jangled nerves made it hard to breathe. "*Jah.* We'll talk later." She reached for the doorknob, but Thad got it first and opened the door.

"I'll walk you out."

"*Nein.* I'm okay. Stay in here with Leah."

Gumdrop was waiting in the drive. He stomped his feet, snorted and shook his head when she approached. *Jah*, she felt that same way.

She rubbed a hand down Gumdrop's nose, then put her arms around his neck and gave him a hug. "I want someone to *liebe*, so it looks like you're stuck with the job." His sympathetic big brown eyes looked at her. "You have *gut* intuition."

She climbed in and tapped the reins on his back. "Let's skedaddle, big boy. I feel a *gut* cry coming on." He took off as if promised a big bucket of oats.

She turned him onto the road, and urged him into a faster trot. The fence posts flashed by and field after harvested field disappeared as Gumdrop flew down the road.

Her heart felt like those fields…picked clean.

A knife stuck in his heart when May walked out the door. She was the air that he breathed. He didn't want to let her go, but this time he needed to do what was best for her. For them. Thad could tell by May's eyes when she spoke about finding April's diary that it was more a matter of she *wanted* to believe. Not what she actually *did* believe.

Thad wandered through the *haus*. What had he done? He knew he'd been selfish to have married her, he should have waited, but *nein*, his heart had ruled over his head and all reasoning had fled. What was he thinking of to put her through it again? Her eyes held a sadness that cut to his core.

He had to be the dumbest man on earth when it came to women.

When Leah awoke, he fed her, then left her with his *mamm* while he attended the dairy meeting.

He shuffled around three men sitting at the end of a row, and sat next to Caleb. He plunked down on the chair as if he didn't really want to be there.

Caleb eyed him. "Is everything okay? I drove by your place and saw you carrying out some suitcases."

"It's nothing to worry about." He stared straight ahead. He wasn't ready to explain it to Caleb or anyone else.

As they called the meeting to order, he had to shake the image of May from his head.

The president of the dairy association stood wearing a somber face and waved a letter that Thad could see had the USDA logo. The president wasn't smiling. Thad's heart nearly stopped. The dairy was a big part of his livelihood. The knife plunged deeper and twisted. No doubt, that reply was going to mean he'd lose business on his dairy cows. They had the co-op cheese business that May started, but now he had no *frau* to make his cheese and sell it.

Finally, a smile broke out on the president's face. "The USDA has agreed to review the information brought to them regarding the big producers violating the organic rules. The letter also states the USDA inspection agency would write a citation to those producers who knowingly violate the regulatory definition of organic. Each producer could receive a fine for each violation, which means if the producers are not meeting the grazing requirement, their milk will not be classified as organic."

A roar of whooping and hollering went up. After a few minutes, the room buzzed with talk. Caleb patted Thad on the back and raised his voice over the noise. "Hopefully, we will see big results from this action."

A huge wave of relief washed over Thad. "I'm praying that this is the fix for the small dairy farmer."

The noise in the room grew louder with all the men talking at once. Thad leaned back in his chair and pretended to listen to what others around him were saying.

His mind wandered to his earlier conversation with May. What had he done, sending her away? But he wanted her to make the decision about their marriage based on what both her heart and head wanted, not something forced on her by April's diary or the bishop.

May had to forgive him completely and say so, or it wouldn't work between them. If she couldn't, then he was going to set May free.

He owed her that.

# *Chapter Twenty-One*

May worked for days cleaning the attic, sorting and writing a description for each object and piece of furniture, explaining what it was, whom it belonged to and how old it was. If it had a story behind it, she wrote it down.

Leah would know about her *mamm* and all her *grosseldre*. May was going to tell her how beautiful April had been from the inside out. How her *gut* heart shone and that made her outside glow.

When *Daed* had cancer, April had taken care of him day and night. She'd spent all her time caring for and helping him, or sitting next to him in his room sewing. She'd made rag rugs, quilts, *boppli* blankets, and all kinds of doilies and dresser scarves the *Englisch* loved and had placed them in a consignment shop to help pay the medical bills and the mortgage that had to be taken out against the *haus* for *daed*'s bills.

May wrapped up all the things that April had made. They would make a nice addition for Leah's hope chest when she got married. May wiped away the tears that rolled down her cheek. She regretted her jealousy of April. That was hard for her to admit.

The attic was finally organized and cleaned of years of dust and annoying spiders. Working in the attic had given May plenty of time to think about her life. Maybe Thad was right, and she should visit *Aent* Edna.

On Sunday morning, May checked the church schedule. Preaching was at the Millers' farm this week. She hitched the buggy and headed off.

At the farm, she glanced around for Janie, didn't see her but found a spot on the bench next to Sarah and Mary. She searched the men's benches on the opposite side of the barn for Thad. Row after row, she scanned faces. Finally, on the last bench, she spotted him, his head down, probably avoiding her. Her heart jumped at the sight of him.

Bishop Yoder's preaching that day was about finding the perfect mate. He said that meant working together for the future, but also working individually, selflessly, to make the other person happy. Only then could a person have the perfect marriage. His message touched May's heart. It was a *gut* recipe for success. He and his *frau* seemed to have a great marriage. His testimony also spoke to her. *Forgive and move on. Don't allow the past to possess you.* Had she done that? Had Thad been right all along?

The bishop ended the service, then glanced from side to side. "I have a *wunderbaar* announcement to make. Janie Conrad and Jonah Hochstetler will be married in four weeks."

Janie and Jonah? Getting married? May hadn't

thought Gretchen would ever let that happen. She looked around and found Gretchen. She was staring at May and gave her a smile. May returned the affection. *Ach*, it seemed like Gretchen's heart had truly changed. What a blessing from *Gott*.

On the way to serve the meal, May caught up with her mother-in-law and gave her a hug.

"*Ach*, what was that for, May?"

"You know very well, Gretchen. You and Aaron gave Jonah and Janie your blessing."

"*Jah*, and we gave it to you and Thad, too. Now you two need to make up and quit this foolishness."

May glanced away, then back and nodded. Her mother-in-law was right. And May knew what she had to do.

When she sat for the common meal, she glanced over the tables for Thad, but couldn't find him. She walked into the Millers' *haus* and around the yard, but there was no sign of him anywhere. He must have gone home right after church. She hadn't seen Leah either. Her chest felt as empty as a hollowed-out log.

She helped clean the tables and carried leftovers into the *haus*. Making her goodbyes, she hitched her buggy, and urged Gumdrop into a fast trot. Her excitement spurred her all the way home.

Her friends were happy and getting married. And Gretchen was right. She never thought she would be saying that. Now she had to convince Thad that she loved him with all her being.

The next day dawned crisp and bright with only a few clouds puttering across the sky. May hitched Gumdrop. "You have been lazy." She scratched his ears. "You need to get out before it gets too cold. You can sleep all winter, eat oats and get fat until spring."

He shook his head as if he understood her teasing.

She pulled up in front of Bishop Yoder's *haus* and knocked on the door.

Mrs. Yoder answered the door. "*Gut* mornin', dear."

"Morning, Rebecca. Is the bishop in?"

"He's in his office. I'll get him." She swept May with an examining look before she waddled down the hall. There were probably only a handful of reasons most people visited the bishop. *Nein.* Boil that down to two: good news or bad news. Most likely Mrs. Yoder was looking for a hint as to which this was. Amish women liked to spread the news and gossip. May waited by the front door, her hands twisting around in her apron.

After what seemed like an eternity, the bishop finally appeared from a doorway down the hall. "Nice to see you, May. What brings you by?"

"I've need of a *Schtecklimann*—a go-between."

The bishop raised his brow. "Let's go into the kitchen and talk about this over a couple cups of coffee." He closed the front door after May entered.

She took a sip of the strong brew, then added a little of the cream sitting on the table. For the most part, the bishop would know her story. He listened as she talked. When she finished, he chuckled.

May stared at him. "Is this funny to you, Bishop?" Her tart words slipped out.

The bishop reached over and patted May's hand. "*Nein. Nein.* Someday you will look back on this and tell the story to your grandchildren. My advice to you is the same as I give everyone—settle the problem on a buggy ride. You and Thad work all the time. He worries about the dairy farm, you worry about cheese, and you each worry is the other person in *liebe* with me."

May felt heat creep up her neck and burn her cheeks.

"You dwell too much on the past, May. That's why people set the old in the attic. It's past history. We must live in today's world and deal with our present issues. It's okay to go up to the attic and see those old treasures from time to time."

He paused for a moment, his eyes searching her face for a clue to her heart. How did he know she'd been snooping around in the attic?

"The old things were placed there for a reason." He looked at her intently and continued. "Live in the present. Thad is a *wunderbaar* man and he loves you and wants to do right by you. You need to decide what is right for you, then tell him. *Liebe* isn't that complicated. Don't hurt that little *mädel*. She is innocent in all this. Leah loves you unconditionally. You and Thad are all she has right now, *jah*?" The bishop eyed May.

She knew he wanted an answer but she was fresh out of words.

"I'm always telling folks, go on a buggy ride and get to know each other." He patted her hand. "I'll talk to Thad."

"Just one more thing, Bishop. My *aent* Edna from Shipshewana asked me to come to Indiana and help run her café and bake shop. She gave me three months to make up my mind. The time is up. I called Edna and told her I would take the train Tuesday, the day after tomorrow. I am packed and ready to go, so if Thad wants to see me about our marriage, it will need to be before then."

Before May climbed into the buggy, she gave Gumdrop a few pats on the nose. He raised his head up and down. "*Jah*, you are a smart horse. You knew all along. I think *Gott* whispered in your ear. He probably whispers in mine, too, but I'm too busy talking to listen. What I wanted was right under my nose all this time. Let's stretch your legs."

The bishop's words helped her put her life in prospective. The fall fields were bare and lifeless. They were in a state of restful sleep, a time to replenish strength by letting the natural course of nature wash over the land.

She jerked her head around when Gumdrop turned into the drive. She hadn't even been paying attention; she was home already. The horse passed the *haus* and trotted to the barn. She unhitched and fed Gumdrop, then hurried into the *haus*.

May needed to keep her hands busy and her mind off Thad until it was time to get on the train. Why not start ripping up April's dresses so she could take the strips with her to make rag rugs and save them for Leah.

She was going to miss Leah…and Thad terribly.

Ever since Thad had seen May at church, she kept appearing in his head. Her smoky-gray eyes and auburn hair set a fire in his heart that was hard to put out. Every time he saw her, he wanted to take her in his arms and never let her go.

Gott, *I don't know what you want from me. I felt called to marry April and give her and Leah a chance at a family. Yet the woman I loved and wanted most to have a family with, I alienated.* Gott, *I'm drowning here. I wanted a family with May, and now I'm afraid I've lost her forever.*

Buggy wheels churning the dirt in Jonah's driveway pulled Thad from prayer. He peered out the window. It was Bishop Yoder. Must be important for him to drive all the way out here in the country, and it couldn't wait until Church Sunday.

"Bishop, *gut* to see you. What brings you out here?"

The bishop didn't smile. "Thad, I'd like a few words with you."

He motioned the bishop inside the *haus*. "What's going on?"

"May stopped by to see me. She told me everything. She said you tricked her into marrying you by leading her to believe there were many complaints about your living arrangements."

Thad's heart almost stuttered to a stop.

"You fibbed to her. *Jah?* You will need to talk to the Lord about that. Do you truly *liebe* May or did you marry her just because Leah needed a nanny?"

The words slammed into Thad's chest. "I regret saying all that. I *liebe* her, and I've done nothing but hurt her. That's why I wanted to make it right by setting her free."

"Thad, she still wants to be your *frau*. You must go talk to her and make it right. But she said to tell you her *Aent* Edna gave her three months to make a decision on whether she was going to move to Shipshewana. She has a train ticket for Indiana for the day after tomorrow, and she will leave if you do not contact her." The bishop looked him squarely in the eye. "You know what you have to do, Thad."

* * *

May heard a buggy come up the drive and peered out the window. It was Ethan, one of the *youngies* who helped do chores.

Her heart felt like a hollowed-out tree stump without Leah and Thad as part of her life. Tears were blurring her vision and she could hardly breathe. As soon as she arrived in Shipshewana, she'd get settled and start to work at the café and stay busy.

She couldn't imagine life without Thad and Leah. The life that she once never wanted, and now she couldn't imagine how she would get along without it.

She waited hour after hour. But Thad didn't come and ask her to stay. Tears welled in her and an ache tore through her heart.

When she heard wheels crunching over the rock in the driveway, she ran to the window. But it was only the SUV that was taking her to the train station. Her throat clogged with emotion as she took one last look around the *haus*.

She told the driver she had luggage, and he said he'd be happy to come into the *haus* and help her.

May walked toward the kitchen door, and stopped. Footfalls sounded coming up the porch. She took a deep breath. A knock sounded loud and firm. The knock of a man who knew what he wanted.

She smiled and slowly opened the door.

Thad stood there holding Leah.

"You didn't have to knock," May said.

"I did, just this once. I needed you to open the door and let me in, not just into your *haus*, but into your heart. I *liebe* you, May. I always have and always will.

I know I hurt you by trying to do what was right for someone else. I hope I never have to do something like that ever again."

"*Nein*, Thad. I know why you married April. It took me a long time to come to terms with it, but I promise you, I have. Our belief is that we serve our *Gott* and our community above ourselves. You did what was best for the community, and I wallowed in my own self-pity. I wasn't living our faith. But *Gott* is *gut* and faithful. Marrying you was always my dream and losing you my worst fear come true. I *liebe* you, and now I can live my dream."

She stepped forward. "We both wanted the same thing but worried that the other would say *nein*. You're an honest man. I wouldn't want you any other way. *Ich liebe dich*, I love you, Thad Hochstetler, and always will."

May took Leah from his arms and hugged her tight. Leah smiled and giggled. May shifted her to her left hip. She raised her hand to Thad's cheek and stepped toward him until their lips met for a tender kiss.

He put his arms around May and pulled her and Leah both into a hug. "*Ich liebe dich*, May Hochstetler. We are *ehemann* and *frau* and always will be. And nothing will ever separate us again, for sure and for certain. That's a bargain that I will never be sorry for making."

She stepped back and held up her Amtrak ticket to Shipshewana. "Shall we tear it up?"

Thad paused. "*Nein*, we will give it to the driver, along with his payment."

"When I bought the ticket, an overwhelming fear of losing you came over me. Then I knew what April must have felt like losing Alvin. When I thought about her being pregnant and knowing that she and her *boppli* would be shunned, I realized what she was going through. How desperate her life must have felt like to marry someone whom she didn't *liebe* to give her *boppli* a name. But I'm sure she found some kind of satisfaction in knowing that you, Alvin's *bruder*, was going to marry her, and that you would take care of her and Leah, and raise her like Alvin would have wanted."

She caught her breath. "You asked me a couple of questions a few days ago that I wasn't prepared to answer. But I am now. You asked me if I'd forgotten about the past and that April and you were married. *Nein*, I haven't forgotten, at least not yet, but in time I believe that it will dissolve into the past and become like ashes. It just won't matter, because I tried to put myself in April's situation, and I hope that she would be willing to make the same sacrifice for me. I forgive you, not just because Christ said that if we do not forgive men their sins, our Father in heaven will not forgive our sins, but because we live in community. And I'm glad that you loved your *bruder* enough to marry April and take care of Leah."

He crossed the distance between them and wrapped May in a hug and kissed her tenderly again.

"Me, too, *Daed*. Me, too," Leah called out.

Thad kissed Leah's cheek. "Pumpkin, you will always be part of our hugs."

May wiped the tears from her eyes. "I will always *liebe* you both, and we will always be a family."

# *Epilogue*

"Bishop Yoder!"

May tried to hurry but the bishop could step lively when he had a mind to do it. Perhaps he didn't hear. "Bishop!"

She glanced around at the congregants after preaching to make sure no one else could overhear her request.

She stepped a little faster. "Bishop!"

He stopped and turned around. "May, did you call?"

"Bishop, you seem a little hesitant to talk to me."

"My dear, you and your *ehemann* at times like to stretch the authority of the *Ordnung*. I tell you that you can't work outside the home in your cheese factory, so you get the whole community involved so I can't say *nein*. And you organize it during the common meal on Church Sunday. When I wanted to matchmake you and Thad, you resisted. Then when you decided you'd marry him, you two fight and want a divorce." He scowled. "No one I have played matchmaker for has ever had a complaint or asked for a divorce. Just the fact that you even asked for one sets a precedent I don't like. If news of that ever got out, the other bishops would think I have lost control of my community." The bishop whisked out his handkerchief and blotted his forehead. "Now that I got that off my chest, what can I assist you with?"

"Bishop, there are six of us in the cheese factory and one cell phone for the business is just not enough. We would like permission for all of us to carry a phone."

"Certainly not." The bishop waved his hand as if to wave the idea away. "There can be one per business. You will need to designate someone to carry the phone."

"But we all make different kinds of cheeses and have our own orders. For each of us to have a cell phone would be so convenient." She laid a hand on her belly. "And since Thad and I are expecting, he worries about me when I'm away from home."

"And how is your business? Is it all you hoped it would be?"

"It is a blessing, Bishop. It not only pulled us out of debt, but all those who are in it with us have no financial worries. The farm is looking better than ever after all the repairs. And we are thinking about expanding the business and getting on the Iowa Cheese Roundup and getting a star put on the Roundup Map."

"And when is your little one due?"

"In two months."

"So." He rubbed a hand down the breast of his coat. "I have time to think about the additional cell phones."

He turned to walk away, then glanced back. "*Jah*, I think my matchmaking hat has not lost its credibility. *Gut* day." He turned, raised his hand in the air and waved.

The clip-clop of the horse pulled May's attention to

Thad pulling the buggy up next to her and stopping. She stepped up and slid in next to Leah.

Leah tapped the rein against Tidbit's back. "Look, *Mamm*. Get going, Tidbit."

"*Jah*, you are a *gut* driver."

Thad helped Leah sit back in the seat. "Okay, Leah, the horse is trotting so no more tapping. What did the bishop say?"

"He'll think about it. But I'll keep working on him. I think he'll change his mind. I just have a feeling."

"Is that like the feeling you first had about us when we married?"

"*Nein.* After I learned what true forgiveness was, I could trust again and that unlocked the door for us. I asked the Lord to guide my steps, and they led right back to you."

Thad slipped his arm around her, and she slid closer to him. His dark blue eyes locked with hers and stole her heart once again. "*Ich liebe Dich*, I love you, May." He leaned over and gave her a tender kiss.

"*Ich liebe Dich*, Thad."

"*Daed*, I want to drive."

Thad raised a brow and glanced at May. "She's taking after you more and more every day."

Peace filled May as she glanced toward Thad with a smile. Her dream had come true. She let her gaze wander to the sky. She had a wonderful *ehemann* and family; who could ask *Gott* for anything more?

* * * * *

# FINDING HER AMISH LOVE

Rebecca Kertz

For my aunt Betty, my grandmother's sister,
with love. You are a wonder,
and I'm glad I have you in my life.

Ask, and it shall be given you; seek, and ye shall find; knock, and it shall be opened unto you.

—*Matthew* 7:7

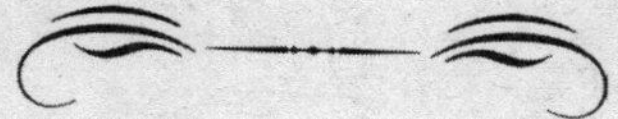

# *Chapter One*

Crickets chirped and frogs croaked, filling the stillness of the night, as Emma Beiler eyed the Amish farmhouse across the road. It was late, and she realized that everyone inside the house was asleep. She'd come to see the young Amish woman who'd helped her after she'd escaped briefly from her foster home fourteen months ago. She'd have to sleep in the barn until morning, a place she'd sought refuge previously.

Cold, she buttoned up her lightweight navy jacket. She had the feeling she was chilly because she hadn't eaten a decent meal in over a week. Leah, the Amish woman she'd come to see, told her to return if she ever needed her help. Well, she desperately needed assistance now. She had to find a job and a place to live. Maybe Leah could give her guidance.

Emma crossed the street, then entered the barn by the back door. It was pitch-black inside, and once she closed the door, she pulled out a small penlight, the only thing she'd taken with her when she'd left Maryland besides some loose change. She switched on the light and made her way to the stall where she'd slept before. It was empty but laid with fresh straw. The last time, she'd slept with a dog. The puppy had made her feel better as he'd slept beside her when she'd been terrified of discovery.

She stepped into the stall, closed the half door and got comfortable. The scent of the straw soothed her. She was grateful that a horse hadn't taken up residence there. The temperature was dropping, and she shivered. Ignoring her sore feet and legs, she curled onto her side. *Soon, I'll see Leah again.* The knowledge eased her mind, and she allowed herself to relax.

She woke to daylight filtering in through the window over the loft. She'd slept hard and well. She started to rise when she heard the main door open, then the sound of male voices that grew louder as men approached. Emma slunk low into the far corner of the stall and covered herself with straw.

"Do you think 'tis a *gut* idea to build on to your house, Reuben?" a man said. "Surely it's big enough. You'll have no problem with church service. Missy and Arlin managed to fit everyone inside the house or the barn when they hosted here."

"I don't know, Daniel. Our congregation is growing. I want to do my part."

"You can and you will," the man called Daniel insisted. "Now what did you want me to see?"

Emma froze, terrified, as their voices grew louder. She didn't want them to find her. She wanted to get out without anyone seeing her, then go up to the house to politely knock on the door, not get caught sleeping in a barn stall.

"Back here," the man called Reuben said. "I thought you might want these for your harness shop."

The men's voices were close, and Emma relaxed only slightly as the sound grew distant again.

"Where did you get these?" the man called Daniel asked, sounding awed.

"Picked them up at a mud sale last year. Thought I'd use them, but I find I don't need them. Take them. If nothing else, you can hang them next to the ones you carry once you open up shop."

"*Danki.* If you're sure you don't want them."

"Nay, Ellie has been after me to get rid of them."

"I'll use them," Daniel said. "It won't be long before I have enough money to rent a place."

"Once you open your shop, then what?"

"Then I'll see about finding a wife."

The other man laughed, but she couldn't hear his response. Emma heard the sound of the barn's back door opening and the conversation receding as the men stepped outside. She didn't budge. She hadn't heard the sound of the closing door. Heart thumping hard, she lay as still as she could. After several moments of silence, she thought it might be safe to leave. Relief that she hadn't been caught overwhelmed her, making her feel giddy. Or was the swimming sensation she felt from lack of food? She hadn't eaten since yesterday morning when she'd finished the last of the granola bars she'd bought in a convenience store.

She sat up, then abruptly sneezed as a piece of straw tickled her nose. She stilled, listening for the noise of someone approaching. When all remained quiet, she started to stand, then froze as she sensed someone's presence. She glanced toward the door and saw with mounting horror an Amish man staring at her over the half door of the stall. The man wore a black-banded straw hat, royal blue long-sleeved shirt and navy pants held up by dark suspenders. He had light brown hair and brown eyes. Their gazes locked. The frown on his face eased into amusement as he took in her appearance.

Shame made her hug herself with her arms. She scrambled to her feet, aware of her ragged jeans and the faded green T-shirt under her jacket. When his eyes shifted upward as if seeing something in her hair, Emma instinctively reached up, felt straw and blushed as she pulled it off. When his gaze met hers again, she stared back at him, refusing to be intimidated. She wasn't afraid that he would hurt her. Her only fear was that he'd call the police and she'd be sent back to her foster family, the Turners.

"Did you have a nice sleep?" His deep, pleasant voice rumbled along her spine.

Daniel, she realized, and wondered why it had been easy to recognize his voice. "Yes."

He eyed her narrowly, all signs of his amusement gone. "Who are you and what are you doing here?"

"I came to visit someone who lives here."

The handsome man arched an eyebrow. "Who?"

"Leah," she said. She saw a brief flicker of recognition in his gaze.

"Leah Mast?"

Emma bobbed her head. "She told me I could come back to see her." She bit her lip. "So here I am." She eased across the stall a few steps toward the door, but since he was blocking her escape, there was no place for her to go.

"There is no Leah Mast here."

His tone made her tense. "I don't know her last name, but she has blond hair and blue eyes. A pretty girl."

"You know Leah." He sounded doubtful, but the look in his eyes changed after she'd described her.

"Yes. We met last year." She studied him carefully. He was an attractive man, a fact she couldn't help noticing. "Are you her brother?"

"Nay." He tilted his head. "Come out of there."

Fear washed over her as she shook her head vigorously. He looked nice, but since moving in with the Turners, she'd learned that looks could be deceiving.

He frowned. "You believe I'd cause you harm?"

"No," she breathed, and she believed it, but she couldn't be too careful. "I just need to see Leah. Can you get her for me?"

"Leah no longer lives here," Daniel said.

All her hopes quickly disappeared. Feeling faint, Emma closed her eyes briefly and swayed. Her stomach hurt, and she felt dizzy. "Then I'll go," she said.

He watched her carefully. "I can take you to her, if you like." His smile appeared, but it was gone so fast that she wondered if it had been genuine. "She married and moved into Henry's house. She's Leah Yoder now."

She eyed him with misgiving. Dare she trust him? "Where is she?"

"Not far. Leah and Henry run Yoder's Country Crafts and General Store." Daniel opened the door, and Emma backed into the other corner, hugging herself tighter. Concern entered his expression. "I won't hurt you."

"I know."

"Then stop backing away from me."

She didn't know what to say. Logic told her that he wouldn't hurt her. He was Amish and religious, right? Then she recalled attending church with Bryce Turner and his family, and she knew people pretended to be Christian when they weren't.

Daniel Lapp studied the bedraggled girl in front of him with compassion. The fact that she described his cousin accurately eased some of the concern at finding her in the barn, but not all of it. Leah had lived here with her parents and sisters until each sister had wed and moved away, leaving their parents with a house that was too big for them. After his cousin Ellie married Reuben, the couple had switched houses with his aunt and uncle, her parents, Reuben's smaller house a better fit for the older couple. The trade had worked well since Ellie and Reuben had a son and needed the larger space to expand their family.

Reuben had asked him to come. His cousin's husband had been thinking of adding on to their great room. Daniel thought the expense of a renovation unnecessary, and he hoped that Reuben now agreed with him.

The girl's clothes were torn in several places. He saw a rip near the pocket of her jacket and one across one knee of her jeans. She still had straw in her hair and a dirt smudge across her right cheek. What was her name? How old was she? He scowled at his interest. Did it matter?

"I'm Daniel Lapp," he said, opening the door and stepping inside the stall. "Leah's cousin."

Surprise flickered in the girl's brown eyes, but she didn't move. "You're her cousin?"

Daniel inclined his head. "And you are?"

"Jessica Morgan." She bit her lip. "Jess."

"Well, Jess Morgan, if you come with me, I'll take you to Leah."

She didn't move, and he realized that she was afraid to trust him. Something shifted inside his chest. *What happened in her young life to make her afraid?* Why was she here in his cousin Ellie's barn? Was she a runaway? Was her family half out of their mind with worry over her?

He softened his expression. "If someone vouches for me, will you let me give you a ride to see her? Leah's sister Ellie lives here now with her husband."

"You don't live here?" she asked warily.

"Nay." Daniel headed toward the back door. "Reuben!" he called. "Would you get Ellie for me?"

Reuben entered from outside. "Why? Is something wrong?"

"There's someone I'd like her to meet." Daniel sent him a silent message with his gaze.

"*Ja*, I'll get her for you." Curiosity glimmered in Reuben's gaze, but he didn't approach. Moments later, Ellie entered the structure, followed by her husband and her sister Charlie.

"What's wrong, Daniel? Reuben said you wanted to see me."

Daniel waved inside the stall. "I'd like you to meet someone and to tell her that I am who I say I am."

Frowning, Ellie approached with Charlie following until the sisters could see inside. Ellie saw the girl in the corner who hugged herself with her arms. His cousin met Daniel's gaze with raised eyebrows. "Who is she?"

"She says she knows Leah. Said they met last year."

Charlie stared at her. "Jessica?"

The girl jerked and looked stunned. "How do you know my name?"

Charlie smiled. "Leah." Her eyes twinkled as she glanced at Daniel before turning back to the girl. "Come outside, Jess. My cousin Daniel is harmless," she said with a casual gesture in his direction. "Most of the time," she added teasingly.

"Who is she?" Ellie asked.

"She's the girl Leah found sleeping in the barn last year." Charlie studied her with compassion. "Are you all right?"

The girl bobbed her head. She started toward the stall door until her gaze fell on Daniel and she halted. Understanding, Daniel stepped back to give her enough space to comfortably leave the stable. "Leah talked about me?" she said, looking upset as she inched toward the door.

Charlie nodded. "She told me not long after she married. She was worried you'd come back and find her gone. She wanted us to know so we could bring you to her if you ever returned. But then you never came back. I told my sister Ellie just in case. She and Reuben live here now." She looked thoughtful. "Leah left a bag for you in the barn for over a week, but you never came for it."

The English girl blushed. "I'm sorry. Something happened and I couldn't come back." She shifted her gaze briefly toward Daniel. "Besides, I'd already taken too much."

Daniel stiffened. Had she stolen from his cousin?

As if sensing his thoughts, Charlie laughed. "She didn't steal anything, Daniel. Leah gave what she wanted her to have." She smiled at her. "Come and be *willkomm*."

His cousins headed toward the door, and he followed. The English girl hesitated as if afraid, until he smiled at her gently and motioned her to join them.

He observed Jess in the bright sunshine and saw a young woman who was vulnerable…and beautiful. Startled by his thoughts, he looked away. When he glanced back, he saw that she avoided his gaze. "Will you let me take you to Leah?" he asked softly.

She didn't say anything but eyed him nervously as he locked gazes with her.

"'Tis fine to go with him, Jess. Daniel is a *gut* man." Charlie eyed her cousin with amusement.

Daniel pretended to glare at his cousin then heard Jess's sharp intake of breath, as if she didn't understand that he'd been kidding with Charlie.

"Would you like some breakfast?" Ellie asked. "I have plenty of muffins and fresh bread. And I can make you eggs and bacon."

"We can get breakfast on the way," Daniel said impulsively, much to his own surprise. He wanted to be the one to feed her. He felt a surge of protectiveness toward Jess unlike he'd ever felt before, and he had no idea why.

"Thanks, but I'm not hungry," Jess said, but he didn't believe her. "I'm fine."

Softening his expression, Daniel captured the girl's gaze. "Are you ready to go?"

"Yes."

"We're pleased to meet you, Jess," Ellie said. She slid a glance toward her husband, who watched curiously. "I'm sorry. I didn't introduce my husband to you. Jess, this is Reuben. Reuben, Jessica, a friend of Leah's."

"Nice to meet you," Reuben said. He handed Daniel the two harnesses he'd given him.

Jess smiled. "Same here."

"Reuben," Daniel said, "Thanks for the harnesses."

Reuben nodded agreeably. "I'll see you when you get back," he said quietly. "If you don't have time today, don't worry about it."

Daniel watched as Ellie shifted closer to her husband. He could feel the love between the couple and felt a longing for a relationship like theirs. Charlie had the same loving relationship with her husband, Nate Peachy. As did his married brothers, Noah, Jedidiah, Elijah, Jacob and Isaac, with their wives. Soon, he thought, after he'd opened his harness shop.

He set the harnesses in the back of the buggy, then turned to Jess, who now stood quietly beside him. When she would have climbed in, he stopped her. "Nay, over here."

She approached him slowly, cautiously, toward the other side of the buggy where he waited. He glanced at Charlie and saw her compassion for the girl in her eyes. He turned back and held out his hand. "Let me help you," he said.

She hesitated but then let him take her hand. Her fingers felt small within his grip. He reached to place his other hand under her elbow, then heard her gasp and felt her stiffen as he lifted her easily onto the front passenger seat. He climbed in through the other side, grabbed the leathers, waved at the others, then drove out of the yard.

The girl remained silent as he pulled onto the road toward Yoder's Country Crafts and General Store.

"Are you all right?" he asked softly. She shot him a wary glance, then inclined her head. "We can stop somewhere and eat."

"No." Jess glanced away. "I'm fine," she said, but he sensed that she wasn't.

Daniel wondered again why she'd come. Was she in some kind of trouble? He had so many questions, but he wasn't going to pry. *Yet.*

Less than fifteen minutes later he flipped on his right turn signal and steered the horse into the parking lot next to the store. He felt Jess tense beside him. "Leah and her husband, Henry, own the store. They live in the house on the hill behind it."

She exhaled on a sigh. "I hope she remembers me," she murmured, looking nervous.

Her vulnerability made his heart melt. "She will."

He saw her swallow hard. She seemed to pull into herself, and he felt the strangest urge to offer comfort. He steered his horse up to the hitching post. "Stay put," he said.

Daniel climbed out of his vehicle, tied up his horse, then went to her side and extended a hand to help her. She looked at his fingers, then at him, then placed her small hand trustingly within his grasp. He was gentle as he set her onto the ground before releasing her.

"Are you ready to see Leah?"

Her lips curved slightly. "Yes."

"Come," he said, leading her into the store's interior, which appeared dark after the bright morning sunlight.

Henry and Leah stood behind the counter, going over papers. They both looked up as the bells over the door rang and he approached with Jess. Leah smiled at him before her gaze settled on the girl next to him. She stared a moment as they came closer, and Daniel felt the tension in Jess beside him. Suddenly, his cousin's eyes widened, and she grinned. "Jess!"

The girl beamed at his cousin. Witnessing the pure delight and warmth in her expression took his breath away. In that moment, he realized that she must be older than he'd first thought. A young woman. Something shifted inside him.

"You came back," Leah said.

Daniel saw Jess nod. "I hope it's okay," she said.

"*Ja*, of course. I told you to come see me whenever you..." Her voice trailed off and a look of concern settled on Leah's features.

It seemed to Daniel as if they were silently communicating.

"Come with me," Leah said. She turned to her husband, who eyed Jess warily. "Henry, we'll be up at the *haus*."

Henry nodded. Leah gestured for Jess to round the counter and follow her. As she obeyed, Daniel saw Jess take in Leah's pregnancy and freeze. "I'm sorry. I shouldn't have come. You're about to have a baby."

Leah arched an eyebrow. "And that means I can't talk with you?"

Jess blushed. "Of course not."

"I'll wait for you here," Daniel told the girl.

She opened her mouth as if she would object. She promptly shut it without a word and nodded.

When both women had left, Henry turned to him. "Who is she?"

"Someone apparently Leah knows."

"Where did you find her?"

"In Reuben's barn. It looked as if she'd spent the night there." Daniel's gaze went toward the back of the store where the women had disappeared. He could already envision his cousin making Jess sit and forcing her to eat.

"Should I be worried about Leah being alone with her?"

Daniel hesitated. "I can't say for sure, but my gut says that she'll be fine. She was terrified when I found her. She came looking for Leah, said they'd met last year. Same way I found her probably. She says Leah discovered her in the barn asleep and offered to help her. I believe she's a runaway."

Henry frowned. "Maybe we should go up to the house."

"We could, or we could trust that your wife is fine and knows what she's doing. Clearly the women were happy to see each other."

Daniel noted Henry's softened expression and affectionate smile. "Leah is something. I still can't believe I'm married to her."

"Believe it, Henry. You're not only wed to her, but she'll be having your *bobbli* soon."

A worried look came to Henry's eyes. "I'm scared."

"Of being a father?" Daniel was surprised.

"Nay, I want those babies more than anything. I worry for Leah and all she'll have to endure to give birth. Reuben's first wife..."

"I know," Daniel said softly. "She died right after giving birth, but Leah isn't Susanna, and she's your wife. She'll be fine."

Henry looked as if he needed to be convinced. "I hope so."

"I know so," Daniel said with a grin. He glanced at the wall clock. He should head to work, but he had to stay to make sure the English girl didn't need a ride. It seemed like an hour had gone by but was probably only ten minutes when he became concerned. "Want me to go up and check on them?"

"And anger Leah? Nay. I'll stay right here. You don't want to be on the wrong side of my wife. I was once, and I vowed to myself never to be there again."

He needed to get to work. If he was ever to earn enough money to quit construction and open a business of his own, he had to show up at the job site.

But Daniel recalled Jess's vulnerable expression and knew he couldn't leave no matter how long it took for the women to return. He was torn between wariness and longing, an odd combination of feelings for a woman he barely knew—and an *Englisher*.

If the two women didn't return after a half hour, he'd go up and risk Leah's ire. He would ensure that both of them were fine. The mental image of Jess's face lingered, and he felt anxious for some unknown reason.

## *Chapter Two*

Feeling guilty for deceiving her Amish friend, Emma followed Leah out of the back of the store and up a small incline to a white house. They entered through the kitchen. The room was spotless, with oak cabinets and a pie on the white kitchen countertop. She glanced at it briefly, then looked away and prayed that her stomach wouldn't rumble from hunger.

"Have a seat." Leah gestured toward a trestle table. It was large, rectangular and made of oak with six chairs. "How do you like your hot tea?"

Emma blushed. "I don't know."

The Amish woman studied her with surprise. "You never had hot tea?"

She shook her head. "I've had iced tea a couple of times." Emma managed a smile. "I liked it sweet."

Leah grinned. "Then you'll want sugar in your hot tea."

She watched silently as her friend filled the teakettle with water and set it on the stove. Emma felt like she should do something to help. She was never allowed to simply sit for a moment and be idle in the Turner household. "Can I help you?"

"Nay, I've got this."

"I'm sorry to barge in on you."

"I'm happy to see you, Jess. 'Tis been a long time." Leah paused. "I was worried about you."

Warmth rushed through Emma, overriding the guilt that had crept in hearing her false name on Leah's lips. "You were?"

The woman nodded. "I knew something was wrong when we met. I wanted to help."

"You did," Emma whispered. "More than you'll ever know."

"Tell me what you've been doing since I last saw you."

"When you found me, I'd run from my foster family." Her throat tightened as Emma thought of her deceased parents. "I lost my parents when they were killed in a car accident." She blinked against the tears that always came whenever she recalled that horrible time. "I was eleven. There was no family to care for me, so I was put into foster care. The Turners are the second family I've been placed with." She shuddered and hugged herself. "They're not nice people, so I've run away from them again." She paused as Leah placed a cup of steaming tea before her.

"Be careful," Leah warned. "'Tis very hot."

Emma nodded. She added sugar and stirred it into her cup. She stared at the swirling liquid for a long time.

"Jess?"

"Yes, sorry." She swallowed hard. "I don't want to go back, but if they find me, I'll have no choice." She stopped. "A few days after I left the safety of your barn,

I was picked up by the police in downtown Lancaster." Embarrassment made her blush. "I was searching for food."

"For food?"

"Yes, near a dumpster," she murmured, ashamed. But she'd been hungry, and hunger had made her do things that she normally wouldn't do. "The Turners filed a missing persons report." Emma laughed harshly. "Once I was returned to them, my situation there got worse." She didn't want to confess about the abuse, and Leah didn't need to know what she'd endured before she'd escaped. Leah's ignorance would keep her friend safe from harm should Bryce Turner find Emma again. She gingerly took a sip of the hot tea. The warmth felt good in her throat. The taste was delicious, just sweet enough to make the brew go down easily. She felt stronger with that one sip.

"You ran away again," Leah said. "Tell me about them."

She looked up from her tea mug. "If it's okay, I'd rather not." She took another fortifying sip. "All I can tell you is that they don't care about me. They are only interested in the money the state of Maryland pays them for my care." She gestured at her clothes. "I was unhappy there. I had to leave, and I need to find a place to work and live until I turn eighteen, when I'll be free from the foster care system."

Leah frowned. "Jess—"

"Please, Leah," Emma said. "I think it's best if you don't know." Without thought, she rubbed her arms.

Frowning, Leah rose and skirted the table. "What's wrong with your arms?"

Emma blushed and looked away. "Nothing."

"I want to see your arms, Jess. If there is nothing wrong with them, you won't mind if I take a look. There is something you're not telling me." Leah paused. "Please?"

She sighed. "If I show you, will you promise you won't tell anyone?" Emma regarded Leah solemnly. "Not even Henry or Daniel?"

"I promise," Leah said, although she looked extremely uncomfortable.

She stood and took off her jacket. Her long-sleeved T-shirt was thin, and Emma resisted the urge to put her jacket back on. Instead, she hesitated, then pulled up her right sleeve as high as the inside bend of her elbow. Her arm was covered with bruises, but the worst of them remained hidden near her shoulders. When she saw Leah's changing expression, she knew she'd already shown her Amish friend too much.

Leah gasped. "*Ach*, nay, Jess. Who did this to you?"

"It doesn't matter now. I'm not going back."

"Your foster father did this?"

Emma nodded.

"I'm sorry."

"For what?" Emma gazed at her, confused.

"For what was done to you."

She smiled. "You've been very kind, and you've made a difference in my life from the first moment I met you." Emma held her gaze. "You gave me food and the twenty dollars you left for me when I came back the next night."

Leah arched an eyebrow. "What twenty dollars?" But there was warmth in her pretty blue eyes and a smile on her lips. Leah Yoder was genuinely beautiful inside and out.

Emma was relieved to be here with the young Amish woman. She'd never felt so safe since she'd been sent to live with the Turners. It was as if Leah was a true friend, and she definitely needed one. She thought of Daniel Lapp and the way he'd looked at her, as if she'd come to cause trouble for his cousin. But then his expression had changed as he'd watched her a little while later. As if he worried about her, despite his concern for his family. She was wrong. She shouldn't have come back, bringing her problems to Leah. She just hoped for some advice, then she'd leave Leah in peace…and safety.

"How long is it before you turn eighteen?" Leah asked.

"Five weeks."

"And you need a job," the Amish woman said.

Emma nodded. "Yes."

"And a place to live." Leah looked thoughtful. "You also need a place where you can hide until you're free of the foster care system."

Looking away, Emma stood. "Yes. I'm not here to cause you trouble. You can imagine what my foster family is like. But you know the area well, so if you could point me in the right direction, I'll get out of your hair." Dread and sadness filled her as she stood. "I shouldn't have come. You have your family to worry about."

"Please sit down, Jessica."

She blinked and obeyed.

"I have a solution to your problem."

Hope flickered in her heart. "You do?"

"Henry and I need help. I'm going to hire you to work

in the store. You can live with my parents, who have a spare room. I only ask that you help them with chores if they need it." She paused. "Is that agreeable to you?"

Emma allowed the tears to fall. "Yes," she whispered. "Very agreeable." She inhaled sharply. "But I shouldn't accept. If my foster father comes here looking for me..."

Leah covered Emma's hands with her own. "I'm not worried about him. Besides, he won't find out you're here among us." She smiled. "You'll be a big help to me. Before long, I won't be able to work for a while." She patted her belly. "I'm having twins."

"Twins!" Emma held her gaze. "You must be so happy about them."

"I'm thrilled. I love Henry, and I already love our babies," Leah said gently.

She grinned. "I'm happy for you, Leah. You deserve everything good life has to offer."

*"Danki."* Leah rose and went to the refrigerator. "Now before we do anything else, I'm feeding you, then you can take a shower."

It sounded wonderful to her. She must have said it aloud because Leah laughed.

Emma hesitated. "May I wash my hands before I eat?"

Leah directed her to a small downstairs bathroom. Emma continued to fight tears as she washed her hands and face. Feeling overwhelmed and emotional, she experienced hope for the first time in a long time. Hope tinged with a feeling of concern for accepting her friend's offer. There was no mirror in the room, but she could imagine how awful she must look after days on the road and having slept in the barn.

Emma managed to gain control of her emotions as she wolfed down the turkey sandwich Leah fixed for her. After she finished, she then ate the piece of an apple pie that Leah pressed on her.

"Come with me," Leah said after Emma was done eating.

She followed Leah out of the kitchen, then upstairs to a bathroom with a shower. She glanced down at her dirty clothes and grimaced at the thought of putting them on again.

Leah turned on the shower and adjusted the temperature. "Wait here a moment." She returned within minutes with clean clothes.

Emma eyed the royal blue Amish dress, and her throat tightened with emotion. "Leah, I can't take your clothes."

"Of course you can. Until we can get you several garments of your own." To Emma's surprise, Leah took her hand. "Jess, think about it. Hiding in plain sight, you can live among us freely. No one would suspect an Amish girl of being a runaway foster child."

Emma hadn't thought about that. "That does sound like a good plan."

*"Gut,"* Leah said, pronouncing it with an accent. "*Gut*, not good. But don't worry, I'll teach you a few phrases that will make your place here convincing."

"Thank you."

*"Danki,"* Leah instructed.

*"Danki,"* Emma said, and the Amish woman beamed at her.

"When you're done here, come downstairs. I'll be in the kitchen."

"Okay. *Danki.*"

*"Ja, danki,"* Leah corrected with a laugh.

Emma grinned at her before the woman closed the door, leaving her alone to ponder her new temporary life. She cleaned up and changed into the Amish clothes Leah had provided. She knew she wouldn't have trouble fitting in. After all, she'd been raised in an Amish community until she was six years old. She knew how to speak high German, although she couldn't let on. She'd have to allow the others to teach her a few words or they would suspect that she and her parents had left their Amish community for the English world and been shunned by their family and friends for their decision to leave.

"We need to come up with an Amish name for you," Leah said. She looked thoughtful for a moment. "How about Emma? You can be my cousin Emma Stoltzfus from New Wilmington, Pennsylvania."

"Emma?" she breathed, shocked by Leah's choice.

Leah smiled. "*Ja*. What do you think?"

Emma smiled back. "I think it will be easy for me to answer to that name."

"What's taking them so long?" Daniel said. He'd brought a stranger into Leah's life and home. He was worried, although Leah said she knew the girl.

"Knowing my wife," Henry said, "she's feeding Jess over a long conversation."

"You're not concerned?"

His cousin's husband shook his head. "Nay, I know Leah. She has *gut* instincts. If she trusts the girl, then I do, too."

"Maybe I should go up to the *haus*." Daniel couldn't

shake the uneasy feeling that had come since the discovery of the girl in the barn.

"You'll upset not only Jess but Leah as well. Do you want to upset your cousin?" Henry asked with a look of amusement.

Daniel couldn't help a smile. Henry had hurt Daniel's brother Isaac, who had been his best friend, and his cousin Leah had resented him because of it. Even though Henry and Isaac had become close again, Leah hadn't liked or trusted Henry until she'd gotten to know the man's true nature. After forgiving Henry, she'd fallen in love with him. Leah had never been happier as Henry's wife. The fact that she would give birth soon added a new, higher level of happiness to the man on the other side of the counter.

"Are you hoping for a *soohn* or *dochter*?" Daniel asked.

"One of each or two of either," Henry said with a smile. "As long as they are healthy."

He laughed. "That will take time."

Henry shook his head. "Nay. We're having twins."

"Twins!" Daniel grinned. "You're in for it as a parent. You do know I have twin brothers, *ja*? I remember all the trouble they got into."

"We'll handle them," the other man said with confidence. "You forget who their mother is."

Daniel laughed. "I'm sure you're right. Leah is one determined woman."

"Praise be to *Gott*," Henry breathed. "They're back," he said as if Daniel hadn't heard a door open and shut in the back of the store.

He waited for Leah and Jess to appear.

Leah entered first. "I'd like you to meet someone. Her name is Emma." She looked back. "Emma? Come in and meet my husband, Henry, and my cousin Daniel."

Daniel frowned. What had happened to Jess? Had she left as he'd expected? Then Emma entered the room and he stared. It was Jess but not. The young woman standing before him was clean and wore a blue Amish dress, white cape and apron. Leah had rolled and pinned Jess's hair in the Amish way. On her head, she wore a prayer *kapp*. Her hair was brown with golden streaks.

"Jess?"

"Emma," the girl who now looked like a woman said. "My name is Emma." She glanced at Leah, saw his cousin's nod. "Emma Stoltzfus."

"What?" Daniel looked to his cousin.

"Emma, my cousin from New Wilmington, has consented to be our new employee. She will be staying with my parents and helping them with chores."

Henry locked gazes with his wife, then looked at "Emma." "Welcome, Emma. We can use the help around here. Once you get settled in with my in-laws, we can discuss your work hours."

Leah gazed at her husband approvingly before she captured Daniel's attention with a look that pleaded to trust her. Daniel gave a little nod. "Will you take her to my *eldre*?" she asked him.

*"Ja."* He turned to "Emma." The girl looked different enough for him to almost believe that she *was* Emma, a totally different person from the one he'd found in the barn. Emma Stoltzfus was a young woman while Jess Morgan had been a bedraggled girl. "Are you ready to go?"

She nodded shyly. *"Ja,"* she replied.

Leah grinned. *"Gut!"*

Emma's lips curved into a smile that stole his breath. *"Danki."*

Daniel chuckled. "I'll bring her back tomorrow morning. What time?"

"You don't have to bring me," Jess, alias Emma, said. "I can walk."

"I'll bring you." Daniel kept his tone gentle. "'Tis too far for you to walk." He turned to Leah. "Will you please reassure Emma that she can trust me?"

Leah appeared as if she were struggling. He saw Emma studying his cousin with concern until Leah laughed. "I wouldn't send you with him if I didn't trust him. He's family." She refocused her gaze on him. "Nine? *Dat* will be able to show her what to do for morning chores."

Daniel nodded. "Nine o'clock, then." He gestured for Emma to precede him, then followed her to his buggy. He hoped his cousin knew what she was doing. Emma looked like an Amish woman, but the fact remained that she was still an Englisher—a homeless Englisher who, up until a short time ago, looked as if she'd been on her own for a long while. He'd be keeping his eye on her. Leah might have good instincts, as Henry had suggested, but Leah was pregnant, and her outlook on life had softened with her impending motherhood.

He couldn't let the strange feelings of protectiveness he started to feel for Emma stop him from observing her closely. Until she proved trustworthy, he'd be watching her like a hawk.

# *Chapter Three*

Emma was silent as Daniel steered his buggy toward his uncle's house. The way she'd worked her way so easily into his cousin's life bothered him. He glanced at her numerous times, but she wouldn't look at him. She kept her gaze toward the side window. The fact that she didn't interact with him only increased his suspicion of her.

"Emma," he said, drawing her attention. "If you hurt Leah, her parents or anyone else within this community, I'll see that you're tossed out of it. Do you understand?" Expression serious, although he thought he'd detected a brief flash of fear, she nodded. "And I'll call the authorities."

She gasped and paled, her face so white that he feared she would faint. He hadn't expected that reaction. Startled, he pulled his buggy off the road and parked, then faced her.

"Emma," he said gently, "what's going on? Why are you afraid?"

"The police can't know where I am."

He stiffened. "Why not?"

"Because I can't go back. I *won't* go back. They'll hurt me, and I'll just run away again."

Daniel instinctively reached out to touch her arm. She flinched and shifted away from him. Something was seriously wrong. He eyed her with compassion. "Go back where, Emma?" he asked, purposely using her new name. "Who will hurt you?"

"My foster family."

He felt chilled. "They hurt you?"

She nodded.

"How?"

"It doesn't matter."

He frowned. Something was fishy.

"I wouldn't be here if I didn't have to be."

"How did they hurt you, Emma?"

She shook her head. "It doesn't matter."

Daniel felt anger, even though he knew it was wrong. How could he not when clearly someone had hurt her? She wouldn't tell him, and that was fine. But someday he'd learn the truth. He couldn't stop his protective instincts from roaring up in full force.

"I won't press you," he said. He could only hope that she wasn't lying.

To his surprise, she smiled, a small, shy smile that lit up her face and made him startlingly aware of how pretty she was. *"Danki."*

"How old are you?" he asked, curious. "Sixteen?"

She shook her head.

He experienced warmth as he studied her. "Seventeen then."

She stared at him with surprise. "How did you know?"

"You're seventeen. You've taken a job at my cousin's store and you'll be living with my aunt and uncle. You obviously have no family, and Leah is clearly protective of you. You don't want the police to find out that you're here. That could mean one of two things. Either you're in trouble with the law or you need a place to stay until you turn eighteen when you'll be free of the foster care system." He held her gaze. "I'm inclined to believe you haven't committed a crime." He turned his attention back to the road before him. "Am I right?"

She blinked rapidly, clearly disturbed by his deduction. "*Ja*, you're not wrong."

He smiled. "*Gut* accent."

*"Danki."*

His amusement died as she carefully played with the edge of her dress sleeve. "Leah is right. This is the best place for you." Although the secret deception felt wrong. "How about I take you to meet Leah's parents—*eldre*?"

"Are they nice? Leah's *eldre*?"

"*Ja*, you'll like them." And he knew they would accept her into their home without a moment's hesitation. "Missy and Arlin Stoltzfus are fine people. Arlin is my *mam*'s brother."

As he drove on to his aunt and uncle's house, Daniel tried further to engage her in conversation and get her to open up. She might be only seventeen, but he had a feeling that everything she'd been forced to endure had made her seem much older than her years.

"What happened to your family?"

"They died in a car crash when I was eleven," she said.

"Brothers or sisters?"

She shook her head. "I was an only child. I have no other family."

Daniel couldn't imagine being alone with no family. He'd been raised with seven siblings. That Jess—Emma—had suffered such loss as a child was more than a little upsetting to him. "You lived with your foster family all this time?"

"No," she said. "My first foster parents were wonderful." She grew quiet for a moment, then said, "They couldn't take care of me after my foster father got sick." He saw her blink rapidly as if fighting tears. "I don't know if he is alive or dead," she admitted.

"I'm sorry," he said softly.

Talking about her past was painful. Emma stared out the side window and sensed the long sideward looks that Daniel gave her. She faced him. "What?"

"I'm impressed by your courage," Daniel murmured.

"What courage? I ran away from a bad situation."

"*Ja*, you did, and it was the best thing for you. You didn't know what would happen when you left, yet you went. You were brave."

She looked at him and was amazed to see that he meant what he'd said. She gaped, speechless.

He grinned, then turned onto a dirt driveway that led up to a small white two-story house. "Relax," he told her with a smile. "My aunt and uncle are *gut* people. Remember they're also Leah's parents."

She felt her tension dissipate. If this couple had raised Leah, then they had to be good people. A woman doesn't turn out that kind without having a loving family and home.

Emma stared at the house without moving. Daniel's sudden presence on her side of the buggy startled her. His gentle expression eased her fears. He held out a hand, and she accepted his help. Did he suspect that she was bruised? No, he couldn't possibly know about the bruises. It would be some time before they'd be healed enough to no longer be sensitive, but the dress covered her arms enough to keep them hidden until they disappeared. Daniel startled her when he kept gentle hold of her hand after she got out. He released it to knock on the side door of the house. Within seconds, the woman who appeared saw Daniel, and her eyes lit up as she smiled. "Daniel! Come in."

"I've brought you a houseguest," he said. "Leah sent her."

The woman who must be Leah's mother opened the door wider with a huge inviting smile for her. "Come in."

"Emma," Daniel supplied for her.

Emma hesitated until Daniel's hand on her back urged her forward.

"Tea?" Missy invited.

"I could do with a quick cup," Daniel said. "Emma?"

*"Ja, danki."*

Missy looked at her strangely before she turned to put the kettle on.

"There is something you need to know," Emma began when the woman took a seat across from her and Daniel, who had chosen to sit by her side. "I'm a runaway. Leah is my friend. She's given me a job at the store and invited me to stay in your spare room." She paused. "And I'm now a cousin from New Wilmington."

Missy studied her intently. "Emma?"

*"Ja?"* She tensed.

Leah's mother smiled. "Welcome home," she said, and Emma was unable to control the tears that overflowed to trail down her cheeks. Tears of relief and happiness that she'd been given a second chance to feel safe and loved.

Daniel studied his aunt, then observed the young English woman seated next to him. He was startled that she'd been so forthright with his aunt. If anyone would be able to make life better for Emma, it was Missy and Arlin Stoltzfus. He drank his tea, ate two homemade chocolate brownies, then rose. "I need to talk with Reuben briefly before I head to work this afternoon." He met the Englisher's gaze. "Emma," he said, "you'll be *oll recht*?"

She smiled. "*Ja*, I'll be fine."

*"Gut."*

"I'll see you on Sunday if not before," he told his aunt.

"*Ja*, give your *mudder* my best." Missy smiled. "Please tell her that I might not be able to make it to quilting on Wednesday."

"I'll tell her." Daniel's gaze slid over Emma, and he was glad to see her relaxed with a small smile on her face as she moved to stand next to him. He addressed her. "You, I'll see in the morning. I have to be at work at nine tomorrow, so I'll pick you up at eight thirty." He turned toward his aunt. "Will that give Emma enough time to do morning chores?"

Surprise flickered across his aunt's expression, then came understanding. "More than enough time."

To Daniel's surprise, Emma excused herself to his aunt and followed him outside.

"Daniel," she whispered. He halted and faced her. "*Danki* for everything." Her expression was earnest, open and honest.

He smiled. "I'll see you tomorrow."

To his satisfaction, she simply nodded and went back inside. He left with the image of her bright brown eyes gazing at him with gratitude. He didn't want her gratitude. He wasn't sure what he wanted, but it wasn't for her to feel beholden to him.

He drove back to see Leah first. It wasn't afternoon yet, so he had a little time to talk with his cousin about the young woman in her parents' home. When he pulled in next to the hitching post on the side of the building, he waited a moment, his thoughts whirling with questions that needed answering. He got out, tied up his gelding, then went into the building. Henry was behind the counter.

"Is your wife here?" he asked.

"She went up to the house, but she'll be right back."

"I'll wait. I need to talk with her." He paused. "About Emma."

"Leah's idea," Henry supplied.

Daniel blinked. "What?"

"She picked Emma as Jess's identity while she's here, because 'tis a fine name for an Amish girl."

"What did Leah tell you about her?"

"That she lost her parents when she was eleven."

Daniel nodded. "*Ja*, she told me."

Henry looked surprised. "What else did she say?"

"That she ran from her foster family." Daniel

frowned. “She didn’t say much, but what she fears most is being sent back to them.”

“I’m shocked that she told you about her past. She had a hard time telling Leah, and she considers Leah her friend.”

“I think Emma feels vulnerable.” Feeling sheepish, Daniel averted his glance. “I warned her against hurting anyone. Told her I’d call the police if she did.”

“*Ach*, nay,” Henry breathed.

*“Ja.”* He met the man’s gaze again. “She was terrified and explained.” Something about her drew him in to help her. He didn’t know why. She was an Englisher with different ideals and morals. She could be lying to them, but still he sensed something innocent about her.

Her cousin’s husband agreed. “Here’s Leah now.”

“How do you always know when your wife is near?”

Henry’s lip curved, and his eyes glowed with warmth. “Because she is my life.”

Daniel stared at him. It was clear that Henry meant every word. “You’re most fortunate to have such strong love in your marriage.”

“You shouldn’t marry for anything but love. I know some members of our community accept arranged marriages, but never settle for that. Love might come in time in an arranged union, but to know it beforehand? To feel it deep in your heart? That is *everything*.”

“Daniel!” Leah entered the room with a look of concern. “Did something happen to Emma? Is anything wrong?”

“Nay, nothing’s wrong. Your *mudder* welcomed Emma into her home with open arms.”

Leah smiled. "I knew she would. *Mam* is an amazing woman."

"I agree," Henry said.

Daniel smiled. Missy Stoltzfus had been an Englisher who'd accepted the Amish way of life and joined the church to marry his mother's brother, his *onkel* Arlin. If anyone understood the concerns of a young English woman in an Amish community she wasn't born into, Aunt Missy would be the one. "Leah," he said, "I have some questions about Emma."

Sighing, Leah gestured toward the chair they kept next to the counter.

"Sit and put your feet up," he told her. "The chair is for you. I'm happy to stand."

His cousin sat. "What do you want to know?"

"First, I'll tell you what she told me, and you can add from there if you can, *ja*?"

Leah eyed him with surprise. "She talked to you about her past?"

He nodded. "Because I scared her, and I'm sorry for that." Then he explained what happened, watching as his cousin's expression went from horror to understanding to pleasure as he said, "She told me she ran from her foster family. And that she would never go back. I don't know what happened to her, but it must have been something bad."

Leah nodded. "I think it was." His cousin smiled. "She trusts you."

"You think so?"

"*Ja.* I'm surprised that she told you anything. She must feel safe with you."

Daniel swelled up with emotion. "Now tell me what she told you."

Leah frowned. "I can't. I'm sorry, but I promised I'd keep her secrets."

"What kind of secrets?" He stared at her, hoping that she'd give them up.

"I promised. You know I don't like secrets. And while I don't like pretending that Emma is my cousin, I will do it to protect her. She's afraid of her foster father, and I'll do what I can to make sure she is safe until she won't be forced to go back after she's eighteen."

He understood, but he was still bothered by the girl's secrets. What if she wasn't telling the truth? Doubts about her slid in to disturb him as he drove back to see Reuben.

Emma had been so distraught when he threatened a call to the police that he sympathized with Emma once she'd told him why she was afraid. He sighed. He didn't need the complication of her in his community right now. He needed to concentrate on work and his ultimate goal of opening his harness shop. He'd been saving for some time, and he nearly had enough money to look for rental property. Daniel knew that Elijah would give him space in his carriage shop for his business, but he didn't want to take help from his brother. He wanted to be self-sufficient in his business. His brothers had made it on their own. He would, too.

The time spent with Leah after dropping off Emma gave him little left to talk with Reuben before he had to head to the construction site to work. He and the crew he worked with were starting a new job this afternoon.

A number of subcontractors were working the site this morning. They would take over at noon.

It was late September. Soon the temperatures would drop, and work would ease up. He wanted to get in as many hours as possible. A few weeks working for the construction company should net him enough to quit.

Emma's vulnerable features swam in his memory. He didn't know what to believe about the Englisher, and until he knew he could trust her for certain, he would have to put his family first before his business…even if it meant his plans would be delayed a little longer.

Daniel scowled. He didn't want to put off his plans, but how could he not? The Yoders and Stoltzfuses were family, and if he learned that Emma was a liar and a thief, he'd do everything he could to protect them. Even if it meant doing something he didn't want to do—like call the police.

## *Chapter Four*

Emma gazed at the kind couple who owned the house she'd be living in for the next five weeks. "I'm a stranger, yet you've taken me in."

Arlin studied her with warmth. "Missy explained the situation. The best place for you is here." He smiled at her. "And we could use the help if you're up to it."

"I'd be happy to help. I don't mind work." Relief hit her hard as she gazed at Leah's parents with gratitude.

"Then 'tis the ideal arrangement," Arlin said.

Missy eyed Jess with a frown. "'Tis chilly in the morning. If you're to help with morning chores, you'll need a jacket and a sweater." She narrowed her gaze as she studied her. "I have a sweater that should fit you. You can wear Charlie's old jacket until I can make you a new one."

Emma opened and closed her mouth. "You're going to *make* me a jacket?"

"*Ja.* It will be getting colder outside in the coming weeks, and I don't want you to get sick." The woman eyed her with affection.

"I have a jacket." She cringed. "It's not in the best shape, but if you have a needle and thread, I could fix it."

"I'd rather make you a new one," the woman said.

Arlin caught and held Emma's gaze when Missy turned to put a kettle of water to heat on the stove. "No sense arguing with her," he said. "She'll do what she wants, and you'll not be stopping her." The twinkle in his eyes showed amusement. "We have grandchildren, but she misses having a daughter in the *haus*. You being here means the world to her," he whispered. "She's going to want to spoil you."

"I heard that, husband," she said sharply, but there was a smile on her lips as she faced him. Her smile remained in place as she turned to Emma. "He's right. I'm happy to have you here."

Overcome with emotion, Emma blinked rapidly. *"Danki."*

"We don't say thank you often. We show our gratitude in other ways. With a smile or a nod or by doing something special for someone," Arlin told her.

Emma nodded. It had been a long time since she lived among the Amish. It wasn't surprising that she'd forgotten a few things. "I guess I have a lot to learn."

"And you'll do well."

"I—ah—does it bother you that I'm pretending to be a cousin? I know it's wrong, but—"

"'Tis the only way to keep you hidden and safe. We are fine with it," Missy assured her.

"Arlin, where's Jeremiah?"

"I left him in the barn."

Missy frowned. "Why?"

"I didn't want to frighten Emma."

"Jeremiah?" Emma asked. "Your dog?"

"*Ja.* We had him at our other *haus* and brought him with us," Missy said.

"Is he black and white? A little fluffy thing?"

Arlin studied her thoughtfully. "He is. How do you know that?"

She blushed. "I slept in your barn when you lived in the other house. He kept me company during the night. I was afraid something had happened to him."

"Something happened to him, *oll recht.* He's captured the heart of my husband. Arlin, go get him and bring him inside before he chews something he shouldn't."

The man rose stiffly and headed toward the door. "*Ja*, wife."

After he left, Missy laughed. "Don't think he's downtrodden. That man does nothing he doesn't want to do."

Emma felt her lips curve. "I see."

Missy's eyes twinkled. "I'm sure you do. We are going to get along just fine, you and I. Let me show you to your room before Arlin returns and you get reacquainted with Jeremiah."

The bedroom was small but lovely with a beautiful brightly colored homemade Amish quilt on the double bed. There was a nightstand on one side and a tall dresser against the wall next to the doorway. The sun shone through the window, brightening the room. Emma had never stayed in such a nice room. The warm feeling from being in Missy's presence was the best Emma had felt in a long time.

Emma felt hope well up and surround her. God had

led her here, and she would thank Him every day for what He'd given her. She smiled as she sat on the bed while Missy looked on. "Perfect."

A loud bark from downstairs had Missy gesturing for Emma to follow her. "Jeremiah is back. Come and say *hallo*."

Emma followed Missy downstairs. The little dog saw her, and as if recognizing her, he sprang forward and placed his paws on her legs. She laughed, scooping him up to cuddle. Aware of being watched, she caught Arlin studying her and suddenly felt self-conscious. "I'm sorry." She bent to put him down.

"Nay," Arlin said. "He likes you. You can hold him whenever you want."

She grinned and straightened with the little dog in her arms. "Do you want me to take him for a walk?"

Arlin nodded. "*Ja*, I'm sure he would like that."

Emma saw the leash hanging from a wall peg in the kitchen. "Does he sleep in the barn?"

The man shook his head. "Nay, we usually keep him in the kitchen. I had him outside with me since earlier when I was working in the barn." He exchanged looks with his wife, who gave a nod. "If you'd like to take him into your room tonight, I'm sure he'll like that."

Emma felt misty. "I'd love that." She smiled her thanks, then grabbed the leash and clipped it onto the dog's collar. "When I get back, can we talk about my chores?"

"*Ja*, we can talk about them," Missy assured her. "Hold on a minute." The woman left, returning in a moment with a sweater. "Put this on. 'Tis too chilly today to be without."

She immediately obeyed, pleased that someone cared enough to worry about her.

The air was nippy, but the day was beautiful. She allowed Jeremiah to run, and she laughed as she followed his rapid pace. She walked toward the back of the property, noting the farm fields and the way the leaves were starting to change on the trees on the property. She made sure Jeremiah was ready to go back inside before she started back. She felt different in her Amish clothing, like she'd stepped back in time to when she was six years old and had visited with her grandparents. When she'd gone to school in Maryland, she'd stuck out like a sore thumb in the awful garments the Turners had insisted she wear. But here? She felt more at home than any other place except Indiana, where she'd lived so many years ago.

She wondered if the Turners were unhappy she left. Or had her foster father realized what she'd seen? She hadn't stayed long enough to see him after witnessing that drug deal and altercation behind the small shopping center in the center of town. Bryce would probably file a missing persons report again. But this time he wouldn't find her. Not living here among the Amish. He would be unhappy with her. Taking her in had ensured he received eight hundred dollars a month from the state of Maryland. He'd look for her for that reason alone. But if he had pegged her for an eyewitness to his and his son's crime? Then she was in danger. If she thought for one moment that he would find her here and hurt anyone who had hidden her, she would leave now. And she would do so if she learned that someone was in the area searching for her. These kind people didn't deserve to be harmed for taking her in. But after what she'd seen, she knew it was a possibility, so she would stay as long as she could and hope that it would be enough time. Right now, the police would be on the Turners' side. But once she was eighteen, they would stay out of it, for she would legally be an adult and no longer be anyone's responsibility. She'd be free to come and go wherever she pleased.

Emma refused to think about Bryce Turner and his son any longer. She was safe among the Amish. She'd live and be happy until the time came for her to go. A sensation of sadness filtered through her joy as she recalled that her life here was only temporary. The Stoltzfuses were doing so much for her. She wouldn't take advantage of them. She'd make herself useful, starting right away.

The sound of buggy wheels caught her attention as she led the dog toward the house. She blinked as Daniel Lapp parked near the house and got out as she reached the grass before the walkway to the side door.

"Daniel," she greeted, suddenly wary. "Is something wrong?"

He approached with a large paper bag. "Nay, I left Ellie's and am heading into work. I saw Leah again earlier and she wanted you to have this."

Curious, she approached, took the bag and looked inside. "Clothes?"

Daniel nodded. "Just until she can get you new ones."

"I don't need new clothes." The garments she'd been given were way better than anything she'd owned at the Turners'.

His expression softened. "Need them or not. You'll

be getting new garments if Leah has anything to say about it."

Emma laughed. "That's what Missy said, and it sounds like her daughter is just as determined." Her amusement faded. "You think I'm taking advantage of them. Your family. I wouldn't have come, but I have nowhere else to go."

"I wasn't thinking that at all," he replied quietly. "Everyone needs help on occasion. We are always willing to help others. It's the Lord's way."

She nodded. "Will you come in?"

"Just for a minute." He followed her and Jeremiah into the house. "I see you have a new friend," he said.

"Jeremiah and I have met before, and I think he remembers me." She opened the door and held it for him. "This little guy kept me company and warm the first time I fell asleep in that barn." She stepped inside and he followed her. "Look who's stopped by."

"Daniel," Arlin greeted with warmth.

His wife smiled. "What brings you back?"

"Your *dochter*'s need to see that Emma has enough garments to last her until spring."

"Leah shouldn't worry about me," Emma replied.

"Just accept it," Missy suggested. "'Tis Leah's nature to be concerned." She addressed Daniel. "Tell her that I'll take care of anything else Emma needs."

Emma's gaze locked with Daniel's, but she couldn't read his expression.

She unclipped Jeremiah's leash, then unbuttoned her sweater and hung both on a wall hook. She would take her sweater upstairs later. After Daniel left, she'd have to ask Missy and Arlin about her chores. She'd always loved feeding the animals at her grandparents' farm. Doing chores for the kind couple was the least she could do to repay them for their generosity.

"Would you like anything?" Missy asked him, ever the welcoming hostess. "Tea? Cookies?"

"*Nay, Endie* Missy. I'll be heading over to the construction site. I have to work today."

"Is Reuben still set on building on to the great room?" Arlin asked.

"Nay, I convinced him an addition isn't necessary. It helped that Ellie wholeheartedly agrees with me. Your son-in-law accepted the truth with *gut* grace."

"How's little Ethan?"

"He's fine. Hard to believe he's standing and taking steps. Ellie is *gut* with him."

"*Ja*, he took to her right away. Ellie is happy to have such a wonderful family."

"Not as happy as Reuben, I imagine," Daniel said with a smile.

He left minutes later after promising to pick up Emma to take her to work. "I'll be by at eight thirty tomorrow morning," he reminded Emma.

"I'll be ready," she promised, and then watched as he drove away. There was something about the man that drew her. What, she didn't know.

Emma awoke before dawn and went downstairs. She was shocked to see Missy and Arlin already up and seated at the table with Daniel Lapp. He looked nice in a green shirt, black suspenders and navy pants. His hat sat on the chair beside him. His brown gaze slammed into hers, and her eyes widened until she managed to control her surprise.

"You're all up early," she greeted. "Daniel, I thought you were coming by at eight thirty?"

He nodded. "I woke up, got a few chores done and decided to stop by for breakfast with my favorite aunt and uncle." He grinned at Arlin and Missy.

"And we love having him," Missy said with an affectionate smile. "'Tis not the first time he's come to break his fast with us."

"I thought I'd get a head start on my chores before I eat," Emma said. She had her borrowed jacket draped over her arm.

"Why not have something to eat first?" Missy said. "There's plenty of time to feed the animals."

Emma hesitated, then, not wanting to disappoint the woman, she pulled out the chair across from Daniel and sat down. Missy pushed a plate of muffins in her direction, then poured her a cup of coffee. "I can do that, Missy," she said. "You don't have to wait on me."

"I told you she'll want to spoil you, Emma," Arlin murmured with a grin.

She sighed and accepted the coffee before she sweetened it the way she liked it. Watching her, Daniel slid a pitcher of milk closer to her. Emma added a dash of the thick liquid, stirred it in, then took a sip. The coffee tasted wonderful. She closed her eyes and enjoyed another sip before she opened them to find Daniel staring at her. Suddenly feeling flustered, she blushed. "What else would you like me to do this morning besides feed the animals?" she asked as she buttered her muffin.

"Not a thing," Missy assured her.

"Can I help with the wash? I can wash and hang clothes with the best of them."

"We'll do laundry tomorrow."

The room grew quiet as the four of them drank their coffee and ate buttered muffins. Emma couldn't remember tasting anything so good since she'd eaten in her grandmother's kitchen. When she was done, she rose and put her dishes in the sink. She grabbed a flashlight from a kitchen drawer. "I'll feed the animals and come back to do the dishes," she said.

Daniel stood. "I'll go with you."

Emma felt her breath hitch as she locked gazes with him. *"Oll recht,"* she murmured, easily slipping into the language she'd learned as a young girl. She felt his presence strongly as she left the house and headed toward the barn.

"You learn our words quickly," he said.

She tensed, pausing before she entered the outbuilding. "Why are you *really* here so early?" she asked.

There was barely a hint of light in the sky. But it was enough illumination to see Daniel's face.

He gazed at her a long time. "To enjoy breakfast with my aunt and uncle." He paused. "And to see if I could help you with chores this morning, being your first day here."

She felt herself soften toward him. "That's kind of you."

He didn't say anything. Something odd shifted in his expression before Daniel reached past her to open the door.

Emma entered and switched on the flashlight. She waited as Daniel headed toward the back of the barn.

She followed. She knew what to do but was willing to take his direction first.

"We'll let the horses out to graze," he said.

She opened her mouth to object, then shut it as their gazes locked. Was he expecting her to argue? Instead, Emma went to the barn's rear door that opened directly into a fenced pasture. Emma started to pull the door but then Daniel was there tugging it with her. It slid open, and she went back to let the first of three horses out into the paddock.

Daniel followed her and led the other two horses together. Emma sighed. She knew how to do this. She'd learned as a child while helping her grandfather. Of course, Daniel didn't know that. Once the horses were outside. She went over to check the horse water trough and saw that it needed to be refilled. As she turned to head back, Daniel stood waiting for her. "The water trough needs to be refilled."

He nodded at her and waved her to follow him. They found buckets inside the barn and left through the front door. Daniel showed her where there was an outside water pump. He pumped the handle after she set a bucket under the spigot. When pail was full, she moved it out of the way and replaced it with the empty one. When both were filled, Emma grabbed a bucket while Daniel picked up the other. She felt sure he had planned to carry them both, but these were her chores, and she wasn't about to allow him to believe that she didn't have the gumption or the strength to carry them out.

They emptied the buckets into the trough. After that, Emma looked to Daniel to see what he wanted to do next.

"Chickens?" she asked.

He nodded. This time she didn't wait for him but went inside and filled a pail with chicken feed. "Can I let them out before I feed them?" she asked, knowing that she'd done it when she was a young girl.

A flicker of surprise in Daniel's brown eyes as he nodded gave her a feeling of satisfaction. She opened the fence around the chicken coop and threw down feed in the yard. Emma watched with a smile as the hens and one rooster gobbled it up. When she was ready for them to go back inside, she tossed some grain into the fenced enclosure and watched as they headed back in.

"You've done that before," Daniel said after she'd closed the gate and faced him.

Emma nodded. "When I was little, my grandparents lived on a farm." They most probably still did, but she didn't know for sure whether or not they were even alive. A sharp pang in her heart hit her hard as she remembered how much she'd loved her mother's parents. Had they missed her at all? According to her mother, her *grosseldre* would have pushed thoughts of their shunned relatives from their mind. That leaving the community had made them shunned sinners hurt Emma. She'd had a hard time adjusting to the English life as a young child. Eventually, she'd gotten used to it. But she'd still missed her Amish family and friends.

*You can never go back.* Her parents had drilled it into her over and over, especially when she'd begged to visit her grandparents. After her parents died, she'd felt more alone than ever before. No mother or father. No aunts or uncles. No grandparents or cousins. No one.

"Emma?" Daniel's concerned voice drew her attention, and she realized that he'd called her name several times before she'd looked at him.

*"Ja?"*

He eyed her with a gentle expression. "Are you *oll recht*?"

She managed a smile. "I'm fine," she lied. "What next?" she asked, trying to distract him from asking any questions.

"We can let the goats out with the horses, then we should be finished."

"That doesn't seem like enough work for me to do," she murmured.

Daniel regarded her with a smile. "I'm sure Missy will think of something else for you to do eventually. 'Tis your first morning. Enjoy it while you can."

Emma chuckled. "I will."

When they were done, they headed toward the house. Emma was conscious of Daniel beside her. Had he come early just to help her get acquainted with her chores? She realized that she should have asked Arlin the night before how he liked the animals cared for, but she'd taken care of farm animals in the past. She didn't think she'd have any trouble. Still, having Daniel beside her as she worked this morning helped. She hadn't given a thought that Arlin and Missy might do things differently here. Emma knew she wouldn't be quick to assume they did anything the same in the future.

"Do you have some time for another cup of coffee?" Missy asked as Emma, followed by Daniel, entered the kitchen.

Emma glanced at Daniel, saw him nod. "That would be *wunderbor*," he said.

A quick note of the time on the kitchen wall clock showed her that it was only seven. Daniel originally hadn't been due to arrive for another hour and a half yet.

"Sit," Missy ordered when Emma hovered, wanting to help.

She took a seat, and this time Daniel sat next to her.

"Did you get the animals fed?" Arlin asked as he cradled his coffee mug.

*"Ja,"* Emma said. She felt self-conscious. "'Tis still early. Surely there is something else you'd like me to do."

Missy smiled as she set down two mugs of coffee. "Did you make your bed?"

Emma nodded. "Of course." She'd made her bed since she'd been old enough to learn how.

"Then relax. Keep my nephew company. You can help with the laundry tomorrow if you'd like."

After flashing a quick, shy look in Daniel's direction, Emma took a small sip from her coffee. "I can do laundry." She could feel Daniel's gaze on her. She avoided looking at him but couldn't ignore his scent—of soap and outdoors.

"Do you need help getting your corn in?" Daniel asked Arlin after a moment of silence.

"Are you offering?"

"I'd be happy to help. There isn't much. With a little help, we could get it done in a morning."

"I could ask my sons-in-law."

"You've got other nephews, too," Daniel pointed out.

"True. James will be busy at his vet clinic, and Henry will be helping Leah at the store."

"I'll be there to help Leah," Emma pointed out.

Daniel captured her attention. His brown eyes warmed as he studied her. "That would work." He turned his gaze on Arlin. "Joseph could use the experience. Not that he hasn't had any, but he'll be taking over the farm someday, so the more experience he gets the better."

"I'll ask Reuben," Arlin said. "He'll want to help."

Emma immediately pictured the man who was married to Leah's sister Ellie. The woman and her husband were both blond-haired and had blue eyes. *They will have beautiful children.* She felt a longing for something she most probably would never have. A husband and children. What man would want a runaway foster child with no extended family? She thought longingly again of her mother's Amish family, and her chest hurt. Even after all these years, she still felt the loss.

She sat listening quietly to Arlin and Daniel's discussion. At first tense, Emma soon relaxed and enjoyed sitting at a kitchen table with people who obviously cared about one another. Whenever someone asked her a question or her opinion, she felt included, something she hadn't experienced in years. Feeling accepted. Although her time in Happiness would be short, she knew that once she left she'd never forget everyone's kindness.

She enjoyed hearing the conversation among Daniel and his aunt and uncle. She learned about his siblings, especially his sister Hannah, the youngest and only girl, who had seven older brothers. Daniel expressed concern about the fact that it was time for Hannah to go on *rumspringa*. Apparently, Hannah had always been bold, and he was afraid she'd get into trouble in the English world.

Emma was amazed by Daniel's concern for his family. She wished she had siblings to enjoy. A brother or a sister. Either one would have made her childhood less lonely. Her first foster family had grown children who didn't live at home. The Turners' children, Kent and Melanie, didn't want her as a sibling. In fact, they hadn't wanted her at the house at all.

"I guess we should go." Daniel stood abruptly, drawing her glance.

She was surprised that it was just after eight thirty. Emma was startled that the time had gone so fast. "Are you done with your coffee?' she asked Arlin and Missy.

"Nay," the older bearded man said. "I think I'll sit a while longer with my wife."

Emma smiled as she stood and picked up her and Daniel's mugs. She took the dishes to the sink and washed and dried them. After putting them away in the cabinet, she reached for her sweater, which she'd hung on a wall hook, then met Daniel's gaze. "I'm ready."

"Wait!" Missy said. She got up and pulled two paper bags from the refrigerator. "Lunch for each of you." She handed her and Daniel their lunches. "Fresh roast beef on homemade bread. I put a bag of potato chips in there as well." She smiled. "And an apple. You need to get your nourishment." Her eyes crinkled with warmth. "Have a *gut* day. Emma, enjoy your first day at work."

Emma stared down at the paper lunch bag and was overcome with emotion. *"Danki,"* she whispered. She heard Daniel talking with the Stoltzfuses as she headed outside to regain control of her emotions. Daniel stepped outside moments later. She followed him to his buggy and waited, knowing that he would insist upon helping her get in.

"Are you ready for your first day at work?" Daniel asked after she was seated.

"I'm a bit nervous, but I'll learn quickly. I'll make sure that Leah is never sorry she hired me."

Daniel didn't say anything, but she could tell he was worried.

Emma sighed silently. No doubt worried about Leah and Henry, she thought. He'd been reluctant to trust her from the first. *I'll prove to him that I'm a good worker.*

Fifteen minutes later the store loomed ahead and to the right. Emma was quiet as Daniel pulled in front of the building and waited for her to get out.

"*Danki*, Daniel."

"I'll be back for you at four thirty. Leah said you'll be done working by then."

His sudden cool, detached tone made her want to refuse the ride home. "I can walk home."

"Nay, it will be nearly dark by then. I'll be here when you're ready to leave."

She frowned. If she couldn't walk to work, how could she get to the store without inconveniencing anyone, especially Daniel? Emma thought of the times her grandfather had briefly allowed her to take the reins of his buggy. She'd been fearless and *grossdaddi* had been pleased with her. Could she drive herself?

Daniel was at her side of the buggy before she could move. He helped her out.

"I'll see you at four thirty," he told her again before he climbed back in, then drove away.

"Not if I find another way home first," she muttered as she watched his vehicle disappear from sight. The man confused her. She liked him. How could she not? But yet she knew he saw her as an inconvenience.

She scowled as she headed toward the door in the storefront. Did he come to help with the animals because he hadn't trusted her to handle the job?

Emma briefly closed her eyes as she recalled Daniel's kindness since she had told him about her foster family.

Or had he come because he cared?

## *Chapter Five*

Emma was nervous as she entered Yoder's Country Crafts and General Store. Bells jingled as she walked through the door. She hesitated a moment, then moved toward the counter where Leah and Henry stood, blond heads close, bent over something between them. Henry was dressed in a maroon shirt with black suspenders but no hat, and Emma recalled that Amish men took them off whenever they came inside any building, except perhaps a barn. Although she couldn't see, she suspected Henry's pants were also black. Leah looked lovely in a purple dress with white cape and apron. A white prayer *kapp* rested on her pinned-back blond hair. She and Henry made a striking couple.

"*Gut* morning," Emma greeted.

Leah looked up, smiled. "*Hallo*, Emma."

Emma met her friend's husband's gaze. "*Hallo*, Henry." His expression wasn't as welcoming as it had been yesterday, and she wished she could read his thoughts. "Where would you like me to start? Do you need me to restock the shelves?"

Surprise flickered in Henry's blue eyes. "That sounds like a fine idea."

Emma smiled. "I'll be happy to help with that. If you'll show me where to find what I need…"

Leah frowned. "Emma, I don't want you carrying heavy boxes."

"I'm stronger than I look." She locked gazes with Henry, pleaded silently with her eyes.

She saw his lips curve. "I'll show you what needs to be done." He turned to his wife. "And I'll carry any heavy boxes out for her," he assured Leah.

"*Danki*, husband," she heard Leah whisper. The love in her friend's eyes for Henry was clearly heartfelt.

Emma followed Henry into the back room. He showed her a small room filled with stacks of boxes. "This is our storage room." He held the door open for her to precede him.

Emma stepped inside. "Henry," she said, "I'll work hard for you and Leah." She inhaled sharply. "I promise. Leah has been a friend when I really needed one."

Henry gazed at her silently for a long time. "She cares about you," he murmured.

"I know. And I care about her. Someday I'll be able to repay her—and you—for everything you've done for me."

"There isn't any need," he said. As if the topic made him uncomfortable, Henry became businesslike. "Those boxes hold nonperishable food items. You can start with those. I'll carry them out for you."

Emma nodded. "Okay."

*"Ja,"* he corrected with a little smile.

"Sorry."

Henry arched an eyebrow. "No need to apologize." The man grinned.

He carried out two boxes for her, one at a time. The first box held packages of dried corn mix. When she asked him about them, he explained, "Englishers like to buy it. 'Tis the easy way to make dried corn casserole. Have you ever had it?"

"I've tasted it." She'd done more than that. She'd eaten it many times, even after her family had left their community. They'd loved dried corn casserole. Emma hadn't had it since her parents died.

"Did you like it?"

Emma nodded.

"Leah will have to make it for you," he said with a smile. "She's a *gut* cook."

"Missy is, too. I've never eaten as much as I did last night at dinner with your mother-and father-in-law," she confessed. In fact, she wasn't used to being properly fed.

"All the Stoltzfus sisters are fine cooks," Henry said as he set the second box close to where she needed to unpack it.

Emma smiled. "I've met them—Charlie and Ellie."

"Leah has four sisters."

"Four!" she exclaimed.

"*Ja.* Nell is the oldest. She's married to James Pierce, a veterinarian. He was an Englisher who joined the Amish church because he loved her."

"That's..." *Sweet*, she thought, but didn't say it.

"It has worked out for them."

"So, Nell is the oldest, then who? Leah?"

"*Ja.*"

"Leah what?" The woman in question approached with a smile.

"Henry is telling me about your sisters. I thought you only had two, but he said there are five of you."

"*Ja*, Nell is first, then me, then Meg is in the middle. She's married to Peter Zook. They have a little boy, Timothy."

"Who is next?"

"Ellie, then Charlie."

"I like them," Emma said. "They were kind to me." She bit her lip. "You told them about me."

"I told Charlie." Leah looked slightly uncomfortable. "I know I said I wouldn't tell anyone, but I knew I wouldn't be at the house after I married, and I wanted someone to be there for you when you returned."

Feeling emotional, Emma blinked rapidly. *"Danki."* She bent quickly to pull four boxes of dried corn from the case."

"When you're done with the shelves, find me and I'll show you how to ring up sales," Leah said.

Nodding, Emma went to work, grateful that the couple left her alone to do the job, as if they trusted she wouldn't mess up. She put out stock and rearranged shelves, moving the older product forward while putting the new in the back. It didn't take her long. She picked up one box with the merchandise there was no room for and carried it toward the back of the store.

"Emma, you don't have to do that," Leah said.

Emma hefted the box higher. "'Tis light. Only a few boxes left inside."

Leah looked relieved. "When you're done putting that away, join me behind the counter."

She nodded, put the box back into the storage room, then returned out front to get the other one. The box wasn't as light as the first one since it held canned goods, but it wasn't too heavy that she couldn't manage it. She breezed past the counter into the back where Henry saw her.

"All done?" he asked.

"*Ja.* Leah wants me behind the counter as soon as I put this away." She paused. "I moved the older items up front before I added the new. That's the right way, *ja*?"

Henry regarded her with approval. "'Tis correct."

She beamed at him, feeling ten feet tall, then went to join Leah.

Daniel steered his buggy toward the main office of the construction company where he worked. Today they would be starting a new project. The office meeting was to let the crews know where they would be working in the coming weeks. As he drove into the lot next to the building and parked, he couldn't help but worry how Emma would make out at the Yoders' store. Was it a good idea to trust her? How could they be sure she wouldn't steal from them and then flee? If not for work, he would have hung out at the store for a while, see how Emma was doing. *As if she wouldn't guess what you were doing?*

The room in Rhoades Construction was filled to capacity. The company had grown over the past few years. His brother Jedidiah had started working with them first after Matt Rhoades, his former foreman, had formed his own company. Daniel and his brother Isaac had come to work for Matt next. At one time or another, all of his older brothers had worked for the company, even if for just a few days here and there. Joseph would join them eventually, he figured. His youngest brother would be looking for work to earn some extra cash. He would continue to work on the farm since he was the youngest son who would inherit the property.

Daniel sat in the third row of chairs in the room, waiting for Matt Rhoades and other construction managers to speak. He didn't particularly like working construction, but he reminded himself that it wasn't a bad way to earn money for the business he wanted to open. He needed to work as many hours as he could to raise the money in record time. Except now that Jess Morgan had joined his Amish community, he wondered how he could work as often and as much as he wanted. He had to keep his eye on her. No one else seemed to see the danger in her presence. Leah trusted her, but he didn't. If he kept his eye on her, he'd be able to discover the truth about her.

"We have several jobs in the works," Matt Rhoades told the group of men. "Fred is going to give you your assignments. Fred?"

Fred Barnett stepped front and center. "We have several places we need workers today. I'll call out the job and the names of the men we'd like on the project. Daniel Lapp. You'll be at the new house we'll be building just off Old Philadelphia Pike."

Daniel nodded, waiting as others were called, the crew who would be working alongside him. He was pleased with the location of the job site as it was just a short distance to Yoder's Country Crafts and General

Store. He'd be able to stop in and buy a soda—and check up on Emma while he was there.

He climbed into an SUV with the rest of the crew. When they got to the job site, Daniel saw the first order of business was to lay block. Someone had already dug footers and poured in concrete. Cement blocks were on pallets close to what would soon become the foundation of the building.

He went to work with the others. It was tedious work, but it wasn't bad. He worked in the front near the road with an English man, Edward Wyatt.

"Time for lunch," Edward said a short time later.

Daniel looked up with surprise. The morning had gone more quickly than he thought it would. Maybe because they'd been in the office for over an hour before leaving for the job site.

"I'm heading over to the store to get a soda," he told his foreman.

"Want Billy to drive you?"

Daniel shook his head. "Nay, it isn't far. I don't mind walking." He walked quickly. The day was warm with a light breeze to keep it from being hot. He hadn't gone far when he caught sight of the store. He paused near the entrance before he opened the door. He heard the jingle of the cow bells on the door as he stepped inside.

There was a woman at the counter paying for her purchases. She was tall, and Daniel couldn't see who was working the counter because of her size. He approached, expecting to see Emma, when he realized it was Leah who worked there instead.

"We appreciate your business," he heard his cousin

say as the woman grabbed her bags and left. "Have a nice day."

Leah sighed, looking tired. Daniel suffered a flicker of anger. Why was Leah working the counter? Where was Emma? Had she skipped out? Leah glanced in his direction, and she smiled. "Daniel, what brings you here?"

"Leah, I have everything you need from the house," a feminine voice said as Daniel caught sight of Emma entering from the back room. She froze when she saw him. "What are you doing here?"

"Buying a soda."

She narrowed her gaze as if she didn't believe him.

"Emma, will you get Daniel his soda? I'm going in the back to sit for a few minutes."

Daniel saw Emma's features soften. "*Ja*. I'll be happy to. You go and rest. Would you feel better if you lie down up at the house?"

"Nay." Leah smiled. "I'll be fine. I'll just make a cup of tea and take a few moments of quiet time." She grabbed a cup and poured water from the teakettle she must have heated up just minutes earlier.

"Leah, go and sit. I'll bring you your tea." She shot him a look as if daring to object.

He watched with amusement as she helped Leah into the back before she returned to make her tea. Only after she fixed it—as if she knew Leah's preference—and took it back to her did she meet his gaze squarely.

She stared at him hard. "What kind of soda?"

"Cola."

"Brand?"

"Doesn't matter."

She reached into the refrigerated case for a cold can. “Anything else?”

He shook his head. “That’s all.”

“One dollar.”

He handed her a dollar bill. She rang up the sale. “Want a paper bag?”

He shook his head, then popped open the can and took a long drink.

“Did you really come here for a soda or to check up on me?”

He studied her, noting her high color. And how her blue dress made her eyes look a different shade of brown. “Both,” he admitted. Then he took his soda and headed toward the door. “I’ll be back for you at four thirty,” he said. He heard her growl of frustration and smiled as he left.

## *Chapter Six*

Her heart thumped hard as Emma watched Daniel leave the store. He had come to check up on her. The fact that he'd admitted it should have made her angry, but it didn't. How could she be angry when she would have felt the same way if their situations were reversed?

Emma fought back tears and raised her chin, determined to make the best of things. She was only here in Happiness a short time. She went to check on Leah and saw her relaxing in a chair, enjoying her cup of tea. "Leah?" she ventured without getting too close. "Is there anything else I can get for you?"

The woman rose from her chair. "I'm sorry. I've sat here long enough."

"Nay, you stay. It's quiet out front. Enjoy it while you can."

She spent the rest of the afternoon cleaning the store. She swept the floor, wiped the counters and dusted the shelves. She even cleaned the glass on the cold case. Emma ate a quick lunch at one thirty, then went back to work. Leah had come out front for a while and at Emma's encouragement, the mother-to-be went up to the house to rest in her own bed. Henry entered the store a few minutes later.

"Everything *oll recht*?"

Emma nodded. "Not many customers today."

"I'm sure you can handle anyone who comes in. I'll be in my workshop across from the house if you need me."

"Will you be back before I leave?"

He nodded. "*Ja*, I'll be back.

She learned today that her hours would be nine until three each day. She wondered how much money she'd be able to save working part time, especially after she paid Leah for her garments. She didn't mind the shorter hours. It would give her a chance to help Missy in the house more. Daniel wouldn't be able to accommodate her work hours. She'd have to find another way to get to the store.

Daniel returned at four fifteen. Emma saw him immediately as he entered through the front door. Her pulse raced as he approached. "Are you ready to go?" he asked pleasantly.

"I'll let Henry know that I'm leaving."

As she was headed toward the back door, she encountered Henry. "Daniel is here."

"Have a nice night." He smiled. "You did *gut* work here today."

Emma felt a rush of warmth and satisfaction. *"Danki."*

Henry and Daniel chatted while Emma grabbed her sweater. "I'm ready when you are," she said to Daniel.

He inclined his head. "See you later, Henry." Daniel

followed her out of the store. She quickly climbed into his buggy without help and waited for him to settle in next to her. He didn't say a word as he picked up the horse's reins and with a flick of the leathers steered his buggy onto the road.

As the silence between them lengthened, Emma felt a familiar tightening in her chest. She closed her eyes and breathed deeply. When she felt no relief, she sighed and gazed out the side window. Her arms ached, and she rubbed them. Fortunately, she wore long sleeves so no one would see the lingering bruises aggravated by the day's work.

"Are you cold?" Daniel murmured.

"Nay." She settled her hands in her lap and stared out the front buggy window.

"Did you have a nice day?" he asked.

"*Ja*. It was enlightening, especially when you came to buy a soda."

He sighed loudly. "I didn't come to spy on you, Emma. I needed something to drink." He shot her a glance. "Does that make you feel better?"

"Maybe." She bit her lip. "I know you don't trust me."

"I don't *know* you," he said. "I can't help but feel concern for my family.

Emma studied Daniel's profile, noting the strong lines of his face. He was a good-looking man. "Henry was very pleased with my work today."

"*Ja*, he told me."

"Does *that* make you feel any better?"

He shrugged.

"You want to believe the worst of me," she accused.

Daniel pulled onto a packed dirt-and-gravel driveway. He parked his vehicle. "Nay, I'm just cautious."

"What does that mean?" She frowned. "Never mind, I don't want to know."

He jumped down and was on her side of the buggy before she had a chance to get out. His lips twitched with amusement as he extended his hand toward her. Emma eyed his long, masculine fingers as she reached her arms out. He lifted her out of the carriage and set her on her feet. She was conscious of his strength, the warmth of his hand on hers before he let go. The scent of outdoors that permeated him teased her senses.

Missy stood at the door and waved. "Daniel," she called. "Have time for a snack?"

Daniel grinned at her. "Sounds *wunderbor, endie*, but I need to get home. *Dat* is waiting for me to help with one of his projects."

"Don't be a stranger, nephew. Stop in and stay for a while another day." She opened the door as Emma headed toward the house. "Come for breakfast anytime."

"I'll keep that in mind," he said pleasantly. "I'll be by to take you to work tomorrow," Daniel called out to Emma. "Be ready early. I have to be at work by eight thirty."

She stiffened, glanced his way, then nodded before she turned away. As she entered the house, Emma heard the carriage move as Daniel left.

Missy closed the screen door after Emma entered. "Are you up for tea and cookies? Or I have milk if you prefer."

"Sounds delicious." Emma wanted to ask Missy

about her thoughts on walking to the store instead of having Daniel drive her, but on her first full day with the kind Amish couple, she wasn't yet comfortable enough to approach the topic. She became aware of how quiet the house was. "Arlin not home?"

"He went over to his sister's," Missy said with amusement in her gaze, "to help Samuel with a project."

The same project that Daniel would be helping with? "Where's Jeremiah?"

The older woman smiled. "He's in your room."

Later on, Missy told Emma over tea and cookies that this Sunday was Visiting Day. "We're hosting. I'll be cooking on Saturday. We don't cook or work on Sundays."

"May I help?" Emma asked, well aware of what Visiting Day meant.

"As if I'd ever turn down help," the woman said warmly. "I took out chicken to fry. Have you ever made fried chicken?"

"Nay," Emma admitted. She had never been allowed to cook in her foster homes, and she'd been too young when she'd lived in their Amish community.

"It takes time, but it's not hard." She pulled a plate of chicken from the refrigerator. The chicken had been cut into pieces ready for frying. "Would you please grab the canister of flour from the pantry?"

Missy showed her how to coat the chicken with a mixture of egg, flour and cracker crumbs with dry seasonings.

"May I try?" Emma asked, and she followed her instructions.

"That looks fine," the Amish woman praised. "Now we fry it."

Missy had placed a large cast-iron skillet on the stove and filled it with vegetable oil. "These won't take long. About fifteen minutes or so."

"Won't it splatter if we put the cold chicken into hot oil?"

Missy looked at her with approval. "*Ja*, if the oil gets too hot. We won't let it get that way." She struck a match and turned on the gas. The burner flamed to life.

Missy used metal tongs to pick up a piece of chicken and set it into the heating oil. The chicken sizzled but didn't pop. She turned to Emma. "Would you like to try?"

Emma picked up a drumstick and placed it into the skillet.

"Go ahead and put in all of the chicken," Missy encouraged.

"When do you go to church?" Emma asked conversationally as she placed each piece of chicken into the fry pan.

"We attend service every other Sunday. The Sundays in between are Visiting Days like the one this weekend."

After she'd set the last piece of chicken into the frying pan, she looked to Missy for direction. The woman beamed at her. "*Gut* job. Now we watch carefully and turn the chicken a few times while it cooks to ensure the outside becomes a crispy golden brown."

When the chicken was done, Missy gestured toward the oven. "Go ahead and put the skillet of chicken inside. It will help keep it warm until we're ready to eat."

"Okay." She went to grab the skillet.

"The handle is hot, Emma." She handed her two oven mitts. "Use these."

Emma slipped on the oven mitts and reached for the skillet. She grabbed it using both hands, but the weight of it made her stagger. She breathed deeply as she placed it into the oven, then sighed with relief as she pulled off the oven mitts. She didn't realize that she'd been rubbing her arms until she caught Missy watching her with a frown.

"Emma. Did you hurt your arms today?"

She shook her head. "Nay, I'm fine."

"Let me see."

Emma backed away. "I'm fine."

"Emma." Missy's tone was sharp.

She pulled up a sleeve. She heard the woman's sharp gasp.

"You're bruised. How did it happen? I shouldn't have asked you to pick up that skillet."

Emma smiled. She couldn't help herself. Missy fussed over her like she cared. *Like a mother would fuss over her child.*

"I'll have to talk with Leah."

"Nay, please. I'm fine." She thought what to say and decided on the truth. "This didn't happen at the store."

Missy's gaze grew sharp.

"It happened before I came here," Emma admitted. "Please don't tell anyone. I'm okay. I don't want anyone to feel sorry for me. I can work and pull my own weight. And the bruises don't hurt much anymore."

"I don't like this."

She placed a gentle hand on Missy's shoulder. "*Danki* for caring. I'm truly fine. I need to work. You've all been *gut* to me. Please don't let a few bruises make you see me differently."

Missy's expression softened. "I'll not tell anyone if you take a bath later this evening and soak those bruises. And I may have something that will help. Will you let me help you?"

Emma nodded. *"Ja."* She thought for a few seconds as she looked around the kitchen. "Mashed potatoes and peas," she suggested. "You wanted to know what to have with the chicken."

"Sounds *gut*."

Later, after supper, Missy made Emma take a bath. She added Epsom salts into the warm water, then left her to soak. As Emma went to bed that night, she felt much better. It was a while before she relaxed enough to fall asleep.

When the sun rose the next morning, Emma was eager to start the day fresh. Then she remembered that Daniel was coming for her again, and she promised herself that she'd talk with him about another way to get to and from work. He might object, but he wasn't the boss of her, and she'd be fine on her own.

Daniel had found her in the barn, helped her to find Leah and stepped in to assist her whenever she'd needed him. Unbidden came the knowledge that if she didn't continue to accept rides with him, she wouldn't see him every day. She drew a sharp breath. The realization bothered her far more than she'd ever expected.

# *Chapter Seven*

Before dawn, Emma fed the animals, then went into the house to help Missy with laundry. With Missy's help she stripped beds, gathered the dirty laundry and put everything into the machine to wash. An hour later she stood at the clothesline in the backyard and hung up the damp garments and linens to dry in the fresh air.

It was close to seven thirty when she finished with the laundry and went back inside. Daniel had promised to pick her up just after eight. He had to be at work at eight thirty, but fortunately his construction job site wasn't far from the store. Unfortunately for her, she would be almost an hour early for work.

The distance to the store couldn't be that far. She could walk. She wanted to walk. Emma knew that she would have to discuss it with him first, though. But she had to remind herself, he wasn't in charge of her. If he didn't agree, then she'd find a way to approach the topic with Arlin and Missy. They would no doubt find nothing wrong with her walking to work. She had to be careful that the police didn't recognize her and send her back to Maryland. Dressed in Amish garments, she doubted they would see her as anything other than a member of the Amish community. It was a common sight to see Amish walking down the road either alone or with others.

It was a warm September. After her hard work that morning, Emma decided to wash up and change into fresh clothes. She wouldn't need a sweater or jacket today. The weather at the end of September was often changeable, sometimes warm, sometimes cool. Today promised to be a warm one. When she came back downstairs, she heard Daniel's voice from the direction of the kitchen. He was seated at the kitchen table, a cup of coffee before him.

"Emma," Missy said with a smile, "Daniel's here."

"Daniel," she greeted. There would be no ignoring the man. She glanced quickly at the wall clock and felt slightly annoyed that it was only seven forty-five with Daniel already there. She started to bring up the subject of walking to work, then thought better of it. She'd talk with Daniel about it later.

"Did you want coffee?" Missy asked.

"Nay, but I appreciate the offer," Emma said. She locked eyes with Daniel. "I'll be outside when you're ready." Her heart pumped hard as she exited the house and went out in the backyard where they'd tied up Jeremiah earlier. She unclipped his tie-out line, then put on his leash. Then she walked him around the yard a bit before Arlin appeared at the door to the barn. "Would you like him inside?" she asked.

Arlin shook his head. "I'll take him into the barn with me."

Emma had recently learned that Arlin liked to make birdhouses, small tables and shelves as well as other wooden items. She'd seen the items in one back corner of the barn set aside for his workshop, and she'd been impressed not only by the craftsmanship but the way he'd painted some of them to sell in local gift shops for tourists. She smiled as she handed Arlin his dog's leash.

"I see Daniel is here. You ready for work?"

Emma nodded. "I know it was only my first day, but I enjoyed yesterday."

*"Gut,"* the man said with gruff affection. Emma heard a screen door open as Arlin looked past her before he met her gaze again. "Daniel," he murmured.

She turned to watch with skittering nerves as Daniel approached. *"Onkel,"* he said with a smile. To Emma's surprise, the younger man bent down to pet Jeremiah, spending a few moments lavishing attention on his uncle's dog. Both surprised her. Not all Amish cared for animals that didn't serve a specific purpose like a horse pulling a carriage or chickens laying eggs or cows providing milk. Emma had always loved all animals, but this little black-and-white furry creature held a special place in her heart. The dog had been kept in the barn and had offered Emma the comfort she'd desperately needed as she'd tried to get a good night's sleep in a stranger's building. Only they were not strangers anymore. Now she knew that the house and the barn had belonged to Arlin and Missy Stoltzfus.

Daniel rose to his feet. "Ready?" he asked Emma as he placed his straw hat onto his head. He looked handsome in a light green shirt with denim pants and black suspenders. He wore heavy-duty tan work boots.

Everything about him proclaimed him a strong male personality. Emma thought of her father, who'd been more studious and quieter, but she and her mother had loved him dearly.

Missy came out of the house. "Don't forget your lunches," the woman said as she approached. She handed Emma and Daniel each a paper bag. "Chicken salad sandwiches," she told him.

Daniel grinned. "My favorite." The sight of his sparkling eyes and smile hit Emma like a brick to her midsection.

"Mine, too," she murmured truthfully.

"We should go," Daniel said. Near the passenger side of the buggy, he held out his hand to her. She drew a calming breath and accepted his help, aware of his warm fingers around hers.

"Did you sleep well?"

She got situated in the front seat of the buggy, then stared at him. "Why do you ask?"

He sighed. "You look tired."

"I'm fine," she said shortly.

Daniel remained silent as he skirted the buggy and climbed into the other side. "'Tis going to be like this, is it?" he said stiffly.

"Like what?"

"You don't like me, I get it, but can't we be…kind to each other?"

She blinked rapidly, suddenly on the verge of tears. Her intention wasn't to be unkind. She'd suffered enough unkindness in her life and hated the idea that she made someone feel that way. "I'm sorry."

He looked surprised as he met her gaze. "I understand. I'm sorry, too. I wasn't exactly kind to you. It was rude of me to suggest that I have doubts about you."

Emma suddenly felt vulnerable and didn't know what to say. "We can start over," she suggested softly after Daniel had climbed onto the driver's side.

His lips curved as he regarded her with warmth. "We could."

Emma decided to wait until the ride home to discuss another way for her to get to work. She wanted to prolong the easy moment between them. Once she told him what she wanted, Daniel would be unhappy with her once more.

The drive to the Yoders' store took less than fifteen minutes. Emma took notice of the speed of the buggy. Fifteen minutes in a carriage that went how fast? Not fast at all, she realized. Therefore, the store was how far? Two miles? She could walk two miles easily enough.

Daniel pulled in front of the store and waited for her to get out. She'd seen his instinctive move to get out to help her, but he'd held back, probably because of her reaction earlier.

She hesitated a moment, then regarded him softly. "Thank you, Daniel," she said sincerely. Without waiting for his response, she headed toward the store. The front door was locked, so she went around to the back entrance, which was open. Upon entering, she immediately saw Henry at the table, drinking a cup of coffee.

"*Gut* mornin', Henry."

He looked surprised to see her. "You're early."

"Daniel had to be at work by eight thirty this morning, so he dropped me off early."

The man nodded. He held up his mug. "Would you like coffee?"

*"Ja."* He started to rise. "I can get it," she said. She grabbed a mug and went out front to the pot resting on the small single gas propane burner. She poured coffee into her cup, then added one sugar before going into the back room again. "How's Leah feeling?" she asked.

Henry smiled warmly. "My wife is fine. Slept in this morning, and I didn't have the heart to wake her."

"She needs her sleep," Emma murmured with a smile.

He nodded as he gestured to a second chair at the table. "Have a seat."

She stiffened. Had she done something wrong the previous day?

"You're not in trouble. You did a *gut* job yesterday."

She gaped at him. *"Danki."* She frowned. "Then what?"

"I need to take Leah to the doctor today."

"Is she *oll recht*?"

Henry inclined his head. "*Ja*, just a routine visit."

She felt an overwhelming sense of relief. "What do you need from me?"

"Can you handle the store by yourself?"

"*Ja*, of course—"

*"Gut."* Henry smiled. "We'll be gone for most of the morning. I want to take her out to lunch afterward."

Emma grinned. "She'll like that. She works too hard."

The good humor left his expression. "She does, but she doesn't think so."

"Give her a day to remember. It will be *gut* for her."

"I will."

Henry left through the back door, and Emma checked that everything was ready for her to open the store. She felt confident as she unlocked the door.

Her morning was uneventful. No customers came by until it was close to ten. Then Missy and Arlin Stoltzfus came into the store together. Emma eyed them warily as they approached the counter. Had they come to check up on her, much as Daniel had done the day before? Still, she greeted them warmly.

"We wanted to see you at work," Missy said with a smile. The woman looked genuinely happy to see her. "And frankly I need a few things."

Emma nodded. "Can I help you find something?"

"Nay, I know my way around."

She chuckled. "I'm sure you do."

Arlin stood at Missy's side, watching his wife fondly as she pulled a list from beneath the waistband of her apron. "Is Leah up at the *haus*?" he asked.

"Henry took her for her doctor's appointment this morning." Emma met his gaze. "Then he's taking her out to lunch."

The man's eyes warmed. "He's a *gut* man."

"Coffee?" When Arlin nodded, Emma fixed him a cup of coffee and set it on the counter close to him.

A few minutes later, she rang up Missy's purchases and watched as they headed out. "We'll see you at home later," the woman said.

*Home*, Emma thought as she watched the couple leave. Arlin and Missy considered their house her home.

Wasn't that wonderful?

* * *

Daniel was silent when he came to pick her up after work at three. Emma wondered if he'd had a bad afternoon or if it was just her that bothered him. Then she recalled that Henry had set three o'clock as the end of her workday. That would greatly infringe on his own work hours. Another reason to insist on her finding another way to and from work.

"Where are we going?" she asked with concern when he'd gone in a direction opposite from the Arlin Stoltzfus residence.

"Into town. I need to pick up a few items at the supermarket. Things that Leah and Henry don't carry."

"Downtown Lancaster?" she asked, growing anxious. What if Bryce had filed a missing persons report and the police were searching for her? Worse yet, what if Bryce, having recalled where she'd been found the last time, decided to come looking for her himself?

Her heart began to race in fear. She clutched the side of the buggy, her chest tightening as she struggled to breathe. "I need to get home," she said. "Please take me home." Emma swallowed hard. "I have chores to do."

Daniel must have recognized her fear, for minutes later he had steered the horse into the parking lot of a shopping center and turned the vehicle around. He didn't say another word as he drove her home.

Fifteen minutes later, Daniel drove his vehicle onto the Stoltzfuses' dirt driveway. He didn't say anything at first. Emma wanted to get out. In fact, she went to move, but his hand on her arm stopped her. "What are you afraid of?" he asked softly.

She closed her eyes, seeking God's guidance. When

she opened them, she saw concern and caring in Daniel's golden-brown gaze. "The last time I was in downtown Lancaster," she said, "the police found me and sent me back to my foster family." She drew a sharp breath. "I can't risk it happening again."

He studied her thoughtfully. Then he nodded, and Emma could feel only relief. She turned to get out.

"Wait," he said. Suddenly he was beside her, waiting to help her get out of the vehicle.

His hands encircled her waist as he gently lifted her from the carriage and set her down.

"Daniel—"

*"Ja?"*

His intense gaze made her blush. "I appreciate the ride home."

He nodded, his eyes still focused intently on her. "I'll be by for you in the morning. Sleep well, Emma."

She remembered she'd wanted to talk about her walking to work. "Daniel—"

He shook his head. "We'll talk tomorrow. *Mam* needs groceries."

Emma felt guilty for keeping him from the grocery store.

"Have a nice night, Daniel," she breathed softly before she headed inside.

She looked out the window once she was inside and saw that Daniel hadn't driven away yet. He stared at the house with an odd expression. Their gazes locked, and she pulled back from the glass, stunned by the riotous feelings inside her.

"Emma?" Missy called from the gathering room. "That you?"

"*Ja*, 'tis me," she said before she made her way to where Missy sat, sewing, in the great room.

"Did you have a *gut* day?" the older woman asked.

"*Ja*, I did." Emma realized that she meant it, although the drive home had been fraught with tension and worry. Was Daniel still outside in the buggy? Or had he finally left? She ignored the urge to check as she joined Missy by taking a chair next to hers. "What are you doing?"

"Making squares for our quilting bee next Wednesday at my sister-in-law Katie's *haus*." She smiled. "You'll meet her on Sunday. Katie is Daniel's *mudder*."

Would she see Daniel on Sunday as well?

"Tomorrow is your last workday at the store for the week. On Saturday, if you'd like," Missy said, "you can help me with the baking for Visiting Day."

"I'd love to help you."

Missy smiled. "I'll show you how to make an upside-down chocolate cake and a couple of pies."

"I'll look forward to it," Emma said. And she realized that she wanted to learning everything Missy was willing to teach her. She loved that everyone in this community was so warm and friendly. She hadn't felt this safe in a long, long time.

Daniel couldn't get Emma out of his mind all night. That a simple trip into town frightened her continued to haunt him. What must she have endured to be so scared? She told him she'd been brought into police custody and returned to her foster family. He felt an anger boiling up that he knew was wrong. He said a silent prayer to the Lord to calm himself. He found it difficult as he realized that her foster family had hurt her. What had they done to her?

He dozed a few hours before waking well before sunrise. He wanted to talk with Emma, learn the truth. He didn't know why, but he felt protective of her. He would never fight anyone. It wasn't the Amish way, but if someone threatened her, he'd do all he could to ensure she was safe.

With the knowledge that he'd be up well before the rest of his family, Daniel got ready for his day, then quietly went downstairs. He put the coffeepot on the stove and waited for it to perk. He took down several mugs for himself and the rest of his family. He'd drink a quick cup, then take care of the animals before heading over to his aunt and uncle's house to get Emma.

Daniel couldn't see her revealing any more information to him. If he was correct in his thinking, reliving her time with her foster family would be too hard. The coffee finished brewing, and he poured himself a cup, fixing it to his liking. He sat for a moment at the kitchen table sipping coffee, his mind wandering in several directions, consumed with Emma. Today was her third day of work, and according to Henry, she'd been doing well. She had proven trustworthy and hardworking, both traits he valued highly.

Finishing up his coffee, he rose and debated about having another cup. As he reached for the pot, his brother Joseph entered the kitchen. "You're up early."

"*Ja*. Couldn't sleep," Daniel said. "What about you? Something on your mind?"

"Nay. Fell asleep early last night. Thought I'd get a head start on my chores."

"Want coffee first?"

*"Ja."* Joseph took the filled cup from him.

Daniel poured himself a second cup, then sat down across from his younger brother. "What are you up to today?"

"Thought I'd help *Dat* around the farm. You?"

"Have to take Emma to work, then head over to the construction site."

Joseph stared at him. "Tell me about Emma."

Daniel stiffened. "What about her?"

"What's she like? I heard she was staying with Missy and Arlin."

He nodded. "She is. She's a…" He wasn't sure what to say.

"Some kind of distant cousin, I'm told."

"That's what they say."

"Why do you need to take her to work?" his brother asked.

"She's helping Leah and Henry at their store. I'm trying to help Missy and Arlin."

"That makes sense." Joseph took the last swallow of his coffee and set the mug down. "I'm going to head out to the barn. Take care of the animals."

"You need help?"

"Nay, I can handle it."

The sound of footsteps on the stairs drew their attention. Their little sister Hannah entered the kitchen. Daniel took one long look at her and realized that she wasn't little any more. She was sixteen, an age that worried him.

"Mornin'," Hannah greeted.

"There's coffee," Daniel said, motioning to the coffeepot and mugs on the counter. He watched her nod and fill up a mug.

"I'll see you later, Daniel," Joseph said.

*"Ja."* He returned his attention back to Hannah. "What are your plans for today?"

"Helping *Mam* with chores."

Daniel breathed a sigh of relief.

"Then I may take a ride into Lancaster," she added, and Daniel nearly groaned.

"You are going there alone?"

"Nay, I thought I'd take Ruth Peachy with me."

His eyes widened. "Why?"

Her eyes gleamed as Hannah lifted her chin. "Because I'm allowed."

The arrival of his parents forestalled any further conversation about his sister's *rumspringa* plans. Daniel looked at the wall clock and realized it was time to pick up Emma.

Minutes later as he pulled onto his uncle's property, he saw Emma sitting on the stoop, watching as he drove in. He got out of the carriage and approached her.

"Emma, you ready?"

She nodded. "Daniel, I need to talk with you first."

He eyed her with concern. "What's wrong?"

"I can't keep bothering you for a ride. Starting tomorrow, I plan to walk to work."

Daniel shook his head. "Not a *gut* idea, Emma. 'Tis dark until nearly seven forty-five. You don't want to walk when it's dark."

"But it won't be dark when I leave at three. Remember I don't have to be at work until nine. It will be bright by that time."

He still didn't like the idea. What if something happened to her before she made it to the store? Everything inside him wanted to argue with her, but he knew it wouldn't do any good. "Can we talk more about this after work?"

"*Ja*, we can, but my mind is made up and you won't be able to change it."

*We'll see*, he thought. Somehow, he would convince her that walking to the store wasn't wise. He could talk with his aunt and uncle, see what their thoughts were on Emma's decision. "Where are Missy and Arlin?"

"They left for Meg's an hour ago. Something about babysitting for Timothy while Meg and Peter head into town for an appointment."

"Do you have your lunch?" he asked.

Emma arched an eyebrow at him. "*Ja*. You?"

He couldn't stop the small smile that cropped up at the sight of her sassy spirit. "*Ja*. Made myself a sandwich last night."

"Let's go, then," she said sharply.

Daniel gazed at her intently. "You're being bossy."

She blushed. "Sorry," she murmured.

Hiding his urge to laugh, Daniel watched as Emma climbed into his buggy unaided before he got in and drove to Yoder's Country Crafts and General Store.

## *Chapter Eight*

Today was Thursday and payday. Henry paid Emma, who refused to take the money. "I owe Leah for the clothes," she said.

"Nay, you don't, Emma," Henry said pleasantly. "Take it. You've earned it. If you won't take your pay, then I'll not have you working at the store. You've made things easier for us. You deserve the little money we can pay you. The garments were a gift."

Emma blinked rapidly as a lump rose in her throat. "Please take it back."

Leah's husband shook his head. "Nay."

She saw the firm resolve in Henry's expression and finally accepted the cash. Henry smiled in approval. Since he and Leah refused to take her money, she'd find another way to repay them. Did he really believe that during her short time working for them she'd made their lives easier? It was true she'd worked alone at the store while Henry had taken Leah to the doctor, but that was nothing compared to what they'd done for her.

Her first purchase from Leah and Henry's store was

a wallet. She slipped the remainder of her money inside for safekeeping, then cleaned up the counter. At the end of the workday, Emma realized Daniel hadn't stopped by to check up on her, but he would be coming soon to take her home. The knowledge that she had a little money went a long way in improving her outlook for the future.

Just then, the bells on the front door jingled. Emma's stomach began to flutter as Daniel approached. Would he want to bring up the topic of her walking to work again?

"Are you ready to go?" he asked.

She inclined her head. "I'll tell Henry I'm leaving for the day."

Henry came out from the back room. "*Hallo*, Daniel. Come for Emma?"

*"Ja."* Daniel locked gazes with her.

"I was just coming to let you know he was here."

Henry smiled at her. "See you tomorrow, Emma."

Emma smiled. *"Ja."* She glanced at Daniel and saw his thoughtful look. "We should go," she whispered. She followed him out of the store.

He didn't say a word until they were outside in the sunshine. "Emma—"

"I'll be walking to work tomorrow, Daniel. You'll not change my mind." She saw him scowl, but he didn't argue right then, but she knew it was only a matter of time before he did. Emma felt triumphant as she sat back and enjoyed the ride home, until she realized that Daniel wasn't going to accept her decision. Soon, possibly tomorrow, they'd be arguing the safety of her walking to work.

* * *

The next morning Emma got ready for work. She would be walking to the store today. She figured it was two, maybe three miles at the most. At least, she hoped so.

"Did you make your lunch?" Missy asked.

"*Ja*, I used some of the chicken salad that was left. That's *oll recht, ja*?"

The older woman smiled. "*Ja*, you can have anything you'd like from the kitchen." She pulled eggs and butter from the refrigerator. "What time is Daniel coming for you?"

"He's not," Emma said. "I told him I'd walk to work this morning."

Missy frowned as she melted butter in a pan then cracked open the eggs into it. "Do you think that's a *gut* idea?"

"I walked here from Maryland," she told her.

"If you're certain..."

"I'll be fine," Emma assured her. "I don't have to be at work until nine. I'll leave at eight. Once I know how long it will take me, I can adjust my departure time."

Missy nodded, but Emma could see the worry in her expression. "Missy, I can't keep putting Daniel out. He has to work. I know he usually works later than I do, yet he's had to leave early to bring me home."

"I don't think he minds."

Emma wasn't so sure of that. She'd heard what he'd said when she'd been hiding in the barn. He was saving to open a business. The earnings from his current job would finance his future harness shop.

At eight o'clock, Emma grabbed her lunch bag and

started to walk in the direction of the store. She hadn't walked far when she heard the sound of buggy wheels behind her. She didn't stop. The carriage drew up next to her, finally snagging her attention.

"Emma." The shock of Daniel's voice halted her.

"What are you doing here, Daniel?" She continued walking, and he steered his buggy alongside her.

"You wanted to walk so I'm following along beside you to make sure you arrive at the store safely."

She jerked to a stop. "Nay, you're not."

Daniel arched an eyebrow. "*Ja*, I am."

"Daniel—"

"'Tis for the best, Emma. Let me do this, *ja*?"

"But you have to go to work."

"*Ja*, I do, but I'll go in a little late. It will be worth it to know that you reached the store without incident."

"But you've got a business to save up for."

He looked surprised. "And how did you know that?"

"I heard you that first day in the barn." She was across the road from him, but he kept even with her, slowing the horse's pace to hers. "Daniel, you need to go."

"Nay."

She heard a car come up behind her. She turned, saw it was a patrol car and experienced a moment's terror. She kept her head down, hoping the police officer wouldn't stop. He didn't. He seemed to be in a hurry. Fortunately, Daniel had pulled off to the side of the road. He halted the horse and stared at her as if he saw and understood her fear. Once the officer passed, Emma met Daniel's gaze, then closed her eyes briefly before opening them again. "Fine, I'll accept a ride from you, but only because I don't want you to be late for work," she said. Daniel started to get out. "Nay," she warned, "I can get in by myself. 'Tis too dangerous for you to get out and help me. Cars drive past too fast along this road."

Emma climbed into his buggy and settled in the seat. She didn't look at him, and he didn't drive on.

"Emma..."

"We should go."

He sighed before he finally flicked the leathers and drove back onto the road. Minutes later he steered the horse into the store parking lot, close to the hitching post. Daniel didn't say a word. Emma met his gaze, saw emotion in the brown depths of his eyes and felt something swell inside her.

"Daniel..."

"I'm sorry, Emma. I had to follow you," he said before she could continue. "I was worried."

She softened toward him. "That's sweet of you, but—"

"But you no longer need me to take you to and from work," he finished for her.

Emma hesitated. It was true that she didn't need him for transportation, but mostly she was worried about taking advantage of his generosity, especially when he had a job that was important to his future. "*Ja*, although I appreciate the concern." She recalled her reaction to seeing the police cruiser and shuddered.

"My brother Joseph will pick you up at three today," Daniel said. "He works on my *dat*'s farm and he'll be finished well before then."

She didn't like that he'd dictated who she should ride

with. She hadn't met Joseph. She didn't want to ride with anyone. "Daniel—"

"Please, Emma."

His soft, imploring tone startled her, and she shot him a glance. How could she resist? "Fine, but today only."

His grin made her breath catch. *"Gut."*

He started to climb down from the buggy. "I can get out on my own," she told him. She knew he was trying to be kind, but she didn't want that. Her feelings about him already confused her.

He nodded, and she could feel his regard as she stepped down from his vehicle. "*Danki*, Daniel."

"I'll see you again sometime soon."

*"Ja,"* she said. Visiting Day was this weekend. She knew she would see him there.

The workday went quickly for Emma. Customers entered the store, buying items for the weekend. She was kept busy helping them find the things they needed.

A quick look at the clock revealed that it was nearly three. Would Daniel's brother come for her as promised?

Minutes later, a young man with dark brown hair and blue eyes entered the store. He smiled as he approached the counter. "Emma," he said, "I'm Joseph."

He was good-looking but in a different way than Daniel. His smile remained on his face as he studied her. It didn't appear as if he felt put out by coming for her. "I'm sorry that you got stuck with me today," she said. "I could have walked home."

Joseph frowned. "I don't think that's a *gut* idea. Besides, I don't mind. 'Tis nice to get out and about."

Leah came out from the back of the store. She'd been

up at the house taking a nap. Her blue eyes lit up when she saw Daniel's brother. "Joseph! What a pleasant surprise!"

The young man grinned. He seemed to be close in age to Emma. "I've come to take Emma home."

Leah glanced in her direction. Emma gazed back, trying to keep her thoughts hidden. "That's nice of you," her friend told Joseph. She turned toward Emma. "I'll see you on Sunday if not before," she said.

Emma only smiled.

"Ready, Emma?" Joseph asked.

"*Ja*. Take care, Leah," she said before she preceded Joseph out of the store.

Unlike Daniel, he didn't offer to help her into his vehicle, a large open carriage with four huge wheels. He simply untied his horse from the hitching post as Emma climbed into the high seat. Joseph got in. Emma held on tight as the carriage lurched as he flicked the leathers before he steered the horse onto the road.

He was quiet as he drove toward the Stoltzfus house. Finally, he turned to her. "How old are you?" he asked.

Emma looked at him, trying to figure out why it was important for him to know. How much of her background was he told?

"Seventeen," she murmured.

Joseph smiled. "I'm eighteen." He returned his attention to the road. "So, you're a cousin of *Endie* Missy."

Emma didn't know what to say and realized he'd been told only her cover story. *"Ja."*

"First time visiting Happiness?"

"*Ja*. My parents are gone, and I have no *bruders* or sisters."

He studied her briefly with concern. "I'm sorry."

She smiled. "Don't be. I'm fine. Besides, they are with the Lord now, *ja*?" She hoped so, anyway. Her parents had been labeled sinners. She prayed that God had taken them home to reside in heaven with Him.

The house rose up on the left. Joseph made the turn and pulled up by the side door. Missy was taking clothes down from the line. Emma frowned. "I told her I'd help with those."

"Then 'tis a *gut* thing I brought you home," Joseph said with good humor.

She saw the teasing twinkle in his eyes and decided she liked Daniel's younger brother. "I appreciate the ride."

"You're most *willkomm*. Shall I pick you up Monday after work?"

"I don't want to impose. If I haven't made other arrangements, I'll let you know."

The young man nodded.

Emma went to the clothesline. "Missy, I'll help with this. I'm not doing enough chores," she said.

Missy glanced at her. "You do more than enough, Emma." Her gaze went beyond her. "Joseph!"

Emma was surprised to see that Joseph had followed her. "I couldn't leave without saying *hallo*," he said. "I'm the one who brought Emma home today."

Missy looked from one to the other. "That was nice of you."

"Daniel insisted," Emma muttered.

"It was my pleasure," Joseph assured her with a smile.

Emma began to unpin the remaining garments from the clothesline. She ignored the conversation between aunt and nephew. When she was done, despite Missy's protests, she picked up the wicker laundry basket and took it inside the house. Missy followed moments later.

"'Tis important for me to help," Emma said.

Missy looked at her with a soft expression. "You help out plenty. But you can help me cook for Visiting Day if you'd like."

She nodded. "*Danki.* I'll be happy to."

The next morning she and Missy baked the upside-down chocolate cake, one of Missy's well-known and sought-after specialties, and a number of pies. Emma enjoyed working with the pie crust, kneading it on a floured table, then rolling it out into two circles. She made an apple pie first.

"The apples this time of year are fresh and crisp," Missy told her. "Perfect for pie making as well as eating."

"It smells delicious," Emma said with a grin.

"I'll teach you to make a shoofly pie next." Missy smiled at her. She wore a quilted apron tied around her waist. She gave one to Emma, which she quickly donned. Both aprons had been handmade by Missy.

"What is shoofly pie?"

"It's thick and sugary and delicious. We call it shoofly because if set on the windowsill to cool, flies swarm around it eager for a taste."

Emma wrinkled her nose. "Eww."

Missy laughed. "Don't worry. We won't let that happen."

By late afternoon, she and Missy had made not only cake and pies but four loaves of bread, macaroni salad and a roast beef. "We don't do any cooking or housework on Sundays, Emma." She pulled the roast beef from the oven and set it on a hot mat on the worktable. "As I explained earlier, tomorrow we'll have visitors. It's not a church service day but a day when family and friends get together to enjoy one another's company. My sister-in-law and her family will be coming. So will Leah and my other daughters. It should be a nice day."

Emma was nervous. Would she be able to act like she belonged? How much did the family know about her background? Daniel knew and so did Leah, Charlie and Ellie. But what of the others? Of Leah's sisters Meg and Nell? She hoped and prayed that she fit in well enough that everyone would accept her as one of them.

Sunday morning Emma got up and dressed in clean garments before she rolled and pinned her hair, then covered it with a white prayer *kapp*. Their visitors would be coming at 10:00 a.m., Missy had told her the day before. It was seven now, later than usual for her to rise. She descended the stairs and found Missy in the kitchen setting out muffins and jam for breakfast.

"I'm going to feed the animals," Emma told her.

Missy shook her head. "Arlin got a head start. The animals are taken care of."

Emma flushed guiltily. "Where's Jeremiah?"

As if recognizing his name, the family dog lifted his head from his dog bed in the corner of the room.

"Ah, there you are!" Emma exclaimed. "Would you like to go for a walk?" She grabbed his leash and the dog ran toward her, eager to be outdoors. "Let's go, then."

She took him across the yard, waiting a minute for him to do his business before she took him into the barn. Arlin was inside watching his horses eat with their noses deep in their feed buckets. “Good morning, Arlin.”

The man turned and smiled at her. “Mornin’, Emma.”

“I’m sorry I overslept.”

“You needed your rest.” The warmth of his expression relaxed her.

“I hope you don’t mind that I brought Jeremiah with me.”

The man smiled affectionately at his dog. “Nay. I’m sure he was ready for a stroll.”

“Missy said that breakfast will be ready in a few minutes.”

“I’ll head over, then, and wash up.” He started toward the door.

“Arlin.”

He turned to her with raised eyebrows.

*“Danki,”* she said softly.

“Nothing to be thanked for, Emma. You’re always welcome in our *haus*.”

Emma felt overwhelmed with emotion as she accompanied Arlin on the walk back. As she entered the kitchen, she felt her mouth water. She was hungry, tempted by the fresh muffins on the table accompanied by several jars of jams and jellies. Since she’d moved in with the Amish couple, she’d been well fed. Just shy of a week, she was already feeling stronger than when she’d first arrived. And this simple breakfast, she thought, was only the start of a day that would be filled with food and fellowship.

The day was unseasonably warm but not humid. After breakfast, Missy and Emma opened all the windows to let the fresh air into the house. Emma was pouring glasses of cold tea when she heard the sound of buggy wheels on the dirt driveway. The first of their visitors had arrived. She picked up a glass and went to the window as a gray family buggy pulled in near the barn.

She waited with bated breath to see who was in the vehicle, expecting—and hoping—it would be Daniel. A man she hadn't met before climbed out, then helped the others get down. A woman with a baby stepped out with his assistance, followed by a little boy, who was lifted into his father's arms. They headed toward the house. Emma opened the door as they approached. The man froze a moment as he saw her before he continued his approach with his wife and baby.

"*Gut* mornin'," she greeted. Her heart raced as she held the door open for them to enter.

"You must be Emma," the woman said. "I'm Sarah Lapp. This is Jedidiah, my husband, and these two are our children."

"Jed," he invited. "I'm Daniel's brother." The man studied her thoughtfully.

The mention of Daniel's name gave her an odd little thrill until she began to wonder how much of the truth Daniel had told his family about her.

The man smiled. "You're a cousin from out of state, I hear. *Willkomm.*"

She hid her discomfort at the necessary deception. She managed to smile. "I'm grateful that Missy and Arlin put up with my company."

"I'm sure they love having you here."

"We do," Missy said as she entered the room. "Jed, Sarah, I'm glad you could join us today."

Jed's expression softened. "Wouldn't miss a visit with my favorite *endie* and *onkel*."

Missy laughed. "You're a charmer like your *bruders*." She reached for the baby in his arms.

"Noah and Rachel can't make it," Sarah said. "Susanna is sick, and they thought it best to keep her home."

"Poor girl. I hope she feels better soon," Missy said.

"Isaac and Ellen won't be coming either," Jed added. "They're with Ellen's *eldre* today."

Missy nodded. "Leah and Henry will be over later after a brief visit to Ellen's parents." She explained to Emma, "Isaac is married to Ellen. Henry and my nephew Isaac are best friends."

"Ellie and Reuben will be here any minute with Ethan." Missy paused. "Meg, Peter and Timothy are with Horseshoe Joe and Miriam today."

An open carriage pulled in, and two couples and a child got out. "Charlie and Nate," Missy said with a grin of satisfaction. "And Ellie, Reuben and Ethan."

Another vehicle entered the property moments later. Jed grinned. "My *mudder* and *vadder*." Emma waited patiently beside Missy while Jed approached the family buggy and opened the door for his parents and siblings.

"Daniel, Joseph and Hannah are with them," Sarah said.

"Where's Elijah?" Jed asked as his family entered the small home.

"He and Martha are at the Masts'," Daniel said. His gaze locked with Emma's, and she felt a fluttering within her chest.

She reluctantly pulled her eyes away from him. "May

I get anyone something to drink?" she asked everyone. She held up her cup. "Iced tea?"

Sarah, Jed and Hannah wanted some.

"I'll help," Ellie said. "Reuben?"

The man smiled at her lovingly. *"Ja."*

"I'll have some as well," Joseph said.

"I'll get it," Hannah said.

Emma grabbed a few plastic cups and poured tea for those who wanted it. Daniel entered the house, carrying a large bowl in each arm. His sister Hannah followed him inside.

"I'll help," Hannah said. The girl had pretty blue eyes and blond hair. Emma saw the resemblance between Daniel and his sister in the shape of their eyes. She handed two cups to Hannah.

Daniel placed the bowls of food on the kitchen counter. He watched Emma fill two more glasses with iced tea. Emma gave them to him. *"Danki,"* he murmured as he held her gaze.

She rewarded him a small smile and breathed easier as he carried them outside. She took another pitcher from the refrigerator and filled four more cups, which she set on the counter.

"Thank the Lord 'tis a nice enough day to eat outside," Ellie said with a smile. "This *haus* is too small for all these people." She grabbed two of the cups and left the house.

Despite Ellie's belief, Emma secretly thought the house perfect for any number of people, as Missy and Arlin filled it with love for their family and friends.

Daniel returned. "I thought there might be more," he said, reaching around her for the two plastic cups. His nearness made her heart rate spike. He stepped back but didn't move. His eyes warmed as his lips curved. "Emma, earlier you didn't say *hallo* to me." He looked amused. "I'll say it first, then. *Hallo*, Emma. Nice to see you."

"*Hallo*, Daniel." She blushed. "I should go out and see if anyone wants something other than tea." Without waiting for his response, she brushed by him and exited the house. She was aware of him following close behind her. She asked around, but no one else needed anything. She went back into the house. To her surprise, Daniel followed her inside.

"I need to take Jeremiah for a walk," she murmured as she grabbed his leash and headed toward the barn. Arlin had put the dog in the barn so that the animal wasn't overwhelmed with all the company. Inside the barn, she went to Jeremiah's stall. Arlin had supplied his pet with plenty of creature comforts—his bed, some chew toys, a bowl of water and one of dry dog food.

"Hey, boy," she whispered as she unlatched the stall door and went inside, then closed it behind her. Emma approached the little dog and crouched down to pet him. "Are you lonely in here, buddy?" she asked as she ran her fingers through his fur. She laughed when Jeremiah flipped onto his back for her to rub his belly.

"You have a kind owner," she said softly. "You're lucky." She grinned. "Missy and Arlin love you." She sighed. "I do, too." She continued to stroke the dog's belly. "Want to go for a walk? We can walk through the fields toward the back road. What do you think?"

"I don't think that would be a *gut* idea," a familiar voice said.

She gasped and looked up to see Daniel leaning over the half door.

"You left in a hurry," he said. "Has it been that long since Jeremiah went out last?"

Emma blushed. She'd taken him for a walk less than two hours ago. But she needed the comfort Jeremiah gave her. Everyone had been so kind to her, but she reminded herself that she was only living here temporarily, and she felt guilty and out of place. Daniel's expression was unreadable as he studied her.

"Does it matter when he was out last?" she asked, her tone crisp.

"Maybe. What if Missy needs your help?"

"Oh, I..." Embarrassment made her look away. "I can tie him outside and keep him from being underfoot. He'd like watching everyone, and he won't make a pest of himself." She clipped on Jeremiah's leash. This man did something to her. She was attracted to him although he made her feel off-kilter.

Daniel stepped aside to make room for her and Jeremiah to exit the stall. She took the dog out into the yard, aware of Daniel behind her.

Missy was in the yard chatting with three women. It didn't look like Missy needed help. Emma flashed Daniel an accusing look, but he merely arched an eyebrow at her.

She approached Missy and her friends. "Emma," Missy greeted with a smile. "Come and meet my sister-in-law Katie."

She was suddenly the focus of three kind gazes. *"Hallo,"* Emma murmured. She recognized Katie

Lapp, Daniel's mother, in the similarity of her features with Daniel's.

"'Tis nice to meet you," Emma said.

Katie smiled. "Daniel has talked about you."

Emma stilled. "Nothing bad, I hope."

The woman shook her head. "All *gut*. And Leah and Henry have said nothing but nice things about you. I've been told you're a hard worker, and your help at the store allows my niece to get off her feet and rest."

Relaxing, Emma gave her a genuine smile. "I enjoy helping Leah and working at the store."

"I'm glad you like working there," Missy said. "Leah will need you more in the coming weeks."

*"Ja,"* Katie agreed. "She'll be tired. I remember when I carried Jacob and Elijah. My twin sons," she explained. "I was exhausted by noon every day."

"Henry urges Leah to nap in the afternoon. She didn't want to at first, but now she gets so tired that she listens to him when he urges her to go up to the house and lie down."

"Are you taking Jeremiah for a walk?" Missy asked.

"I thought I would tie him up outside away from everyone. Unless you think it would be better if I put him in my room."

Missy nodded. "That might be a better idea."

Emma excused herself to take Jeremiah upstairs to her room. She took off his leash, then refilled the bowl of water for him, setting it next to the makeshift bed she'd made for him.

When Emma returned downstairs, the women were gathering food from the kitchen to take outside. She grabbed a large bowl that Daniel had carried in earlier and took it to the table that Arlin had set up outside for food. The men had also set up tables made from plywood laid across sawhorses. Kitchen chairs had been brought outside for people to sit on. Everyone else searched for a comfortable place to sit. When it was time to eat, Emma filled her plate and sat on the small stoop near the side door of the house.

Watching Missy's family interact from a distance, Emma saw the love among family members. She experienced an intense longing to belong in some way. She sat and silently ate from her plate with her cup of lemonade next to her on the step.

Daniel came over to her, and she tensed. "Mind if I sit down?" he asked.

She shook her head and moved her glass of lemonade to her other side, shifting over to give him room.

He sat close beside her, and she struggled to appear at ease.

"The food is delicious."

Emma managed to smile. "*Ja*, I especially like the salads your mother made."

The air grew tense with silence.

"Did you have a *gut* first week?" Daniel asked.

"Daniel—"

"'Tis a simple question, Emma."

She faced him, found him studying her with an intensity that startled her. "*Ja*, it was a *gut* week. I learned a lot from Leah and Henry."

He nodded, then went back to eating. "Was it a problem for you to have Joseph to bring you home yesterday?"

"Nay." She took a sip from her lemonade.

"Then you won't mind if he comes to take you home every day."

"Daniel—"

"I'll take you to work and he can bring you home."

She sighed. "I don't think so."

He scowled at her. "What? Why not?"

Something about his tone made her breath catch. "I don't want to bother either of you."

"You won't be bothering us. We offered."

"It doesn't seem right."

"But we *want* to help," he said, his expression sincere.

Her heart melted. "I'll accept your help for now," she said, "until I can make other arrangements."

His grin warmed her heart. "That's fine."

Daniel surprised her by staying close to her for a time. Emma found that she didn't mind his company as much as she thought she would. He was entertaining as he told her stories about each of his relatives. "Charlie used to be a wild child," he said.

"Charlie?"

"*Ja*. Nate didn't know what to make of her until she convinced him she was perfect for him."

Emma chuckled as Daniel smiled at her.

A short time later, he excused himself to discuss something with his brothers. Emma headed toward Missy and Katie, who stood talking with Leah and Ellie in the shade of an oak tree.

"I tell you 'tis a shame," Missy said. "David knows better. No technology. 'Tis against the Ordnung. 'Tis no wonder the elders want him to be shunned."

"The bishop believes 'tis the right thing to do," Katie Lapp said.

"David understands our rules and what's expected of him."

Overhearing, Emma froze, waiting to hear more. They were about to shun someone? In this community? She suddenly felt sick to her stomach.

"David says he found it, whatever it is. I think it's a tablet. He works in a supermarket in Lancaster. His sister said he bought it."

"And it runs on electricity," Katie pointed out.

"And I heard he plugs it in to charge it at Whittier's Store. Bob Whittier has some code that David puts into the tablet so that he can view the English world on it," Leah said.

"He clearly doesn't think he did anything wrong," Leah's sister Ellie added.

"Bishop John spoke with David and he's not sorry for owning one."

Emma stepped closer, needing to know more.

"Emma!" Sarah Lapp exclaimed. "Come and join us."

Her heart fluttered in her chest. If these people ever learned the truth about her shunned family, she'd be ostracized like they planned to do to this David. "I didn't mean to intrude."

"You're not," Katie assured her with a smile. "We were chatting about a member of our community who has gone against the Ordnung. 'Tis a terrible thing. Our bishop and church elders have decided that he should be shunned, especially since the man feels no remorse for what he's done."

Emma nodded as tension rose within her. "If he were sorry, would he still be shunned?"

"If he said he regretted what he did—and meant

it—then he would be accepted back into our community," Missy said. "Shunning is simply the Amish way of tough love. David Fisher can remain in Happiness, but no one will sit or eat with him. Nor will members of the community do business with him."

"I see." And Emma truly understood for the first time about shunning. One had to do a terrible wrong to be shunned. She realized she never really understood what shunning—or ostracizing a person—meant. Only that her parents told her that they could never return to their Amish community. Never see her grandparents, other relatives and friends. Now she knew that if they had, her family would have rejected them.

*I shouldn't stay.* As much as she would have liked to, she didn't truly belong here.

When it was time for everyone to leave, Emma watched Daniel and his family climb into their buggies. His hands holding the leathers, Daniel saw her and smiled. She eyed him warily, then turned away, unable to bear the thought of his rejection should he learn the truth about her.

In a few weeks, she'd turn eighteen. She wasn't sure where she'd go, but she knew she had to leave now. She couldn't stay. She would work one more day and pay for the clothes that Leah had provided for her. Then she would leave Happiness and the Amish community here. *And Daniel.* She would never forget any of them. And she'd always remember Daniel and how kind he'd been to her. It would hurt to go, but if he ever learned the truth about her, she was sure he'd reject her.

That would be more painful than anything her foster father had done.

# *Chapter Nine*

Daniel arrived at the house the next morning as Emma pinned the last of the wet laundry on the clothesline. She heard the sound of wheels on the dirt driveway and turned to see him climb out of his buggy and head toward the house. Aware that he hadn't seen her, she approached the house and entered within seconds of Daniel's entry.

"*Hallo*, Daniel," she said.

He eyed her with surprise. "You were outside?"

"*Ja*. I was at the clothesline."

Missy handed her a paper bag. "I made you lunch."

*"Danki,"* she said solemnly. She grabbed her sweater from a wall hook. It was chilly outside, and the temperature would likely drop later in the day.

She was quiet as Daniel drove her to work. Her throat felt tight as she stared through the side window. She could barely swallow. She was saddened by the realization that today would be the last time she would see or spend time with him.

The Yoders' store loomed ahead on the right side

of the road. Daniel steered his horse to the parking lot. He sat a moment without a word until Emma started to get out.

He caught her by the hand to stop her. “Emma, wait,” he said.

She stiffened.

“Something is bothering you,” he said.

“I’m fine.”

He shook his head. “Nay, you’re not. We had a nice day yesterday, *ja*? Then at some point, something changed and you seemed upset. You became quiet.”

“Daniel, I’m fine.”

He studied her for a long time. There was something in his expression that made her heart race. “You’d tell me if you were upset?”

Emma shifted uncomfortably. She didn’t want to have this conversation. He seemed genuinely concerned about her, which only made her feel more guilty and sad. “You need to get to work, and I should get inside. Leah and Henry are waiting for me.”

He inclined his head. “Joseph will bring you home this afternoon.”

*“Oll recht.”* She got out of the vehicle but paused at the front entrance of the store. “Take care, Daniel Lapp.”

He frowned. “I’ll see you tomorrow morning, Emma.”

Despite her decision to leave, Emma experienced an odd warmth in her chest from Daniel’s concern for her. She entered the store and approached the counter. “*Gut* morning,” she greeted the Yoders.

“*Gut* morning, Emma,” Leah said, and Henry smiled.

“Should I restock shelves today?”

"Leah has another doctor's appointment," Henry told her. "Can you handle the store for us?"

"*Ja*, I'd be happy to."

Henry smiled. "*Danki.* I'll carry out some boxes for you."

She quickly hurried to the door that led to the back room. "I'll manage."

The man started to object.

"If it's canned goods or jars, you can carry them for me. But I'll start with the lighter items." Emma brought out a number of boxes and set them in the corner to grab when she needed them.

The morning passed quickly. Henry left with Leah for the doctor's appointment at noon, and with them gone Emma chose that time to pay for the garments Leah had given her. She opened the register drawer and put in a hundred dollars. The rest she would need if she didn't want to find herself living on the streets again.

The front door opened with a tinkling of bells as Joseph Lapp stepped into the store. Flushing with guilt, Emma slammed shut the drawer and smiled at him. "Joseph, is it that time already?"

"*Ja.*" He didn't return her smile. "Are you ready to go?"

She stared at him. Something felt wrong. She looked away. "Let me lock the doors and we can slip out the back." Emma brushed by him on the way to lock the front door.

"Where are Leah and Henry?"

"Leah had a doctor's appointment."

Joseph nodded. He watched her lock the front door, then waited while she grabbed her wallet from under the counter. He followed her out through the back of the store. After ensuring that the rear door was locked, she faced Daniel's brother.

"You didn't have to come to take me home."

He narrowed his gaze. "Why not?" He opened his mouth as if he wanted to say something else, then promptly shut it.

Emma followed him to his buggy, then climbed in. Joseph got situated in the seat next to her and picked up the leathers. He sat a moment without moving. Finally, he turned and met her gaze. "Tell me that you didn't take money out of the register."

Emma gaped at him in shock. "I didn't take money out of the register."

"Then why did you open it? There were no customers in the store."

She blinked back tears. "I didn't take money from the register," she insisted.

He stared at her. She faced him with glistening eyes. "I put money *in* the drawer," she admitted hoarsely, her throat tight. "Leah won't take any payment for the dresses she gave me. I needed to repay her, so I thought I'd—"

"Slip it in the register when she wasn't here?" Joseph said softly.

*"Ja."*

She braced herself for his response, but he just smiled at her. "Let's go. I'm sure you're tired and ready to go home." He believed her, she realized.

Emma nodded. She wished the Stoltzfus residence was truly her home. But it wasn't, and it never would be. So she would leave tonight. She settled her wallet in her lap and hugged herself. Despite her sweater, she was cold. The temperature had cooled, and there was a hint of dampness in the air. The distant sky was dark, as if threatening rain.

Joseph noticed the change in temperature and the dark sky as well. "I need to get you home before it pours."

"Will you be *oll recht*?" she asked with concern. "Or will you stay with us until the rain passes?"

"I don't live too far. I'm sure I'll make it home before the storm hits."

It had started to drizzle by the time Joseph drove his wagon onto his uncle's property.

"Are you sure you won't stay?" Emma asked.

He gave her a genuine smile that warmed her inside. His willingness to believe her about the register meant a lot to her.

Emma climbed out of his vehicle and waved to him as he drove away before she ran to the house. She burst into the kitchen. "A storm's coming."

"I saw," Missy said. "Thank the Lord you're home." The woman eyed her damp garments. "You're shivering, child. Take off your sweater. Tea? It will warm you up."

*"Ja."* She would miss these moments with Missy. She would miss her and Arlin and their married daughters and family. And the Lapps. But she'd miss Daniel most of all.

As she spooned sugar into her tea, Emma thought about leaving. Should she leave at night? Or in the morning? She wouldn't go in the rain. She'd get sick if she did. If she became ill and out of sorts, the police would have a better chance of finding her.

She'd have to plan her departure wisely. She was safe here until someone learned the truth about her identity and her past. Then she'd be shunned and tossed out of Happiness. She wished there were a way to work at the Yoders' store for a little longer so she could save a bit more money for food and shelter until she could figure out what to do next.

"Emma." Missy's urgent calling of her name alerted her to the woman's concern that she'd said Emma's name several times without a response. "What's wrong?"

Emma shook her head. "Nothing. I'm fine."

The older woman looked as if she didn't believe her, which made Emma feel all the more guilty. Emma remembered well the ideals of her Amish community, and she knew that she rarely thought much about going against them. Until now. Because of Missy and Arlin and Leah and the others. Until Daniel.

"May I help you prepare supper?" Emma asked, hoping to distract her.

"We're having leftovers. You can help me make a dessert if you'd like."

Emma grinned. "What will we have?"

"I thought we'd make custard."

"Sounds delicious." Emma put thoughts of leaving from her mind for now and concentrated on spending the rest of the day with the woman who had come to mean so much to her. Her thoughts continually remained on all she'd be leaving behind when she left.

Daniel and his construction crew stopped work early because of the rain. He climbed into his buggy and headed home. Joseph would have taken Emma home by now. He thought of her too often lately. Why? It wasn't as if he could wed her. The fact that she looked as if she fit into his Amish community didn't negate the knowledge that she was an Englisher who would soon leave.

He'd had a good week at work. Next week would prove to be better, moneywise. He had saved a lot of his pay. It was time for him to look for a place to rent for his upcoming business. What if all the places he liked were more expensive than he'd anticipated?

Instead of going straight home, he decided to drive through the area to see if there were any locations that might work for him. The ideal spot would have a house and a decent outbuilding he could use as his harness shop. He thought of Emma again as he passed by some houses with outbuildings. What would she think of the homes in the area? Would she come with him to look at places if he asked? He wasn't sure what was for sale. He would have to ask around or contact a real estate agent. He might have to rent first, but he really wanted to buy a place.

He gave up after a half hour and steered his horse toward home.

Daniel drove onto his father's property and pulled the buggy close to the barn. He undid the horse and took him to his stall. After he fed and watered him, he took care of the rest of the animals before he headed in.

His *mam* was in the kitchen making supper. His father sat at the kitchen table with a steaming cup of coffee before him. They both looked over as he came in. *"Hallo."*

"Daniel," his mother greeted.

Then he turned his attention to his father. "Did you get what you wanted done today, *Dat*?"

Samuel Lapp nodded. "*Ja*, Joseph and I worked on the new outbuilding we started."

"Do you want to work on it tonight?" He couldn't take off from his job, but he could work on it after hours.

"No need. Another day's work is all we need."

"I took care of the animals," Daniel said. "What's for supper?"

"Can't you smell it?" his mother teased.

"Fried chicken." Daniel loved fried chicken. Did Emma know how to make it? he wondered.

"With mashed potatoes and green beans."

He grinned. "My favorite. Any coffee left?" When his mother nodded, he took a mug from the cabinet and filled it. He sat next to his father and fixed his coffee. "Where's Joseph?"

"Upstairs washing up."

"Did he take Emma home?"

Samuel shrugged. "He said he did."

As if on cue, Joseph entered the kitchen, his hair wet and in freshly laundered clothes. "Said he did what?" he asked.

"Take Emma home."

Joseph nodded. "*Ja*. Got her there before the rain hit hard."

"I appreciate it."

"Did she give you any trouble?"

"*Nay*, but—" His brother's brow furrowed. "Would you come outside with me for a minute?" He shot his parents a quick look."

Daniel frowned. "Is something wrong?"

"Not really, but there is something I'd like to discuss."

He followed Joseph onto the covered front porch. "What's so important that we can't talk about it in front of *Mam* and *Dat*?"

"'Tis about Emma."

Daniel chest tightened. "What about her?"

"When I went to get her, I caught her in the cash drawer." Joseph paused. "There were no customers in the store. I asked her if she had taken anything."

"If she was stealing money?"

Joseph nodded. "*Ja*. She denied it. Said she was putting money in the drawer because Leah and Henry won't let her pay for the garments Leah gave her. Daniel, I believe she's telling the truth, but I wanted you to know." There was concern for Emma in his expression. "I feel terrible for questioning her like she was a thief. I don't really know her so I had to ask." He met Daniel's gaze directly. "She had tears in her eyes, Daniel. She was hurt that I doubted her innocence."

Daniel listened, unsure what to think. "I appreciate that you told me." Daniel wanted to trust Emma, but like his *bruder*, he would have questioned her. Still, he wanted to believe her, so he would until she proved herself a liar.

"I think she'll tell you. She was really upset."

Daniel could only nod. "We'd better go in before *Dat* comes looking for us." He managed to smile. "I'm hungry."

Joseph grinned. "I'm starving."

Daniel's mind was on Emma as they went back into the house. He hated the idea that she might have stolen from Leah and Henry. It made more sense that she'd tried to pay for the clothes that Leah gave her. It probably bothered Emma not to give back what she felt she owed the Yoders.

The young woman fit in well with his community. What if it was all an act on her part? She was English, and Englishers could be deceitful. *Everyone is human and capable of deceit.* He was upset at the thought that Emma could deceive any of them.

After dinner, he could go to see his *onkel* and *endie* and visit for a spell. Arlin was like a second father to him, so it wasn't unusual for him to drop by uninvited.

He'd also get to visit with Emma, too. Daniel felt a burst of happiness as he pictured her living in his community, in his home, having his children…

*She's an Englisher. She will never stay.*

Daniel sighed. He had to confront her, make her tell the truth about whether or not she'd taken money from the store register. And what if she didn't? *I'll have to apologize for asking.*

He didn't want her to be guilty of stealing. He appreciated how hard she worked for his aunt and uncle, and for Leah and Henry. *She has no family. Is she happy here?*

He didn't need the distraction of his growing feelings for her. He needed to concentrate on getting his harness shop up and running.

"*Soohn*, you seem pensive. Are you *oll recht*?" his mother asked as he sat at the kitchen table.

"Just thinking about work," he said.

"Work?" his father teased. "Or the business you want to open?"

Daniel smiled. "The business," he confessed.

"I have some money set aside," *Dat* began.

"Nay, *Dat*, I need to do this on my own."

"There is no shame in accepting a little help when you need it," Samuel insisted. "You can pay me back once you're established and earning a good living."

Daniel regarded his father thoughtfully. "I'll keep that in mind."

His father nodded approvingly. *"Gut."*

Joseph took the seat across from him. The only one missing from the table was his sister. "Where is Hannah?" Daniel asked.

"She's visiting Rose Ann," his *mam* said. "But I expected her back by now."

Samuel frowned. "I should look for her."

"I'll look for her after supper," Daniel said.

"She's old enough for *rumspringa*," Joseph pointed out.

Though Daniel knew that, he was as concerned as his *mam* and *dat*.

A sound at the door drew their attention, then Hannah bounced in, smiling. Her eyes widened as she saw that her family was already seated for supper. "I'm sorry I'm late. I lost track of time."

"We just sat down," his mother said, looking relieved.

*"Gut."* Hannah seemed reassured.

"Come and eat." Daniel motioned to the empty chair.

"I'll wash my hands first." She walked over to the kitchen sink. "What's for dinner?"

"If you'd been here—" her father growled.

"Samuel," Katie said gently. "Would you pass the fried chicken, please?"

Hannah dried her hands with a kitchen towel, then sat in her usual seat, on Daniel's right. "Smells delicious. You're right, *Mam*. I should have been here to help," she said sincerely. "I won't be late again."

"'Tis fine, *dochter*," their *mudder* said. "You can help me with tomorrow night's supper."

Daniel observed his family while he ate. He felt warm and comfortable with them. Emma didn't have a family who made her feel that way. Had she ever? he wondered. He silently groaned. Why couldn't he stop thinking about her?

He thought of postponing his visit, but he wanted to see Emma this evening. To see Emma? Or Arlin and Missy? He'd visit with his relatives *and* Emma, he decided.

# *Chapter Ten*

The scent of vanilla wafted in the air, teasing her taste buds, as Emma learned to make custard. "It smells delicious."

"'Tis one of my favorite desserts," Missy admitted.

"What else can I help with?"

"You can take the ham and the sweet-and-sour green beans out of the refrigerator," the older woman said. "Then would you check on Arlin? He's been in his workshop for most the day."

"Okay. Should I set the table first?"

Missy smiled. *"Ja, danki."*

Emma put out plates, then placed the food in the center of the table. When she was done, she walked to the barn to where Arlin kept a small workshop in the far back corner. He liked to build birdhouses and other small wooden items. Missy had told her earlier that Arlin had started his woodworking to earn extra money to pay off medical bills after their daughter Meg had been hospitalized with a serious illness. Their Amish community, which was in Ohio at the time, had given them financial help, but Arlin had been determined to do what he could to pay off some of the bills himself. While doing so, he'd discovered he enjoyed making things, so now he did it for the joy of it rather than necessity.

Emma entered the barn and approached Arlin at his workbench. He was sawing a block of wood with a handsaw. The scent of slightly burnt wood lingered in the air. As she studied Arlin before he knew she was there, she blinked back tears. She would miss him and Missy. She had to go, but she would be leaving a huge section of her heart behind.

Arlin set down his saw and picked up a piece of sandpaper. As he sanded the newly cut wooden edges, Emma shifted closer. "Busy, I see," she said softly so she wouldn't startle him.

He smiled at her. He didn't seem in the least surprised to see her, as if he knew she'd been there all along. "Come and take a look at what I've been making."

Emma leaned closer to see a small wooden box, which was beautifully handcrafted. She saw that the lid opened and closed on tiny brass hinges. "It's lovely."

"I'm glad you like it," Arlin said. "I made it for you."

She gasped. "For me?"

*"Ja."* The man had affection in his gaze as he handed it to her.

"'Tis the most wonderful thing I've ever seen," she breathed as she cradled the box lovingly in her hands. "I've never had anything this nice before." She swallowed against a tight throat. *"Danki."*

"You are most *willkomm, dochter.*"

Her eyes filled with tears. He had called her daughter. She turned away before he could see them. "Missy said to tell you that supper's ready."

"I'll be in shortly," he promised, his voice soft.

She nodded, then quickly headed to the house, holding her precious gift. She let out a sob halfway there and paused to wipe her tears and get control of her emotions. She was leaving. She didn't want to go, but she knew she couldn't stay. This Amish community practiced shunning, and the knowledge urged her to leave town before they learned the truth about her.

She'd have to write a note to soften the blow and thank them. She would confess that her time with them, as short as it was, had been the best time of her life. She would go, and she would take this handmade box with her, a memory of when she'd been regarded as a daughter by a kind man and his wife.

Emma entered the kitchen, showed Missy what Arlin had made for her, then took it to her room, where it would stay for only a few hours more. Then she went downstairs and joined Missy and Arlin at the supper table, where she pretended that everything was fine. Her heart was breaking as she smiled and ate supper, and then as she helped Missy clean the dishes and put them away afterward. She was about to plead tiredness and head up to her room when a knock on the side door stopped her. Seconds later, Daniel greeted them as he let himself in.

"I'd like to take Emma for a ride while there is still a hint of sunlight," he said. "We won't be gone long." He locked gazes with her. "Emma?"

Because she cared for him, she agreed. "I'll get my

sweater," she said, and went to retrieve it from her room. She wanted—needed—to spend a little more time in his company before she left. She heard him talking with his uncle as she reached the bottom stair landing.

"I thought I'd take Emma for ice cream at Whittier's. Do you want any?"

She couldn't hear what Arlin said. She entered the room, and his uncle was smiling, so he must be fine with Daniel's plans.

Daniel met her gaze. "Do you like ice cream?" he asked.

"*Ja*, of course." It felt like there was something more beneath Daniel's invitation. If this wasn't strictly a social call, then what was it? Had Joseph told him what he'd seen earlier today? Would Daniel believe her innocent or guilty of stealing from the Yoders?

Suddenly, it was important to her that she and Daniel be on good terms when she left.

Daniel reached his carriage before her. This vehicle was open with two large wheels to support the body, which had only enough room for two to sit in. Was it a courting buggy? From what she remembered, Amish couples courted in secret until they decided they were ready for the next step. That was when a young Amish man would approach the bishop with his intentions. The bishop would then reach out to the girl's family to gain permission on behalf of the young man for them to wed.

She didn't realize she'd stopped by the carriage, frozen in place, until Daniel lifted her into the buggy with his hands at her waist. Her heart thumped wildly. She didn't know what to make of his evening visit, but she had a bad feeling it wasn't because he wanted to buy her an ice cream.

* * *

Daniel felt Emma's tension as he settled into the seat next to her. He turned to her. "What kind of ice cream do you like?"

She shrugged without looking at him. "I like all kinds," she murmured.

He kept his tone light. "Favorite flavor?"

Emma met his gaze then. They hadn't left the property, and he wouldn't until she answered his question. He searched her pretty brown eyes for any clue to what she was thinking and found nothing except perhaps sadness. The realization floored him. "Chocolate chip mint," she breathed.

He laughed. "Mine, too."

She beamed at him, her happiness stealing his breath away.

"Let's go get some," he said. He flicked the reins and headed the buggy toward the road. A quick glance at the house showed his aunt and uncle standing at the window. When they saw he had caught sight of them, they waved and grinned, then disappeared.

Daniel suddenly felt lighthearted as he drove the short distance to Whittier's Store. He was spending time with Emma. He liked being with her. He pushed the thought of her stealing from his mind. She might tell him on his own. Joseph believed her. But then why did his brother tell him what he'd seen? In case she mentioned it, Joseph had said. And if she didn't?

He focused on her sitting beside him, on the way the light breeze teased the tendrils of her hair that escaped from beneath her prayer *kapp.* Whittier's Store loomed ahead. Owned by Bob Whittier, an Englisher, it was a frequent stop for many in his community. He wondered if Emma had ever visited, but one look at her face showed him that she hadn't.

Daniel pulled up to the hitching post, got down and tied up his horse. "Nay, Emma. Please wait," he said when he saw Emma move as if to climb down. She waited while he skirted the buggy and reached up to lift her down. The warmth of her waist beneath his hands reminded him that she was someone he could care about. He released her quickly and stepped back in his attempt to put some emotional distance between them.

Without prompting, Emma entered the store with him following.

"Daniel," Bob Whittier said.

*"Hallo,"* Daniel greeted warmly. "We've come for ice cream." He looked at Emma. "Cup or cone?"

She glanced up at him shyly. "May I have a cone, please?"

He couldn't help but smile at her. "Two cones with chocolate chip mint ice cream."

"Coming right up," Bob said with a grin. He fixed their cones and handed each of them one with a couple of napkins.

"Thank you, Bob." Daniel paid the man. "Have a nice evening."

"Be careful to get home before the storm hits," the man warned. "The weather forecast is calling for a severe thunderstorm."

Daniel nodded. "We'll eat our ice cream and then be on our way." He and Emma went outside. He gestured toward a picnic table at the side of the building.

It was still bright. Fortunately, the earlier rain and cloud cover had disappeared. The sun shone on the horizon. The evening was cool, but Emma should be warm enough with her sweater. Of course, that could change once she started to eat her ice cream.

"Do you want a soda or a bottle of water?" Daniel asked, just thinking of it now.

"Nay, I'm fine. *Danki*." She took a lick of her cone. "I haven't had ice cream in a long time."

Daniel gazed at her. "You haven't?"

She shook her head. "I appreciate this, Daniel. More than you'll ever know."

He frowned. Her voice was wistful, as if she were already thinking about the time she would leave. "We'll have to do this again," he said with conviction.

She merely smiled, looking sad.

They ate in silence for a time. Her sadness was a tangible thing. He could sense it and realized that she was in pain. "Emma," he began carefully, "what's wrong?"

"I'm fine," she said quickly. Too quickly.

He stayed silent. He wanted her to tell him about what Joseph had seen today.

Suddenly, she stiffened. "He told you," she said. "Joseph told you he thought I was stealing from Leah and Henry."

"*Ja*, he did," Daniel said, "and he also said that you said you weren't stealing but trying to pay for the garments Leah gave you."

She glanced at him with surprise. *"Ja."* There was only innocence in her beautiful brown eyes.

He smiled. "I know." He hadn't believed her capable of such deceit—not when he thought about it on the way over to the house. He felt as if he knew this woman inside and out, and he liked what he saw.

Her eyes warmed as she grinned at him. "*Danki*, Daniel."

He shrugged but held her gaze. He glanced down at her hands again. "Your cone is dripping."

She gasped and bent to lick it. And he laughed. Because he liked having her near. *She is an Englisher*, he reminded himself. *But she fits in so well*, a little voice inside argued. Only time would tell what the future held. He hoped it meant more of him spending time with her, but there was a big chance that she would leave and never return once she turned eighteen. Unless he could convince her that his Amish community and his family was where she belonged.

"We should get going," Daniel said.

Emma saw him eyeing the horizon. "Okay." She reached for his soiled napkins and threw them out.

He smiled at her as they walked back to his vehicle. He helped her up, then climbed onto the other side. The sky in the distance had darkened. It was far enough away that she thought they could both get home safely. Would the thunderstorm go on all night? If it did, she wouldn't be leaving this evening. She could go in the morning or tomorrow night. She preferred to leave before the sun rose and not after sunset, with the long night of darkness making her feel unsafe.

Would she ever feel safe again once she left Missy and Arlin's home? She wished she could stay but knew she couldn't. Would Daniel be angry once he realized that she'd gone? She would try to explain everything to him in a note. She only hoped that he would understand and forgive her.

Emma was conscious of him sitting beside her, his competent hands on the reins. The night air had warmed considerably, which might have been due to the approaching storm. "Will you have enough time to get home safely after you drop me off?" she asked with concern.

Daniel met her gaze. "I'll have plenty of time."

She felt the tension of worry leave her body. *"Gut."* She thought of what she'd done in the store today. "Do you think Leah will notice that I put money in the register?"

"When they run a register accounting, they'll know."

She gasped and closed her eyes. She felt him shift beside her. She looked at him and was surprised to see him watching her through narrowed eyes. "How can I ever repay them if they refuse to take my money?" she said.

His expression softened. "Leah gave with her heart. She doesn't want to be repaid."

Warmth settled in her chest. "You are all so generous and giving." She sighed. "I've never met anyone like you…and your family." Emma saw his curiosity and averted her gaze. "When I was little, I had family who loved me, but that was long ago."

"Emma."

She hugged herself with her arms.

"Emma, look at me." She faced him, and he said, "You deserve more than you've had. You know that, don't you?"

Did she? "I guess so."

Daniel steered the carriage onto Arlin's property.

"Know so," he stated firmly. He pulled close to the side door. He came around to help her down. "You look tired. I hope you sleep well."

She paused before going to the house. "*Danki* for a lovely evening, Daniel Lapp."

"You are more than *willkomm*, Emma Stoltzfus," he replied with a smile. "*Gut* night."

"*Gut* night." She turned away before he saw the tears in her eyes. Emma Stoltzfus, he'd called her, as if she already belonged to the family. She wouldn't see him again, and the knowledge pained her. She heard him leave, the sound of horse hooves and the contact of the metal buggy wheels against dirt and gravel.

"Farewell, Daniel Lapp," she breathed softly.

Emma wiped her eyes, drew herself up, pasted a smile on her face and entered the house, where she greeted Missy and Arlin and told them of the evening she'd spent with Daniel.

Three hours later, when she was in bed, the storm started as a low rumble of thunder. Emma had never been fond of thunderstorms. From an early age, she'd been frightened of the thunder. When her parents' deaths had occurred one rainy, stormy night, she'd become terrified instead of just scared. Every storm since then reminded her of the loss of her mother and father. She lay on her side with the covers pulled up over her chin, waiting for the full force of the storm to hit. When it did, she jumped every time there was a flash of lightning followed by a sharp crack of thunder. The rain fell in torrents, beating against the roof and obscuring the view outside. She pulled the covers up over her head but found little comfort. Were Missy and Arlin awake with all the noise? Emma didn't want to be alone. If they were up, she wanted to get up, too. Maybe then she'd find comfort in the safety of their kindness and caring.

She threw off the covers and got out of bed. Emma opened the door and peered into the hallway. There was no light in the room down the hall. Could they be downstairs? What of the animals? Would they be all right in the barn?

She went back into her room and grabbed her penlight. Switching it on, she left her bedroom and went downstairs. The penlight was slowly dying. *Please don't die yet.*

Emma made it to the bottom of the stairs. A light shone from the kitchen. Relieved, she rushed toward the room, halting when she saw Arlin and Missy at the kitchen table with steaming mugs. She was trembling when she entered.

"Can I join you?" she asked shakily.

"Emma." Missy took one look at her and hurried to her side. Slipping her arm around Emma's shoulders, she led her to a kitchen chair. "Sit, and I'll make you tea. Unless you want something cold?"

Emma hugged herself with her arms. "Tea is fine. *Danki*."

"You don't like storms," Arlin said.

She shook her head. "I hate them."

"My Leah is—was—the same way. She's been afraid since she was caught in a storm when she was only three."

Emma widened her eyes. "Leah afraid?"

"She was." He nodded. "Probably still is, but Henry

has helped her tremendously. 'Tis funny how the love of a good man cures a lot of things."

Missy and Arlin exchanged loving looks. Emma thanked Missy when she placed a cup of tea on the table before her. She took a sip and realized that Missy had fixed her tea just the way she liked it. "I've always disliked thunderstorms," she admitted. "And it only got worse after my parents were killed in a car crash during a storm."

Missy took the seat beside Emma's. "I can't say I'm too comfortable with them myself. This one is particularly noisy. Neither one of us could sleep."

"*Ja*. I can't either."

"Tell us, Emma," Arlin urged with a small smile. "What do you think of our Daniel?"

Emma blushed. "He's nice."

"He's a fine young man."

She nodded.

"I think he likes you."

"I'm an Englisher," she reminded them. "He's polite because that is his nature."

"I don't think that's entirely true." Arlin took a sip from his cup. "Didn't you like going for a ride with him?"

"I did," Emma murmured.

"You need to stop worrying about where you came from," Missy scolded kindly. "You're here with us now."

"*Ja*, I know, but—"

The woman shook her head to stop her. Emma sighed. If they ever found out who she was and what her family had done, she'd lose their kindness and respect. "Tell me about your daughters growing up," she asked, hoping to change the subject."

Arlin and Missy were more than willing to tell stories about each of their daughters. Emma was shocked to learn that Leah was their niece before they'd adopted her as their daughter. Missy's sister Christine had given birth to a baby girl but had been unable to care for her. Christine would come to visit her child—as an aunt. But then Leah's birth mother was killed in a car crash shortly after Leah's adoption was final.

Emma felt for the woman who had died. She'd been so young to have a baby, too young to die before she'd ever really lived.

Fortunately, Missy and Arlin loved Leah as if they'd given her life. The couple spoke lovingly of Charlie and Ellie and Nell and Meg. Before Emma knew it, the storm had moved away, leaving the night quiet and peaceful. It was close to midnight when they went back to bed.

Missy stopped Emma at the top of the stairs. "'Tis late and you've barely slept. You should sleep in tomorrow morning. Don't worry about getting up to tend the animals."

"I don't mind."

"If you can sleep late, sleep, Emma," Arlin said with affection. "I'll handle the animals in the morning. You'll need to be well rested before you go to work."

Agreeing because she had no other choice as far as Missy and Arlin were concerned, Emma went to bed. She'd planned to leave tonight, but the storm—and the knowledge that Leah needed her to work—had her postponing her departure. What if she left and it stormed again? Where would she find shelter or sleep? How would she eat? The idea of sleeping in a barn again after enjoying a comfortable bed didn't sit well with her. She'd stay a little longer, and for now, she wouldn't think about being shunned or her departure.

As she lay in bed, Emma thought of her parents and how they hadn't regretted leaving their Amish church community. Now that she was living in Happiness as an Amish woman, she had so many questions for them.

She could stay until her eighteenth birthday. She liked the idea because it meant that she would see Daniel again until she had to leave. He said he'd buy her ice cream again. Would he take her before she left for good? She didn't care how she spend her time with Daniel, as long as she could enjoy more moments in his company. Moments she could store as precious memories before she had to go.

# *Chapter Eleven*

Now that she'd decided to stay for the time being, Emma felt that her week was flying by quickly. Daniel took her to work each morning. Joseph picked her up each afternoon. The day after she'd put money in the register, Henry had done a register accounting. Joseph was in the store waiting for her when Henry had confronted her about what he'd found.

"The register tape doesn't match the cash in the drawer. There is too much money."

Joseph chuckled. "I know why," he said before Henry could accuse her of overcharging someone.

Emma glared at him. "Joseph."

"She put money in the register to pay for the garments Leah gave her."

Henry narrowed his gaze at her.

"I had no choice. You wouldn't take back my pay," she said softly, his look making her avert her glance.

"Because you earned it, Emma," he replied quietly.

He sounded more resigned than angry. She met his gaze. "Please keep the money. 'Tis not much. *Please.* 'Tis important to me."

Leah's husband gazed at her steadily for a long moment, then sighed. She caught his reluctant nod. She grinned at him. *"Danki."*

When payday came around on Thursday, Henry paid her. "Don't even think about returning a single penny of it."

Emma smiled. *"Oll recht."*

Sunday was church service day. After helping Missy in the kitchen on Saturday, Emma rose while it was still dark and stared out the window as dawn was but a promise in the sky with barely enough light to see. She thought of how much her life had changed since coming to live with Missy and Arlin.

Emma dressed quickly, then went out to feed the animals. Sunday or not, taking care of them was a necessary task, thus allowed by the bishops. She did the work quickly, then returned inside to find Jeremiah asleep in his bed in the corner of the kitchen. As she shut the door behind her, the little dog woke and looked up at her. He stretched his black-and-white body before he came to her with a doggy grin and eyes that pleaded for attention.

Emma beamed at him. Jeremiah waited at the door for her to attach his leash. Then she opened the door and watched as the dog bounded outside, dragging her behind him. She laughed. "Jeremiah, stop, boy! Hold up. I'll get you where you want to go." She took him on a brisk walk and returned to the house. Missy and Arlin were in the kitchen when she came in. "What time do we need to leave for service?" she asked.

"Church is at nine. My sister and her husband are hosting today," Arlin told her.

Emma's belly began to flutter. "Daniel's parents?"

*"Ja."* Missy smiled at her. "Breakfast is ready—muffins and biscuits."

Her lips curved. "Sounds *wunderbor*." Emma sat in her usual place at the table across from Missy with Arlin beside her at the end. A cup of coffee steamed from its place above her plate. Emma saw it, then smiled at her Amish foster mother with gratitude.

"Eat," Missy urged with a small smile.

Emma grabbed a muffin, then reached for the butter that Arlin had passed to her. She took a bite, and the sweet taste hit her tongue, causing her to make a sound of appreciation. When she realized that Missy and Arlin were staring at her, she blushed and carefully set the muffin on her plate. "I'm sorry. It's delicious."

Missy beamed while Arlin studied her with affection. "I'm glad you like it," Missy said. "'Tis *gut* that you enjoy your food, Emma. You were too thin when you first came to us."

Emma couldn't deny it. She hadn't been given enough to eat at the Turners'. She slowly picked up the muffin for another bite. The three of them enjoyed their breakfast in silence. When they were finished, Emma helped Missy put away the leftovers and threw out the paper plates they'd used.

"Why don't you get into your church clothes? I laid them out on your bed for you."

Emma stilled. "You got me new garments?"

"Just church clothes."

She blinked rapidly, close to tears. "*Danki*, Missy. I don't know what to say."

"You can say 'I'm getting ready for church,'" Missy said with good humor.

She grinned and headed upstairs.

The royal blue dress that lay on her bed looked brand-new, as if it had been specially made for her recently. Emma studied the garment and noted the tiny neat and even stitching. Missy's handiwork, she thought. She washed up, then changed into her new clothes. Over the dress, she donned a white full-length apron. She undid her hair and brushed it, then rerolled and pinned it before covering it with the new white prayer *kapp* that had been on the bed next to the dress.

After putting on black stockings and shoes, Emma went back downstairs and entered the kitchen. She felt suddenly shy in her new garments. Arlin glanced at her as she came into the room, nodding his approval. "Wife," he called, and Missy turned from the counter, saw Emma and smiled.

"It fits you well."

Emma nodded.

Missy held up an iced tea pitcher. "Would you like some? There is still time for a cup before we need to leave."

"Is there any coffee left?" she asked.

*"Ja."* Missy poured her a fresh cup before Emma could do it herself. Emma sat.

"You took care of the animals this morning," Arlin said gruffly as he watched her pour some milk into her cup.

*"Ja."*

"And you took Jeremiah for a walk. For a little one,

he has a lot of energy. 'Tis nice to have you pitch in with him."

Warmth filled her that Arlin was willing to share his precious pet with her. The three of them chatted to pass the time, which easily slipped by them. Missy glanced at the clock and stood. "We need to go if we don't want to be late for church service," she said.

Emma felt a sudden rush of nerves as she picked up a huge bowl of potato salad and carried it out to the buggy.

There would be a lot of people at the service. People she'd never met before. Daniel would be there along with his brothers, their wives, their children, his sister and his parents. And who knew what other members of the community. The thought of meeting so many new people scared her.

It was a short ride to the Samuel Lapp property. Arlin pulled his family buggy in at the end of a long line of parked carriages. Emma waited for him to tie up the horse, then she grabbed the potato salad they made for the midday meal and climbed out of the vehicle after Missy.

Her Amish foster mother carried a sheet cake. "There's Katie," she said, and started toward her sister-in-law. Emma immediately followed. She stopped when she caught sight of Daniel surrounded by three young women in the backyard. He was chatting and smiling as if he were enjoying their company.

Emma's gut clenched. Daniel was way too handsome for her peace of mind. He was dressed like every other Amish man there, in a white shirt with black vest, black pants and a black felt wide-brimmed hat. She watched as one of the women said something to him and he laughed, drawing attention to the fact that he'd done very little laughing in her company. She liked the man, and she shouldn't. Their outing for ice cream had been the most fun she'd had in…forever. She looked away and continued toward the house.

"Emma?"

Emma turned and flushed when she saw Daniel's mother. "'Tis *gut* to see you again. We're glad you could come," Katie Lapp said. "Missy was telling me how much of a help you've been to her and Arlin."

"I like to help." She eyed Missy worriedly. "I'd like to do more."

Missy blinked. "Dear child, if you did anything more, there would be nothing at all for me to do." She placed a gentle hand on her shoulder. "You do more than enough. I wish you wouldn't work so hard."

Emma gazed at her with wide eyes. "I don't want you to have to work so hard." While she was here, she thought. For she'd be leaving soon. She sighed and looked away, toward the backyard—and Daniel.

Arlin joined them. He smiled at his sister. "Katie."

Katie grinned. "Always *gut* to see you, *bruder*."

"Arlin!" Katie's husband Samuel waved him over to the group of men he was chatting with.

"They'll talk about the weather," Missy confided, "and who knows what else until 'tis time for service."

Emma managed a smile. She refused to look in Daniel's direction again, because seeing him with those other women hurt too much. "Shall I take the food inside?" she asked as she reached for the sheet cake with her other arm.

Katie smiled. "Of course." Emma nodded. "You can put the potato salad in the refrigerator if you can find room."

Balancing the large potato bowl and the sheet cake in a metal pan with lid, Emma climbed the porch steps, wondering how she would open the door with her hands full. She set the bowl on the arm of a porch chair and tugged open the door. With her hip holding it open, she leaned back for the potato salad. As she stretched to reach it, she saw a masculine hand pick it up for her. Emma looked back and drew a sharp breath. It was Daniel.

"May I carry this in for you?" he said with a twinkle in his eye.

She nodded, then entered the house.

"Straight through toward the back of the house," Daniel instructed from behind her. Heart thumping hard, she found the kitchen and set the cake on the counter. Conscious of Daniel behind her, she turned for the potato salad, but he had already placed it inside the refrigerator for her.

Soon he faced her. *"Danki,"* she murmured. Why was she comfortable with him one moment and uncomfortable the next?

Daniel nodded. "Nice dress," he said pleasantly.

She flushed with pleasure until she recalled him in the backyard with the other women.

Before she could formulate a response, the back door that led directly into the kitchen opened, and a young woman entered. Emma immediately recognized her as one of those women he'd been chatting with.

"Daniel! I wondered where you went," the woman said.

"Maryanne," he murmured.

She was blond, blue-eyed and beautiful. She made Emma feel like the ugly foster child in comparison. "Who is this?" Maryanne said with a long look at Emma.

"This is Emma. She is a cousin from my aunt's side of the family." His expression softened as he met Emma's gaze. "Emma, meet Maryanne Troyer. Her family moved into our church district a few months ago."

Emma shifted uncomfortably under the woman's blue gaze. "'Tis nice to meet you," she murmured.

"Same here," the woman said without warmth.

Something flashed in Daniel's expression. Emma couldn't read his thoughts, but she suddenly felt as if she were intruding. She needed to get away. "Excuse me. Missy is waiting," she said, and headed toward the back door.

"I'll walk you out," Daniel piped up, shocking her.

Emma caught a glimpse of something dark flash in the woman's blue gaze. "Daniel," she called out as he followed Emma. "You'll be attending the singing this evening, *ja*?"

"I might be," he said. "But that will depend on Emma." Then to her surprise, he reached for Emma's hand and tugged her to exit the house, only releasing her to grab the door and hold it open for her.

Emma rushed ahead of him toward Missy, who was still talking with Katie.

"Emma," Daniel said, halting her, prompting her to face him. "Don't let her upset you. She's immature for her age."

"*Danki*, Daniel." Emma noticed that Katie and Missy

were moving toward the barn. She hurried to join them for church service.

Missy turned as Emma caught up with her. "Just in time."

She nodded, following Missy and Katie into the barn. To her surprise, Daniel caught up to her and entered the barn alongside her.

The pulpit was surrounded on three sides by benches. Daniel parted ways with her to take a seat in the left section where men were already seated. Missy waved for her to follow toward the right where women and their children sat. Emma sat next to Missy and watched as others quietly filed in. A man moved to the pulpit and waited for everyone to enter and be seated. Women and children filled the middle and far side while the men sat with their older sons in the section where Daniel had taken a seat.

Once all church members were seated, the preacher started to speak. Emma listened carefully and watched the others in the room who looked intent, engaged. Everyone stood and began to sing, an odd chanting sound without musical instruments. The song—a hymn—spiked a childhood memory. The way the hymn was sung might be different, but she remembered the words as clearly as if she'd sung them yesterday. Her lips began to move as she joined in. When the hymn ended, she listened closely to the preacher and felt a strong sense of God in the room. Just like when she'd been to service with her *mam* and *grossmamma.* Memories of the past flooded her. Fighting tears, she closed her eyes and offered up a silent prayer for everything she'd lost and everything she wished for. A life with a family like the

Stoltzfuses and the Lapps. A life filled with love and caring without the terror and threat of the Turners, her foster family.

The service continued with another hymn and the deacon adding a few words of wisdom before church finally ended at midday. Emma rose and followed Missy outside. The day had begun with cool temperatures but had warmed up considerably. She looked for Daniel, but didn't see him.

Missy touched her arm, drawing her attention. "Follow me. We need to put the food out."

She nodded and trailed after her toward the house. As she crossed the yard, she saw Daniel standing alone, leaning against a buggy. Their eyes met, and Emma's cheeks grew warm. She forced her attention on being part of the community and found she liked the feeling of belonging. It brought back memories of her time in Indiana and the love of her family.

Emma helped the other women put out all the food, then sat with the Stoltzfuses and their daughters and their families at one of the makeshift tables that the men had set up in the yard. A large plate of food lay before her on the table, but she wasn't hungry. Her stomach churned as she attempted to eat. Her thoughts centered on Daniel. She tried not to stare in his direction, but he continually drew her attention.

"Are you *oll recht*?" Leah smiled as she sat down next to her.

Emma nodded. "I'm fine. How are you feeling?"

"Big."

She grinned. "Have you been getting enough rest?"

Leah chuckled. "I have, thanks to you."

"Leah, I don't know how to—"

"Emma, don't say it," Leah warned with a frown.

Dread filled her stomach. "What?"

"Don't tell me how grateful you are and how you need to repay me."

She averted her gaze. "But I do."

"From what Henry told me, you already did. You put money in the cash register. Over a hundred dollars!"

"You gave me a job, clothes and a home with your parents." Emma would leave another hundred dollars for Missy and Arlin when she left. She'd be fine now that she'd earned a second week's pay. With nearly three hundred dollars, she'd be able to travel farther than if she'd left on Monday when originally planned.

Leah regarded her with a soft expression. "You deserve everything, and I'll keep telling you that until you believe it."

"Anyone for dessert?" Leah's sister Charlie said as she approached.

Leah and Emma grinned. "We are," they both said together.

She would enjoy her time here, know that God had blessed her with these people, and she would thank Him every day while here and after she'd gone.

"I want the chocolate cake," Emma said.

"Me, too," Leah declared. "But why don't we try a little of everything?"

Emma smiled. "Sounds *gut* to me." She stood and followed Leah to the dessert table, catching Daniel's eye as she did. Her heart stopped beating as he continued to watch her, his expression unreadable, until she forced herself to move on and focus on enjoying dessert with Leah and the Stoltzfus family.

A short while later, with a dessert plate on the table before her, she rose to pour herself an iced tea. Standing at the drink table, she sensed Daniel beside her.

"Emma," he said warmly. "Would you like to take a ride after lunch? I'll ask Joseph and Hannah to come with us," he added, as if she needed convincing.

She looked up into his brown eyes, and she couldn't say no. "*Ja*, I'd like that."

His smile made her heart beat faster. "I'll tell Joseph and Hannah. Let me know when you're done with dessert."

Emma nodded, watching as he headed to his family table where he spoke briefly with his brother and sister. She saw both smile as they gazed in her direction.

Anticipation ran wild as she enjoyed her dessert. When she was done, she put her paper plate and plasticware in the trash, then turned to look for Daniel. He was already approaching her. She smiled at him as he reached her.

"Ready to go?"

"*Ja*, just let me tell Missy and Arlin."

"Joseph is telling them now."

Surprised, Emma saw that Joseph and Hannah were talking with their aunt and uncle. "What is he saying to them?"

A small smile of amusement played about his lips. "Who knows? As long as we get to go, I don't care what they tell them."

Emma raised her eyebrows. "Daniel…"

"I'm teasing, Emma. They're simply telling them we're going for a ride to check out locations."

"Locations?" she asked.

"I'm looking for a place to open a harness shop."

"I remember that," she said.

"I should be able to open it by next month at the latest."

*After I'm gone*, Emma thought. She would have liked to see his business, watch him at work. He would be talented and dedicated, intent on providing excellent service to his customers.

"Is that why we're going for a ride?"

"I want to take you on a ride because I like spending time with you," he admitted.

Her breath caught. "I don't know what to say."

"Tell me you won't change your mind."

"I won't."

"We'll take the open wagon," Daniel said to Joseph as his brother and sister reached their sides.

"Sounds *gut* to me."

"You'll ride in the back with Hannah," Daniel whispered to his brother, but Emma heard him.

Daniel wanted her to ride in the front seat with him. She felt lighthearted and happy. It was if God were smiling down on her and granting her secret wish. That Daniel would like her and want to be close to her. But no matter what happened in the future, she felt forever changed by her time here.

# *Chapter Twelve*

The afternoon started out pleasantly. Emma sat in Daniel's open carriage and took in the scenery. The air was fresh and she took a deep breath...detecting a pleasant masculine scent that was Daniel's.

Joseph and Hannah sat behind them. Daniel's siblings teased each other mercilessly and made amusing comments about various members of their family. Joseph teased Daniel for a long while about making Emma sit up front with him.

"Where are we going, *bruder*?" Hannah asked after he turned onto a country lane with vast open farmland on both sides of the road.

"No place special. Just taking a drive to show Emma the area," he said.

Emma met his gaze. "Is there someplace in particular you want me to see?"

He grinned at her. "Nay, but if I see something interesting, we'll stop and take a look."

Daniel steered the horse through several turns that took them onto a number of country roads. They passed an ice cream shop in the middle of nowhere. "They make great ice cream here," he told her. "We'll come back when the place is open. 'Tis run by members of our community, and therefore it's closed on Sundays."

Emma loved that Daniel had suggested another outing together. If things continued to go well, she'd be able to enjoy going for ice cream with him. If not… she didn't want to think about her situation and how she could be long gone before she ever had a chance to drive back for ice cream.

Thoughts of Bryce Turner gave her chills, and she rubbed her arms.

"Cold?" Daniel asked after a glance in her direction.

"I'm fine." His concern made her feel good. She was safe with Daniel. Bryce would never search for her in an Amish community. She was sure of it.

Daniel drove through a few turns, then headed back toward the main road. Before they reached it, Emma saw it—a white house set back from the country lane about a hundred feet or more. Next to it was a small barn and beyond that a smaller outbuilding. The house was plain enough for her to believe that it belonged to an Amish family. There was a for-sale sign in the front yard.

Without thinking, Emma instinctively put her hand on Daniel's arm. "Daniel…"

"I see it," he breathed. He pulled over to the side of the road. The sign had a phone number and said the house was for sale by the owner. "Joseph, would you come up front and take care of the horse?"

Daniel climbed down from the vehicle. "Emma?" He reached up a hand, and she allowed him to lift her down. Together they both walked down the fine gravel driveway toward the house.

"Do you think anyone is home?"

He stared at the house. "I don't think anyone is living here at present."

Emma nodded. She accompanied him to the house. They went to the front door, and he knocked. After waiting a few moments, Daniel knocked again. "You're right. Looks like no one is here."

Without saying anything, they went to a window and looked in. There was no furniture. The vinyl floors looked as if they had been installed recently. They walked around to the back of the house and saw a kitchen with a refrigerator and stove as well as oak cabinets. "It looks nice," Emma murmured.

*"Ja,"* Daniel said quietly. Emma could sense his excitement. As if he liked what he saw and was considering buying it. Emma envisioned Daniel living here with a wife—some other woman—and felt a sadness wash over her. But she couldn't worry about that. She was here with Daniel right now, and she was glad that he allowed her to share this with him.

"Shall we look at the barn and outbuilding?" Emma asked.

"*Gut* idea." But Daniel was already moving in that direction. He went to the barn first and opened the door. The inside was empty, the stalls clean. So far everything was in move-in condition. Then he led her to the small building in the backyard. It was a ten-by-ten building with a window. The door opened easily, and whatever he saw inside made him gasp. "Perfect," he said. "This place is perfect."

Emma knew then that Daniel wanted this place—and badly. She said a silent prayer that he would be able to afford it, that no one jumped in to purchase it out from under him before he had his chance to make an offer.

He shut the door. "We should go," he said quietly. His expression was thoughtful, worried. At that moment, Emma wanted to give him all the money she had—just under three hundred dollars. If it helped him realize his dream, she'd be fine with giving it all away. She'd figure out a way to get by once she left Happiness. She'd done it before, and she could do it again.

The ride home with Daniel back at the reins was quieter than when they'd started out.

"Nice place, Daniel," Joseph said. "Going to buy it?"

"If I can, *ja*," Daniel muttered, his grip tight on the leathers.

Emma felt the urge to cover his hand with hers. "You'll find a way," she murmured, believing it to be true.

He shot her a surprised look. Staring at her a moment, his face erupted into a genuine smile. "*Danki*, Emma."

She frowned. "For what?"

"For believing in me."

She blushed and looked away. He was more than competent in anything he did. Why did he question it? Unlike her, who couldn't decide what to do. The best thing she'd ever done was come back to Happiness to see Leah. She sighed. Her temporary place with the Stoltzfuses was nothing she could take credit for. It was because of Leah and Henry and everyone else.

* * *

Daniel heard Emma sigh. "What's wrong?"

She smiled at him reassuringly. "Nothing to worry about." She paused. "My birthday is in three weeks."

"And you'll be eighteen," he said gruffly. The thought of her leaving bothered him, although he'd always known that the day would come. "It's too bad you couldn't stay here…" he murmured.

He felt her tense and sensed her gaze on him. "Forever? Daniel…"

"I know. You can't stay." *You don't want to stay*, he thought bitterly.

"I don't belong here," she whispered.

Daniel looked in her eyes, saw the sorrow in them, the tears. Something jolted inside him. "Emma—"

"Hey, look!" his sister exclaimed, pointing toward a vehicle parked on the side of the road close to the dirt entrance to his family's property.

"That's David Fisher," Joseph said with surprise.

Hannah started to stand up to better see. "Do you think he's come to ask forgiveness?"

"Could be," Daniel said, but he doubted it. The man was seated in his buggy, and he hadn't made a move to get out. No doubt he missed his family members who were in his parents' house.

Daniel turned on his left blinker and turned into the lot. "Don't look at him. Don't make eye contact," he told Emma and his siblings. "I hate this, but 'tis not allowed since he was shunned."

Emma hadn't said a word, but he could feel her withdraw from him, her shoulders so tense that he wanted to reach out and rub them for her. Which, of course, he would never do, as it wasn't proper unless they were husband and wife. Daniel's jaw tightened. Which they'd never be, as she would be leaving them—*him*—in three weeks. Suddenly, the excitement of finding the perfect place for his business and new home disappeared. But he would work for it anyway. Whether Emma stayed or not, he would start his harness shop business, and eventually wed and start a family.

Emma didn't wait for his help getting out of the carriage. He watched her stride toward his aunt and uncle and their family, watched her speak to Leah, who frowned and stood up to follow Emma, who moved away from the others.

What was she telling them? Was she reminding them that her birthday was just around the corner and she'd be leaving soon? Was she telling them about David Fisher, the shunned man who had parked his buggy in the street in front of the house?

Emma left Leah and went to the beverage table. He watched her pour two cups of tea. To his shock, she headed in his direction. "I thought you might be thirsty," she said softly. She held out a cup to him.

He held her gaze, begging to know her thoughts, as he nodded and took the cup from her. He smiled his thanks.

"I had a nice time today, Daniel," she began carefully, and he sensed a "but" coming. "I hope you get the house and the property. It's perfect for your business and your home. I'll be thinking of you living there someday, happy with a wife." She stopped. "And children."

"Emma, we still have time to spend together."

She shook her head. "Do you think that's wise? Knowing that I'll have to leave?"

"I don't care if 'tis wise. I want to see you and take you for ice cream again. We can go to that ice cream shop we saw today, or we can go back to Whittier's." He took a sip from his cup. It was all he could do to keep his hands steady as he lowered his drink. "Think about it, Emma."

She nodded. "I will."

And he could only hope and pray that God would allow him to find a way to keep them together, because Englisher or not, he wanted Emma in his life—as he was realizing more and more that she was already in his heart.

She remained by his side for the next hour until Missy and Arlin decided it was time to go home. She'd been overly quiet since their conversation about ice cream and spending more time together.

"I'll see you in the morning, Emma," he said as he walked her toward Arlin's carriage.

Emma frowned as she looked up at him. "In the morning?"

"To take you to work? At the Yoders' store," he gently reminded her.

"Ah, *ja*. Sorry."

"Emma, are you *oll recht*?"

"I'm fine." Her smile—which didn't quite reach her eyes—didn't reassure him. "I'll see you tomorrow."

As he watched her leave with his aunt and uncle, he felt an ache inside his chest. And a sense of foreboding he didn't understand.

Daniel joined his parents, who were talking with

Bishop John. David Fisher was a relative of the bishop's, and John was unhappy with the man. "You saw the buggy parked out front, Bishop?" he asked as he came close.

The bishop nodded. "I'd hoped that he would come in, but if he expects us to accept what he's done when he shows no repentance, it's not going to happen."

"Would you like me to approach him?" his father asked.

"Nay, he knows the rules. We are not to talk with him, look at him or do business with him. If he wants to enjoy the delights of the English world, he should have thought of that before he joined the church."

Daniel couldn't imagine being ostracized by his family. He loved and needed them too much to ever give them up. Plus, he couldn't think of any reason he'd ever go against the Ordnung. He excused himself with a nod toward the bishop and his parents.

Daniel sought out his cousin Leah, who was there with her husband Henry.

Leah saw him heading her way. She left her sisters and family to meet him halfway. "You look as if you have something on your mind."

Daniel nodded. "May I talk with you?"

*"Ja."* She settled one hand on her protruding stomach while the other one waved him away from anyone who remained.

When they were alone on the side of his father's barn, Daniel met her gaze. "I like Emma."

Leah laughed. "No kidding."

His expression grew serious, concerned. "She'll be eighteen soon, and then she'll be leaving."

"I know," his cousin murmured with sympathy.

"Tell me what they did to her. Her foster parents."

"Her foster father and brother," Leah said.

Daniel felt his jaw tighten with tension. "Tell me."

"That day when you brought her to me? She had bruises on her arms. I made her show me, but I think she hid the worst of them."

"They mistreated her?"

"*Ja*, emotionally and physically."

"She needs to stay with us," he stated firmly. "With me."

"Emma may be hard to convince, but if anyone can, 'tis you." Leah eyed him with a small smile. "She cares for you."

Emotion rushed through him, and he closed his eyes. "I hope so."

"Have patience with her, Daniel," she said. "Love is worth it. I almost gave that up with Henry because I was afraid. Don't let her be afraid, Daniel. She needs you, and you need her."

Daniel smiled as determination rose up in him to give him more than hope. It gave him purpose. He wanted that house and land more than anything. Emma might be English, but he believed she'd be happy within the Amish community. He'd seen her grow from an unhappy runaway foster child to a warm, loving and hardworking young woman.

"I'll convince her," he said, and at that moment he believed it.

It was time. After a wonderful evening at home with Arlin and Missy, Emma went upstairs to bed—and to plan. While she wanted to give Daniel all of her money, she knew it wouldn't make sense for her to do so. She'd need every cent for a safe place to stay until she turned eighteen and got another job. She would miss Missy and Arlin. The thought of leaving them hurt terribly. But it was the knowledge that she wouldn't see Daniel again that broke her heart. She'd never be the same after her time here. Knowing that she'd had the love of these people, even for a short time, would sustain her through the long lonely days and nights ahead of her.

She lay in her bed, still dressed, listening as Missy and Arlin ascended the stairs and retired to their room at the end of the hall. Her heart thumped wildly in her chest. Her stomach burned, and her hands were clammy. She was scared. She wrote a note and placed it on the dresser. After another hour or so, when she was sure Missy and Arlin were asleep, she rose, took her money and put most of it in her shoes. Fortunately, the sky was clear, the stars twinkling brightly against an inky backdrop. There would be no rain tonight, no thunderstorms to terrify her during her journey.

She pulled on her sweater and buttoned it all the way up. She glanced at her Amish garments. Traveling in them wouldn't be ideal, but it was all she had now. She hadn't seen her English clothes since she left them with Leah. If she found a thrift store, she could buy some clothes. She'd draw less attention to herself if she blended better in the English world.

She left a hundred dollars on the bed, covering it with the note. She hoped Missy and Arlin would understand, and that Daniel would forgive her.

Her heart was breaking as she grabbed the new flashlight that Missy had given her recently and descended the stairs. Jeremiah was in the kitchen, curled up in his bed. She figured it was best to leave him there when she went up earlier, but now she wondered if it wouldn't have been better to lock him in her room.

The little dog had received a lot of attention from her when they'd returned home. He was obviously tired, and her crossing the kitchen to the side door didn't wake him. Sending up a silent prayer of thanks to the Lord, Emma opened up the side door, turned the lock on the inside, then pulled the door quietly shut behind her. She headed into the night with her destination unknown. *Daniel.* What she wouldn't give to see him one more time. If she did, she knew her resolve would weaken, and she'd stay. And she would risk losing him when he learned the truth. *It's better this way.*

She was blinded by her tears as she left the property and headed away from Happiness, away from the city of Lancaster where the threat of discovery still remained. She would walk until she found a hotel that she could afford, even if it was just for one night. She had two hundred and sixty-eight dollars after leaving the money for Missy and Arlin. Poor payment for a lifetime of warm and happy memories, she thought. They deserved so much more from her.

The sound of a car behind her made her take cover in the bushes in a neighbor's front yard. When the vehicle roared passed, she walked along the side of the road again, quickening her steps. She needed to get somewhere fast so she could feel safe again.

If she ever would feel safe again.

* * *

Daniel steered his buggy toward Missy and Arlin's house. He was eager to see Emma. He'd been awake most of the night thinking of her, trying to figure out a way to convince her that she should stay in Happiness. And wed him when she was older and ready for marriage. He pulled into his uncle's yard and parked. It was early, but he knew Arlin and Missy would be up. Emma, too.

He tied up his horse and ran to the side door. He tapped on the wood and smiled when as expected his aunt opened it with a grin. "Daniel, come in."

"Mornin', *Endie* Missy." He saw his uncle at the table. "*Onkel* Arlin."

His uncle nodded. "If you're looking for Emma, I'd check the barn. I haven't seen her this morning, but that's where she always is first thing."

Daniel grinned, then nearly ran toward the barn. He burst inside. "Emma!"

No one answered. "Emma! 'Tis me. Daniel. I'd like to talk with you." When she didn't answer, he checked every inch of the structure, then hurried back to the house to see if she'd come down for breakfast. "She's not in the barn," he said as he entered.

"She was tired last night," Missy said. "Maybe she slept late." She set a mug of coffee for him on the table. "Sit. I'll go up and check on her."

Daniel sat down to drink his coffee. He heard thundering on the stairs before Missy appeared, her face distraught, a handful of twenty-dollars bills in one hand and a note in the other.

"She's gone," she cried. "Emma left us. She's gone!"

Arlin stood and took the note from her. Daniel rose, his stomach clenching as he thought of the woman he loved and where she could have possibly gone. His uncle's features changed as he read Emma's note. When he was done, he silently handed Daniel the note and sat down, his face ashen.

*Dear ones,*
*You will never know just how much your kindness has meant to me. I have felt truly happy here, and if things in my life were different, I would have stayed. But I'm trouble. Bryce Turner will no doubt be searching for me. I saw something I shouldn't have seen before I ran away. He is not a* gut *man. Bryce is evil, and so is his son. I love you and will miss you. Please pray for me, although truth be told I don't deserve your attention or your prayers. Please thank Leah and Henry for me. Without Leah, I would not have enjoyed even a few moments of feeling safe and loved. Tell them I'm sorry.*

There was a spot on the page that looked as if it had been marked by a tear. Daniel felt his throat tighten.

*Please tell Daniel that I will miss him. He is* gut *and kind, and I will never forget him. He needs to buy that house and property we looked at. It is right for him, and in the future, as I look back at my time with him—with all of you—I'll think of him happy with his business on the property, and a wife with children in that house. I'm so sorry*

*for all the trouble I've caused. Know in my heart that I'll always look upon you as family. You were there for me when no one else cared.*
*Love, Emma.*

Daniel looked at his aunt and uncle. They appeared as destroyed by the note as he was. "I have to look for her."

"Where?" Arlin said.

"Anywhere. Everywhere," Daniel said. "And while I'd love to ask everyone to search for her, I believe if she sees any of us, she'll bolt again. I need to do this on my own. If I can't find her, I'll let you know." He drew in a sharp breath. "I don't want to involve the police. Emma is terrified of them. She's afraid she'll be sent back to her foster family, and we can't allow them to do that to her."

Arlin nodded. "Whatever you think is best."

"How can I help?" Missy said hoarsely, her eyes filled with tears.

The sight of their tears brought home how much the young runaway Englisher had worked her way into their hearts. *Especially mine.*

He chose Emma over his job at the construction company. There was no question in his mind that he needed to find her. He stopped by Whittier's Store first to call his foreman from Bob's phone to explain that he wouldn't be able to make it in to work today. The man was pleasant enough, although Daniel knew he wouldn't be happy if he called out for more than two days straight. But he would if he had to. He could get the property, but without Emma nothing would be the same.

And if he didn't find her today? He would keep searching for her—and he would make an offer for the house and have it ready for when he eventually found her.

As he steered his buggy to the edge of the parking lot at Whittier's, Daniel thought about where to look first. How much money did she have? She probably had made one hundred eighty dollars the first week and two hundred eighty-eight dollars her second week at the Yoders'. She'd put a hundred from her first week into the register. Then left Missy and Arlin a hundred dollars on the bed. After two weeks of work, that would leave almost three hundred dollars that she took with her.

He drew the horse to a halt and thought hard. Where would she go? She had enough money for a hotel room. At least for one night, he thought, maybe more. Daniel remembered how she didn't want to enter the city of Lancaster. *She'll go in the opposite direction.*

He flicked the leathers and turned away in the direction he thought she'd head. "Emma, where did you go?"

# *Chapter Thirteen*

Emma walked through the night without incident. Every time she heard a car or truck, she hid so no one would see her. She was cold, but she'd be fine as soon as she found a room for the night she could afford. She paused to rest a moment and realized she'd been foolish not to bring food with her. But she'd never steal from Missy and Arlin.

Emma walked until she reached a small hotel that promised a free breakfast and a room for sixty-eight dollars a night. She hadn't gone far, but it didn't matter. She was ready to get out of the night air. The hotel belonged to a familiar chain, and she figured she'd be safe there. The light was on in the front office. She entered with her small bag of belongings and approached the reservation desk. Wearing her Amish garments, she didn't look as bad as when she'd first arrived in Happiness in her threadbare English clothes. And she had money.

"I'd like a room for one night, please," she told the night manager.

The woman looked at her. "Credit card?"

"Nay." Emma shook her head. "But I have cash."

"All right. It's your lucky day. You have a choice—first or second floor?"

"Second floor, please."

"That'll be seventy dollars," the woman said.

Emma handed over the money, and the manager handed her a room key. "Breakfast is in a room off the lobby between six and nine thirty."

Emma nodded, then with key in hand, she headed toward the elevator. She found her room on the second floor and let herself in. The room was clean and had recently been scrubbed, the scent of cleaning products still in the air. A virtual paradise to someone who thought she'd have to stay in a dirty hotel somewhere. And with the added benefit of breakfast. She glanced at the alarm clock on the night table and saw that it was nearly eleven. She put her things inside a dresser drawer and hid her money in a sock, which she shoved between the mattress and bedspring. She'd put out a do-not-disturb sign whenever she left the room until she checked out. She just needed a place to rest and recharge and figure out what to do next. She set the alarm for 6:00 a.m., hoping that there would be no one at breakfast at such an early hour. Then Emma slipped beneath the covers and closed her eyes. All she could think about was Daniel and how upset he'd be once he learned she'd left.

If she didn't have the threat of Bryce Turner—or if she hadn't been shunned by her former Amish community along with her parents—she might have found a way to stay. Because she'd loved it there. But she had to keep focused on the future. Maybe tomorrow after she'd eaten and returned to her room, she could make some plans past this one night. She wouldn't get far on the money she had. Maybe she could find a job in a small town. She knew how to work a cash register. And she could wait tables. Except she was underage, and she didn't have anything to prove how old she was.

She slept until her alarm went off, then she got up, got dressed and went downstairs for breakfast. As she hoped and prayed for, there were no other diners at that early hour. Emma nodded to the night manager who was still on duty, then proceeded to fill up a plate. There were trays of eggs and sausages. And there was a waffle iron with a pitcher of batter if she wanted waffles. She chose eggs, sausage, a biscuit and an apple. She filled a cup with hot water and grabbed a tea bag, then headed upstairs to eat in her room.

As she ate breakfast, she thought of Daniel and the people she'd left behind. *Why did I leave? I had people who cared for me.* A safe place to stay until her birthday. She was doubting herself, wondering if she'd made a mistake leaving Happiness. After finishing her food, she made another cup of tea using the room's electric coffeepot. As she sipped her tea, she thought of Missy and their tea times together. She closed her eyes as she fought back tears. She'd let down everyone—Leah and Henry. Missy and Arlin. Daniel and the Lapps.

Could she go back? Apologize and ask for another chance? Would they welcome her with open arms or send her away?

"What do I have to lose?" she whispered aloud. She finished her tea, packed her few belongings and stowed her money in her shoes. She hadn't come that far. Maybe she could return before they missed her.

She went downstairs, handed in the room key and left. Emma realized that she needed to get back to Happiness. She would ask for another chance and hope they would understand that she was confused.

Emma exited the hotel and headed back the way she'd come. While she walked, she prayed and pleaded for another chance and hoped that God would lead the way back home.

Daniel drove east on Route 340, away from Bird in Hand toward Intercourse, where he pulled into the parking lot near a coffee shop. He went inside to order a cup of coffee and some pastries to share with Emma when he found her. A police officer was at the counter, waiting for his order. Daniel thought nothing of it until he saw the officer show a photo to the girl behind the counter.

"Have you seen this teenager?" the officer asked.

The girl shook her head. "I'm afraid not."

Daniel stepped up and gave his order to the girl, then turned to the officer. "You're looking for someone?" he asked casually.

The officer met his gaze. "Yes. A teen runaway from Maryland." He shoved the photo in Daniel's direction. "Her foster family is eager to get her back."

Daniel took the photo and studied it with a calm gaze while his heart beat faster and his stomach started to burn. It was Emma. Dressed in English clothes. He handed the photo back. "Can't help you." He paused. "What's her name? In case I see her," he added. He expected to hear Jessica Morgan and was stunned at the name the officer gave.

"Emma Beiler."

"Why did she run away?" Daniel asked.

The officer frowned. "That's the thing. I found her the last time she ran away. Running away a second time makes me wonder if everything was as it should have been at her foster home." He tucked the photo in his shirt pocket. "I was hoping to find her and talk with her. Find out how things really were for her there."

Daniel received his order and followed the officer outside. "What should I do if I see her?"

The officer hesitated. "Get in touch with me." He handed Daniel a business card with a phone number and the address of his police station.

"I'll do that." Daniel gave him a nod. "Have a nice day, Officer." He untied his horse and debated which way to go next. He doubted she would continue east. Maybe south? There were a lot of hotels and motels along Lincoln Highway. Would she have looked for a cheap place to spend the night?

*Emma Beiler.* Her name was Emma Beiler. He didn't know if he should be angry or not. She could have lied about her identity because she feared getting caught.

Would she check into a hotel under her own name? Use Jess Morgan or a different alias?

Daniel steered his buggy south. It was still early. Looking for her was like searching for a needle in a haystack. He sighed. He could head back in case she decided to return on her own, although he doubted she would. Fear for her safety rose within him. He needed to find her and convince her to return. Why did she leave?

What triggered her sudden desire to go? Because he'd told her he enjoyed spending time with her?

He continued to search for her, driving south and then heading north again. Then suddenly he saw her. An Amish girl walking along the road. There was something about the set of her shoulders, the way she moved, that he instantly recognized her. He pulled up beside her.

She stopped walking and faced him. "Daniel?"

He stared at her. "Get in, Emma."

"I was on my way home," she told him.

He felt something inside him soften, but he needed answers, not only for himself but for Missy and Arlin and Leah and Henry.

Emma didn't move. "Please, Emma," he said. "Get in and I'll take you home."

She blinked rapidly but raised her chin. Then she crossed the road and climbed into his vehicle.

"Where did you spend the night?" he asked.

She released a sharp breath. "In a hotel. It came with free breakfast."

"What made you decide to return?"

"Because I realized that I was letting everyone down—Leah and Henry. Missy and Arlin." She sniffed. "You."

"I'm just glad you're *oll recht*," he said huskily.

"You were looking for me?"

"*Ja*. Ever since I went to the house to take you to work and discovered that you'd left." He ran his gaze over her, hoping to read her thoughts. "Why did you leave, Emma?"

"Because I don't deserve to stay."

"Yet you were coming back to us."

"*Ja*. Because I couldn't stay away."

He was more than a little upset with her. But could she blame him? She'd left without a word—just a note. It must have hurt Missy and Arlin terribly to find it. To know that she'd left them after they'd given her a home, love…

Emma took surreptitious glances at the man sitting beside her. Would Missy and Arlin be angry as well? She wondered what time it was. Did Leah and Henry know that she'd left, abandoned them in their time of need? She closed her eyes.

The Arlin Stoltzfus house loomed ahead. Daniel turned onto the property, and Emma's heart started to hammer. She felt sick to her stomach when she saw that there was another buggy on the property. Leah and Henry's?

Daniel pulled his vehicle behind theirs. He jumped down, tied up his horse, but didn't come around to help Emma out. He was angry with her, she thought.

Expecting worse inside, Emma headed toward the house, knocked on the side door and waited. The door opened, and Missy stood there as if in shock. Then with a cry, she opened the door and pulled Emma inside. The woman hugged her. Arlin sat at the kitchen table, looking haggard. Henry and Leah had taken the chairs across from him. They took one look at her, then as one, they stood. "You're back," Leah said.

She nodded.

"Where did Daniel find you?" Henry asked.

"On the road. I was on my way back here. I…" Tears

filled her eyes. "I shouldn't have left." She turned away. "I'm sorry," she whispered brokenly.

Daniel had come in behind her. Emma was aware that everyone was staring at her.

"When did you leave?" Missy asked.

Emma blushed. "Last night, after you were asleep."

"Where did you spend the night?" Leah asked.

"At a hotel. I… I didn't want to sleep in a barn." Her head was throbbing, and she lifted a hand to rub her temple.

Missy nodded. Arlin hadn't said a word. Emma knew that she had hurt him. She shouldn't have left but since she did, maybe she should have stayed away.

"I know I shouldn't have left, but I think 'tis for the best. You don't need me here."

Arlin stood abruptly. "Nay, you will not leave, *dochter.* You will go upstairs and think about what you did and how your disappearance affected the rest of us."

Emma gaped at him. Joy hit her hard when she realized he'd called her his daughter. "*Ja*, Arlin."

When she left the kitchen, it was silent. No one said a word. Clutching her small bag, she went up to her bedroom. She went inside, set down her bag, then lay on the bed, staring at the ceiling. She wouldn't hurt them by leaving again. Not until she turned eighteen and they expected it from her. She felt emotionally overwrought and exhausted. Emma closed her eyes and slept.

"The police are searching for her," Daniel said.

Missy and Arlin exchanged concerned glances.

"You spoke with an officer?" Leah asked.

"*Ja*. I stopped in a coffee shop for something to

drink. The officer was showing her photo to the girl behind the counter."

"What did he say?"

Daniel pulled out a seat and sat at the table with the rest of them. "That she's a runaway foster child from Maryland." He rubbed the back of his neck wearily. "The officer did express concern that despite her foster father's eagerness to get her back, things might not be what the man is claiming. That she is his daughter in every way except by birth."

"*Ja*, we know the truth. It was a terrible situation for her," Leah said.

"There is something else you should know."

"What is it?" Missy asked. Arlin leaned forward with his arms on the tabletop.

"The girl lied to us about her identity. Her real name is not Jess Morgan. 'Tis Emma Beiler."

Leah smiled, seemingly unconcerned. "No wonder she said she could easily answer to Emma. The name was my idea."

Daniel hesitated. He was hurt by the way Emma had left and the fact that she'd lied to all of them. He had confessed that he liked to spend time with her—and she'd run away. "Are you going to keep her at the store?"

"*Ja*, she's a *gut* worker," Leah said.

Daniel glanced at Henry.

"I don't have any problem with it. She's proven trustworthy at work."

Something shifted inside him. "Why did she leave?" He hoped that they had an answer and it wasn't the same one he'd come up with on his own. "Her birthday is in less than three weeks."

"I know." Missy appeared concerned as she took a sip from her tea. "Something is troubling her. I thought she was happy here, but something in her past has hurt her badly, and she's afraid to care."

Daniel stared at her. "But what?"

"I don't know. Ever since Visiting Day, she's seemed quiet. I don't know what happened that day, but she was upset by something."

He thought of his time with her. Had he upset her? He hoped not. She would be leaving, and he couldn't be emotionally involved with her. He needed to distance himself from her. To concentrate on work and looking into the property he'd viewed. That he and Emma had viewed. Daniel stood. "I need to get to work. I called in, but Fred wasn't too happy with me. I don't want to lose this job." He paused. "I don't think I can take Emma to work in the morning." *Or any other morning.* Not if he wanted to spend less time with her so that when it was time to go, it wouldn't hurt so much.

"Not to worry. I'll take her," Arlin said.

Daniel picked up his hat and headed toward the door. Leah and Henry followed him outside. They needed to open the store. Concern for Emma had brought them here. Emma. Not Jess. *Emma.* It bothered him that she hadn't trusted him enough to tell the truth. *She's an Englisher. She'd never be happy here.*

And that knowledge hurt.

She heard the sound of buggy wheels through her open bedroom window. Emma got up from the bed and went to peer outside. She didn't have a view of the yard. She could see the street, though, and she watched as one buggy left the property and turned left toward Yoder's store while the other one pulled to the road and stopped. She didn't know why, but she knew it was Daniel. He waited until a car passed, then turned in the opposite direction of the store.

Daniel was upset with her, and she didn't blame him. Would he ever forgive her? The loss of his friendship would hit her hard. If things had been different, she would have liked to be more than Daniel's friend, but she knew that it wasn't meant to be. Her life was destined to be in the English world, a far cry from his life within the Amish community.

She drew away from the window and sat on the bed. Tears stung her eyes, but she refused to give in to them. She bent over and cradled her head in her hands. A knock on her bedroom door had her sitting up straight.

"Emma?" It was Missy.

She got up and opened the door. "Missy."

"I'd like to talk with you."

Emma nodded. "*Ja*, I figured you would." She sat down on the edge of the bed.

Missy entered the room and sat next to her. "What made you decide to leave now? Your birthday will be here before you know it, *ja*?"

She nodded. "I… I don't deserve to be here," she whispered. "You have all been so nice to me, and… there are things you don't know about me."

"That your real name is Emma Beiler?"

Emma gaped at her with shock. "How did you find out?"

"Daniel told me. He went looking for you this morning," Missy said. "He met a police officer who was displaying a photo of you in a coffee shop. He asked the officer questions but didn't let on that he knew you. He was surprised when the man told him your name was Emma and not Jess."

She closed her eyes. "I'm sorry. When I first met Leah, I didn't know who to trust. I thought it best if I gave a different name. Jess Morgan was a friend from school."

Missy studied her thoughtfully. "Emma, what made you leave now?"

"I felt bad. I was deceiving all of you, and I felt terrible..."

"I don't hold that against you. Arlin doesn't hold it against you. Leah and Henry would like you to come back to work at the store if you want. They trust you."

Emma blinked back tears. "Why?"

"Because they know your character. Do you think many people would *add* money to the register to repay someone for their kindness? You did. And Leah has always had *gut* instincts. I do, too. You need to stay here, Emma. If you leave again, you may be picked up by the police and sent back to your foster family. If you wait till your birthday, they can't make you go back."

"I know." Emma gazed at her with sorrow. "I'm sorry, Missy. I never meant to hurt you and Arlin. Or anyone." She thought of Daniel and knew that she'd hurt him most of all.

"You may work this afternoon if you'd like, but you don't have to. If you want to go back tomorrow, Arlin will take you. But the choice is yours."

"Arlin?"

Missy inclined her head. "Daniel has to work. He missed—"

"Work because of me." Emma averted her glance. "He is upset with me, and I don't blame him." She met the older woman's gaze. "Why are you being so nice to me?" She felt terrible. She still had secrets, which she couldn't confess, for she feared the consequences if she did.

"I was upset that you left, but you came back on your own," Missy said. She smiled. "You didn't want to leave, did you?"

"Nay, I like it here."

*"Gut."* Missy stood. "Because we like having you here. Why don't you come down for lunch? You can decide while you eat if you want to work this afternoon or head in tomorrow morning."

"Missy," Emma began, "Arlin called me *dochter*."

The woman smiled. "Daughter. *Ja*, he considers you one of his."

Warmth filled Emma, and her heart overflowed with joy. "I haven't felt like a daughter in a long time," she whispered.

Missy eyed her with compassion and understanding. "Come. Arlin will be hungry."

Emma rose and followed the woman downstairs. Arlin was at the kitchen table. He looked over at her as she entered the room. "Arlin—"

"Sit, *dochter*. I'm hungry, aren't you?"

And just like that, Emma was forgiven. If she continued to feel guilty for having been banned from her own Amish community, she decided to make the best of it, for she knew she'd never again feel as included as she did right here in Arlin and Missy's home.

Would Daniel ever forgive her? she wondered. Or would she leave here with the knowledge that she'd lost the friendship and respect of the one man she longed to have in her life?

# *Chapter Fourteen*

Emma climbed out of the family buggy after Arlin and Missy. Today they were spending Visiting Day with Meg and Peter Zook, Missy and Arlin's daughter and son-in-law. When the three of them approached the house, the door opened, and a familiar young dark-haired Amish woman with pretty features that clearly resembled Missy's stepped out.

*"Mam!"* Meg greeted with a smile. She held a young boy on her hip.

Missy smiled. *"Dochter."* She held out her hands. "Is that my Timothy? It can't be! This young man looks like he's three years old."

The boy reached for his grandmother with a big toothy smile. "*Grossmamma.* I am three," he said, holding up three fingers as Missy pulled him into her arms.

"Such a big boy," Emma said.

Timothy looked at her. "You are Emma, *ja*?"

She nodded. "That's right."

"You like cake? *Grossmamma* makes *gut* cake."

"*Ja*, I know. She's been teaching me how to cook and bake."

His face brightened. "Then you will be able to make cakes, too?"

*"Ja."* Emma caught Meg's gaze and smiled. The young woman looked amused, then love filled her eyes as she studied her son.

"Come in," Meg invited. "There is no reason for us to talk in the doorway.

A man came from the back of the house. "*Hallo*, Missy, Arlin. And 'tis Emma, *ja*?"

Emma nodded.

"Emma, do you remember my husband, Peter?"

"*Hallo*, Peter," she greeted with a smile. He was an extremely handsome dark-haired man who clearly loved his wife and young son.

Emma realized they were the first of the guests to arrive when she entered the kitchen and Meg invited Missy and her to sit at the kitchen table. Would any of the Lapps be coming? she wondered. She longed for a glimpse of Daniel. Arlin had taken her to and from work all week. She hadn't seen Daniel since he'd brought her home on Monday.

"Iced tea or soda?" Meg asked.

"Iced tea," Emma said. She rose. "May I help?"

"Nay, 'tis not necessary."

Arlin entered the room with Peter moments later. "Ah, iced tea. That looks *gut*."

Peter grinned as he went to a cabinet and pulled out two glasses. "We'll both have some," he said, and proceeded to pour his father-in-law and himself each a glass.

The five of them along with little Timothy, who climbed into his grandfather's lap, leisurely enjoyed their drinks until a knock on the front door heralded the arrival of Meg's sisters and their husbands—Charlie and Nate, Nell and James, and Leah and Henry.

Charlie grinned when she saw her. "You're looking much better than the first time we met."

Emma flashed the other couple an uneasy look. "*Danki*. I'm fine." She managed a smile for Nate, who placed a hand on Charlotte's shoulder.

Capturing Emma's gaze, Leah pulled her aside and smiled at her with warmth. Despite Emma's concern over how things would be between them after she'd left, Leah had been gracious and forgiving—almost like her departure and return had never happened.

"I'm so glad you came back to work with us." She smiled. "Henry is forever making me rest."

Henry chuckled as he joined them. "*Make* you?" He gazed fondly at his wife. "I don't *make* her do anything. Every afternoon, when she's dead tired on her feet, I simply steer her up to the house so that she can fall asleep at home rather than in a chair at the store counter."

"I appreciate that you allowed me back to work in the store."

"Nay," Henry said with a suddenly serious expression that made Emma's heart lurch with concern. "We appreciate you. We don't know what we would do without you."

"Henry..."

"He means it, Emma," Leah said softly.

Emma felt her throat tighten. *"Danki."* They both had been quick to forgive her. Would Daniel ever? She had not seen him in almost a week. Was he avoiding her? Hoping he wouldn't have to see her again before she left?

Henry nodded. "See? Emma understands."

The kitchen door opened and Katie and Samuel Lapp entered with Daniel, Joseph and Hannah close behind. Emma met Daniel's gaze, and her stomach filled with butterflies. He didn't smile at her. He greeted everyone but her, and she experienced a sadness that she knew she'd never get over. Daniel's parents greeted her, then were commandeered by Missy, who offered drinks and a light snack to start off the day. Much to her disappointment, Daniel and Joseph moved into the other room, leaving her with only their sister Hannah.

"Hannah, 'tis nice to see you," Emma said.

She tilted her head curiously. "So you ran away then came back, did you?"

Emma couldn't deny it. *"Ja."*

"Why?"

"I left because I thought I should. I came back because I realized I regretted leaving. I'm only here for a short time. Leaving the way I did hurt people I care about."

"Like Daniel," Hannah said.

She shrugged, then admitted, "*Ja*, like your *bruder*."

"He's upset, but I don't think he is really angry with you."

Hope filled Emma's heart. "He has every right to be."

"Maybe, but I'm glad you came back."

Emma blinked. "That's kind of you."

"Leah needs you. She's happy that you're here, so I am, too."

Joseph entered the room. “Emma. Daniel said that Arlin has been taking you back and forth to work.”

“*Ja*, he’s been generous with his time.”

“I didn’t mind taking you home.”

She gave him a genuine smile.

“I enjoyed our rides together,” he admitted.

The look in his eyes startled her. “Joseph, I’ll be leaving in less than two weeks.”

Daniel’s younger brother appeared surprised. “I didn’t know.” He seemed regretful but not upset. “Doesn’t mean I can’t give you rides until then, *ja*?” he said with a little grin.

Emma chuckled. “I suppose. I can talk with Arlin.”

“Talk with Arlin about what?” Daniel said from behind her. She’d felt his presence immediately. He was the only man she’d ever felt a connection to. And he’d avoided her since the morning he’d found her walking back along the road.

Emma tensed. Then slowly turned toward him. He wore a green shirt that brought out the green flecks in his brown eyes. “Daniel,” she acknowledged him.

“What about Arlin?” he asked, addressing Joseph without meeting her gaze once.

She felt the insult from head to toe. Was this what it was like to be shunned? To be ignored this way? “Excuse me,” she said, and started to leave.

To her shock, Daniel grabbed her arm. “Where are you going?”

She tensed. “You don’t want me here, so I’m leaving.”

“Joseph, will you excuse us? I need to speak with Emma. Alone.” Daniel hadn’t let go of her arm, but his grip was gentle. “Emma, walk outside with me?”

Emma shot him a glance. He looked calm, determined, but she couldn't read his thoughts. "Fine."

He took her through the front door and walked toward the side of the house where there were no windows. There was a stand of evergreen trees there, a windbreak of sorts, although it was next to the house and not a farm field. Daniel stopped her there and stood face-to-face with her.

He gazed at her a long time without a single word. Then finally he asked, "Why did you run, Emma?"

Feeling ashamed, she averted her glance. "Daniel—"

"Why, Emma? Tell me. Was it because of me?"

Horrified by his assumption, she studied him with widened eyes. "What? Nay, Daniel—"

"Then *why*?"

"You wouldn't understand."

He narrowed his eyes. "Try me."

She rubbed a hand over her face. "There are things you don't know."

"What things? That your real name is Emma Beiler?"

Emma nodded. "Missy told me that you knew. But that's not all of it, Daniel, and I'm afraid I can't tell you. I can't. Please don't ask me to."

"You're leaving soon. What does it matter now?"

It mattered to her. If he—or anyone—knew, they would kick her out of their community, shun her as her own family had done. "It matters."

The fact that she would be leaving soon was hard enough. She couldn't bear it if he learned the truth and rejected her.

She heard him sigh heavily. "What are we going to do with you?" he whispered.

"What do you mean?" she asked shakily.

"Take a walk with me," Daniel said. He started toward the back of the property. He was quiet as they walked.

She grew tense to the point of pain. "Are you mad that I didn't tell you?"

"I was upset at first," he admitted, "but then I realized that you did so because you were afraid to trust anyone."

She closed her eyes. "You're not angry."

He seemed to hesitate. "Nay."

It had been the longest week for Daniel. Knowing that she was near yet choosing to ignore her made him feel worse, not better. She would only be here a little while longer. Why deny himself her company until she left? All week he'd prayed to the Lord for guidance. He asked what he could do to get over her. He prayed that he could convince her to stay.

But it was clear to him that Emma still had secrets. The fact that she wouldn't tell him let him know that they had no future together, because she didn't trust him enough.

She looked pretty in a purple dress with white cape and apron with a white *kapp.* He was conscious of the fact that at full height she stood only to under his chin. As they walked, he stifled the urge to hold her hand. They weren't sweethearts, and she would be horrified if he took the liberty.

They strolled until they reached the back end of the stockade fence that contained Peter's livestock. Peter had taken over his father's farm. Horseshoe Joe, a blacksmith, had moved into the *dawdi haus*, but he continued to run his farrier business with Daniel's brother Jacob, leaving Peter with control of the main house and farm property.

Daniel took her to a quiet place behind the barn and halted where it was safe from prying eyes. "Emma, I want you to listen to me."

"What is it?" she asked, her voice shaking.

He felt himself pulled into the depths of her beautiful brown eyes. "Your birthday is coming up soon, and I know that you'll want to leave…but Leah is due to have her babies, and I was thinking that it would be a big help to them if you stayed until she gives birth. I know you've been handling the store alone while Henry takes Leah to her doctor's appointments and while she rests in the afternoons. Consider staying a little longer. Once the babies are born, other arrangements can be made."

Daniel wanted her to stay indefinitely, but he knew that wouldn't happen.

She appeared to give it some thought. "I do want to help Leah," she finally said.

She gazed out over the fields. There was a peacefulness about her features. He liked seeing her this way. Daniel held his breath as he waited for her answer. It would give him more time with her. Leah wasn't due to give birth until a few weeks after Emma's birthday.

"*Oll recht.* You make a good point. I'll stay until Leah gives birth."

He exhaled in relief. Daniel smiled. "*Danki*, Emma." Her agreement meant the world to him, although he couldn't let her know.

"I guess we should get back to the *haus* before Joseph and Hannah come looking for us." He started to walk away, but her hand on his arm stopped him. She released him immediately.

"Daniel?" she said quietly.

*"Ja?"* He gazed at her raised eyebrows.

"I'm glad you're no longer angry with me."

"Me, too, Emma."

Daniel took her back to the house, where they spent a quiet afternoon. Emma blended in well with his family. But he knew that unless he could convince her that Happiness was where she belonged, she would leave, and he'd never see her again.

Emma sat in a barn stall while Jeremiah slept, curled on her lap. She closed her eyes and leaned back against the wall, trying to stop her brain from thinking. Daniel entered her mind again, and she prayed for a sense of peace for what she had to do and for what surely would come after she left. It was late Monday. Despite Joseph's offer, Arlin continued to take her back and forth to work. They had gotten home about a half hour ago. She'd come here for a few minutes contemplation, to think about her promise to stay until Leah gave birth. She refused to hurt everyone by leaving abruptly, so she would do what she could and leave Happiness on good terms.

Emma heard a sound in the barn, letting her know that someone had entered. She straightened away from the wall as Leah appeared above the half door. Emma was surprised to see her.

"Leah, what are you doing here? Is something wrong?"

She greeted Emma with a smile. "Nay, I'm fine." She

opened the door and came in. Emma noted how radiant her friend looked in a purple dress that enhanced her blue eyes and fit her swollen belly. "I thought I might find you here." She started to lower her pregnant self onto the floor next to Emma.

"Don't. I can stand."

Leah laughed as she studied the sleeping little dog and got down anyway. "I may need a hand getting back up."

"Why aren't you home resting?"

"I wanted to see you. What with all my doctor's appointments, we've barely had time to talk."

The little dog opened his eyes and perked up at the sound of Leah's voice. He swung his head, saw Leah and sprang from Emma's lap to greet her. Jeremiah stared at Leah's belly and hesitated as if he'd realized there was no room for him on her lap. Leah laughed, a melodious sound that spoke of joy as the Amish woman patted her side in invitation.

Emma watched with a smile as Jeremiah cuddled against Leah's side, enjoying the fingers that rubbed through the fur on his neck.

Emma saw Leah grimace. "Are you in pain?"

Leah smiled. "I'm fine. Just Braxton-Hicks contractions. My doctor warned me about them."

"Are you sure?"

*"Ja."* She smiled and appeared to relax. She resumed stroking Jeremiah's head and neck. Suddenly the little dog stood, trembled and stared at Leah.

"It looks like he wants something." Emma checked his water bowl. "He has plenty of water." She frowned as she eyed the dog. "What's wrong, boy?"

Suddenly, Leah gasped and cupped her belly. She tried to stand, and Emma immediately reached to help her. Her friend gave her a trembling smile. "I think I may be in labor."

Emma swallowed hard. "Where's Henry?"

"Up at the house."

"Stay here," Emma urged. "I'll get him." She stopped. "Is it *oll recht* to leave you alone for a minute?"

Leah nodded. "I'm fine." But she looked a bit shaky and a lot scared.

"It's not too early, is it?"

"Not for twins."

Emma drew a sharp breath. "Do you need a chair? Do you want me to help you outside?"

"Nay, just get Henry."

She nodded and raced to the house, bursting in through the kitchen to a number of startled gazes. "Leah is having twins!" she gasped.

Missy glanced at her with a smile. "*Ja*, we know."

"Nay! Now! She's in labor! Where's Henry?" Emma looked around the room frantically.

Having heard the commotion, Henry came rushing into the kitchen from another room. "What's going on?"

"Henry, you have to come now! Leah is in the barn and *she's in labor*!"

Henry paled and ran from the house.

Emma turned to see Missy following Henry. She wondered what she should do. Boil water? Get blankets? She wasn't a member of the family. She didn't have the right to interfere. *But Leah is my friend.*

Daniel entered the house a moment later. He walked

in casually, clearly unware of what was happening. "Where is everyone?"

"In the barn," Emma said, overcome with a sudden dizziness.

Suddenly, Daniel was by her side. He placed his hand lightly on her shoulder and slipped his other arm about her waist. "Don't faint on me."

She shook her head. "I won't. I'm fine." She gave in to the sensation of having him near, then promptly pulled away. "But Leah isn't," she gasped. "She's in the barn and she's in labor. *Leah is about to give birth!* I need to check on her." She pulled from the circle of Daniel's arms and ran from the house and sprinted toward the barn. Suddenly scared, she paused midway to catch her breath and stared at the outbuilding. Leah was inside. She desperately wanted to help her friend.

To her shock, Daniel was suddenly beside her. He captured her hand and gave it a light squeeze. "Leah will be fine. She's strong."

Emma nodded as she met his gaze. "What do we do?" She bit her lip. "Why are you here?"

"I wanted to see you," he said. "We have a few things to discuss. Arlin has been taking you to work. I want to give you a ride in the morning again. Joseph wants to bring you home, but I want to take you home, too."

"But Daniel, your work..."

"'Tis fine." He nodded. "I'll not be working there for much longer."

Henry and Missy came out of the barn holding Leah up between them. "I'm fine, Henry," Leah insisted. "Don't baby me!"

"Leah," her mother said patiently, "you need to be inside the *haus*," her mother said.

"Nay, I need to be at home." Leah turned her gaze up to her husband's. "Please, Henry, I want our babies to be born at *our* home."

Henry eyed his wife with concern. "Leah—"

Leah clutched at his arm. "Please, husband."

He nodded his head. He didn't look happy about it, but Emma knew that he would do what he could to please his wife.

Emma approached as Henry carefully eased Leah into their family buggy. His movements were loving, tender, and Emma felt a lump rise to her throat. She shuddered out a sigh and was surprised when Daniel put his arm around her. "Wouldn't it be better if we called a driver?"

She felt Daniel stiffen. "'Tis fine. They don't live far," he said crisply.

She met his gaze. "It's just…the road bumps might…"

His gaze softened. "I understand."

Emma wondered what would happen now. She'd promised Daniel that she would stay until Leah gave birth. Did that mean he wanted her to go before her eighteenth birthday? Or would Henry want her to run the store during Leah's recovery? She hoped so. She didn't want to leave yet. She wasn't eighteen, and the danger of being reunited with the Turners still loomed. But as painful as it would be, she desperately wanted a little more time with Daniel.

Missy approached her. "I'm going to follow them to the *haus*," she said. "Do you want to come with me?"

Surprise flared inside her, surprise and joy that

Missy had included her as family by asking her to go. She flashed Daniel a glance to see that his expression was unreadable. Did he matter? She wanted to be there for Leah whether she had his support or not. But he didn't argue against her going, so maybe he didn't mind.

Everyone had come out into the yard to see Henry and Leah off. Missy murmured something to her daughters, and soon Missy and Emma were in a separate buggy following Henry and Leah with other family members bringing up the rear. As Missy steered the horse away from the house, Emma glanced back at Daniel. His features were taut with concern. For Leah? Or for her?

They arrived at Yoder's Country Crafts and General Store. Henry steered the carriage close to the house behind the store, and Missy parked beside him. She and Emma jumped out of their vehicle and followed the couple into the house.

"I'm fine," Leah assured them. "I can't be in labor."

"Your water broke. You will be feeling those pains within the next twenty-four hours," Missy said.

Emma watched as Henry pulled a chair from the kitchen table before he gently helped his wife to sit. "What can I do?" she asked.

Leah smiled at her. "You can sit and keep me company."

Henry and Missy nodded their approval, and Emma sat. "I'm sorry I'm not much help."

Leah scowled at her. "How can you say that? You ran for Henry."

"I shouldn't have left you," Emma insisted.

"Nonsense! And if you did, then where would I be? Giving birth in a barn."

"It wouldn't be the first baby born in a barn," Henry said softly.

Emma understood immediately and nodded. He was referring to the baby who was born in a manger when there was no room at the inn.

The back door opened behind them, and Leah's sisters spilled into the kitchen. They had left their husbands back at the house. The men had told their wives that they would follow soon. The women were there for Leah. The men would come to support Henry.

"I'm hungry," Leah complained.

"Nay, *dochter*," Missy said. "'Tis better if you wait until after the babies are born. Eat now and you'll get sick to your stomach."

Leah looked at her mother with horror. "And if they stay inside me for another week? I'll starve!"

Leah's sisters laughed. Emma cracked a smile, because if the situation was amusing to the Stoltzfus sisters, then it meant that Leah would be fine.

The women spent the afternoon with Leah. There were no additional signs of labor. Finally, Leah told everyone to go home. "Doesn't look like it will happen anytime soon. *Mam*, I'd appreciate it if you'd stop by to tell Mary Smith, our midwife, then she'll be ready when we need her."

Missy looked as if she would refuse to leave. "We'll go now, but I'll be back later."

Leah nodded. Her gaze softened as it settled on Emma. "*Danki*, Emma."

Emma jerked with surprise. "Why are you thanking me?"

"Because you were there for me."

She leaned toward Leah. "You've always been there for me, Leah. I'd do anything for you." She paused. "Do you understand?"

Leah smiled. "*Ja*, I understand. Now go home and get some rest." Her gaze turned to encompass every woman in the room. "All of you. I may need you later."

Emma shot Henry a worried glance before she followed the women outside. Henry seemed composed, but in that quick look she noticed a flicker of anxiety in his blue gaze. Her belly fluttered with nerves as she climbed into the buggy beside Missy.

"Henry is scared," Emma said.

"We won't stay gone long. He's going to need us." Missy pulled into the paved driveway of a small house. "I won't be but a minute."

"The midwife's?"

*"Ja,"* the older woman said with a smile. She was back within seconds. "Mary has all the details. She'll stop by later in an hour or so to check on Leah. We'll head back as soon as we can."

Emma thought about Daniel and her longing to stay in Happiness and be his wife. She wondered how it would feel to be in Leah's shoes with Daniel as her loving husband and she soon to give birth to his child. Would he be frightened or calm when she went into labor? Would he gaze at her lovingly after she gave birth, look forward to raising their baby together?

## *Chapter Fifteen*

Less than two hours later, Emma waited with Leah's family in the Yoder house. Missy excused herself to check on Leah. The women were in the kitchen. There was excitement in the air, as Leah's sisters were excited for the birth of their sister's twin babies. Ellie and her husband Reuben with their son Ethan were the first to arrive. Nell and James arrived minutes later. The men immediately went outside to chat after exacting a promise from their wives to keep them up to date on the babies' progress.

Daniel with his parents and siblings arrived next. Emma caught sight of him and longed to go to him. He had a way of making her see things clearly, and right now she was confused and felt like a mess.

Meg came with Peter and their son Timothy. The sisters greeted Meg and urged Reuben to join the men outside.

"Reuben is nervous about Leah's babies," Ellie murmured quietly. "His first wife, Susanna, died after giving birth to Ethan." She smiled and touched her belly. "He's going to have to get used to it. I'm with child."

Everyone beamed at her. Emma smiled. "Congratulations."

Missy had returned and eyed Ellie with joy. "You'll take care of yourself, and Reuben won't have anything to worry about." Her daughter agreed. "I think I should go check on Leah."

Missy came back immediately. "It will happen soon. The midwife should be here any minute."

Mary Smith, the midwife, arrived, and after a quick hello she headed upstairs to see Leah. The women decided to put food on the table to distract themselves, and because the men were probably hungry. Ellie went to get the husbands, and they filed in, eager to eat.

There were muffins and biscuits and fresh bread. Everyone dug in. They were worried about Leah but eager to put their minds elsewhere even for just a few moments. The men filled up their plates and retreated into the great room.

Emma sat with the women at the kitchen table and reached for a chocolate chip muffin. The breakfast treat had become a favorite after Missy had made them during her first week with them.

The midwife appeared in the doorway. "She's in labor now."

Missy nodded and stood. "Emma," she said, "Come with me."

Wide-eyed and heart beating wildly, Emma followed Missy up the stairs. When she entered the room, she found Leah in bed, propped up on pillows.

Leah smiled at her mother and Emma when she caught sight of them. "'Tis starting now, *Mam*."

Her mother smiled back. "It will be fine, *dochter*. I

can't say I'm not surprised they're coming a little early. Twins usually come before they are due. You've carried them long enough. They should be fine."

"*Ja*, and you kept your doctor's appointments, took prenatal vitamins and had plenty of rest in the afternoons," Emma pointed out. "You will soon have two beautiful, healthy babies."

Leah's gaze went soft. "That's what Mary said." She shifted on the bed pillows. "Who's here?"

"Everyone," Emma said with awe. "Your sisters and their families. Your cousins and aunt and uncle."

Emma went downstairs to leave mother, daughter and midwife alone. She immediately spied Daniel leaning against the wall near the base of the stairway. She locked gazes with him.

"How is she?" he asked.

"She's doing well. The midwife thinks it won't be long now." She looked away. "Are you hungry?"

"I already ate, Emma."

She blushed. "*Ja*, of course."

"You seem nervous."

"Nay, just a bit taken aback." The evidence of Leah and Henry's love for each other was about to make an appearance. Emma wanted that. A husband to love and his children to love and nurture. But she'd never have that, because what she wanted was here and she couldn't stay. She didn't deserve to stay.

Emma peeked into the great room. Young Ethan lay on the floor close to his father's chair. Peter Zook, Meg's husband, held little Timothy asleep in his lap. Everywhere she looked in the room, there was evidence of love and family. Something that Emma didn't have.

Daniel approached. “Did you get any sleep?” he asked, studying her with his liquid brown eyes.

“Not much,” she admitted. “I napped for fifteen minutes or so before we decided to come here.”

“I thought as much.” His tone was gentle, his expression warm and understanding.

She stiffened. “I look that bad?”

He frowned. “Nay. You look…beautiful.”

She blinked. He was so confusing. Why was he being so nice? She’d run away and come back, and it seemed as if he’d forgiven her, but did he really?

Time passed slowly, and the twins hadn’t arrived yet. It was now morning and close to 8:00 a.m. Emma decided that she would go open the store. Henry would want her to. Leah would be glad that she’d stepped in. And it was just for today. She had no idea what would happen tomorrow.

She sought out Henry, who stood near his father-in-law. He was understandably tense and on edge. “Henry,” she murmured as she approached. “I thought I’d open the store. It’s almost time.” Henry blinked as if in a daze, as if he didn’t understand what she’d said. “The store,” she repeated. “I’m going to open Yoder’s for you.”

He blinked. “You don’t mind?”

Emma shook her head. “Nay. There are more than enough women here to help with Leah. She needs her mother and sisters with her.” She wasn’t a sister. She didn’t belong. “Where’s the key?”

Henry grabbed the key from a kitchen drawer and

gave it to her. "You know where to find me if you need help with anything."

Emma left the house and walked to the store. No one noticed she'd left, but it didn't matter. The sun lit up the morning sky, displaying autumn in its full splendor. She unlocked the back door and started the daily routine of getting ready for customers before she unlocked the front door. She doubted that anyone would come in the next hour or so, but she was prepared in case they did.

She pulled out two loaves of bread—one of German rye and the other a loaf of sliced white bread—from the storage room in the back. She carried and stashed them with the other lunch supplies under the counter near the wall end. Then Emma put on water to heat on the single gas burner for tea. When the water was hot, she fixed a cup of tea and sipped it leisurely as she looked around the store, deciding what else she should do today.

Her mind wandered to everyone back at the house. Would someone come tell her when Leah had her babies?

She heard a sound as someone entered the store through the back door. Had she forgotten to lock it?

Daniel appeared in the door opening, his gaze settling on her immediately. "I thought you might like some company."

"Leah hasn't had the twins yet?"

He shook his head.

While she more than cared for Daniel, she didn't trust his motives for being here. "Water still hot?" he asked. When she nodded, he went behind the counter and made himself a cup of tea.

She wanted to spend time with him but also wondered if it wasn't wise to put distance between them so it wouldn't be so hard when she left.

"Don't you have to work today?" she asked more sharply than she'd intended.

# *Chapter Sixteen*

Daniel was shocked by her attitude. "Is something wrong?"

Emma averted her gaze. "Nay," she said quietly. She appeared ashamed of her outburst.

"I don't believe you. Something is bothering you that you feel you need to take it out on me."

"Maybe you're the problem."

He narrowed his eyes. "Excuse me?" He saw her blush. "What have I done?"

She shook her head. "Sorry. I guess I'm just worried about Leah." She eyed him over her cup as she took a sip from her tea. "I appreciate your checking up on me, Daniel, but as you can see, I'm fine."

"Emma."

"Go back to the house, Daniel. I'm fine here alone. You belong with your family. You should be with them."

"And you don't belong?"

"You said it. I didn't."

"Emma—"

"You don't need to worry about me. I'll be leaving soon."

He studied her, noting the sudden change in her brown eyes. She gazed at him blankly, as if she had no feelings for him, and it hurt. Despite her behavior, he caught a glimpse of vulnerability in the quiver of her pink lips and in a quick blink of her eyes. He inhaled a breath and realized that he loved her. He loved her, and she wouldn't stay.

"Daniel," she said sharply. "You're staring."

It was his turn to be embarrassed.

"Go up to the house. I've got this."

He struggled with disappointment. He wanted to stay and keep her company, but she wanted him to leave. She didn't need him. She'd only needed a place to hide in plain sight until she turned eighteen. Didn't she understand that she'd still be vulnerable, even after she came of age? That she could stay, and he could love and protect her?

He left the way he'd come, through the back door, and headed to the house. Because she was right. He should be there waiting with his family. And she didn't feel a part of that.

He wanted her to feel included. He wanted her to be a part of his family and his life.

Emma felt dejected after Daniel left the store. She'd told him to go, but still she missed him. She didn't deserve to have Daniel in her life…or the family who loved him. She'd leave and look back on her time here as something special, a moment when she'd enjoyed what she might have had if her parents hadn't left their Amish community. Mostly, she'd never forget Daniel

Lapp, and she'd always wonder what happened to the man who'd stolen her heart.

In an effort to keep busy, she worked to clean the store. She swept the floor although there was little dirt to warrant the use of a good corn broom. She removed items and dusted shelves before putting the merchandise back. Then she went to the counter again where she found paper and pen, then jotted down the items that needed to be reordered.

The front door jingled. Emma looked up from the paper with a smile on her face with the hope that Daniel had returned despite her efforts to push him away. She gasped in horror as a man approached. He didn't stop until he reached the counter. She'd recognize his smirk anywhere. The man was Bryce Turner, her foster father.

"What are you doing here?" she demanded. She attempted to keep calm as she casually searched for something to use as a weapon in case she needed to defend herself. "What do you want?"

"I've come to take you home, Emma dear." He stared at her, a big brute of a man with an unholy light in his black eyes.

"This is my home now. I have family and friends here."

Bryce laughed. "You're living with the Amish?" His gaze ran down the length of her as if noting her plain clothing and prayer *kapp* for the first time. "I don't think so. I'll have a talk with them. I'm sure they'll be happy to see you go."

"Bryce, please. Just leave. You don't need me. Keep the money from the state. I don't care. The authorities won't know that I'm no longer living with you. I'll be eighteen soon anyway and free to live on my own."

The man's expression hardened. "It sounds like you don't want to come home with me. After everything I've done for you, that's not very nice. You shouldn't talk that way to your foster father." He snarled, "Show some respect."

She flinched. He had edged to the end of the counter, boxing her in. She wondered what would happen if she attempted to bolt out the back door. Emma recalled the pain he'd inflicted on her arm and the resulting bruises. Her arms were finally healing, and she refused to allow him to hurt her again.

She sighed, and her shoulders slumped. She didn't want to cause trouble for her Amish friends. She needed to keep the man as far from them as she could…even if she was forced to go with him. *Keep him talking until you can figure a way to escape him.*

"How did you find me?"

"I had some help. The police were looking for you when they found someone who thought they'd seen you. The tip didn't amount to anything concrete, so I came looking for you myself. I knew you had to be close. After all, you once lived in an Amish community when you were a child."

"How did you know that?"

"We received a file on you. Or should I say, I hired someone to investigate your background. We couldn't have a criminal living in our house."

Then his features darkened. "You saw us, didn't you?" he murmured.

"What?"

"Don't play innocent now. You saw me and Kent in the alley that night. I figured you had because you ran away soon after." His mouth tightened into a thin line. "Let's go," he ordered.

"I'd rather stay here."

"I'm not asking. I'm telling you to get moving or suffer the consequences."

She stiffened her spine. No, she thought, she couldn't go back. She *wouldn't.*

With a suddenness that shocked her, Bryce grabbed her by the arm and dragged her from behind the counter. His fingers squeezed flesh, making her cry out with pain. "Move!" he commanded. "Did you honestly think I wouldn't come after you?" He pulled her the length of the store.

"What are you going to do with me?" she gasped.

"Why, dear Emma, I won't do anything. You're my daughter, and I take good care of my children."

"I'm not your child and I don't want to go!" she cried, struggling against his hold in an effort to get free.

"Sorry, sweetheart, but you're going. Get moving or I'll force you."

She fought harder, but Bryce only laughed as he dragged her out of the store and toward his car.

Emma saw a little English girl playing across the street and quickly looked away. Bryce must have sensed the direction of her gaze, because he hollered across the street to the child. "Hi, honey," he said. "My friend and I are going for a ride."

"No!" Emma screamed.

The girl jumped up and backed away.

Bryce cursed. "You tell anyone what you've seen, little girl, and I'll come back to get you," he warned.

The child crouched on the lawn to play with her dolls, as if he hadn't spoken. Bryce stared at the child a long moment, then, assured of the little girl's silence, he opened his car door and pushed Emma inside. "Get in! Now!" he ordered when she tried to resist him.

Emma was terrified. She'd never get to see Daniel again…or any of the others here she regarded as family. She could only imagine what would happen to her if she didn't find a way to escape. Bruising would be the least of her worries. There were other things that Bryce could do to ensure her silence.

Daniel was upset. He stood in the great room in the house, waiting for Leah to give birth while Emma was working alone in the store. He frowned. Why didn't she want him there? They'd been friends, and he felt sure she had feelings for him. What made her behave that way? Why wouldn't she tell him what was bothering her?

Leah was in labor. The men were chatting like they were at a picnic outside. Except for Henry. Leah's husband looked ill with worry. No doubt, he wanted to be upstairs with his wife.

Emma. He wanted to see her. He needed to be with Emma, because he loved and needed her. Now if only he could convince her of that.

He decided to head back to the store to see her. He loved her. He would convince her to talk to him. If she cared for him even a little, he'd work to convince her that he was the right man for her. That the Amish community was the right home for her.

This time he entered through the front entrance. “Emma?” There was no sign of her.

Calling her name repeatedly, he checked in the back rooms but couldn’t find her anywhere.

Would she leave without a word? Nay, she wouldn’t! She’d promised to stay. And Leah had yet to give birth. Besides, Emma was still only seventeen. Those were two good reasons for her to stay.

She’d left the store unlocked. That wasn’t like her. He grew more concerned. Where was she? If she had left of her own free will, she would have locked up the store and put the key where Henry could find it.

What if the police had found her? Or worse yet, her foster father?

Daniel burst out of the store toward the street. He looked both ways but saw no sign of her anywhere. A little girl played in the yard across the street. Had she seen Emma? He approached her.

*“Hallo,”* he said gently. “Did you see a woman leave the store?” He smiled. “An Amish woman?”

Fear entered her green eyes as the child looked up at him. She nodded but didn’t speak.

Encouraged, Daniel crouched beside her. “Was anyone with her?”

The girl nodded vigorously.

“Can you tell me what you saw?” He frowned when she shook her head. “But you saw something?”

She bobbed her head.

“Was she with a man?”

“Yes,” she whispered.

*"Please,"* he begged, "she may be in danger. I need to know what you saw."

The child looked thoughtful. "A bad man took her," she finally said.

"A bad man?" His stomach roiled with dread and fear.

"Yes, they came out of that store together, and he shoved her into his car." She clutched her doll tightly to her chest. "She didn't want to go. The lady didn't want to leave with him, but he made her."

"What color was the car?"

"Blue." She looked up at him with rounded eyes. "She didn't want to go," she repeated, clearly frightened. "She tried to get away, but he wouldn't let her. Then he saw me and said he'd come back to get me if I told." She trembled. "You won't let him get me, will you?"

"No one will hurt you," he soothed. "Where is your mother?"

"She's at work. My babysitter is inside."

"I'm going to get help from the police. Why don't you go inside where it is safe? When I bring a policeman, will you let us in? Tell your babysitter—what's her name?"

"Patty."

Daniel nodded "Tell Patty that we'll be coming to talk with you. Will you do that?"

"Yes."

"Get your dolls and take them safely inside with you."

He rose to his feet. "Thank you for telling what you saw. The lady—she's special to me."

"You're going to get her back?"

"Yes. I'll do everything I can to get her back."

He gave her a gentle smile. "Now go inside." Daniel watched as she ran to her house, then he sprinted across the street and up to the house. He burst in the room where the men waited. "Henry, do you have your cell phone? I need to use it."

*"Ja."* Henry frowned at him. "Something wrong?"

"Emma has been kidnapped."

# *Chapter Seventeen*

Emma sat in the back of Bryce Turner's sedan, amazed that he hadn't tied her up, that he believed she wouldn't attempt to escape. But he was wrong. Yes, she was scared, even terrified, but the first chance she got, she'd escape and return to Happiness, to those she cared about.

She pressed her face against the rear passenger window. She studied her surroundings. They hadn't gone far, so they were still in Lancaster County. She heard the ding that accompanied the low-fuel light in Bryce's car. It was only a matter of time before he'd have to pull into a gas station and refuel. As the man drove down the road, Emma recognized the restaurant across the street. Thank the Lord that they were still on the main road.

She longed to go back. Home, she thought. Happiness was the first place to feel like home since she'd left Indiana.

She heard Bryce curse and watched with satisfaction as he pulled the car into a gas station. Emma hid a smile as he got out to fill up the car with gas.

He leaned in and glared at her. "Stay where you are," he ordered. "Or there'll be consequences."

She waited with patience as Bryce pumped gas. When he was done, he growled with anger when he wasn't given a printed receipt at the pump. She sat back and closed her eyes and pretended to have fallen asleep. She waited a few moments until Bryce entered the building to get his receipt.

*It's now or never!* Emma threw open the door and bolted down the street back the way they'd come. When she heard Bryce's outraged yell, she raced across a farm field toward a large house set off from the road. She prayed for help as she ran, begged God to find her help.

She banged hard on the farmhouse door. When no one came to open it, she hammered her fist against the wood. *"Answer the door. Please!"* But no one came.

She looked back. Bryce was near the edge of the road, searching for her. She knew the exact moment he spotted her and headed her way. She changed direction, skirted the house and raced back to the road. She heard him bellow at her to stop, but she kept on going.

*Daniel.* Thoughts of him comforted her until Emma felt a strong, punishing grip on her arm. Bryce's furious face loomed above her. His fingers tightened painfully above her forearm. "Let me go!"

"Shut up! Stop or I'll punch you out so you can't yell for help!"

She slumped as if defeated. She wanted him to think that she was biddable, for if he decided to tie her up, she'd never ever be free of him.

Emma prayed as he dragged her toward his car.

*Please, Lord, help me. I'll do better, I promise. I'll apologize. I'll do whatever You want. Please.*

"No sense praying, girl. He won't listen to the likes of you."

She ignored him and closed her eyes as she continued to pray. She ignored the pain of his hold and put her trust in the Lord.

Suddenly, she heard police sirens. Bryce seemed surprised, and Emma took the opportunity to be free of him again and run. Bryce chased after her, catching her before she got more than a few yards. Two police cars roared up to surround her and Bryce. She froze. Would he convince them that she was his misbehaving daughter? Would they insist she go home with him? She wouldn't be forced this time! She'd hold her ground and demand they listen to the truth about Bryce.

Officers encircled them with drawn guns. Bryce smiled. "I'm glad you came, officers. I've been searching everywhere for my daughter. I'm grateful I found her. Thanks to you, I have her back."

"Step away from the girl, Mr. Turner," an officer ordered.

"Why are you aiming your gun at me?" Bryce said with outrage. "I haven't done anything wrong. She's the one who ran away. I only came to bring her home."

"I don't know, Doug," one officer said to another. "The girl sure looks Amish to me. Doesn't look like she's this man's daughter."

"I'm not," Emma said, then cried when Bryce dug his fingers into her arm. The pain made her waver dizzily.

"Release her and put up your hands, Turner," a third officer said.

When Bryce didn't move, he stepped closer, gun aimed directly at Bryce.

Bryce released her and held up his hands. "You're making a mistake," he warned.

Out of breath, Emma leaned over and gulped for air. Tears ran down her face, and she couldn't stop them.

Someone knelt at her side, gently touching her shoulder. "Emma," said a familiar voice.

She turned her head. "Daniel," she breathed.

"*Ja*, dear heart." He was careful as he helped her to straighten. He put his arm around her, and Emma felt safe and protected…and loved. Overwhelmed with emotion, she sobbed, and Daniel pulled her into his arms.

"Emma, 'tis *oll recht*. I'm here now. I won't let anyone hurt you again."

Daniel held her close as she answered the police officers' questions truthfully about her life with the family, about what crimes she'd witnessed involving the man and his son. Once she'd finished answering questions, the officers took Bryce into custody and loaded him, handcuffed, into the back of a police cruiser.

Daniel was silent as he drove her back to Leah and Henry's. She wondered what he was thinking.

"You came for me," she whispered. "Why?"

Daniel shot her a concerned look. "You were gone. The store was open, and I knew you wouldn't leave it unlocked. Then I saw the little girl across the street. She told me what she'd seen. So I called the police and then I followed them." She felt his shudder. "Fortunately, you hadn't been taken far."

Emma sighed. "Thank you. I was shocked to see

Bryce." She shuddered and hugged herself. "I… I don't think I would have gotten away from him alive."

"You never told the police what you saw until today."

"Because the police never believed me. When I ran away the first time, I tried to tell them how bad things were for me at the Turners', but they wouldn't listen. Bryce convinced them I was a troubled teen who needed love." She paused as she fought tears. "I was just a runaway foster kid, and Bryce was a law-abiding citizen. The physical abuse wasn't obvious back then…"

Daniel remained silent as he steered the horse into the driveway and up the hill toward Leah and Henry's house. As she followed Daniel into Leah and Henry's house, Emma saw pleased smiles on everyone in the great room. Charlie rushed over and reached for her hand. "Are you *oll recht*?"

Emma smiled, sensing her genuine concern. "I'm fine."

Henry approached, his features filled with happiness. "Leah delivered our babies. We have twin sons! I'm a *dat*!"

Emma beamed at him. "Congratulations."

Daniel rested a gentle hand against her lower back and asked Henry, "When can we see them?"

"As soon as Arlin and Missy come downstairs. I thought it best to not overwhelm them with too many at one time."

"How is Leah?" Emma asked. Leah had been a true friend to her. She wished the woman every happiness that life had to offer.

"She's well," Henry said with a bright smile. "Happy."

Everyone had to wait their turn. Her sisters and their

husbands were allowed to go in together before the others. When it had come time for the actual birthing, the midwife had asked everyone to leave except Missy, the babies' grandmother. She'd stayed until Arlin came into the room with Arlin's sister Katie and her husband Samuel. After they had enjoyed the sight of Arlin's new grandsons, they had rejoined the others downstairs. Finally, Leah's cousins were allowed in. Emma was prepared to hang back until everyone had enjoyed their turn. Hannah, Joseph and Daniel were called up to take a peek.

Daniel turned toward Emma. "Come with us," he urged softly.

She blinked with surprise. She looked at Henry, who nodded and smiled his approval. Overjoyed to be included, Emma accompanied him up the stairs to the second floor.

The sight that met Emma nearly stole her breath. Her friend was propped up by pillows with a tiny newborn in each arm. Her gaze met Emma's as the four of them entered the room. Her eyes suddenly lit up as Henry came in behind them. He went immediately to Leah's side and stared at her adoringly. Emma was overwhelmed with emotion when Henry reached out to stroke a gentle finger over each of his tiny sons' foreheads.

Leah waved the four newcomers closer. "Come and meet our sons, Isaac Henry and Daniel James."

Emma felt Daniel tense, and she smiled when Leah explained, "Isaac for Henry's closest friend with his middle name after Henry. Our other son is named after you, Daniel. You have always been there for us when we needed you. And James? It seems fitting that we give him the name of a man who gave up his English life because he loves my sister."

Daniel seemed overcome with emotion. Emma wanted to reach for his hand but didn't dare. He had offered her comfort when she needed it, but this was different. This wasn't pain or sadness. This was joy.

The cousins were enjoying their visit with the newborns. Daniel pressed her forward to get a closer view of the tiny little boys in Leah's arms.

As she studied their little features, then turned to observe their parents, who were in love and overjoyed with their family, she felt a longing so deep she was on the verge of tears.

She stepped back, and Daniel came to stand by her side. She loved the man next to her, but unfortunately her time here in Happiness with everyone, with Daniel, was coming to an end.

"I want that," Daniel whispered in her ear as he leaned close, "with you."

She gaped at him. "What?"

His smile was warm with affection…and love. She shook her head, for she couldn't believe what she'd heard. Had he just admitted that he cared for her? Maybe even loved her?

"Daniel—"

With his mouth close to her ear, he whispered, "I want a life with you, Emma. I want to marry you and have a family with you."

She wanted this so badly, she couldn't believe it was happening. "Daniel, there is something you don't know, and it might change how you feel about me."

Daniel frowned. "I don't believe that, Emma. You won my heart with your determination to do the right thing." He reached for her hand, murmured that they were going downstairs so others could see the babies. "Leah. Henry. *Danki*. I'm honored that you chose to name your son after me."

Then he pulled Emma from the room. Daniel tugged her through the house and then outside.

Emma halted him as soon as they stepped out. "I can't stay. I…"

"What, Emma?" he asked gently.

She felt her face crumple as she started to cry. "You won't want me here, Daniel. Promise me that I can say *gut* bye to everyone before I go."

He frowned. "Tell me."

"I've been shunned."

Daniel studied the distraught woman before him and wondered what she was talking about. Emma was regretful. That alone made him wonder why she thought she'd been shunned.

"I used to live in an Amish community in Indiana. When I was younger, my parents left the church and took me with them. They told me that we could never go back to visit my *grosseldre* or any of our relatives, because we'd been shunned."

"Emma, you were how old?"

"Six," she breathed.

He smiled at her warmly. He saw her confusion and went on to quickly explain. "You were six years old, Emma. You were not a member of the church. You were never shunned. Your parents were, because they joined the church and decided to leave anyway. That is an offense against the Ordnung. Going with your parents because you were six and had to remain with your parents is not, Emma. You are not shunned."

She reeled as if in shock. "But they told me—"

"They couldn't go back, but you could have."

Her eyes filled with tears. "After they died, I could have gone back to live with my family in Indiana?"

*"Ja."*

Emma began to weep.

"I hate that you went through this, believing as you did. That you had to endure the Turners and what they did to you. But if you had gone to live with your *grosseldre*, then I never would have met you."

She blinked. "*Ja*, you're right," she breathed with awe.

"Do you want to go home to Indiana, Emma? Or would you consider staying here in Happiness with me? I love you, Emma Beiler. I want you here with me. When you're ready, I want you to be my wife." He smiled at her. "Earlier today I put an offer in for that property. The owner accepted it, and I put down a deposit. That's why I didn't pick you up this morning. I had to work this afternoon, but I came to see you as soon as I got off work." He took hold of her hands. "I won't be working for Rhoades Construction for much longer. In fact, I put in my two weeks' notice. I'll be opening my harness shop. I thought that once we marry, we'll live in the house we looked at. What do you think?"

Her eyes shone with happiness. "I'd like that very much."

*"Gut."*

"Daniel?" she murmured softly.

*"Ja?"*

"I'd like to see my family in Indiana."

"*Ja*, you should," he said approvingly. "And we can invite them to our wedding."

"*Danki*, Daniel."

"And you no longer have to worry about the Turners. I have a feeling Bryce and his son will be put in jail for their drug dealing and the abuse you suffered at their hands."

Emma beamed at him. "I love you, Daniel."

"I love you, Emma."

# *Epilogue*

A year later, Emma and Daniel wed before the Amish community in Happiness. Only weeks before, Daniel and Emma had joined the Amish church. Daniel with Emma's help had set up his harness shop on the property he'd purchased. He'd accepted his father's help with financing because he wanted to own his home before he married Emma.

Emma stood beside Daniel as they made their vows. She was overwhelmed with love for her new husband. He had proved time and again over the last months how much he loved her. He found her first foster parents whom she'd loved. John Bowden's cancer was in remission, and he and May were happy to attend the wedding.

Emma's family from Indiana were seated among the congregation. They had been stunned to hear what happened to her and were happy to be a part of her life again. Their pleasure was twofold when they saw that Emma had found love and a new life in an Amish community.

After the wedding reception was over, Daniel and

Emma, alone in their new home, gazed at each other in the waning light of a beautiful autumn day.

Emma smiled at her husband. “I love you. More than you’ll ever know.”

“Wife, I’ll love you forever.” Daniel pulled her into his arms and kissed her.

As she leaned into him, Emma sent up a silent prayer of thanks. She had everything she’d ever wanted—Daniel, a family and the promise of a future blessed by God.

* * * * *